ANGEL'S ROAR

FEATHERS AND FIRE BOOK 4

SHAYNE SILVERS

ARGENTO PUBLISHING

CONTENTS

Shayne Silvers

Angel's Roar

Feathers and Fire Book 4

ISBN: **978-1-947709-11-9**

© 2018, Shayne Silvers / Argento Publishing, LLC

info@shaynesilvers.com

CALLIE PENROSE MUST DIE.

*C*allie Penrose – a wizard with a splash of Angel's blood flowing through her veins – kind of broke the Vatican and their band of Holy-warrior, wizard-priests, the Shepherds. Officially, the report stated *Callie forgot to turn the other cheek, and things escalated...*

She returns home to Kansas City to find new gangs of supernaturals roving the streets, preying on the innocent while the local factions do nothing. Although not unified, everyone seems to agree on one point...

Callie Penrose must die.

And she's still hearing those strange Whispers in her mind – much more frequently than before, and not nearly as... *forgiving.*

But when an epic betrayal blindsides her and she discovers the truth of her birth – why Heaven and Hell have been so interested in her – Callie's world begins to crumble, and she must decide whether she wants to be a good girl...

Or if it's time to be a little naughty.

No matter how hard you try, you can't make an Angel cry...

They just *roar.*

DON'T FORGET! VIP's get early access to all sorts of Temple-Verse goodies, including signed copies, private giveaways, and advance notice of future projects. AND A FREE NOVELLA! Click the image or join here:
www.shaynesilvers.com/l/219800

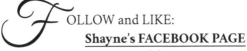

OLLOW and LIKE:

Shayne's FACEBOOK PAGE

www.shaynesilvers.com/l/38602

I try my best to respond to all messages, so don't hesitate to drop me a line. Not interacting with readers is the biggest travesty that most authors can make. Let me fix that.

CHAPTER 1

*T*he rickety bench was cold and uncomfortable, still wet from the chilly downpour of rain earlier. Claire was studying the brick wall behind our bench while my eyes focused on the gang of thugs across the street. Sirens wailed in the distance, but they weren't anywhere near us.

Because police didn't typically patrol this part of town. They only came if someone called them, and even then, they would arrive armed with assault weapons, riot gear, and body armor. Gangs owned these streets. Police actually discouraged vehicles from coming to a complete stop at the stop signs, because gangs were known to target obedient drivers. Follow laws too closely here and you were liable to see the barrel of a shotgun pointing at your face from outside the window. New age highway robbery.

I took a deep breath, tucking some stray hair back under my hood. Even though the heavy rain had ceased, constant drizzle still fell from the leaden-gray night sky.

I heard the hiss of air brakes from a nearby Greyhound bus and the heavy scent of exhaust was like a stale perfume in the air – almost enough to overpower the smell of wet trash and refuse. This part of town was neglected, forgotten. At least the rain attempted to wash away some of the grime. The beautiful skyline in the distance was a mockery of the poverty festering here.

Almost like this place wasn't a part of Kansas City.

But it was.

I studied the street of leaning brownstone homes before us, marking the parked cars lining both sides of the street. Many of the bulbs in the lampposts were broken – whether they had burned out or been shot out by local hoodlums, I wasn't sure. Regardless, they hadn't been replaced. I clenched my fists as I watched the thugs breaking into the cars, stealing the stereos and any other valuables inside. They did this without shame, unconcerned with anyone witnessing their crime.

On the upside, the distant sirens wouldn't be close enough to save these assholes from me.

"What is the... *Chancery?*" Claire asked thoughtfully, pointing at some graffiti on the wall.

I shrugged, continuing to watch the brazen thieves. "Someone really ought to tell them about an *eye for an eye...*" I mumbled.

"What about this one? Think it's talking about Nate?"

I ignored her, not wanting to talk about Nate Temple. I leaned forward, gritting my teeth as the thugs shattered another car window, laughing as they congratulated each other. What if the owner of that vehicle had kids? That would fuck with their sense of security in the morning when they were getting ready to leave for daycare.

"Oh! I think this one's talking about *you*—"

"Please stop, Claire," I said in a tight voice, turning to face her. I was getting annoyed with her fascination with the graffiti. She didn't seem concerned about the hoodlums across the street, just the shitty graffiti. She was pointing at a section on the brick wall behind us. It was a crude sketch of a fist – two blades extending out from between the knuckles. A halo floated above the fist, like some kind of logo.

I jolted in recognition. It *was* about me.

How had anyone heard about *that?* I had first used those blades months ago, but that had been in Rome, not here in Kansas City. It was pretty obvious the sketch was referencing me, unless we had an Angelic Wolverine in town that I hadn't yet met.

Seeing that image, scrawled on a shitty wall in a shitty part of town made me uneasy. Like a sniper had me in his sights.

I stood hastily, my eyes latching onto one of the other graffiti tags Claire had pointed out. *Chancery wuz here.* I frowned, dismissing the street art.

Stupid name, I thought to myself. "These assholes are pissing me off," I said, openly glaring at the seven hoodlums.

Sinners... a soothing purr filled my ears.

My skin pebbled instinctively at the sensation, but I no longer flinched when they spoke to me. The *Whispers* were something to do with the Angelic blood flowing through my veins. They offered constant commentary to my life, like my own personal narrator. Sometimes they were pleasant, other times obnoxiously creepy. Like someone was staring through my eyes and passing judgment on these thieves. I muted them. I didn't need them for what I had planned.

I felt Claire standing beside me, watching me with concern. I waved a hand and put on a shallow smile. "Just tired," I said. "And pissed."

Her breath puffed out before her face in a brief cloud. "Are they Freaks?" she asked, scrutinizing the thugs.

I nodded, tightening the straps of my small backpack so it wouldn't be a hindrance in a fight. "Saw some fangs. And that one ripped a door off with one hand," I said, pointing openly. Two of the thugs were now watching us, their predatory gazes full of warning. Two young women shouldn't be out alone in this part of town at this time of night. And they definitely shouldn't have any hobbies remotely related to the automotive industry.

It was a threat. They were strong, hardened, dangerous men. And we were two cute blonde women, obviously in the wrong part of town on the wrong night. We weren't welcome.

Claire openly snorted at their silent threat and their eyes narrowed, lips pulling back into snarls. "I'm bringing Teddy," she said, waving a small white teddy bear towards the dangerous thieves. "It's only fair to warn them. Did you bring your scarf?"

"I'm not a Knight Templar," I murmured disgustedly under my breath, not wanting to think about the scarf I had stolen from them in Rome. The one that blocked magical attacks.

Claire shrugged. "It's more for *their* benefit," she said, waving her white teddy bear at them more blatantly. "To give them fair warning of what we *really* are." I nodded absently.

The stuffed animal to let them know she was really a shifter polar bear.

She turned the bear to face her. "Right, Teddy?" she asked it, staring into its button eyes.

"Right, Clairebear," she answered herself in a tinny voice.

I shot her a baffled look. "Really?" I shifted my eyes to study the bear, thinking. "If you're going to talk to a stuffed animal, shouldn't you at least make his voice deep and rumbly?"

"My bear, my rules," she said defensively. She jerked her chin at the thieves, her green eyes twinkling with anticipation. I turned to see them now forming a line. Brass knuckles glinted in the dim lamplight on a few pairs of hands. Others sported outright claws, proving my point about them being Freaks, and that they didn't have a sliver of concern that anyone might see them. People kept their heads down in this part of town. Even if they didn't know about Freaks – supernatural beings – the Regular criminals were ruthless enough. The wrong look could earn you a bullet and a shallow grave.

I rolled my shoulders, plucking out my Crucifix necklace so it could hang freely before me. Maybe Claire had a point. It *was* only fair to warn them. Then I stalked closer, shoving my hands in the pockets of my Darling and Dear coat.

Claire chuckled at my necklace, matching my stride. "There. *Now*, they've been warned."

I grunted. I wasn't particularly religious – at least I didn't attend Mass like a good little Catholic girl or anything. But... I had *seen* things. Been shown that I literally had some kind of bond with Heaven. My father had been a Nephilim, and I'd once had a minor Angel blood transfusion. So... it felt kind of childish to deny that the Crucifix didn't hold power. Still, it made me feel like a poser.

Because I was no saint.

"Hey, boys. Like my teddy bear?" Claire asked, pouting her lips.

A tall, pale, gangly man stepped forward. Water dripped from the stubble on his chin as he sneered back at Claire, ignoring me. "The only teddy I want to see is you in skimpy lingerie in the back of my truck, where I can show you where a tiny woman like you belongs late at night. On her back—"

I shoved my fingers in my ears in anticipation, right before Claire exploded into a massive white polar bear. She was easily ten feet tall, and her roar threatened to shatter window panes in the nearby homes. Her thick, snow-white fur whipped back and forth as she shook off the misty rain.

Like any woman should do in a similar situation, she slapped the offensive little prick.

I'm pretty sure he was a vampire.

And I'm pretty sure she broke his spine in three places.

At least, it sounded like muffled firecrackers had erupted under his skin before he flew back into one of the cars, shattering the windshield. He groaned in a very unmanly way, staring up at the misty night with wheezing, shallow breaths. Surprisingly, the car alarm didn't go off. Then again, maybe the thugs had somehow deactivated them. Made sense. Hard to rob a whole street full of cars if all the alarms were going off.

The street was silent as the other thugs stared at us in stunned shock. "One Brokeback vampire, served cold. *Sooo* cold," I chuckled.

Clairebear made an amused chuffing sound.

I pointed at the teddy bear – miraculously still gripped in Claire's massive claw. "We're not really into foreplay, but we did try to give you a heads up," I said, shifting my finger from the teddy bear to Claire. "Practically a flashing sign, really." I was mildly surprised that the werewolves in the back hadn't noticed her scent. Maybe they hadn't ever met a shifter bear.

"And what the fuck are *you*? A Ninja Nun?" a squat bald man asked me, his jowls quivering like a wet plate of tapioca Jell-O as he indicated my Crucifix. A few of his crew chuckled, but the rest frowned thoughtfully.

I let my hood fall back to reveal my unique white hair, and the single braid hair extension I had chosen for the night's activities. Most Freaks in town had seen a video of me kicking demon ass with my long white hair and recognized me by it. Those who hadn't initially laughed along with their pals froze, their previous hesitation now confirmed horror, but the leader just stared, not noticing their reaction or recognizing me. At least *some* of them recognized me.

"Have you heard about our Lord and Savior?" I asked in a soft tone, shaking out the thick, white braid. I had cut my hair off at the jaw recently, and the familiar weight of the extension made me feel more… me, I guess. I missed it, so had picked up an extension for nights like this when I was bored.

I took a casual step closer, my polite smile turning menacing as I flashed my teeth.

"Because he sure as fuck's heard about *you*," I said.

The three furthest away turned and ran. "It's her!" one of them screamed as he fled, tossing his brass knuckles to the street in a sign of surrender.

Sometimes, it was nice for a girl to be recognized. To have a reputation.

Claire didn't let them get very far before tearing after them on all fours, her teddy flopping in her paw at the sudden motion, splashing through the puddles and ruining the beautiful white fur. I smiled at the remaining hoodlums.

"Oh, no. Whatever shall I do?" I said in mock fear.

CHAPTER 2

The three formed an arc before me, brandishing fangs and claws. A motley crew of the unwashed – tapioca-face looked like a werewolf, a bearded blonde guy that sported fangs from his lips looked like a vampire, and the last was a short, stunningly handsome Fabio lookalike with long, blonde hair below his shoulders, and... *pointed ears*? A Fae? Huh. Color me surprised.

Faebio, not *Fabio*.

I hadn't ever run across one of his kind before. Faebio was the *heavy*, in my opinion – the unknown variable.

Proving my suspicion, Faebio flung out a hand in my direction and a swarm of strobing lights zipped through the space between us. My black fan appeared – a defensive spell I could call up by instinct – and slapped most of them from my vicinity, but a few struck my coat with a hissing sound. I felt the impact, but it wasn't any harder than if someone had thrown wads of crumpled paper at me. I glanced down, watching as the embers puffed out like pinched candle wicks to reveal... finger-length pixies. Several of them lay dazed on the wet pavement, gasping and wheezing, eyes dazed. They were female, naked, and had butterfly wings.

I glanced up at Faebio, who had retreated closer to Claire's Brokeback vampire on the windshield – who was still emitting whimpering wheezes, if it mattered. Faebio seemed stunned that his fiery sprites hadn't burned through my coat. I knew I was. "Would you look at that," I murmured, carefully stepping around them so as not to crush their tiny bodies under my boots. "Naked and flat on their backs," I laughed, repeating Brokeback's comment from before Claire had sent him hurtling into the windshield like a piece of wet laundry.

I smiled at Faebio. "My turn..." His pixies had given me an idea.

I flung my hands wide, tilted my head back, and then clapped them together before me, the rain making the slap of skin on skin crack like a whip – or a Sister's ruler on a rebellious church boy's wrist. A dozen silver butterflies exploded from my fingertips like droplets of water. The quicksilver butterflies tore through two of the thugs like hot knives through butter – especially the werewolf – emitting a pleasant chiming note with each strike.

The vampire and werewolf collapsed, gasping, whimpering and groaning.

With the others down, my butterflies had latched onto Faebio, forming what resembled a chrome feather boa around his throat – except one made of slowly flapping butterfly wings. Right over his vital veins and arteries. He stood as still as a statue, knowing anything else would mean execution by butterfly – a potential cautionary tale he would never be able to live down, ironically speaking. *Razor-fly? Butter-flay?* I thought to myself. I'd think on it.

I slowly approached, locking eyes with him. I accidentally stomped on the werewolf's hand as I made my way closer. I might have even ground my heel a little, judging by his gasp.

The ground rumbled as Claire came bounding back up beside me, claws skidding on the wet pavement. She stumbled, clumsily slamming into the car holding Brokeback vampire. The blow knocked him off the windshield and...

The poor bastard struck a fire hydrant.

With his *face!* I winced instinctively.

Then his legs knocked over a nearby lidless trashcan, spilling the goopy muck all over his chest right as he opened his mouth to gasp in pain from the blow to his face.

I frowned at Claire. She managed to look a little embarrassed – even for a bear – but maybe that was just because all the blood on her muzzle resembled a comical blush. Her lips curled back as she gave Faebio a low warning grumble. He looked properly terrified, but also incredulous. These two women had taken down more than half a dozen of his fellows? I saw his face pale and realized he was staring down at Claire's lower body. I followed his gaze to see Claire still clutching the teddy bear, which explained her clumsiness with the whole brakes thing.

Teddy was liberally coated with blood. He had also lost one of his eyes and his arm was ripped at the seam, a bit of stuffing hanging out.

I turned to look at Claire's face again – at all the blood.

"You *ate* one of them?" I asked her, frowning in disapproval.

She shook her head *no*, but lifted the teddy bear to wipe across her muzzle as if to tamper with the evidence. She glanced down at it afterwards, letting out an indelicate snort. Then she lumbered over to Brokeback vampire. His prognosis now included a shattered face, and he was probably a high-risk for infection from all the slimy trash painting his body. Well, he was a vampire, so maybe *no* on the infection. He appeared to be unconscious or heavily dazed, because he didn't react as Claire lovingly tucked the bloody teddy bear under his arms, folded them, and then grunted, somehow sounding amused.

I jerked my chin for Faebio to go stand beside… Count Brokeback Trashula.

"On your knees, Faebio," I purred.

His face darkened at the nickname I had given him. The butterflies around his throat abruptly ceased flapping their wings, and his defiance coincidentally evaporated as he sensed their grips tightening on his flesh.

He couldn't get on his knees fast enough. Right beside Count Brokeback Trashula.

I studied the street, tapping my lips thoughtfully as I pulled out my phone. Then I shook my head. "No. This just won't do."

Faebio's face paled in terror. "I'll do whatever you want. Please, don't kill me. I was only with them for the protection they offered! The only safety these days, is in numbers!" he looked about ready to cry, and a distant part of me frowned in disappointment at his lack of dignity. He was Fae, and he was so scared of being alone that he joined a local gang? The streets weren't *that* bad.

But I didn't really care, all things considered. He'd been robbing the poor and innocent. He was scum. "Lie down. You're the big spoon." He blinked in confusion, not understanding. I sighed, then pointed a finger at Count

Brokeback Trashula, explaining. "Little spoon." Then I pointed my finger back at Faebio. "Big spoon," I said. With utter shame on his face, he did it, clutching the vampire like they were long lost lovers. I circled them, glancing at the street thoughtfully for a few breaths.

"That was all of us," he pleaded, assuming I was checking for threats. "Please, you proved your point. Don't give us to them," he begged.

My lips tightened, but I didn't really care about whatever rival gang he was so scared of. I found the perfect spot and smiled reassuringly. I crouched down, finally meeting his eyes. "Say *Thank you, Callie*, and then give your friend a smooch on the cheek." And I lifted my phone, ready for the money shot.

Suddenly understanding that I wasn't going to kill him, he let out a sigh of relief and obeyed. I snapped a few pictures. Claire let out another chuffing laugh. I climbed back to my feet, scrolling through the images. The streetlamp gave off the perfect ambiance – the chaos of the fight and the beauty of love. Like a rose growing from a crack in the sidewalk. One of the pictures had a perfect angle for one of the butter-flays, showing the ever-beautiful Faebio kissing Count Brokeback Trashula on the cheek.

The bloody teddy bear clutched in the vampire's arms really brought it all together.

CHAPTER 3

I showed it to Claire, who actually doubled over. Then I showed it to Faebio. "This goes public if I ever see you in my city again. Even if it's at the beauty salon getting a blow out, getting a fresh manicure at the mall, performing community service at the homeless shelter, or helping a little old lady cross the street." He nodded adamantly. I knew he was embarrassed, horrified, and distantly angry, but his gratitude vastly outweighed those other emotions. He must have really pissed off this other gang to prefer my treatment to handing him over to them, but I hadn't heard about any other gangs in town since I got back from St. Louis.

"You'll also find a way to pay for damages to this car," I said, indicating the probably totaled vehicle. "And reimburse whatever you stole from the others. How you do that is up to you. But you have forty-eight hours. Or else my butter-flays will get you." I blew him a farewell kiss and motioned for Claire to follow me.

I took off my backpack and passed it over to Claire, guiding her towards a nearby alley that might provide a modicum of privacy, even though she likely didn't care. Shifters were very comfortable in their skins – no matter how they had felt when merely human. Like some switch was flipped turning them into a nudist the moment they became a shifter.

Proving my point, Claire was suddenly naked as a jaybird before we hit the alley, chuckling as she reached into the pack for the pair of sweats and hoodie I had stored inside. We pretty much carried spare clothes every-where, now, since she was a shifter and her changings forced her clothes to rip beyond salvation. She tugged the replacements on, still laughing as her head popped through the neck of the hoodie. "Faebio!" she muttered.

We left the alley after a glance back at our fallen foes – who were still on the ground, probably waiting until they were confident we were gone.

"Bye, Teddy..." Claire murmured sadly as we left the alley, sounding entirely sincere.

I felt myself smiling satisfactorily. "Let's go shower up. You can crash at my place."

"This is way more fun than bar hopping," Claire said, skipping down the sidewalk on bare feet, aiming for every single puddle. "And at least my walk of shame isn't during the morning commute!" she chuckled, tucking her arm into my elbow. I inspected her outfit and the blood on her face. Then sighed, nodding. "No *happy ending*, though..."

"It was happy ending enough for me. More pleasurable than most of the guys I've tussled with lately," she added, sounding annoyed.

I grunted. I didn't want to talk about her sex life. I was in my own purga-tory of a dry spell. "You did text Beckett earlier, right? To let him know we were going on a *walk* tonight?" She nodded, smiling at my codename for our occasional girls' night out. Beckett Killian was a local detective, and it was easier to give him a little warning ahead of time so that his cops didn't walk up on a scene they couldn't explain to internal affairs later. "Good. Send him an update. His secure cellphone." Whether it did any good or not, it made me feel more responsible. Working with the only police officer in Kansas City that I was certain knew about supernatural events and beings. And didn't blindly hate us for it.

Claire rolled her eyes at my micro-managing, but nodded. Or maybe her eye roll was due to the fact that I didn't just text Beckett myself. Claire seemed confident that there were tangled sheets between the detective and me, but nothing could have been further from the truth. Maybe I had considered it at one point. But that was before... well, I had different prey now. But I didn't want to even think about that right now. Let alone *talk* about it with Claire – who could extract details faster than a lifelong-vegan-turned-vampire could break his diet regimen.

Simply put, Beckett was better left in the friend zone. I hadn't spoken with him in months, anyway, only just now beginning to reach back out to him via Claire, who had remained in contact with him in my extended absence.

"Just do it, Claire. I'm tired. No lip," I warned her.

"Sure thing, Sister—" The sound of slapping feet made us both stop and spin around, ready for round two. But it wasn't a rematch.

A woman darted out of an alley behind us, running straight for Faebio who was still lying where we had left him, stiffly cuddling his buddy. Count Brokeback Trashula was only just now struggling to get up. Faebio looked suddenly conflicted. Seeing the woman suddenly running straight at him seemed to put him in a very awkward position. Did he dare move out of her way and possibly risk my wrath?

She saved him the trouble, launching over the two just as the vampire was finally propping himself up on shaking elbows. The woman's foot clipped Count Trashula in the jaw, snapping his head sideways. She stumbled a bit, not having anticipated him trying to get up in the middle of her jump, but she caught her balance and resumed her flat-out sprint, brown hair fanning out behind her.

Whether conscious or not – Count Trashula squeezed the teddy bear and let out a pained whimper, as if hoping Teddy would keep him safe from further pain.

Any other time, I would have burst out laughing. But then I heard pounding feet from the same alley which the woman had just fled. Three figures burst from the shadows, eyes flicking over us with a quick threat assessment, but then one of them spotted the woman they were obviously pursuing fifty yards down the street, and still hauling ass. They turned to chase her down like a pack of wolves.

The first man accidentally stomped down on Count Trashula's hand before hurtling over him. The vampire gasped, head rising up instinctively, and was in the perfect position to get clipped in the nose by the second pursuer's boot, sending him skidding into another trashcan.

Faebio, sensing the cloud of misfortune surrounding his buddy, had wisely scooted away to squeeze his back against the broken vehicle, consequences of my anger be damned. He looked absolutely petrified as he stared at the three men racing past him. The three new strangers paid them no mind, sprinting after the woman.

I shared a look with Claire. Then she exploded into her bear form, ruining her spare set of sweats, and we gave chase.

If I had ever seen a woman in need of protecting, it was this one right now.

The trio rounded a corner, disappearing from view as we poured on the speed. When we got to Count Trashula, he let out a shriek, clutching his hands and – incidentally, the teddy bear – to his chest. Faebio was whispering something to himself, but all I caught was *them...* as he visibly shook with fear.

I ignored him, eager to reach the woman in time to help her. We rounded the corner, Claire using a lamppost to slow her momentum, but only managing to tear it loose from the concrete with a squeal of bent metal. The man in the back of the group glanced behind him at the sound, sneering hatefully before slipping into an alley ahead of us. I heard him shout out a warning to his pals, his voice echoing off the alley walls. I ducked into the alley, ready for a sword to decapitate me or something, but found no enemy. I pressed on deeper into the gloomy, putrid alley until I came to a brick wall.

I skidded to a stop, jerking my head to either side, trying to find out where they had all gone. There was no exit. Not even a fire-escape. I quickly checked the doors leading inside some of the buildings, but they were all locked tight. And there had been no other intersections for them to take.

Claire was sniffing a small pile of broken glass near a wall. Then she snorted, backing up a few steps as she shook her massive head. I approached warily, taking in the earthy scent that only barely masked the scent of nearby trash dumpsters. Blue vapor rose up from the glass shards. I shared a long look with Claire.

"Where the hell did they all go?" I said.

Claire glanced up at the walls towering over us, shook her shoulders as if annoyed, and then shifted back into her naked human form, having destroyed the second outfit for no real benefit.

There was no way they'd had time to climb their way out. Unless the three men had scaled a fifty-foot wall in record speed... they had just disappeared. I scooped up a few larger pieces of the glass and noticed an inky blue substance staining the surface. I wrapped them up in a slip of fabric from Claire's sweat suit lying on the alley floor and shoved the bundle in my pocket.

With a tired sigh, I gave up. We only had one change of clothes for Claire and I didn't want to risk calling a taxi with my friend naked and covered in blood. I opened a Gateway on the spot – a ring of fire illuminating the dark alley. Through the center of the fire was a hazy view of my apartment. Wizards knew how to travel in style.

I was ready for bed. Claire hopped after me through the Gateway in silence, letting out a tired sigh as I let it close behind us. I let my backpack drop to the floor, wondering what to feel about this bizarre night.

Did I chalk it up as a win?

Or had that woman died? Or been abducted? I'd have Claire check with Beckett. Then again, I didn't have much to go on. I had only seen her face for a fraction of a second. She had been young and pretty with thick brown hair, but nothing that would make her stand out in a crowd.

At least I had a funny picture for a memento. Maybe I would frame it.

CHAPTER 4

I stood in my living room, lost in thought.

"Well, that was... strange. Think she's okay?" Claire asked.

I snapped out of my reverie, shrugging tiredly. "I didn't sense any magic, so they didn't make a Gateway or anything... Locked doors, no ladders." I sighed. "Hope she's alright."

"I didn't pick up anything either," Claire frowned, tapping her nose as she indicated her heightened shifter sense of smell. "Other than that glass. It smells terrible," she said, eyeing my pocket.

I frowned, taking it out. "It just smells... earthy to me," I said, setting it on the counter.

Claire grimaced. "If by *earthy* you mean a rotten corpse after a week in a hot trunk..."

I scrunched up my face at her ridiculous exaggeration. Or... maybe it was just a shifter thing. Had we picked up different scents? "Were they all human? Faebio looked scared when they ran by, almost like he recognized them. Maybe a rival gang?" I suggested. But my eyes drifted to the bundle of glass. That scent thing didn't seem normal at all.

Claire shrugged. "Human, I think. Not anything else that stood out, anyway. Oh, well. Can't save everyone. You could always ask Roland. He's been in town for a long time. Maybe he's run across them before?" she said doubtfully.

I shook my head adamantly. "He's in Italy still. Meeting with the vampire council."

Claire grinned. "Bet that's fun. They probably consider him a celebrity. The only vampire hunter turned vampire, right?"

I smiled weakly. "That's the way he makes it sound. Unless he's been lying to me on the phone… Either way, I highly doubt his reception is as glamorous as you imagine. Probably has a lot of enemies there, but his notoriety also grants him protection, and he has backup, just in case." Nate's vampire friend, Alucard, was keeping an eye on him. Being a Daywalker, Alucard also had celebrity status. I just hoped it was enough to keep them both safe.

Claire, sensing my growing silence, piped up with another terrible solution. "You could ask the other Shepherds… Maybe they'll recognize the stuff on that glass."

"No way. The Vatican is still pissed about my last visit to Rome. I don't think they'll be in a charitable mood. Or they would suggest a high price for the answers."

Claire muttered something that should have earned her a smiting. I smiled in agreement. "Fabrizio likes you, right?" she asked. "Isn't he in charge now?"

I nodded, smiling to myself. Fabrizio was one of the only pleasant experiences I had from Rome. A larger-than-life Italian man who I had dubbed *Meatball* for purely offensive reasons. In return, he had dubbed me *Girlie Penflower* rather than calling me by my name, Callie Penrose. "Meatball still has bosses. The Conclave."

"Oh, that's right. Your mantra thing," she chuckled, shaking her head.

"Motherfuckingmilkeyedshitweasels," I replied proudly. "The Conclave is a bunch of jerkwads. I need to let them cool off before I approach them again." I tugged off my jacket and threw it over a chair, but not before inspecting where those pixies had struck me. Not a mark on the leather coat. I'd been told it was made of Gruffalo hide, whatever that was. Something magical and lethal, no doubt, and it apparently had purple spots on its skin, judging by the markings on the back of the jacket.

I frowned, thinking about the pixies, and realizing that I was distantly hoping they'd gotten away safely. I doubted they'd had much say in the matter when Faebio had thrown them at me. Then again, I'd heard some war stories from Nate Temple about the vicious Fae, so who knew? Claire was watching me, pointedly not looking at my jacket, but she was shifting from foot to foot eagerly.

"I'll take you to get something soon, don't worry," I said, rolling my eyes as I turned to the kitchen on autopilot.

"Yes!" Claire hooted behind me. "Darling and Dear, forever!"

I paused in front of the fridge, debating whether I was hungry, thirsty, or ready to just go to bed. Claire placed a hand on my shoulder, squeezing supportively.

"The first step is admitting you have a problem," she whispered, flipping my braided hair extension with a finger. "And you should wash this rat tail. You've gotten blood on it."

I lifted it up, cursing as I realized that she was right. I unclipped it from my hair, tossing it on the counter with a grumpy sigh. Hopefully, I could wash it out.

"I don't even know why you wear it," Claire continued. "I like your new hair. Edgy. Bitchy," she said, smiling to herself.

"It helps everyone recognize me. My long hair has a reputation. Everyone talks about it." I gave her a level look. "Like people will soon know about your war teddy."

Claire clapped her hands excitedly. "Teddy's the man," she agreed.

"And I don't have a *problem*," I argued, circling back to her original comment.

"Just grab a juice box. Stop denying yourself."

I finally nodded in resignation. It did sound good. Some girls loved cupcakes. I loved juice boxes. Like a toddler.

"I'm going to update Beckett and then jump into the shower," Claire told me.

I nodded halfheartedly, smiling to myself as I shoved the straw into the juice box and took a sip. The liquid nirvana struck my tongue, and the world became a happier place. I made my way over to the couch, taking another calming sip before plopping down.

The events of the night had me thinking about enemies.

Other than the Shepherds, I had made some other enemies during my trip to the Vatican.

The Knights Templar – or a fragmented remnant of the original Order.

And thanks to the fashionable scarves the Templars wore, they were immune to magic. I glanced at my dresser where a black scarf with a crimson cross on it hung from the mirror. Not the traditional crucifix, but a Cross Pattée – like an ornate *plus* sign. I had obtained a small pile of the scarves during a battle against the Templars in Rome – trophies of the men I had assassinated in my attempt to save Roland. Oddly enough, I didn't feel any guilt about those deaths, which made me absently wonder about myself.

An odd sensation. To have a part of you question why another part of you didn't feel something – an internal form of psychoanalysis.

Not wanting to leave the scarves lying around where anyone could have scooped them up, I had chosen to keep them. After some testing, I had decided to dye one black rather than keeping the faded white color. Something to make me stand out as different from the real Templars if I ever decided to wear it to a fight – because the *immune to magic* ability was pretty incredible. To my happy surprise, the scarf still worked fine – able to nullify any magic thrown at it. Maybe I could dye one in each color so I always had one that matched my outfit.

A magic-proof scarf could come in handy *and* be fashionably chic.

But the Templars – and their Commander, Olin Fuentes – were a problem for a later day. During our last encounter, he'd been infected by a werewolf before fleeing the scene. My best hope was that he had turned, and his fellow Templars had then turned on *him* as a result – because Templars hated Freaks. To find out that their leader was now what they hunted?

Sweet, sweet irony.

Anyway, the Templars were in Rome, and I had some house-cleaning to do here in Kansas City, hence our little adventure tonight. Cleaning up the streets.

I'd need to ask Haven – the Master Vampire of Kansas City – about the vampire we had just throttled. It was a simple courtesy to let him know I had harmed a vampire that may or may not belong to him – even if the man had been a waste of life, robbing from the poor. But it was better than Haven hearing only that I had brutalized a vampire and had forgotten to tell him about it.

Better if he heard my side of the story right from the get go.

I probably needed to reach out to Paradise and Lost, the de-facto werewolf queens of Kansas City, or whatever they had chosen to call themselves. Shared Alphas, perhaps. But I would see them in two days when we met with the real estate agent to check out that old church that Roland wanted to buy.

Because he needed a new home since he was also no longer associated with the Shepherds.

Paradise and Lost – of their own volition, I think – had adopted Roland as their savior, or something creepier, perhaps. Very touchy feely, if you asked me, but they were as loyal as one could possibly be, and anyone that kept Roland safer made me happier.

I wondered how their future pack would take that piece of news – that their leaders were beholden to a powerful vampire. Hopefully, they would see it as an asset. I knew Haven sure did. Not only had he gained an ex-Shepherd, but one with ties to the werewolf pack in town?

Score.

But Roland wouldn't be back for a few more days. He was still in Italy meeting with the Sanguine Council – the Masters of the Master Vampires throughout the world. If I knew one thing about my old mentor, it was that he was probably as uncomfortable around the other vampires as they were around him. The vampire hunter turned vampire-in-law.

I took another sip of my drink, dismissing Roland from my thoughts as I heard the shower turn on in my bedroom.

I was confident that the motley crew of thieves we had encountered tonight weren't beholden to their nations, but rather rogue thugs working together without supervision due to the chaos of leadership in recent months. Still, the current leaders of the city needed to know. I'd also mention Faebio's warning about this mysterious other gang. Whatever could scare a group of Freaks was probably important.

Thinking on Faebio, I pulled out my phone and dialed Nate Temple.

My pulse didn't quicken. I promise. He just had some prior experience with Fae. Maybe he'd know why a lone Fae was gangbanging in Kansas City.

But the call went straight to voicemail. "This is Nate. I'm on a wild vacation, so leave a message!"

I sighed, hanging up. *Wild vacation* was code that he was off in Fae. Again. Dangerous, but I couldn't do anything about it, and he was a big boy. Maybe I could convince him to take me there sometime. All sorts of crazy things happened to those who visited Fae – slumbering abilities awakened inside a person. I shivered as I thought about it. Maybe I *didn't* want to visit Fae. I had enough freaky stuff going on inside my bloodstream as it was.

Because I was part Nephilim and part wizard. Which had interested quite a few beings I really didn't want anything to do wit—

A fist pounded on my door, making me drop my juice box in surprise. It was almost empty anyway, so didn't spill all over my rug, otherwise I would have had a late-night murder to take care of before bed. I glanced down at my phone. It was two in the morning. I heard the shower still running, so knew I had to answer it myself or ignore it. Maybe it was just a drunk—

The fist pounded again. "Miss Penrose?" a muffled voice asked.

I sighed. No such luck. The person knew me. And only something *icky* called me Miss Penrose.

Looked like sleep would have to wait.

CHAPTER 5

A large, tall black man stood in the hallway. Long dread-locks hung down his back, and he wore dark jeans and a flannel shirt with the sleeves rolled back to reveal dense muscle underneath his dark skin. He didn't look entirely pleased to be here. That made two of us.

I knew him, unfortunately.

"Alyksandre," I said sweetly. "What would daddy say if he knew you were calling on an unmarried woman at this time of night?"

This only seemed to further his discomfort. He glanced over my shoulder, and his eyes abruptly widened in alarm. I turned to see Claire standing only a few paces behind me, her pale skin glistening from the shower. She'd, um, accidentally forgotten her towel.

But she had her hands settled on the curve of her hips in case we failed to notice her nudity.

I grinned at her, but forced the smile down as I turned back to Alyksandre, arching an eyebrow. His jaw was hanging open, but I'll hand it to him – he immediately dropped his gaze rather than 'accidentally' getting an eyeful. That alone was proof of his devotion to his cause.

Because he was a Nephilim. The offspring of an Angel and a human.

Claire sighed, almost sounding offended that he hadn't gotten enough fuel for his memory banks later. Because Claire was a sleaze-ball. Alyksandre worked for the Angel in town. In case I ever forgot, it was very easy to remember this Angel's name.

Because it was Angel.

"He needs to speak with you," Alyksandre said in his subwoofer tone, directing his words at the floor of the hallway.

I let out a tired breath. I'd already played cat and mouse with Angel. Railing against him unnecessarily would only cause headaches later. He wanted me to work for him, but he had a funny way of 'asking.' For example, last time I'd heard from the god-squad, Alyksandre had escorted me to a greasy diner with another Nephilim pal of his to meet Angel, who then proceeded to demand my servitude. The meeting ended with me holding a silver blade to Angel's godly scrotum. The time before *that*, Angel had sent Alyksandre to my church with a similar request. In response, I had kicked him out into the street, quite literally. Nothing against Alyksandre – he actually seemed like an okay guy – but I hadn't gotten much sleep the night before.

Because I'd been battling a demon.

And Angel hadn't offered any help. Not even a Nephilim or two for cannon fodder.

Yet like a persistent STD, Alyksandre had returned, asking – again – for me to meet up with his boss. After the blade-to-the-crotch meeting, Angel had given me a week to answer his summons... but that had been months ago, thanks to my recent travels. With a resigned sigh, I decided I'd made him wait long enough to prove my point – since our last visit hadn't done so.

It was probably for the best to get it over with. Let him know – officially – that we wouldn't be coworkers any time soon. I'd had enough of organized religion, let alone signing up for military service to the lamest-named Angel in the family.

But we didn't need to be enemies, either.

"I'll be back soon," I told Claire, suddenly longing for my bed, wishing I had denied myself that juice box. Maybe I would have slept right through Alyksandre's pounding on the door. Or I would have awoken to a murder scene when Claire killed him for trying to break in. Yeah, this was probably the best outcome, all things considered.

Claire immediately opened her mouth to argue. "But—"

I turned to give her a very significant look, silently letting her know I didn't want her to go because I didn't want these guys to have any reason to be interested in her... as possible leverage.

She picked up on my sincerity at least, and finally nodded. "I'll just read a book or something. Because you won't be gone that long."

It wasn't a question. It was a demand. I curtsied gracefully and let the door close behind me. Alyksandre let out a breath of relief to see he was safe from the deadly, wet, naked, blonde temptress. I followed him to the parking lot, wondering exactly how we were going to get to his boss. Some magical Nephilim mode of transport.

I was crestfallen when Alyksandre approached an early-nineties Mazda Miata. A bright red convertible.

I climbed inside, not wanting to mock his chariot of salvation.

I did smile at the custom license plate – *OLTSTMNT*. Like Air Force One.

He pulled out of the parking lot, keeping his eyes pinned to the road as he drove. He even kept both hands on the steering wheel. And he hadn't pulled out of the lot until I had my seatbelt buckled. He even judiciously checked his mirrors in case a demon had slipped into his ride to readjust them while he was knocking on my apartment door.

This confirmed that I could never work for his operation. On principle alone.

Alyksandre cleared his throat after a time, preparing to participate in casual conversation. "You and... you two are *together?*" he asked in a polite, yet clearly uncomfortable, baritone.

I blinked, momentarily wondering if I had missed part of the question. Then it hit me. He thought Claire and I were dating? Because she'd answered the door naked in the middle of the night, obviously fresh out of the shower?

I almost burst out laughing, but instead, I chose to let the awkward question hang unfulfilled in the air, making the drive even more awkward for him. Petty, perhaps, but I was tired and not pleased by Angel's interruption. And silence was a formidable weapon. Also, anything I could do to make his kind uncomfortable would only help discourage them from wanting to work with me in the future. So, he thought I was shacking up with Claire? Perfect.

Sensing I wasn't going to answer, and that my silence *was* the answer, he grew rigid, not risking any further questions.

I turned to face him openly, watching him as he drove, increasing his discomfort. He used his blinkers about a minute before necessary. He rode the brakes if he sensed the wind changing. He was big, filling the space of the tiny car like a gorilla. And he still looked about as uncomfortable as he did when he saw Claire's glistening lady bits. I leaned closer, toying with him.

He recoiled, pulling away as if willing to jump from the moving car if I came any closer.

I frowned. "You're... not comfortable near me."

His jaw tightened. "We should have a chaperone."

I waited for him to laugh.

Then I realized he was deadly serious. That it wasn't acceptable to him to be alone with a woman. I finally let out a sigh. "You know, when I kicked you out of that church it wasn't personal, right? I was upset. A less than reputable gentleman might even say I was cranky..."

His eyebrows twitched, but he nodded solemnly. "I understand. You have nothing to fear from me." He glanced over sharply, but only for a fraction of a second, not daring to take his eyes away from the road for longer than the span of a blink. "I know you're not pleased with us. And I do understand why. Just know that we are soldiers. We are often tasked with less than desirable orders, but we cannot deny an Angel."

I nodded, tapping my lip. "Do you know your father? Or mother? How does that work? Is it always a male bloodline?"

His forehead bunched up in surprise. "You don't know?"

"Missed that day in Sunday School. When the lobbyist for Smiters Anonymous came in."

"I... do not know that group," he said, forehead furrowed. There was a lot of sighing coming from my side of the Holy Miata. "It's all about lineage," he continued. "There are the Firsts, who are directly descended from an Angel and a mortal, but the rest of us have parents who were both Nephilim, as the genes carry down. Not many Firsts these days, they tend to get killed off."

I nodded, thinking. "What if a Nephilim sleeps with a mortal? Does it always make another Nephilim?" I asked, thinking about my own history and what I'd been told about it.

"Sometimes yes, sometimes no," he admitted.

I guessed I was just lucky, then. Maybe I really was a Nephilim, because I sure had received a lot of Heaven's benefits package, even though I didn't toe the line and work for an Angel.

CHAPTER 6

A short time later, we pulled up to an old brownstone near the Plaza – much nicer than the brownstones I had visited earlier. Alyksandre seemed to take an hour and a half parallel parking his toy car in a spot big enough for a tank. He even got out to verify we were the appropriate distance from the curb and the other cars. I wouldn't have been too surprised to see him whip out a ruler.

I followed him up the steps to the front door, but glanced over my shoulder as I heard a catcall. I noticed a jeep swerving down the street with two college guys hanging out the back window, obviously drunk as they hooted at me. A common, but annoying, occurrence.

Unbelievably, they swerved and accidentally clipped Alyksandre's side mirror. They slammed on their brakes abruptly, skidding to a halt, their cheer dying like a popped balloon. I felt Alyksandre looming behind me, muttering furiously.

The car sped off an instant later, their windows rolling back up as they fled the scene.

Alyksandre was panting as he stared at his car, seeming more offended that they had fled than that they had hit his car in the first place. "Drunk driving… have they no sense of responsibility?" he growled.

I patted him on the shoulder and walked past him into the building. "You *were* parked a little far from the curb…" I offered.

His gasp of indignation was satisfying.

Two men stood just inside the doorway, glancing over my shoulder alertly, having overheard part of the commotion outside and likely trying to determine if it was a smite-able offense. Then they seemed to notice me. I heard the door click closed behind me as Alyksandre cleared his throat. The Nephilim stood down, not that they had seemed aggressive towards me or anything, but the sudden relaxed set to their shoulders made me wonder if I had missed the threat.

Alyksandre walked past us and began ascending the stairs. "Please follow me."

I stayed close, but far enough away to be ready for an attack – even though that was highly unlikely. These Nephilim were dangerous, but obviously honorable, judging by Alyksandre. In fact... I hadn't ever really seen them do anything that lethal. Like they were the administrative side of the Nephilim. I knew Nate had run afoul of some Nephilim in St. Louis, and they had left him for dead in a sandwich shop, but to be honest, I was kind of disappointed in the Kansas City crew. All bark, no smite.

They'd avoided almost every confrontation I'd ever been involved in. Or... had been caught and killed when they *did* try to assist.

Maybe I was giving them too much credit. Not sheepdogs, but sheep.

Alyksandre reached a set of double doors and hesitated for a second before knocking. A muffled response came from within before he opened the doors.

Angel sat on a wooden chair in the back of the room near a stained-glass window. The desk was a simple wooden piece, no ornate carvings of weeping angels or anything. In fact, it almost reminded me of a destitute bachelor's pad. Nothing hung on the walls. No elaborate couches or pillows. No fancy rugs. No decorations on the bookshelf near the back of the room.

A few more Nephilim stood on either side of the desk, but hung a few paces back to give Angel space. I approached the desk, studying the space further as I followed Alyksandre. I noticed the bookshelf was actually full of ancient texts – all related to God, Heaven, Scripture, or the Occult. It was the most extravagant thing I had seen so far in the house, but that wasn't saying much.

Thinking back, the entire house had been like this. Stark. Spartan. Functional. Not an Angel lounging in the lap of luxury. But an Angel with a purpose, not a material girl, figuratively speaking.

Angel watched me approach, face devoid of emotion. He was a tall, imposing figure, even sitting down. He had a long, narrow face, but his harsh, godly-clefted chin more than made up for it, and his wavy blonde hair hung to his shoulders, glistening like spun gold.

"I've brought Callie Penrose to see you..." Alyksandre said, eyes lowered.

"Thank you, Alyksandre. Please, leave us. Can you—" he cut off with a smile to find Alyksandre already pulling over a simple wooden stool for me to sit, "thank you."

Alyksandre dipped his head, set the seat beside me, patted my shoulder in an awkward attempt at reassurance, and then left. So did the others. I made sure they all left, turning my back on Angel until the door closed. I took my time turning back around to him, scanning the room for cameras or secret doors.

Nothing. We were alone. I finally sat down. "Okay. What's this about, Angel?"

He tapped a finger on the desk absently, as if considering his response. "First off, you should know that I go by a different name, now. It was apparently confusing to some of the locals," he said, sounding vaguely puzzled, as if not understanding why his name had been confusing.

In a literal fashion, I could understand his confusion. Angel the Angel. What was so confusing about that?

But he didn't understand humans very well. Or monsters. It was like calling everyone on the street Human and then wondering why they gave you strange looks.

"Oh? And what do you go by, now?" I asked, not really caring one way or another.

"Nameless," he replied, watching me.

I looked up, frowning. "That's an unusual choice..."

He shrugged. "I'm not good at coming up with things like that, so it seemed to fit."

"Right," I said, as if it made perfect sense. "Any reason you keep changing your name? Didn't... *He* give you one, originally?"

Angel – Nameless – glanced down at the desk, seeming... tired. "I feel that our original names hold us back. Too long a history attached to them. I feel it has gone to some of our heads. That we expect mankind to drop to their knees in rapture when they hear our names. It... isn't right."

I watched him discreetly, wondering what it meant for the world if an

Angel was having an identity crisis. Or maybe he was a body snatcher. A demon in disguise. Because he seemed entirely different from the last time I had met him. I casually angled the toes of my boots to face him – since they could detect demons – but felt nothing, which was even more baffling.

"Okay, Nameless. I'm here. You're here… The *why* still eludes me."

He nodded. "I realized that authority didn't work with you. That I mishandled you."

"You are never going to be *handling* me, Ang— Nameless," I corrected myself. That new name was going to take some getting used to. "Let's lay that point out front and center, and then proceed from there."

He took a deep, relaxing breath, and then nodded. "Okay."

I waited. Then I squinted suspiciously. "What is this? Good cop tactics?"

He shook his head sincerely, even managing to look mildly guilty. "No. I misjudged you. Old habits are hard to break. I'm used to working with Nephilim who already know what they are. Have known what they are their entire lives, practically. They want this life and consider it an honor. But you… had it thrust upon you. I never took that into account. Or your stubborn, simple-minded Free Will." A faint smile cracked his features, softening his comment. "I have seen the error of my ways, but as you can see, it is not easy for me to admit."

Something about that smile was contagious, and I found myself relaxing. "Okay."

He studied me. "You have lost much for one so young. I do wish we had found you sooner."

Something in my stomach tightened, and I felt the Whispers in the back of my mind, but I pressed them down, wanting to focus entirely on this conversation. I was sitting down with an Angel, and he was nothing like the last time I had encountered him in the diner with his two Nephilim thugs. Which one was the real version? Or was he genuinely remorseful for mishandling me? That sounded Angelic. But… it was more likely – at least in human circles, which I wasn't in at the moment – for one of the two to be a deceit. A ploy.

Something was up, and I was pretty sure I wasn't going to like it.

CHAPTER 7

I looked up, trying to get a read on his motivations, but came up with nothing. "I have," I admitted. "But I don't think finding me any sooner would have changed things. My disdain for authority is pretty much ingrained. Being an orphan will do that to you."

"I know a few things about parental abandonment…" he said with a guilty sigh, leaning back in his chair. I stiffened on my stool. Had that been… a joke, or literal? He wasn't smiling, though. He just looked sad. "Sometimes it is necessary, but it still inflicts a deep pain. I would help you find absolution, but I'm not sure you want it. The offer is there, nonetheless."

I found myself dipping my chin appreciatively. I checked my mind to verify he wasn't softening me up with some power play, but I couldn't even sense his power unless I focused on it.

He smiled knowingly. "I'm containing my power at present. I didn't want to give you a reason to act defensively. This is just a talk. Not a recruitment pitch. I've given much thought to this conversation. Especially after you… well, our last encounter." He looked torn between smiling in amusement and frowning in displeasure, leaving his cheeks to spasm between the two like a mini seizure. I knew Angels weren't accustomed to displaying emotion in the first place, so his reaction was the equivalent of him attempting to pole-vault while quoting Shakespeare.

"I don't think Alyksandre knew it was just for a chat. He made it sound important," I said.

Nameless nodded. "Everything is important to him. Every injustice is a personal slap of disrespect to our cause, in his eyes. But he is also working on mastering his vehemence. His people skills."

Sensing the correlation Nameless seemed to be assuming from my comment, I clarified. "He was the perfect gentleman. Not rude. Just... concerned. Wary."

"And should one not be wary after their first encounter with you sent them sprawling into the street, booted from a church? And when the *second* meeting put their boss in danger?" he asked in a soft, neutral tone. Not sounding amused or angry. Just... controlled, stating the facts. Oh, he wasn't pleased about it. Not at all. But he was keeping his emotions in check.

I felt like I had walked into a Twilight Zone episode.

"You sent Alyksandre to pick me up in the middle of the night because you wanted to tell me you mishandled me during our previous encounters. But... you don't have any further requests for me," I said, summarizing the meeting so far.

He grunted. "To balance my... self-control, I might have relished the idea of causing you a small inconvenience by choosing the time of our meeting," he admitted, smiling down at his hands. "I have plenty of *requests*, Callie, but I have come to realize that we don't share the same priorities."

I studied him. "Well, the way I see it, that's one of the problems. I've taken down two demons. And Gabriel, the only Nephilim who offered to help, died. It seems our relationship could be defined by mistaken priorities. I've been shouldering all the weight, while your crew has been swimming in the piety pool."

The wooden desk cracked, making me jump instinctively. It was only a hairline fracture, and Nameless had gone forcibly still, closing his eyes. I waited, holding my breath. "Yes..." he finally admitted, letting out a breath and opening his eyes. "My apologies for the desk. It is not easy to admit fault. I never claimed to be perfect."

I nodded very slowly, letting a few moments pass before speaking. "This is pretty strange, Nameless. I can't tell if I'm in trouble or not. Or if I should care if I was. If you know you should have helped, why didn't you?"

He nodded. "I haven't always been free to choose my assignments – let alone act at all – in worldly events. But... the walls seem to be weakening. I have more sway now, but not as much as we need to stand against the Armies of Hell. This newfound... freedom to act is likely a result of the demons appearing here in recent months."

"That makes sense." I actively ignored his comment about Armies of Hell on the horizon, wanting to be able to get some sleep later. "So, you knew my fights were important, but were unable to get too involved. Any idea why?"

"No," he said, sounding troubled. "But that is why I might have come across too strongly during our first interaction. I wanted to rectify the situation, and instead took my frustration out on you. I saw power, an unmarked Nephilim slaughtering demons on her own." He lifted his head to stare at me with his intense, pale eyes. "I wanted you to *lead* my Nephilim."

I blinked in disbelief. Talk about bad ideas. I would have gone on a rampage with an army of Nephilim at my back. I hadn't been in a very sane place when I first met Ang— Nameless.

He stood, resting a palm over the desk. The wood groaned as it grew back together. He then walked over to the wall and leaned against it, folding his arms as he faced me.

"If that ever sounds appealing to you, I would appreciate it if you'd let me know..." he said.

I nodded. "I will... consider it. But I'll be honest, I'm wary of abrupt changes of character," I told him, pointedly looking him up and down.

He nodded. "That's why I asked you here. If I met you now, bared my breasts, admitted my past mistakes... then perhaps our healing could begin sooner. Give you more time to trust me before things get worse."

"I won't be baring my breasts, just to be clear, but..." I locked eyes with him. "I do appreciate this. Truly. I won't say I'm convinced, no offense, but I am surprised. And open minded."

"They say women forgive, but never forget," he murmured with a faint smile.

"And men forget, but never forgive," I replied, returning the smile.

A look of genuine amusement crossed his face. "I like that."

"So, that's it? You aren't about to shackle me into servitude?"

"No," he said, almost sorrowful. "You are free to go." He extended a hand towards the door. "I appreciate you giving me a chance to speak my mind. I don't blame you for feeling hesitant."

I studied him suspiciously. This was all too weird. I was a pretty good judge of character. But that was with humans, not Angels. Was I missing something?

"Okay. Nice talk."

I turned and walked back to the door, ready for his hidden card.

I heard papers shuffling and glanced over a shoulder as my hand rested on the door handle. Nameless was reading from a small stack of papers, old parchments of some kind.

I hesitated, calling myself nine kinds of idiot.

"Just out of curiosity, what kind of requests did you have on your plate?"

He looked up at me, not a flicker of victory or surprise on his face. In fact, he looked hesitant.

"We can handle it. I'd rather have your trust, first. But thank you for asking." He resumed reading his papers, not dismissing me, but as if trying to be polite. I knew this tactic, dangling a carrot, but I was still too curious to leave it hanging. I could always decline after he told me.

"I just meant that maybe it would be beneficial to exchange information, at least. A good starting point. We both want the best for the city, right?"

He looked back up at me, nodding thoughtfully. "But I also want what is best for my Nephilim and Heaven. If I can't have all your devotion to that cause, I'm not sure I want any of it. It would only make things worse."

"Just consider us allies exchanging information. I definitely don't want anything bad to happen to your cause. I'm just not sure I want to get the tattoo yet."

He finally set his papers down.

"Do you drink tea?"

"Sure," I said, making my way back to the table, wondering if I had made a mistake. Oddly enough, I could tell that Nameless harbored the same thought.

Were things really that bad in Kansas City?

I sat down, and Nameless began to talk.

CHAPTER 8

I studied Nameless thoughtfully, considering what he had just shared with me. "Just a scouting mission..." I repeated, watching his eyes.

He nodded. I glanced over at Alyksandre who had entered the room halfway through Nameless' explanation. He stood beside the bookshelf, decked out in dark military fatigues with a sword over his shoulder, having dropped the plaid shirt and jeans. I arched an eyebrow.

"Just in case," he said. "We are always ready for the worst."

I leaned back on my stool, tapping my chin with a finger. The tea had helped perk me up, but I knew Claire would be getting anxious soon. I should have been home by now.

"And what exactly are you scouting?"

"We've heard about a powerful object buried in Kansas City. That's one of the reasons we came here in the first place. To find it. So far, no luck."

"So, this is a regular mission you've been doing for months... And you haven't found anything?"

He pursed his lips, likely taking my question as criticism. I hadn't intended it as such, not really, but I let him think so. "Yes. Tonight, will be one of many searches we have done over the last year. All unfruitful, and all without conflict. Although you might get dirty. That's the extent of the danger – at least judging by what we've experienced on our previous excursions."

"Where did you find out about this new location?"

His eyes tightened, not directed at me for asking, but as if not pleased about the answer. "A private party who recently came to town. I'd rather keep their identity classified, for their own safety."

"I have one question before I make my decision." He nodded agreeably. "What were your Nephilim up to tonight?"

He blinked, caught off guard. Then he turned to Alyksandre. "You've all been here, correct?"

The Nephilim nodded, frowning. "Other than when I left to get Miss Penrose. Yes, we've remained indoors. Why?"

I studied the pair, focusing on every facial or bodily gesture. Then I sighed in relief. They hadn't been the ones chasing the woman into the alley. It had been a long shot anyway, but it never hurt to check.

"Okay. We're just going for a looksee. Why do you need me?"

"We don't," Nameless shrugged. "We're just... exchanging information," he said, reminding me of my request. "But you're more than welcome to join. Maybe your... unique gifts will aid us. Maybe not. This is just an olive branch between us with very little risk of danger."

I let out a breath. He was right. If this put me in his good graces – no pun intended – maybe it would be worth losing a little more sleep over.

"Okay. But do you have anything other than Miata's around here?"

Nameless grinned wolfishly.

CHAPTER 9

I had called Claire to let her know everything was fine, but that I would be another hour or so. "It's actually kind of perfect. Maybe this will get them off my back."

"I don't know, Callie," Claire argued sleepily. "They've caused you nothing but problems."

"This shouldn't be dangerous, and it has the potential to solidify trust between us," I said.

"Fine, but I'm coming with you," she said in a commanding tone.

"No, you're not. We're almost ready to leave, now."

"Then you will magic me there."

I clicked my teeth closed. "Magic you... here," I repeated, my tone letting her see how stupid her statement sounded in case her sleep-addled brain had overlooked it.

"Yes," she said, ignoring my tone. "I'll be ready in five minutes."

I shook my head. "This is kind of between me and them. Not sure how they would take it if I brought a bodyguard."

Her voice was much more alert than a few moments ago, and I prepared to argue for all I was worth. Claire could be vengeful. If I denied her, she would make me pay.

"Then you will promise to take me to Darling and Dear, tomorrow."

39

"Claire, I can't—" I froze, having spoken over her comment. "Wait. If I take you to Darling and Dear, you'll get off my back about this?"

"Yes."

I thought about it for a moment. "Fine. Deal." She chuckled on the other line and I scowled. "You set me up! You never cared about joining me tonight. You've been holding on to this card for a while, now."

"You have no idea. I've been waiting for the moment you would have something going down that you wouldn't want me to join you on, but that didn't actually sound dangerous. This is perfect. You fell right into my trap, and now I get to go shopping."

I grumbled unhappily. "I was going to take you shopping anyway," I admitted.

"Oh, great. Then I'll be ready in five minutes. You can come pick me up." It sounded like she was laughing under her breath.

"Sneaky bitch," I muttered.

"Your choice. But I'll raise all sorts of hell if you leave me unsupervised."

Which reminded me of something. Even though tonight was supposed to be danger-free, I realized I would feel much safer if I grabbed a weapon just in case. I was a little tired to rely strictly on magic. "Fine. I'll be there in five minutes. I just need to let the Nephilim know. Be ready or I'll tie you up and leave you in my closet."

She hung up, giggling.

Alyksandre approached from down the hall, seeing that I was now finished with my call. "We're ready. If you will follow me and Kevin."

He turned to head towards the back of the house. I very gently placed a hand on his shoulder so as not to startle him. He glanced back, shifting away from my touch out of habit. "Just the three of us?" I asked him, ignoring his knee-jerk reaction to flee from a woman's touch.

He nodded. "It's just a routine search. No need to waste resources. We've been doing this for months. At first, we brought a large group, but soon realized that not many dangers lurked in forgotten tombs."

I nodded. That actually made me feel better. If the Nephilim had so little concern about this mission, then I probably had nothing to fear. Now, if this had been my plan, the universe would have realigned so that something went wrong. But we had God on our side this time.

Maybe everyone just left the Nephilim alone out of fear. At least I wouldn't have to concern myself with worrying over a surprise attack. "Okay. I've got one change. You're bringing a friend, so am I."

His eyes tightened uneasily, as if not eager to share this update with his boss. "I'll have to check with Nameless. Who did you have in mind?"

I told him. At the sudden flush to his cheeks, I patted him on the shoulder reassuringly. "Don't worry. She'll wear clothes this time."

He blushed darker and turned to go speak with Nameless, who had just entered the hallway to see us off. I studied Kevin, our plus-one for the night. He was an average looking, middle-aged man. Handsome, but in a roguish way. Like he was the uncle that wasn't typically invited to the family reunions, but who had a history of saving your dad from a few bar fights in their college days. He smiled at me. It even looked genuinely respectful.

Alyksandre came back and I saw Nameless nodding at me. "We can pick her up on the way."

"I'll just get her right now. Save us some time. I'd rather get to bed sooner than later. And it would look less suspicious than you guys returning to my apartment. I do have enemies, after all."

He nodded thoughtfully. "We will be around back. How long—"

I opened a Gateway about a foot away from Kevin. He grunted, but didn't flinch at the sudden eruption of white sparks – which I purposely used to remind everyone which side I was on. White magic was tied to Heaven, in a way I didn't fully understand, but still used. Alyksandre looked briefly annoyed that I was already testing his authority by ignoring his commands, but regained his composure quickly.

"Please don't do that without warning. We're twitchy around unanticipated magic."

I nodded in understanding. I thought I sensed Kevin smirk as I turned back to the Gateway, but maybe he was just inspecting the ring of white fire around the hole in the air. Claire stood a few feet away, clutching a pistol in either hand wearing only her panties, and no bra. She also wore my shoulder holsters. I sighed, avoiding Alyksandre's gasp of surprise as I gave Claire a reprimanding look.

Wait. Those were *my* panties. The expensive pair I had just bought from *La Perla*.

Claire stared through the Gateway in surprise, facing us with the pistols hanging at her sides. Kevin grunted from behind me, but when I looked at him, I caught him averting his eyes. He didn't do it as smoothly or as quickly as Alyksandre, which was probably why he wasn't in charge.

"Jesus," Claire hissed, not noticing the winces from the Nephilim at her chosen curse. "I thought I had a few more minutes. Hold on a second."

"That's the new pair of underwear I just bought, Claire. I haven't even taken the tag off yet."

She glanced down innocently, swiftly ripping off the tag. "Oh? I don't see a tag."

"And shoulder holsters go *over* the clothes," I added.

She blushed this time. "Right. I knew that. I was just trying it on for size," she said. "Is that why it's so scratchy in the back?" she asked, bowing her back to reach and twist at the uncomfortable strap. This had obvious effects on her breasts, and I heard Kevin groan as Claire gave us quite the show, dancing back and forth as she struggled with the leather.

"Yes. That's why, Claire," I said, grinning in amusement.

"Can she please put on a bra?" Alyksandre growled behind me. I glanced over to see him staring at his boots again.

"Oh, sorry. I know I told you she would wear clothes, but she's not housebroken yet."

"Time is wasting, Callie," he said through gritted teeth, not lifting his eyes.

"Oh, I don't know. We have a *few* minutes…" I heard Kevin murmur, but when I looked over at him, I saw his chin jerk back down, but there was no remorse in his eyes when they met mine. He had been peeking! Instead of yelling at him, I winked.

It was good to know that not all of the Nephilim were prudes. I had a potential friend in the force. He looked thoughtful, as if wondering why I had a naked chick wearing leather straps in my apartment on standby. I let my grin turn wicked and full of sin.

He finally lowered his eyes, muttering under his breath.

Claire was already tugging on some clothes that had been draped over my couch. I saw what I had wanted to grab hanging from the mirror, but didn't look directly at it. "Can you grab my black scarf? I'm a little chilly from all this rain."

Claire's head popped through the sweater, but she wore a cautious frown, forgetting to tug the sweater down the rest of the way. Or to first put on a bra. Then again, if she needed to shift, I'd rather her not destroy my new bra in addition to the matching panties – *La Perla* was expensive – so I didn't reprimand her. "Your… scarf… The one with a little red on it?" she asked carefully.

I nodded, motioning her to tug her sweater down and end the free headlight show. I hoped the fact that her boobs still hung free had masked our conversation and the look on her face. The prudish Nephilim – well, not Kevin, the pervert – may have missed it.

I sensed his eyes on me, but he didn't say anything.

Claire finished changing, tugged on her boots, and carefully folded the scarf so that the cross wasn't visible.

The scarf I had stolen from the Templars. It blocked magic, and you could never have too much protection. Safety first.

Kevin glanced at it thoughtfully, but didn't say anything. Had he seen it for what it was? Claire was suddenly extending a hand to him, stepping between us with perky cheer. "I'm Claire. Need a cigarette after the free show?" she asked, passing the scarf to me behind her back. I tucked it into my pocket casually.

He grinned in surprise. "I'm Kevin. The Lord gave me eyes to see, but I meant no disrespect."

Alyksandre grumbled under his breath, but didn't directly chastise his fellow Nephilim. So maybe he was the only prude. Claire grinned, shaking his hand hard. He looked impressed at her grip.

"Polar bear," she answered the silent question in his eyes. He grunted warily, probably second-guessing the possible consequences of his wandering eyes.

"Let's go," I said, letting the Gateway vanish.

Alyksandre led us outside to reveal our rides.

Claire began to clap. "Ohhh… nice. I've always wanted one of those between my thighs."

Kevin's face flushed and Alyksandre walked very stiffly down the steps.

"Virgin ears, Claire. You're making Kevin blush."

"I am not!" he argued, laughing.

I stared at the motorcycles before us. I'd seen one of these before and knew enough to remember it was stupidly expensive. Ducati. I didn't care about the model. The brand was enough to let me know we were in for a wild ride.

And I would finally get to see why chicks dig motorcycles.

CHAPTER 10

*W*e stood outside the caretaker's building of a forgotten cemetery. Nothing fancy. Like something you would see in a scary movie set in a small town.

Which made me feel not one bit better.

The Ducatis we had ridden here had been fun – a giant vibrator carrying me around town at lightning speed? Check. The irony that Nephilim had given me this experience was not lost on me.

The six-figure bikes looked out of place beside such a worn-down cemetery. As we studied the small building, I got the impression that the caretaker's building hadn't been opened in quite some time – a hint that the business wasn't attracting new customers.

"What in the world could have caught your attention here? Was your informant a grave-robber?" I asked, sweeping the headstones absently, wondering if any of the graves had been disturbed.

Alyksandre pursed his lips and kicked down the door to the building, ignoring me.

"And the Lord said, *let the door be open. And the door was open*," I whispered to Claire.

Luckily, the two Nephilim had slipped inside the building to keep us safe from cobwebs, and were too busy inspecting the building's interior to notice my comment.

"Why did you want your scarf if this isn't dangerous?" Claire whispered.

"Always be prepared," I whispered back. "And since you were leaving the apartment, I wanted to know it was in safe hands. Not return home to find out that Nameless – the Angel formerly known as Angel – sent one of his goons to scoop up the scarf."

Claire looked suddenly worried, as if the thought hadn't occurred to her. "You think he would have?" she asked, frowning slightly at the building, and the Nephilim inside, as if suddenly doubting their intentions.

I shrugged. "I have no idea who to trust. I find it odd that Nameless has had such a change of heart."

"And a change of name," Claire offered suggestively.

I nodded. "Maybe he's telling the truth about realizing he'd been a dick to me. Or... my suspicion is warranted."

"Do you always think like that? That someone is trying to screw you?"

I smiled at her choice of words. She returned it with a level look. "It's better than being caught off guard by trusting too far," I admitted.

"Well, I'll just have to watch your back. To be your conscience. Just... don't keep things from me," she said meaningfully.

I smiled at her. "You've always been my conscience, Claire. Always."

"Damn right. I'll keep you safe from yourself, since you seem intent to put your neck in the noose every time I'm not looking."

"Clear!" Alyksandre called from the gloom. I rolled my eyes and joined him inside.

My eyes adjusted to the darkness fairly quickly since there wasn't much by the way of streetlights outside the abandoned cemetery. I saw Alyksandre kneeling near the back wall. The building didn't look as disheveled as I had expected. Not often used, but as if someone at least came by once a month to shuffle a few papers, clean the floor, and check the voicemail on the desk. I saw nothing that looked dangerous, and nothing that emanated waves of nefarious magic, so it looked like this was yet another fruitless lead.

Then Alyksandre flung back a rug and hefted. The floor opened up to reveal a trapdoor.

I blinked. "Your informant just *happened* to know about a hidden trapdoor in an old caretaker's building in a forgotten cemetery?" I asked suspiciously.

"The informant seemed... very concerned. Persuasive."

I began to have a very bad feeling about this whole thing as Alyksandre slipped through the trapdoor. I pulled out my scarf, tied it around my face – careful to keep it folded so the red cross didn't show on it – and breathed deeply, testing the draw of air. No point in suffocating to death.

Maybe I should have made Claire grab one, too. But I didn't know if it would have any negative effects on a shifter. I'd have to look into that. At least the scarf would double as a bandana against the dusty, crumbling remains of dead bodies in this forgotten catacomb.

I hadn't heard Alyksandre call back up to us – which would have at least told me it was only a small storage nook or something. The fact that only silence remained meant he had found a space big enough for us to explore, or he was still descending. I heard a knocking sound, and Kevin grimaced, turning to me. "Ladies first?" he asked.

"Scared?" Claire teased him, dropping down into the hole before he could respond. Kevin shook his head in amusement.

"I'm not scared," he clarified, noticing my attention.

"Be a good boy and watch the door. We'll be back shortly. I'd rather not have someone lock us down there," I told him. The look on his face told me he hadn't considered that risk.

Then I slipped down into the hole, my feet latching onto a built-in ladder. Kevin watched me descend, looking suddenly uneasy at the thought that he might be attacked. Not scared, but as if suddenly reconsidering Alyksandre's plan to only have the four of us.

And the question…

What had Alyksandre found down the hole?

"Watch over them, please," Kevin said, not sounding happy about his role, but realizing the importance of it.

I nodded. "I always do."

The earth swallowed me up step by step.

CHAPTER 11

*M*y feet finally reached the base of the ladder. Alyksandre had used a glow stick to mark the end of the descent, so we didn't stumble in the darkness. Claire stood a few paces away from the base of the ladder, staring out at the large dark cavern beyond. Alyksandre was staring up at the ladder, frowning.

"I told him to watch the door," I said. "What if your informant was leading you into a trap?"

He grimaced, apparently not having considered it. "Okay."

It also made me feel better to know we were no longer evenly matched. If this was a trap – for *me* – Claire and I could handle Alyksandre ourselves before taking on Kevin.

"How do you want to play this, Alyksandre?" I whispered. "If I toss up some light, we might scare any… inhabitants."

His eyes were very tight. "We won't need light," he whispered back, sounding troubled. Then he was leading us into the darkness.

Claire gripped my arm as I passed her. "There are lights ahead. And I can smell people. This place hasn't been empty in recent months…"

My eyes might have widened at that. We were about thirty feet underground. Had we actually found something nefarious? Who the hell lived underground? My mind, unfortunately, provided me with all sorts of unpleasant answers.

Feathers...

Fire...

I froze, unable to breathe for a moment. The Whispers were back. Obviously, no one else had heard. But what had their comments meant? Feathers? Fire? And why had it sounded like two different voices this time? Maybe it was the same Whisper, just angrier when it said *Fire*.

I shivered, keeping a tight rein on the voices as I followed Alyksandre and Claire deeper into the cavern. I smelled fresh dirt, obviously. And damp rocks. Like you would expect in a cave. But I soon smelled burning candles. And... herbs? Some kind of incense, maybe?

And a pale-yellow light from up ahead began to illuminate the walls around us. We were in a stone tunnel. I was careful to watch my step, not wanting an echo to alert anyone who might be ahead of us. Obviously, candles meant people. I doubted anyone would leave a bunch of candles burning unless they were still here. Whoever was using this place would likely use a flashlight on the way, and only use the candles while spending time here.

Which indicated we were about to interrupt someone.

Alyksandre held up a fist, silently telling us to *stop*. We did, watching as he lifted a finger one by one, and then we dashed around the corner at *three*.

I ran laterally so we weren't lined up like dominos, my black fan hovering before me as I prepared to launch some of my silver butterflies at any sign of a threat. A large open area yawned before us, dark gray rock covering walls that stretched up thirty feet or higher. No one attacked us. In fact, no one else was present. I turned to see Claire holding both pistols up, aimed into the cavern, waiting for someone to say *hello*.

Great mounds of melted wax dotted the perimeter of the cavern, not in a perfect circle or anything, but spaced far enough apart to illuminate the whole area. Wicks burned atop the masses of candles, letting me know that this place had been used for a very long time – at least at one point in time.

And those early inhabitants were either still around, or someone had discovered this place and brought it back to life. Alyksandre glanced at me, jaw tight. "I don't like this..."

"I never like things like this, but I usually check them out anyway," I muttered. "Now that we've broken in, we should probably look around while we have the chance. They're probably going to know that someone invaded their secret hideout, and will update their security. Now is probably our best and only chance."

He nodded stiffly. "Be wary. Something is wrong with this place…"

Claire was nodding to herself warily, but didn't offer her thoughts. When a shifter acts nervous, it's smart to pay attention. Predator instincts, and all that. I kept my magic close, breathing through the scarf.

We split up to circle the room. I saw cots carved into the rock wall near one of the candlewax mounds, and some dirty, aged blankets. Maybe we had found a homeless camp. Or maybe we were interrupting an archaeological dig site, although I didn't see any modern equipment. No extension cords, stand lamps, papers, electronics, or magazines. Like we had stumbled upon a hideout from the Middle Ages or something.

Alyksandre was inspecting the sleeping area so I focused on the opposite side. What looked like worn steps led up to a small nook in the wall, where a few more candles illuminated some items arranged in a specific manner, like a shrine. I frowned, walking closer to study it, but a sickening feeling suddenly rolled over me.

The focal point was a human skull formed into a cup or bowl, and as I stepped closer, I noticed a red stain in the base. I shivered, eyes sliding away to scan over several ancient golden coins, two badges, and an old broken dagger in the niche. One of the coins featured a worn depiction of two men riding a single horse.

I turned to call out to Alyksandre, my eyes sweeping the entire area out of habit. My voice cut off as I spotted a symbol carved into the wall about ten feet up, so large and worn that I hadn't noticed it until I was on the opposite side of the cavern.

I recognized it, but my brain sort of rebooted for a few seconds, not understanding – or wanting to understand – exactly what this place was doing *here* in Kansas City, Missouri.

That's when the winged man swept down from the ceiling.

Claire started blasting with both pistols, not bothering with any pleasantries or warnings.

CHAPTER 12

*T*he echoing gunshots were painfully loud in the enclosed space, making my ears ring, but I was too busy staring in disbelief at their effect to worry about protecting my eardrums. The figure wrapped his wings around his body and slammed into the ground in a crouch that cracked the floor. Then he whipped his gray wings – made of vaporish smoke and floating chunks of ice – wide, and a ring of force knocked Claire on her ass, cutting off her barrage of gunfire.

A tall, dark-haired, winged man stood before us, wearing jeans, cowboy boots, and a plaid button up complete with pearl buttons. I blinked.

The Angel of country music?

More like the Angel of twang, pickup trucks, and cheap beer. And I *really* hated country music.

The winged cowboy glared at us. "How *dare* you attack—"

"He must be Fallen!" Alyksandre bellowed, eyes wild.

Claire was climbing back to her feet, and I could tell that she was contemplating shifting into her bear form until she heard that little *Fallen* tidbit. Fallen… *Angel?* What the *hell* had we stumbled on down here to warrant a Fallen Angel for security?

"Claire!" I shouted, snapping her out of her hesitation. "Go tell Kevin we need reinforcements! *Now!*"

With a last scowl at the Fallen Angel, she scampered off. I didn't have time to get the old brain working, because Alyksandre was suddenly rushing the winged man with his sword raised. He began spinning and slashing like a miniature tornado. The Fallen Angel's eyes widened in momentary surprise, but he moved like a ribbon of silk in the wind, always just out of reach. Feeling highly uncomfortable with the idea of attacking the supposed Fallen Angel – because I really didn't have any proof, and he hadn't necessarily done anything to hurt us, yet – I flung out my hand, and dozens of silver butterflies swept out in a swarm.

They struck the winged man hard, but where they struck, they bounced away, and a sudden flash of pain struck the exact center of my brain. I fell, crashing into an empty pedestal, knocking it over as my vision swam and tendrils of fire slithered through my brain.

Kill it with fire!

Noooooooo!

Yesssssss!

I stared up at the ceiling, grunting and flinching as I tried to shake off the conflicting Whispers in my mind, which seemed to be arguing with each other. I couldn't tell if they were happy or frustrated with Alyksandre fighting the winged man, because they weren't directing their shouts clearly. Were they saying *No* to Alyksandre or to my failed attack on the winged man? Same with the other shouts. Who were they rooting for?

The fire slowly dimmed in my mind and I gasped in relief, rolling over on shaky arms to see Alyksandre's sword swing towards the creature like a sledgehammer.

The man's elemental wings whipped around his body protectively, and the hardened steel shattered like a fluorescent bulb upon contact, leaving nothing but a puff of powder in the air as if he had thrown a bag of flour.

The winged man placed a boot on Alyksandre's chest – capitalizing on his surprised grunt – and shoved him across the room. Alyksandre struck the back wall with a heavy thud as I managed to climb to my feet, shaking off my wooziness.

"Easy, pardner," I muttered, glaring at him. "The Sheriff's back in town."

The winged creature shot me an incredulous look before his eyes latched onto the broken pedestal at my side. Then his face contorted in anger as he took a step closer, mouth opening to scold me with the Holy Word or something.

But he only managed a step before his head flicked back towards the entrance. I heard a loud *crack* and the sound of many pounding feet racing our way. When I turned back, the winged cowboy was hurtling through the air, slipping through a crack in the stone like a cockroach.

Nameless appeared, glowing with white light. An entourage of unfamiliar Nephilim stood at his side, eyes alert. Claire – in polar bear form and looking ready to rend flesh – jogged up behind them, glaring out at the catacombs as if searching for something to hit. I scowled at her, realizing my expensive new underwear was now shredded as a result of her shift. Nameless bent down to place a hand under Alyksandre's chin, speaking softly. Alyksandre gasped, jumping to his feet, panting desperately.

I blinked. Had Nameless just brought him back to life? Or had Alyksandre only been unconscious?

I was striding up to Nameless before I realized it. I cleared my throat behind him, folding my arms. He turned, locked eyes with me, and then blinked, taking a step back.

"Where did you get that?" he asked cautiously.

Shit. My scarf. The cross must be showing.

At Nameless' tone, the Nephilim suddenly had pointy things aimed in my general direction, but Claire barreled into them like a wrecking ball, bowling them over.

Nameless clapped his hands once and I thought the catacombs might simply collapse down upon us. Everyone froze – even Claire. Then, she slowly climbed to her feet and backed away, never breaking eye contact with the Nephilim as she placed herself in front of me and any danger, a wall of white fur and claws.

I placed a hand on her shoulder and felt her rock-hard muscles shaking.

"Easy, Claire. Let's cool down a second. Everyone's on edge. I'm sure there is an explanation for… whatever just happened."

Nameless was studying me warily – not angry, but suddenly very thoughtful.

"Where did you get that?" he asked again.

"Spoils of war," I answered, keeping my face blank.

His lips pursed for a moment before he gave a brief nod. His eyes quickly flickered to the carving on the wall and then back to mine meaningfully. "Be careful with that. Spoils of war can sometimes be deadly. Just because we found a Templar hideout doesn't mean we should rob it."

I masked my uneasiness with a slow nod. "Understood." I had recognized their ancient symbol – two interwoven triangles that formed a 3D version of the Star of David, the well-known six-pointed star – but to find a Templar hideout in Kansas City? This place looked ancient – which was actually a relief. It meant the Templars hadn't suddenly come to town for me, building a secret base underground. Because I had kind of pissed off their head honcho in Rome.

"Who was that… guy?" I asked.

"An Angel that lacked conviction," Nameless said, sounding both disappointed and disgusted.

"Does that mean he was Fallen like Alyksandre said?"

Nameless grunted, eyes sweeping the cavern again. "We have all fallen short of the glory of God."

I rolled my eyes. "Specificity keeps swords out of the wrong people."

He didn't acknowledge me, instead glaring at the pedestal I had knocked over. "The Ring of Aandaleeb is gone. Did this Angel take it?" Nameless asked, turning to look at Alyksandre.

The Nephilim shook his head, dread locks swinging as he pointed at the pedestal. "Something powerful once rested there, but it was empty when we got here. I didn't notice the sensation until we entered the room itself, as if it had rested here long enough to leave a permanent residue. I checked the area over here to see if someone had hidden it instead of leaving it on display. But I found nothing."

"How long ago? Centuries? Years? Months?" Nameless demanded.

Alyksandre closed his eyes and took a deep breath. "I will try to trace it." Then he began walking, eyes still closed, as he lifted his palms to the air, letting them quest back and forth as if pretending to be a bird.

"Look, Claire," I whispered, patting her back. "An interpretive dance to find Andy's Ring…"

I heard someone cough, sounding suspiciously like Kevin, but the rest of the Nephilim were focused on their leader. Alyksandre reached the pedestal, fingers seeming to caress the air like a harp for a few moments. He took a deep breath, and then murmured. "I've got its aura, now…" Then he slowly walked across the room, eyes still closed, which was honestly pretty impressive since the ground was slightly uneven in places.

He reached the far wall and finally lowered his palms to his side. "Less than a day. It left through here."

I was walking over to him without consciously deciding to do so, wondering how he had tracked this ring down. I didn't realize I had spoken out loud.

"A gift. I can sense objects of power," he admitted, pointing at the wall.

I nodded absently. This ring had slipped through a solid wall? But as I neared, I realized there was actually a fold in the rock, leaving a sliver of a crack. Tight enough for... maybe a small person to slip through. I studied Alyksandre and shook my head. Then I glanced back at the others. They were all too big.

"I can check it out, see how far back it goes," I said, turning to Nameless.

Claire spoke up in a throaty grumble. "I'm smaller."

Everyone frowned at that, but a sliver of a smile crossed Kevin's cheeks as he realized what Claire had meant. She was smaller than me in human form. And that meant he might get another eyeful of her in all her naked glory.

I shook my head. "Unless you want your Nephilim to see a naked woman wriggling through rocks and darkness, it should be me. Also, I have magic. If I get stuck, I might be able to use it to break free."

Nameless nodded his agreement, and I heard a very faint sigh of disappointment from the Nephilim crowd.

CHAPTER 13

I slipped through the crack, ignoring Alyksandre's report of the winged man's form of ingress and egress. The cold stone pressed against me, scraping my shoulders, but it wasn't suffocating. Although dark, I imagined I was simply slipping through a crowd at a concert. The voices behind me faded, but those inside my head grew in volume. Still shouting and snarling intensely, but indistinguishable from one another. I shivered, pressing them down as I squeezed my body through the crack. The space opened up after a few shimmying steps, and the damp rock began to seep through my clothes. I managed to tug down the scarf, not wanting to hyperventilate since the suffocating sensation wasn't helping my mindset while maneuvering through the cramped, pitch-black space.

It began curving to the right, and I let my fingertips guide me, able to shimmy sideways more easily without fear of scraping my face on the rock. Still, I tested the ground beneath me, wary of sudden holes or crevices that could snap my ankle if I fell.

I breathed evenly, imagining sunshine and fields of chirping birds and flying kites, aware that my body was starting to get anxious, my shoulders hitching and fingertips tingling with anxiety as it imagined being stuck in here forever. If the item they were seeking had gone through this place, it had to open up somewhere. Maybe outside the cemetery. A back door. That wouldn't help me, but at least it would get me out of the cave.

Unless it spilled me out onto a camp of Templars or something.

Or if I found that winged cowboy waiting to swoop me up and carry me away. My silver butterflies had not only had no effect on him – they had seemed to recoil and harm *me*. Unless the timing was simply perfect, and the Whispers had decided to turn up the volume at that exact moment.

Or I was just so tired that I hadn't focused my spell properly, and he had some wicked defensive skills. Too tired to keep the Whispers from harassing me.

Still, I hadn't ever heard them sound angry. Sinister, sure. But that had been when I was killing asshole Templars – a far cry from the ones who had founded the Order's humble beginnings. I wondered what form of Templar had occupied the catacombs behind me. More of the twisted, morally righteous assholes I had encountered in Rome, or a bunch of pleasant old dudes reminiscing about the glory days of fighting in the Crusades? Time would tell.

But I was kind of working for an Angel – and he had wanted to steal something from them – so maybe these guys were also assholes. Or the Angel I was working for was an asshole. Or that other winged cowboy was an asshole.

Somebody was a stinker in this equation. And when the assholes had wings, things got messy. I paused, thinking about how *that* had sounded in my head, and sighed.

It didn't slip my mind that the only people I hadn't considered an asshole in the equation were myself or Claire.

And to *really* drive the metaphor home, I was currently sliding through the cold, damp ass crack of planet Earth, well below the surface, thanks to *these* assholes.

But was I sliding away from the assholes or closer?

I reached a thinner, even tighter spot and squinted my eyes closed as I let out my breath, trying to shimmy my way through. But I was still too big to fit. I let out more breath and forced my tense, upper body to relax. Between one moment and the next, I stumbled and fell into open space, but thankfully remained standing. I froze as someone shouted at me in alarm.

It took me a moment to realize I still had my eyes closed, because through my eyelids, I sensed light. I slowly opened them, careful to not appear threatening to whatever scene I had stumbled onto.

And found myself staring at Kevin who looked stunned. *"You're* the asshole!" I gasped. Kevin had double-crossed us, been in on the theft the whole time, even called in the winged cowboy!

He cocked his head and pointed over my shoulder. I briefly glanced back to see the ladder we had originally descended from. I was back at the entrance, the caretaker's cabin above me. "Well, shit," I growled, lowering my hands in defeat as my hypothesis disintegrated. "Might want to go get our sniffer. Looks like Alyksandre missed it our first time through."

Kevin grunted, nodding. He peered at where I had emerged, looking embarrassed that he hadn't noticed it before turning away to jog back to the cavern. The fold in the rock almost fully concealed the narrow crack from view. Without knowing it existed, it was easy to miss. I noticed a piece of rock had broken off a lower fold in the stone. I knew I hadn't kicked free any rocks, so it was yet more proof that someone had made the journey before me, and left evidence behind of their passage.

I heard Kevin call out for Alyksandre to tell him about my appearance. That the crevice had circled the catacomb, and that whoever had stolen Andy's Ring – whatever that was – had left the same way we had entered.

Nameless appeared, listening to the exchange as Claire lumbered up to me, sniffing and then nuzzling her massive head under my armpit. I spotted a piece of shredded lace on the ground and scowled.

"You owe me a new pair of *La Perla* panties," I threatened her. "Your big hairy ass was never designed for couture lingerie." The angry polar bear curled her lip at me and then – without breaking eye contact – sat on the shred of lace. She even wriggled her ass into the ground, grinding the remains of my panties into the earth. I scowled, turning away with a sniff.

Nameless was frowning in disapproval as Alyksandre spoke. "I sensed it before, but thought it was merely the trail of it leading *here*, not the trail of it leading *away*," he grumbled, sounding more embarrassed than anything. As if his own anger at his failure was greater than anyone else's thoughts on the matter.

I let the silence build for a few minutes. "Right. Well, I'm filthy, cold, and tired. This place holds no further importance, so how about we recap tomorrow? Tell me all about Andy's Holy Ring."

"*Aandaleeb*," Kevin corrected.

Nameless nodded, eyes distant. "Yes. Perhaps we can talk about that, too," he said, lifting a finger to point at the scarf hanging from my neck.

He turned back to his Nephilim, obviously not a big fan of goodbyes.

"Search every inch of this place," Nameless told them. "We might find more scarves. Finders keepers," he added with a smile.

Alyksandre and Kevin were both studying me with calculating eyes. They knew I'd had the scarf before we got here, but they hadn't said anything. They very easily could have called me out. Especially since they were likely upset that I hadn't told them what it really was, and had instead concealed the crucifix emblazoned across the front.

Did they know what it did?

Basically, they had many reasons to tattle on me – and they probably should have.

But they chose a life of sin – a lie of omission to their Angel boss.

I was beginning to like them more and more.

CHAPTER 14

*T*he pew was sturdy and vastly uncomfortable, obviously designed for penance. I shifted slightly, trying to find a more pleasant position, but the punishment was evenly spread across the wooden torture rack.

"Stop fidgeting," Dorian grumbled beside me. "Have you no decency? We're at Mass."

Dorian Gray was wearing a pristine dove-gray suit, perfectly tailored to his frame. He even sported a small primrose in his lapel. His hair was perfectly slicked back, it looked like he had colored some gray into his temples – as if hoping it would help him spear-fish the Desperate Housewives of Abundant Angel Catholic Church. And I was pretty sure he was wearing makeup. Then again, he was gloriously beautiful, not the slightest hint of a blemish marring his prettiness.

But he had a painting of himself at his mansion that revealed an entirely different view – depicting him as a leper. He kept that one in a safer place, now. Ever since I had found it and threatened to torch it.

Because Dorian Gray was immortal – as long as his painting was safe. He thirsted for vice and sin, and his appetite was insatiable. Every act of deviance he participated in, each moral or ethical rule he shattered, and any physical wound he received was instead transferred to his painting, leaving him perfectly flawless, but his painting more and more grotesque.

And he was chastising me in Sunday Mass.

The glare on my face only made him smile back, flashing me his perfectly white teeth.

"He has a point," Cain muttered under his breath, leaning closer. "I find it very disrespectful. Personally."

He was a rough-looking kind of guy with messy brown hair and very light eyes that stood out against his bronze skin, as if he never spent a minute indoors. And he hadn't gone out of his way to dress up like Dorian. Cain was a take-it-or-leave-it kind of guy, for the most part. I gritted my teeth, considering elbowing him in the ribs, but quickly dispelled the idea.

Cain – coined the world's first murderer after he killed his brother, Abel, for not sharing his pet rock or something – was *personally* offended? Thinking about it, I kind of understood. He was the son of Adam and Eve. It was probably like watching a home video of his childhood, but none of his friends were paying attention.

So, two morally-flexible people were telling me to stop being inconsiderate. Broken clocks, and all that. "Fine. I'm just tired," I finally admitted.

"Did you know that kid?" Cain murmured softly, not looking away from Father David at the pulpit. We were far enough back to not earn Father David's open displeasure, but I could tell he sensed us and didn't appreciate us talking through his sermon.

Cain slowly jerked his chin towards a young boy who was sitting on the edge of his pew a few rows ahead of us. He looked about ready to explode forward to rush the pulpit, even though his parents kept trying to push him back and make him sit still.

I had pulled the kid aside to ask him to do me a favor just before we entered the church, recognizing him from earlier visits to Abundant Angel Catholic Church – the place that used to be my stomping grounds when I worked with Roland for the Vatican Shepherds – holy warrior wizard monks.

That had kind of gone up in flames after my trip to Rome, but I wasn't about to stop visiting the church. I had a lot of memories here. Hell, Father David had found me as a baby on the church's front steps, later delivering me to my parents for adoption.

Ironically, now that I didn't work downstairs in the secret training area for the once resident-Shepherd, I realized I was more interested in attending church than I'd ever been before. Maybe that was just because I was rebellious. Possibly nostalgic. Tell me I couldn't go somewhere, and guess where I was going next?

"Why is he so excited?" Cain asked suspiciously.

"You'll see..."

Cain and Dorian glanced at me, frowning in unison. The pew suddenly felt more comfortable.

As Father David continued, I could have sworn that his eyes settled on me for a significant length of time. He looked tired. Was he still upset about my adventures in Rome? He did work for the Vatican, in a way. Or maybe he was fearful at the potential reason for my attendance.

To be honest, I would have much rather stayed in bed, but I had thought the soothing drone of the church could do me some good – to put things into perspective. I was neck deep in Angel politics. I realized I was openly glaring at a painting of an Angel in flowing white robes, blowing a trumpet. I sniffed, averting my eyes. *Not at all what they really look like*, I thought to myself.

Perhaps I had come to church for guidance. I felt adrift lately, not sure what my place in Kansas City was going to be.

I'd hunted monsters for the Vatican – briefly – and had never really wanted to work for them in an official capacity. But that didn't mean I didn't want to keep my city safe from monsters. It felt like I had an internal compass pulling me to do it regardless of my employer.

But I'd decided to not be anyone's pawn.

Not the church.

Not Heaven.

And definitely not Hell.

That hadn't stopped the recruitment letters, figuratively speaking. Both sides of the Bible were interested in me. It was getting harder and harder to be a...free agent, so to speak. So, I was making friends with the local monsters – the relatively good ones.

Like taking a few of the monsters to church with me.

Because when Roland returned to find he was officially no longer welcome as a Shepherd – since he was now a vampire – he was going to be forced into monster politics whether he liked it or not. So... I was kind of doing this for him as well. Making sure we both had new allies.

Claire began to openly snore, so I pinched her thigh. "Christ!" she hissed from a dead sleep.

The people three rows ahead of us even turned around at her sudden outburst. Father David pointedly didn't look in our direction, but I could tell he wanted to throw his Bible at us. Dorian was calming those around him down, apologizing for Claire. "She's new to this," he explained in a soft, seductive voice, smiling much-too-devilishly at a married woman.

Not so strangely enough, the woman's husband was eyeing Dorian with a thoughtful smile rather than a territorial scowl about the type of smile Dorian was flashing his wife. I groaned.

I felt like I was sitting in church with the Three Stooges. Or maybe three toddlers.

We managed to make it through the rest of Mass without any further drama, but when we stood to leave, the other members maintained a polite, but obvious, distance. I led my band of heathens to the front of the church, hoping to get out without notice. Then I saw Father David purposely walking my way, and I inwardly cringed. Claire, oblivious, shuffled towards the upstairs offices, sniffing the air anxiously. Using her shifter abilities to find the coffee machine? David fell into step beside me, shooting furtive glances at Cain and Dorian who were speaking in low tones as if about a secret.

"You should join me," Dorian said to Cain, sounding amused. I'd missed the first part of the exchange.

Cain grunted. "I can't. I have a date tonight," he murmured, avoiding eye contact.

"What trouble are you planning, Dorian?" I interrupted, frowning over at him.

Dorian's face tightened, instinctively ready to lie so he could get back to pressing Cain for details on the date he obviously hadn't wanted to discuss. "I have a board meeting tonight."

Cain's eyes momentarily widened in astonishment, but he quickly recovered. I studied the two of them suspiciously as we made our way up the stairs, Father David having given up on me to take the lead – well, more pursuing Claire's uninvited intrusion into his inner sanctum, anyway.

"Board meeting… right. And you think Cain should go. Because… well, he's just such an executive," I said flatly.

"He has a… knack for ending arguments," Dorian offered with a faint grin, but spoke it more like a question. "What about you, Callie? You free tonight?"

I shook my head. "I also have a date tonight."

Cain frowned at Dorian, glossing over my comment. "Wait. You want me to kill your fellow Board members?" he asked, incredulous, but Dorian was staring at me in stunned disbelief.

"I would appreciate it if you didn't talk about killing people in my church," Father David said through gritted teeth, rounding on us now that we were out of public hearing and entering his private quarters. Claire – looking like a zombie – was pouring herself a cup of coffee on autopilot. She got maybe a half ounce of the liquid before it ran empty. She stared at it for a second, not able to process the situation. Then she threw the coffee pot across the room with a shriek of despair.

CHAPTER 15

*F*ather David gasped, but Cain snatched it out of the air – using his superhuman speed to somehow get in front of it even though Claire hadn't thrown it anywhere near him.

David placed his hands on his hips. "Do *not* throw my coffee pot!"

Claire stared back at him through bloodshot eyes that promised murder. "Unless your holy coffee pot can turn wine into coffee, it is of no use to me."

Dorian swept in and placed an arm around her shoulder, guiding her to a couch. He withdrew a slim baggie of something white, murmuring softly.

"Hey!" I snapped at him. "You can't just offer her drugs because she needs a pick-me-up. We'll go get some coffee in a few minutes!"

Cain grunted, gently setting the coffee pot back in place. "That escalated quickly. From coffee to cocaine." He shot Father David an apologetic look. "He's a bad influence, Father David."

This, coming from the man who had just casually discussed killing a group of board members.

Father David was too busy staring incredulously at Dorian – who had swiftly tucked the baggie back into his coat and was smiling crookedly. "Just offering options," he said weakly. "A gift from some old pals downstairs."

This, of course, made Father David livid. "My congregation does *not* deal drugs!"

"I'm sure he wasn't implying that," I said quickly, shooting a warning look at Dorian. He frowned back at me, rolled his eyes, and leaned back into the chair. Maybe he had meant downstairs figuratively, like demons or something. Claire was staring longingly at the pocket with the drugs beneath Dorian's coat.

"Right. We need to go get some coffee," I sighed.

Father David let out a breath. "I'll join you. I have someone you need to meet, anyway."

I frowned at that, but Claire was already tugging Dorian to the door ahead of us.

"What happened to you two last night? You look hungover," Father David asked, not sounding pleased.

"We're not hungover. Just a long night," I answered, walking down the stairs.

"It's not safe for a woman to be out late at night," Cain mumbled behind us, as if speaking to himself. "Else how can she expect to have breakfast ready for her man in the morn—"

I darted back, grabbed a fistful of his shirt, wrapped my arm around his waist, and hip threw him over my shoulder and down the stairs. Father David hissed angrily, especially when Cain loudly rolled the rest of the way down, grunting and chuckling the whole way, the bastard. Conversation downstairs halted as the gathered congregation members hastily turned to check out the commotion. Cain barely missed a vase at the base of the steps.

But rolled right up to a group of older women. The *Three*.

A well-known group of older women always on the prowl for a fresh young stud. They had caused me trouble in the past, but I had eventually turned the other cheek, amused by their antics.

Like right about now.

They couldn't help him get to his feet fast enough, groping handfuls of his body in the process, asking if he needed anything, an ice pack, to sit down, and didn't they just make the best sweet tea in Kansas City? Cain played the buffoon, smiling as they copped feels, squeezed his arms, and patted his shoulders compassionately, admitting to them that he had just taken a fall from sheer clumsiness.

Claire strode up to the group, ignoring the three older women and staring straight into Cain's soul from inches away. "You're delaying my coffee run. Don't do that." Then she turned and stormed out of the church, Dorian hot on her heels.

Cain smiled sheepishly at the women and then followed her and Dorian out the door. I was just happy that the trio hadn't seen Dorian or things would have gotten interesting. He might have even invited the women to one of his famous flesh parties.

I had no doubt they would take over the business after their first visit.

Father David made polite greetings as others noticed him, but one woman in particular caught his attention. An older woman with a sweet, grandmotherly face, but with the eyes of a vengeful goddess. From the looks of it, I don't think anyone else saw past the smiling cheeks.

She wore a simple set of perfectly ironed Sunday Best – a skirt that reached her ankles, and a plain purple cashmere cardigan. David extended a hand to her, and she smiled back at him like a groupie at a rock concert. She let him guide her over to me by the elbow.

I quickly bit back my frown. This was who he wanted me to meet?

The woman took one look at me, and I could have sworn her eyes lit with fire. Not magical, but something much deadlier.

The merciless fires of a grandma who was about to teach me the error of my ways with a quiver of wooden spoons and a bar of soap. All while reciting the Book of Proverbs from memory.

Coffee was sounding better and better.

I opened my mouth to say *hello* when I felt a tug at my hip. I glanced down to see the young boy I had commandeered earlier. He smiled, nodding proudly. I pointedly didn't look up at Father David, but it felt like an oven door had just opened from two feet away. He was pissed.

I slipped the kid a twenty-dollar-bill and he disappeared into the crowd before David could snatch him by the collar – although the good father did try.

Which left me with two angry adults glaring at me.

"You put him up to that stunt?" Father David hissed in a low tone, quiet enough to not be overheard by the rest of the congregation.

I shrugged. "I just encouraged him to always ask questions."

"He *asked* me…" he kept his voice low, trying not to openly snarl, "if God is all knowing, omnipotent, and all powerful, can He make a rock that even He can't lift?"

"From the mouths of babes…" I replied sheepishly.

"He did this in front of new members at the church, Callie. And you put him up to it. You *paid* him to ask it!"

"COFFEE!" a banshee shrieked from outside, full of anguish and misery and frustration – like an entrance to the deepest pit in Hell had briefly opened up outside the church.

"We should probably go," I said, shooting disarming smiles at the frowning congregation members, the mothers suddenly clutching their children to their hips protectively. I quickly shuffled Father David and the older woman out the door. Claire was on the verge of a meltdown. Ever since becoming a shifter bear, sleep was kind of a high priority for her, and I'd kept her out late. Then – without warning – woke her to let her know we were going to church.

"We'll continue our conversation at the drug dispensary," the woman said in a very crisp tone.

"Coffee shop," I corrected, frowning at her.

"Like I said, *drug dispensary*," she replied in the exact same tone.

Thinking about *that*, I wondered if I should get Cain and Dorian as far from the coffee shop as possible while I had a chat with this apparently orphaned ray of sunshine Father David seemed so insistent upon me meeting. I had a feeling she didn't suffer sin well.

CHAPTER 16

*W*e sat in my java joint – the usual haunt for me to pick up my go-go-juice. It was close to both the church and my apartment, and I liked the crew of baristas here, as strange as they were.

Claire had ordered a double-shot of espresso, an energy drink, and a quad-shot latte with more syrup flavors than I could fathom, but I was confident that there was less milk than anything else in the cup.

Dorian was whispering to her, pointing at the energy drink and then the latte, as if encouraging her to mix the two together. She was giving his suggestion serious thought before I reached over and snatched up the energy drink.

"Finish your appetizers first," I scolded her, shooting Dorian a look as well. "When I'm confident you aren't hearing colors, I'll give it back." She stared at me for a few seconds, face devoid of all humanity, before scooping up the espresso in one hand and the latte in the other, double-fisting.

She downed the espresso, set the empty cup down, and began drinking her latte, eyes locked onto the energy drink in my hand.

Father David and the old woman each had a tea in front of them, and she appeared to be listening to Cain with a faint, but appreciative, smile. I hadn't noticed that she had sat down between Cain and Dorian, but I couldn't think of a courteous way to extract her out of the Devil's palms so to speak, so I abandoned her to fate. Maybe they would scare her away before she could pounce on me. I watched in astonishment as she reached out to pat Cain on the hand.

"Such a sweet boy," she said. "We need more men like you in St. Louis."

I blinked in disbelief – at both the exchange, and the mention of St. Louis.

"Thank you, Greta, but St. Louis is a little too... high-brow for my tastes," Cain said, smiling.

Dorian leaned over. "That is a delightful cardigan, Greta." He gently brushed his hand down the fabric. "It truly brings out your eyes. Is it custom fit or do you just make it look that way?"

I hadn't heard her introduce herself, but Dorian and Cain had. I'd been too busy making sure Claire didn't give herself a heart attack. Greta actually blushed, absently straightening the sweater. "I often wonder where all the good men have gone," she grinned. "It seems that two of them are right here in Kansas City. Bless you, boy, even though I should be old enough to shrug off your flattery."

"The Lord works in mysterious ways," Dorian replied with a wicked grin. "But I am just a humble servant, sowing what good seeds I can."

Claire choked on her latte at his double entendre, and Cain began patting her on the back forcefully, asking if she was okay.

I slowly shook my head. This couldn't be happening. This hateful old woman thought the two worst people at the table were good little choir boys? Talk about bad character judgment.

"Well, while Dorian is off sowing his seed, my name is Callie and this is Claire. Greta, right? Pleased to meet you. David said—"

"*Father* David," the woman corrected me, pursing her lips. I felt Dorian and Cain casting disapproving looks my way.

I gritted my teeth, ignoring the two bastards. "I didn't feel the need to specify, because I didn't notice any other David's lurking about the table."

"Here, now, Callie. You should show him the respect of his title," Dorian said gently.

"And respect for your elders," Cain added.

Greta flashed them another genuine smile, but Father David's shoulders were tense, his mouth hanging open as he stared from Dorian to Cain in disbelief. He knew who they were. He was aware of the supernatural community. He was just as shocked as I was. I wondered what the hell this introduction was really all about. And why my friends were antagonizing me.

"Right." I turned to Father David in mock solemnity. "Sorry, Daddy. I've been naughty."

Claire spit out her latte in a coughing fit, and David's face went white as a sheet, in stark contrast to Greta's rapidly purpling face. Dorian was leaning back in his chair, covering his face in mock horror, but I knew he was really concealing his devilish grin.

I frowned at Father David. "Did I say that wrong? I meant, *forgive me father, for I have sinned.* I guess it really *is* all about the delivery," I mused to myself as if at an inner thought. *"Father* David mentioned you wanted to speak with me," I said, pretending not to notice her quivering outrage as I took a sip of my coffee.

"Yes, well..." Father David said, quickly reaching out to pat Greta's hand reassuringly, calming the old bird down. The sooner this was over, the sooner I could get to more important things. I wanted to go have another talk with Nameless to see if he had learned anything about the catacombs or the winged cowboy. I also had a few calls I wanted to make.

I didn't even want to think about the Whispers and their seemingly conflicting comments in the Catacombs. Roland was the only one I dared ask about that, but he was gone. Maybe a little shopping therapy with Claire would make us both feel better.

I noticed a woman a few tables away reading a magazine. Had she been looking at us?

Or was my sleep-deprived brain making me paranoid?

"I want to know what kind of woman you are, child. And so far, I'm not impressed." Greta glanced at Cain and Dorian who were smiling sweetly, leaning forward as if to hang on her every word. "Although these two may help balance out your rough edges." Dorian placed a hand around her shoulders in a brief hug of gratitude at the compliment.

Greta blushed.

I turned to Father David. "Okay. My patience is gone. Who the hell is this again? For a second there, I thought maybe the Pearly Gates had been left unguarded."

Everyone stiffened at that, and Greta's face went right back to that lovely purple hue that matched her *custom* cardigan. I let out a measured breath, closing my eyes for a few moments. Then I opened them and turned back to

Greta. "I've had a long night. Let me rephrase my question. Who the hell are you?"

Cain clucked his tongue, shaking his head in disapproval. Dorian was openly frowning at me.

Claire may as well have had a bowl of popcorn in front of her, her eyes twinkling merrily as she slurped her energy drink loudly. *Wait a minute…* Dorian looked suspiciously innocent. He must have somehow stolen it from me to feed Claire's addiction. I let it go. One fight at a time.

Greta answered through gritted teeth. "I am Greta. One of Father David's friends from St. Louis."

"And that matters to me, why?" I asked with a brittle smile. Something about her just rubbed me the wrong way. Storming in here like the matriarch of women everywhere, holier than thou attitude, and I was expected to prove to her that I was a good little girl? She was obviously a poor judge of character if she believed Dorian and Cain were innocent cherubs.

"Are you a devout woman of God?" Greta asked.

"Can anyone be?" I answered her, waving a hand. "That's a loaded question. I try to do good as often as possible."

"As often as possible…" Greta repeated, not sounding swayed.

I nodded tightly. "I must have forgotten. What job did I apply for again? Why am I being interviewed?"

Father David cleared his throat, cutting off Greta's response. "Let us start fresh. Callie used to work for the Vatican. Although her methods are… unorthodox, she has a big heart and a kind soul." Cain coughed again, and Claire burst out laughing – quickly pretending she had read something funny on her energy drink. She even pointed it out to Cain, but he gave her a frown before refocusing on Greta.

Father David scowled at Claire before turning back to me. "Greta works for Nate Temple's company in St. Louis—"

I slid my chair back from the table, alert for threats. The soothing hum of patrons in the coffee shop seemed to suddenly cease, either in response to overhearing mention of Nate Temple or because of my sudden motion. "What are you?" I asked in a low tone, locking eyes with her. I hadn't sensed a lick of magic on the old woman, but if she worked for Nate, she might be highly dangerous, and she obviously didn't like me much. Had I ever heard him mention a woman named Greta? Now that I thought about it, the name did sound familiar, but I couldn't remember why.

Greta frowned at me. "I'm a humble old woman, girl. Sit back down. Now. You've caused enough problems lately."

"*Excuse* me?" I laughed in disbelief, not realizing I had actually stood up at some point.

"I've heard about what happened at the Vatican. And what you've done in this city. Although you managed to do some good here, you did something terrible last night." Her eyes darted about the room, and she leaned closer, speaking softer but still not that pleasant. "Sit. Down."

"What do you know about last night?" I asked, slowly sitting back down and scooting closer to the table. But I remained alert for an attack.

"Attacking an Angel, of course," she hissed.

I blinked at her. Then it hit me. The winged cowboy?

I suddenly felt very nervous. Was she really who she claimed? Did she really know Nate? Or was she using Father David to get close to me? "If I fought an Angel last night, then he was one of the Fallen..." I growled. "Nephilim fought beside me."

Her lips thinned, and she looked on the verge of having steam burst from her ears.

Despite our intention of remaining quiet, many of the customers were studying us out of the corners of their eyes, pretending not to eavesdrop. The silence made it abundantly clear, though.

"He was *not* Fallen!" she hissed softly, actually quivering as if I had personally offended her.

I met her eyes levelly, forcing myself to think.

She lies... the Whispers cooed in my head. I flinched at the unexpected advice but regained my composure quickly.

"Get out, old woman. I've had enough judgment for one morning." I didn't know exactly what was going on, but my Whispers hadn't steered me wrong yet. They'd actually saved my life a few times. But even without them...

I didn't like this woman. Who did she think she was? I wasn't about to take any crap from this bitter woman. Hell, I didn't even know if she was who she said she was. How could she know about Angels? Especially an attack that had happened only hours ago? An attack that had put Claire and I in very real danger.

When Greta made no motion to move, I stood, snatching up my drink. "We're leaving," I said, staring at Claire.

"We should talk further…" Father David pleaded softly, trying to calm me down. "What could be more important than this?" he asked, holding out his hands, placating.

I walked around the table, grabbed Claire by the bicep, and pulled her to her feet. "Shopping," I told Father David. "Bitches love shopping."

Greta hissed, repulsed by my crass language – especially directed at Father David.

Claire nodded eagerly, understanding what *shopping* meant.

Greta opened her mouth, but I ignored her and pulled Claire after me. Darling and Dear sounded much better than this crap. I had plenty of other people I could call if I wanted to verify details on the events from last night. One person who was definitely getting a call was Nate Temple, to see if he really knew anyone named Greta.

Everyone in the coffee shop watched as I left, likely having sensed the hostility in our exchange with Greta, even if they hadn't heard details. Maybe I had been shouting.

Greta hissed something at me as I walked out the door, but all I caught was …*Solomon…*

I turned to Claire. "Let's go see Darling and Dear."

She squealed excitedly, but I could tell she was distantly considering the conversation at the table. "I don't know if I brought enough money with me to shop there," she finally gasped, sounding horrified.

I gripped her shoulders, smiling. "Don't worry. You don't have to pay with money. Sometimes you just have to sell a part of your soul. Even a sleazy, shattered soul like yours has to be worth at least a bracelet or coin purse."

Claire chuckled weakly, but something about my face made her smile falter and her face pale.

CHAPTER 17

*T*he bell jingled as Darling and Dear opened the door for us. The two owners – possibly in an open marriage, definitely amoral and likely immortal – stood side by side, smiling warmly back at me. Then their eyes turned to Claire and they leaned forward to take a big ol' whiff.

"Hmmm… a woman of the night," Darling hummed. "I approve." He absently combed his fingers through his long, sandy hair, his eyes dancing mischievously against his tanned face.

"A woman after my own black heart!" Dear cooed, bumping her hip – somehow erotically playful – against Darling. Her vibrant red hair was thick and luscious, and only emphasized her perfect alabaster skin. Neither broke eye contact with Claire, who was frowning as if wondering whether she should feel insulted about the black heart comment.

"Um…" Claire replied, glancing from one to the other. "I'm—"

"Claire…" Darling said, licking his lips as if he could taste it.

"Stone…" Dear added immediately, winking knowingly.

"Can we close the door before you two weird her out?" They turned to look at me in unison, arching their brows. "So it's harder for her to escape, of course," I added with an awkward smile.

They blinked, turned to Claire, and then burst out laughing.

They let us enter, closing the door behind us as we stepped inside, the smell of fresh, cured leather swamping me like a comforting blanket.

Darling instantly wrapped his arm around Claire's shoulders as Dear latched hers around Claire's waist. I thought I saw her fingers graze Claire's ass on the way, but my friend must not have minded too much, was too overwhelmed to notice, or I was imagining it. Then they were guiding her deeper into their store, leaving me to find my own way. I scowled, grumbling under my breath as they began telling her what she *simply must have.*

With a resigned sigh, I followed, inhaling the pleasant aroma permeating the labyrinth of a shop these two... beings ran. I wasn't entirely sure what or who they really were, but they had treated me kindly, dealt fairly, and their wares had helped me survive more than one scuffle intact when I very realistically should have just died.

I slowed as I passed a placard that looked new – or at least recently dusted off.

Darling and Dear – Armorers of the Apocalypse. Established...

I frowned, leaning closer to rub off the corner, which hadn't been fully cleaned off.

"Found that in an old box. Even the dustiest of boxes can have hidden pleasures..." Darling whispered directly into my ear.

I gasped, spinning, but he was easily a pace away, not French-kissing my ear canal like he had sounded. His eyes twinkled as he smiled back at me.

His words hit me, and I translated the double entendre.

Darling and Dear were grossly inappropriate. If you thought their comments could be interpreted as dirty or scandalous, that was probably their intent. And you had probably missed a handful of other sleazy references they had uttered. But they rarely spoke casually, their comments usually hiding multiple meanings. And some of those hidden meanings were very important, as if they attempted to conceal their advice in X-rated riddles.

With Darling and Dear, a dirty joke could actually save your life.

Long story short, these mysterious leather workers were into sex. Which kind of made sense, I guessed. They sold all sorts of leather goods to all sorts of interested parties. "Is it true?" I asked, pointing a thumb at the placard.

He shrugged, waving a hand. "Who else would you trust to keep all you silly mortals safe during such a highly violent disagreement?"

I blinked at him. "Disagreement," I repeated in a flat tone. "The Apocalypse."

He smiled.

"Right. I should probably make sure Claire isn't halfway through an orgy."

He shrugged, as if the likelihood was entirely possible, before leading me deeper into the store. I studied the goods around us, nodding absently as we passed the various… departments. Satchels. Bracelets. Armor. Shoes. And several areas that were a hodge-podge of different items, some looking very ancient.

"Did Temple like his satchel?" Darling asked in an amused tone.

"Oh, his purse?"

Darling frowned, glancing over at me. "Satchel," he repeated in a warning tone.

I rolled my eyes, wondering if I would ever see the day where men admitted the truth. Changing the wearer's sex didn't suddenly make a purse a satchel, but it was funny to see that Darling carried the same delusion as Nate.

"He loved it. Got some good miles out of it in Hell, apparently." I watched Darling out of the corner of my eye, waiting for a reaction.

Darling just nodded matter-of-factly, humming to himself as his finger-tips adoringly brushed a whip as he walked by a… darker, date-night section of the shop. I saw a few masks and chained cuffs before I averted my eyes. Right. Freaks needed BDSM gear too, I guess.

Hearing that Nate had gone down to Hell hadn't caused a glimmer of surprise or interest in Darling. Who the hell were these two, really? Even Nate's godly friends had been surprised to hear about Hell.

But Darling? Just fondly fondled a bedroom prop at the comment.

"Waiting for me to compliment your incredibly sexy new hairstyle, or does something else trouble you?" he asked, not turning to look at me.

I smiled at the compliment but continued my search for Claire. How big was this place? I could hear her talking, but the volume hadn't changed, as if we were just walking in circles around her.

"Many things trouble me. Like why all these gangs are forming in town? And why is no one doing anything about them?"

Darling grunted. "Vermin."

I nodded. "I agree. The gangs are vermin, and should easily be handled without me having to step up and slap around a few thugs in the middle of the night."

He turned to look at me. "Oh, right. The gangs are vermin, too." He nodded, continuing on.

I frowned at his back. "Wait. Who were you talking about if not the gangs?"

"Everyone," he replied, smiling over his shoulder. "Both high and low." Then he was briskly walking away again, leaving me sputtering behind him as I rushed to catch up. Was that a subtle nod to Angels and Demons or some other group I wasn't aware of?

"Hey—"

He rounded on me so suddenly that I grunted, skidding to a halt as I lifted my hands out.

My palms struck his chest and I crumpled to the ground like a puppet with cut strings. My vision swam, and then flipped upside down as something squeezed my sides and shoulders. Then the world blurred and my head lolled back. "There, there, Callie. Sometimes I just can't help myself... It will be better if we just go somewhere private and get this over with..."

Despite my fear, I was as helpless as a babe as everything began fading to black.

The last thing I saw was a rack of whips, and a tan hand casually picking one out.

CHAPTER 18

*W*arm, supple leather cradled my body in a loving hug, pressing against my cheeks.

I came to with a panicked gasp. Darling had attacked me! I was restrained! He'd taken—

I saw him sitting across from me, one leg crossed over the other, a blue fire blazing in a hearth behind him. He was smoking a cigar, fiddling with a rust-colored ascot beneath his open collared dress shirt. "I would come closer, but I didn't want to startle you," he murmured in a soft tone.

I let out a breath, trying to gather my thoughts. I wasn't in danger.

"What… happened?" I asked in a whisper.

"Instinct. You ran into me shouting *Hey* and I reacted… prematurely," he chuckled. "I hear it happens to the best of men."

I just stared at him, not rising to the low joke. "You shut me down by… *touching* me?"

He shrugged absently, waving a hand in a whorl of smoke. "You have too much on your mind. You are brimming with questions. You need to hear some questions."

I blinked at him, slowly shaking my head. Maybe I was still disoriented from whatever he had done to me. I had touched him and dropped like a rock. I must have felt him carrying me to the chair, but it had felt so sinister. Just fear from being alone with a dangerous… being? Or was it sound advice? That I really didn't know much about these two leather-makers. I saw a leather whip leaning beside the fire place and flinched, remembering seeing a tan hand picking it up before I passed out.

He followed my gaze and let out an amused chuckle, reading my thoughts. "It was in the wrong spot. From my... personal collection," he admitted with a shrug.

I didn't feel any welts or anything, so let it go.

I was suddenly very eager to find Claire.

"She's fine. Just shopping. You can hear her."

I felt my skin crawl, realizing he had read my thoughts without permission. But he was right. I could hear Claire clearly, speaking with Dear about a pair of leather pants. Like they were just around the corner, but...

We were in a closed room. I glanced over at the door casually, noticing that the walls around it were actually smoked glass and that I could make out vague silhouettes on the other side from the racks of coats, boxes, and shoes outside.

"You're safe. We're all here."

I slowly turned to look at him. He took another long puff of his cigar, and I could have sworn his eyes pulsed blue, like lightning, behind the smoke.

"What did you mean that I'm full of questions, and that I need someone to ask me questions. That doesn't make any sen—"

"Since you refuse to see, let me introduce you to my friend, but I'll warn you, she's expensive." My mind reeled as he interrupted me to use a homonym of my cut-off word *sense* to so adroitly change the topic. He pointed with his cigar to my right.

I turned and almost fell out of my chair.

A beautiful, topless, exotic woman stared at me from the floor. I definitely hadn't ever met her, but almost everyone in the world could have pointed her out, recognizing her face.

But she wasn't *entirely* human.

She lay on her stomach in a familiar pose, feline paws folded one over the other, neck arched regally as she considered me. Her lion's tale twitched back and forth, and her cocaine-white feathered wings were tucked in close to her body. But from the neck up she was a stunningly beautiful, dark-haired woman.

The Sphinx.

"If I poke my finger through your eyes, will your jaws open wide?" she asked in a lazy purr like poured honey.

I blinked. "Um, probably in sheer agony, yes."

She *tsked* disapprovingly, turning to Darling.

He rolled his eyes. "Scissors. Everyone knows that one."

She nodded, lifting a paw to inspect her claws. "Not everyone, apparently."

I blinked. "Wait, that wasn't a threat, but a riddle?" I asked, eyes studying her every detail. She was gorgeous. Like all deadly beings.

She looked back up at me as if bored. "Sphinx. Riddle. I'm fucking expensive. And you're fucking dense." Her tone added *moron*.

I scowled. "Was that another riddle?"

Darling sighed and I shot him a sharp look. "Questions often answer questions," he said, "but the right questions are expensive."

I turned from him to the Sphinx. This was a little too strange, even for me. "I think I'm good."

"Your mind is a nest of thorns, and thrashing your horns shows you only miles and miles of more briars."

I studied her, but finally shook my head. "Like you said, I'm too dense for your expensive questions. They'll only give me a bigger migraine." I took a breath and made to climb to my feet and find Claire.

The Sphinx's head was suddenly resting in my lap. She sniffed rather loudly, getting a primal whiff of eau de Callie, which was about as awkward as anything I had ever experienced. I tried to slide back, but the Sphinx sat up, resting her paws on the arms of my chair, wings flaring out behind her as she leaned in to nuzzle my neck. I remained perfectly still, ready to stab if I sensed even a flicker of danger, although I knew I was already too late if it came to that.

She licked my cheek and I flinched involuntarily. Then she was leaning back, eyes only inches away.

"You'll do. I need a friend. And you taste salty-sweet."

I stared into her purple eyes and felt like I had suddenly been tossed into a river of time. I gasped, pulling myself out of that gaze, shivering. "That's just my sweat. I don't taste salty-sweet."

"No eating her, Phix. We're not finished with this one yet," Darling warned.

The Sphinx – Phix, apparently – cocked her head. "I don't eat friends. Well… not usually."

I nodded as if that was totally acceptable. "So, what brings you here?" I asked lamely, realizing she didn't feel like exiting my personal bubble.

"I typically guard temples, but have recently lowered my standards, lucky for you."

Darling burst out laughing. I scowled at him over Phix's wings, thinking on her words. She was still way too close for my comfort, but the twinkle in her eyes made me think she'd meant more than she'd said outright. Temples… as in Nate Temple? Or was I just jumping to conclusions with her all up in my face like this?

She cocked her head as if listening to something I couldn't hear. Then she turned back to me. "What is light and dark, but neither? Made of shadows but dances in sunlight? Made of sunbeams but frolics in darkness?"

I heard Darling's boots drop to the ground as if he had suddenly leaned forward, interested.

"I…" I thought furiously. I'd never been that interested in riddles. Or, maybe it was more honest to say I'd always been interested in riddles, but after running into a few that I couldn't guess, I usually lost all interest – as a coping mechanism for my frustration.

I thought about it, having a million answers and none. Which was how riddles worked. Was she asking about certain events in town? Me? Or was this another simple childhood riddle where the answer was *time* or something lame?

She shook her head and I shivered. Of course. Mind reader.

I finally shrugged in defeat. "I'm not very good at riddles."

"Your mind is too rigid for riddles, and your body is too tense for diddles."

My face flushed crimson and I realized Claire was now standing in the open doorway. I glanced over at her to let her know I was safe. She smiled at the Sphinx, not looking concerned in the slightest as she grinned widely.

"Oh, I agree. Callie could use a good diddle, and I know just the man for the j—"

"Shut up, Claire," I hissed, glaring at her. She smiled, shrugged her shoulders, and walked over to one of the couches perpendicular to my chair. She studied the sphinx curiously, not remotely alarmed. Was it a shifter thing?

Could she sense something that made her feel safer? Knowing somehow that I wasn't in danger?

"You were saying?" I asked Phix.

"You know too much and miss all else. You see, but don't see, so obsessed with the world's body and not its soul."

I stared at her for a second before glancing over her shoulder at Darling.

"Do you guys have a translator?" I asked, growing agitated. I felt like the Sphinx was only rubbing my face in how ignorant I was, and it wasn't putting me in a good mood. Not even adding in the diddling comment.

The Sphinx suddenly lifted my chin with a paw and I held my breath, feeling the cool tips of her claws pressing against my thin skin. "The answer... it's you. And the Ring of Aandaleeb."

Then she was detaching herself from my chair to saunter over to the fire, where she promptly curled up on her side, stretching her paws out lazily. "Wake me when we are ready to leave, Callie Penrose. I have more work to do with you yet. You're too easily influenced. The bear will help, but you must get out of your own way for a time."

I stared at the creature, mouth opening wordlessly. She knew about the Ring of Aandaleeb? From the Catacombs? Claire looked gob-smacked, as if agreeing with me on the ridiculousness of Phix's comment. I wasn't influenced by anyone. I always fought back against authority. I finally sighed, shaking my head.

Did this make me a crazy cat lady?

CHAPTER 19

*C*laire wasn't subtle about draping her arm over the side of the couch, even shaking her hand unnecessarily until I acknowledged the new accessory adorning her wrist. A band of creamy leather about the size of a watch, but with no face, circled her wrist, and I spotted dark symbols etched into it.

"Oh, this? It's nothing, really," she said in faux boredom. "It just makes me *bulletproof*!" she hooted.

Darling smiled, rolling his eyes. "Like an Aegis," he said, nodding to Dear in approval of her assistance with Claire, and as if also to catch her up to speed on his talk with me. "Not as strong, but close enough to count."

"An Aegis?" I asked. "Like Zeus' shield?"

Dear nodded. "A Godly goat-skin," she said, cackling. "How ridiculous. He had no imagination." She winked at Claire. "Yours is better, my sweet."

Claire was frowning at them, not having been told just how powerful – even though Darling and Dear were downplaying it – her little bracelet was.

"Claire told me the most fascinating story about your underground," Dear said, taking me in with her raptor gaze.

Darling leaned forward with a leer. "Oh? Callie didn't tell *me* about her underground, the sly minx." He winked at me suggestively.

"The Catacombs beneath her city, Darling, not her body's glorious nether regions," Dear chided with a tired sigh.

Darling leaned back with a regretful sigh.

"My glorious nether regions…" I repeated, glaring at Claire for spilling the beans on the catacombs. How much had she told them? She pointedly glanced away, sensing my anger.

"She was quite thorough," Dear answered my thoughts, making my scowl deepen.

"How interesting," Darling said, puffing at his cigar while his eyes roved Claire from head to toe, likely rehashing the details for himself. Pulling the answers from her thoughts.

Since it was pointless to lie to them – they could read our thoughts, after all – I told them everything, hoping they might have some answers for us dim-witted mortals. Phix looked up during my explanation, studying me thoughtfully.

"Yes, it sounds like the old Templar Vault. Lucky you. They've been searching for it for quite some time while you kicked your feet up in St. Louis," Dear finally said, nodding to herself.

I frowned at her. "Wait. The Templars… are here? In Kansas City?" I asked, suddenly tense. I had obviously accepted that a Templar Vault lay forgotten beneath the city – I had seen the signs carved into the rock – but it had all been so old. I'd just assumed it was a historic site.

But to hear that Templars were actually here? Now? Had they been the ones occupying the space? The Templars had every reason to hate me. I was indirectly responsible for possibly turning their leader into a werewolf. "How long have they been here?" I asked.

"Oh, quite some time, I would think. By your measure of time, anyways. I believe they came here for a recruitment rush during your absence. But they've also been hunting for this Vault."

"Is that the one that was here before the Colonial heathens arrived?" Darling asked Dear.

"No, the other one," she replied, standing to pour herself a drink.

He nodded his head in recognition. "Oh, *that* one. With the Ring of Aandaleeb."

I leaned forward. "What *is* the Ring of Aandaleeb?" I asked, not liking how many times I had heard it recently. I definitely didn't like Phix's dumb riddle that implied I had some tie to it.

Darling waved a hand. "A trinket. A trifle, really. Names. Bah. Two sides to the same coin."

My mind raced with possibilities. The Templars were here looking for the same ring that Nameless had wanted, and it had been hidden inside their old Catacombs. Then... who had stolen it? And who had been living down there? And what was it, exactly?

One thing that was blindingly clear, now, was that Nameless and the Templars weren't on the same side. The Templars were zealots. Had Nameless been *trying* to get me to rob them? They already hated me!

And who was that other Angel we had fought? And why had Greta been so offended about us fighting him?

Hadn't she mentioned Solomon before we left the coffee shop? Perhaps she had known about the Templars. They had first started out as the Order of the Temple of Solomon. I really wished I could get a hold of Nate to at least clear up the Greta situation – verify her position. But Nate was off in Fae, so any of his allies I didn't personally know were suspect.

As things currently stood, it was looking like three forces of God were about to meet up for a good old-fashioned war. In Kansas City.

"What can you tell me?" I asked into the silent room.

"That depends on what you can *show* me," Darling smiled.

I scowled at him. Show and tell, the old childhood game from school. Well, I wasn't going to flash him for answers, but I understood that everything was a deal to these two. Which made me wonder what kind of deal Claire had made. "Not happening," I told Darling with a warning look.

"Pity," Dear sighed wistfully. She eyed me hungrily, as if she could see through my clothes. I had to force myself not to blush. I let out a breath, motioning for Claire to join me.

Phix made as if to stand, but I held out a hand. "No offense, but you're not exactly discreet. Mind sticking around here?" I asked her politely, imagining a wall in my mind to prevent her from reading my thoughts. It was taxing, but I was getting sick and tired of mind readers.

A girl needed her secrets to stay sharp.

Phix sighed in amusement, as if sensing my defensive wall, and deciding not to hurt my feelings by telling me it was made of sand. "You know where to find me," she said, curling back down for a nap.

Darling lifted his hand, snapped his fingers, and we were suddenly in a damp alley behind his shop – where I had first seen him and Dear sitting on ornate chairs in a dead-end of brick walls. Two yellow raincoats hung from an out-of-place coat stand.

"What the hell?" Claire asked, taking in the alley, and the random coat-rack.

But I was already tugging on one of the raincoats – *Burberry*, of course – and tying the belt forcefully around my waist, knowing better than to ask. I tugged the hood up as fast as I could.

And like the motion had set it off, rain suddenly poured down from the leaden skies, soaking Claire in moments. She shrieked, darting for the other jacket and frantically tying it on. When finished, she stared at me like a drowned rat.

"We need to go talk to Nameless," I growled.

CHAPTER 20

Claire sat beside me, facing the Angel's desk, listening patiently as I finished laying out our side of the story. Nameless contemplated us thoughtfully in silence.

"What have you found out about the Catacombs?" I finally asked him.

He leaned back in his chair. "We weren't the only ones searching for it, obviously. But no one recognized our... guest. And our whistleblower has gone silent, probably dead somewhere," he said, sounding genuinely regretful. I even heard Alyksandre murmur a prayer across the room.

Like a good Catholic, I swore, clenching my fist. Nameless narrowed his eyes at my outburst, but didn't openly reprimand me.

I kept my mouth shut about Greta, wondering if she had been telling the truth about knowing Nate and the Angel who had attacked us. The problem was, I wasn't entirely sure who was worth trusting these days, but I definitely wasn't going to rely on a bitter stranger's ravings.

"So, who stole the Ring of Aandaleeb?" I asked. "One of the local gangs?"

He grimaced. "The Catacombs seem to have been occupied for quite some time, but nothing had been stolen or damaged, so I doubt it was a gang. Whoever resided there respected the place. I don't think they would have allowed a thief to get in, let alone get *away*." His eyes flickered to my neck, noting the absence of my Templar scarf.

I didn't say anything.

He hesitated for a moment before leaning closer to speak in a soft, barely audible tone. "You're not one of them, are you, Callie? A Templar?"

Claire sniffed, folding her arms.

If he hadn't looked so serious, I would have laughed at him. "The Templars *hate* me, Nameless. They wouldn't take me if I begged them." Sensing his paranoia, I glanced at the other Nephilim in the room. None were close enough to overhear. "Where do you think I got the scarf in the first place?" I added.

His lips tightened in understanding. Because there was really only one other way to obtain a scarf if it wasn't given. Murdering a Templar and taking it. "I have reason to... distrust their Order," he said. "I have heard that they hide Freaks of their own..."

I tried to act surprised, and then decided not to. "A werewolf... They're run by a werewolf."

He blinked at me. "You know this for a fact?" he asked, sounding stunned.

I shrugged. "I kind of had something to do with it, but I don't know if it actually infected him or not. Maybe he walked it off." I knew Commander Olin Fuentes was hundreds of years old, so maybe he was immune to the werewolf gene. I decided Nameless didn't need to know about Paradise and Lost.

"I had hoped it was just a rumor..." he said, sounding troubled. "Being a shifter is not wrong," he suddenly said in an apologetic tone, wincing at Claire. "It's just the antithesis of what they preach, a direct contradiction. Why would his fellow Templars accept it? If he had openly declared a change in their principles, that would be one thing, but to continue hunting Freaks while he himself is one of them... This is not the act of an honorable man."

I shrugged. "I always assumed he was a stinker."

"A stinker..." Nameless repeated, frowning.

"Someone who respected the place moved in, so my guess is the Templars turned it into their new hideout. But if they had already found the Catacombs, why was it vacant when we showed up? Not even a sentry."

Nameless nodded absently, face growing harder. "That's another concern of mine," he said, eyes casually indicating his own Nephilim. I stiffened, but kept my composure well enough for no one to notice. Claire had been studying the bookshelf, so hadn't seen his subtle indication. That perhaps some of his Nephilim had turned coat.

"Well, that is remarkably unhelpful," I sighed, meeting his eyes to let him know I had caught his meaning. Did he really distrust his own men?

"Kansas City is not the same as it was even months ago. All sorts of people stirring up trouble. I even heard a story about a fight last night. Involving a small group of car thieves. Seems a few people saw it all happen..."

I nodded slowly. "Good. Someone is trying to clean up this city, then."

"You've made quite the name for yourself. Taking out two demons – without any help from those who should have been your allies," he added, lowering his chin apologetically to admit his own guilt. Claire squinted at him suspiciously, the conversation piquing her interest again. Especially the admission of fault. "Perhaps you might consider an alliance... mutually beneficial, of course."

"I can handle myself."

"I have no doubt. But it seems those below the equator are not your only enemies. Stories about Rome have reached the city. Everyone whispers about the woman who faced the Vatican. They say her shout broke the walls. And that she lured out the Templars as well... It seems rumor was correct, for once."

I placed my hands on my knees. "What do you know about the Templars?" I asked neutrally.

"They've been around for a few years," he said drily. "As have the Shepherds. Neither are good enemies to have, although they say you can judge a woman by the caliber of her foes." He looked up at me wryly. "Not sure what that says about you..."

I stared back. "I hear men get set in their ways and need to be reminded that times change. We have mobile phones, now, for example. Other annoying things. It all began to crumble after they let women have the vote," I said, straight-faced.

He smirked ever so slightly, catching the tone of my voice, but managing to smile guiltily. He was one of those old-fashioned beings. "You do dress rather provocatively," he added with a frown, but his hand very subtly covered his mouth and nose for a half-heartbeat, like mimicking a scarf. Was that a hint that he respected my accomplishments?

I nodded. "At least I don't walk around naked like my girlfriend, here.

Right, Alyksandre?" I called out in a louder voice, glancing over my shoulder at the door to the room. His face flushed red and he muttered darkly under his breath. Claire turned to smile at him before blowing him a kiss. Kevin chuckled but quickly turned it into a cough at the look on Nameless' face.

"So, what is this Ring of Aandaleeb?" I asked Nameless, walling off my thoughts, not particularly sure what Angels could and couldn't do. Or Nephilim, for that matter. I wanted to see how open Nameless was with me. I could always google the ring when I got home, but I wanted to test him. It would determine the course of events over the next few days. Then there was Phix's bizarre riddle...

"Everyone leave. Except Alyksandre," Nameless said.

"And Kevin," Claire chimed in, glancing back at the Nephilim, not looking remotely concerned with the fact she was attempting to command both an Angel and a Nephilim. "An ass like that was made by God for my viewing pleasure," Claire admitted with an easy shrug.

CHAPTER 21

I coughed into my fist, noticing Nameless' darkening glare. "That will be all, Kevin. Thank you," the Angel commanded.

Claire sighed longingly. Kevin looked torn between smiling back and obeying his master.

Soon we were alone with Alyksandre in the room, who was motioned to approach the desk and pull up a chair. He didn't sit. Just stood beside the desk, eyes alert for dangers, choosing duty over comfort, although I figured with us four in the same room, any bad guys would be in for a long night at the hospital.

Or a quick trip to the morgue.

Nameless pulled out a slip of paper with a familiar drawing on it. Two interwoven triangles, one with the point down and the other with the point up, forming a six-pointed star – the same one I had seen at the Catacombs. The interwoven aspect made the image startlingly different from the typical Star of David that most people recognized. This wasn't a flat, two-dimensional, six-pointed star of solid lines. This was a three-dimensional rendition of two different triangles woven together so that one line of triangle A would intersect above a line on triangle B, but then cross below triangle B on the second leg. A small difference that wouldn't be noticed from a distance, yet it was clear up close.

"The Seal of Solomon," Nameless murmured. He pointed at the downward pointed triangle. "This represents water." Then he pointed at the triangle pointing upwards. "And this, fire."

He checked to make sure we were following.

"Many consider this symbol to be a protection against evil spirits. The interwoven nature of the two triangles was believed to trap, contain, and control demons – rendering them harmless to mortals. Like a maze, confusing any demon who stared at it, let alone one trapped within its lines."

Claire blinked. Then she turned to me. "You mean you didn't have to go all badass against the demons? You could have just drawn one of these fancy stars?" she asked, frowning doubtfully.

Nameless sighed. "A little more complicated than that, but essentially, yes."

"Okay," I said, thinking. "And it was on one of the walls in the Templar Vault. So… they had a demon trapped down there?" I hadn't sensed anything from my boots down there, so it had probably been freed at some point.

But Nameless shook his head. "No demon. The Templars worshipped this symbol. And the man who created it."

"Let me guess," Claire said, leaning back. "King Solomon."

Nameless was nodding. "We believe – based on the evidence found at the Vault – that the Templars of old had hidden King Solomon's signet ring – the Seal of Solomon – there long ago."

I turned to Alyksandre. "That's the object of power you were tracking. This Seal."

"Also known as the Ring of Aandaleeb," he said. "One and the same."

I studied the drawing, thinking over the conversation. "The Templars probably found it, took it, and left," I finally said, shrugging. "And you just said we don't have a demon running amok."

"Nailed it," Claire commented, folding her arms.

Nameless leaned forward, voice very low. "It doesn't just *ward* against demons. It traps them. *Contains* them…"

My stomach felt hollow all of a sudden. "It has demons *inside* it? Right *now?*"

Nameless nodded. "And possibly held by a zealot-turned-werewolf who commands the Templars. A commander who has granted himself immunity from his own judgments… I fear his true intentions."

I considered it, tapping my lips. What kind of trouble could Olin get into with this Ring? Would he dare risk releasing a demon? Why would he? And was he even strong enough to do that? And why was Nameless overly concerned? He was an Angel. Couldn't he just turn them all into pillars of salt?

Then it hit me, and I slowly looked up at him. The tightness around his eyes told me the truth. "Demons… are just one flavor of Angel," I whispered.

Claire frowned at my comment, turning to look at the silent Angel behind the desk. Nameless finally nodded, ever so slowly. "The symbol doesn't have the same power over me as it would a demon, however the Seal itself is powerful enough to trap an Angel – Fallen or otherwise…" he admitted, eyes very cold.

"But this thing isn't new. It's been around for a while. Although missing, sure. What is your sudden interest in it? You said you've been searching for it for a while, now, but only just confirmed the Templars were in town."

Nameless sighed, as if hoping I wouldn't have come to this question for quite some time. "I… wish to interrogate some of the prisoners trapped inside."

I blinked at him, eyes widening.

Alyksandre – although motionless – went so still that he may as well have had a heart attack. But being a good little Nephilim soldier, he didn't offer his opinion on the matter.

Nameless nodded. "Something is coming to Kansas City. I sense a… finality in the air. I don't know if that means the threat is imminent or some time off, but we need answers – to know what they are planning. To know that two demons came after you, and that you somehow managed to defeat them by yourself – although astounding – is unacceptable. True, we should have been on the same side, and that fault lies on *my* shoulders. But maybe if I knew then what I know now, I might have been wise enough to see you as an ally rather than a foe."

He leaned back in his chair, looking exhausted.

"That…" I finally let out a low whistle, leaning away from the table. "Wow. And you haven't told them," I said, thinking back on how he had made the other Nephilim leave the room. "And I had thought you were set in your ways. You might be the most progressive Angel *ever*."

He nodded tightly. "Now you see the full picture. Even my own brothers attempt to stop me. Either… for their own selfish desire to do the same, or because they cannot see what comes, *refuse* to see what comes."

I nodded absently. "How very... human of them," I said softly, not trying to offend Nameless, but to let him know I was well familiar with his plight.

Something about his troubled eyes suddenly made me feel uncomfortable, especially when they pinned me to my chair. "Those demons *found* you, Callie. Even after a lifetime of hiding, they were *still* able to find you. Still *wanted* to find you. We discussed the unique powers at your disposal. How dangerous they are," he said carefully, referring to the Whispers – which he had warned me could be either Demonic or Angelic.

I nodded, a sickening sensation building in my stomach. "I'm managing, thank you. I'm more concerned about the shiny ring that lets anyone waltz up and trap an Angel. That is way too much power in the hands of one person—"

"Unless you are as wise as the fabled Solomon," Alyksandre spoke in a gravelly voice, sounding as if the thought had just struck him. "The only one able to control its influence."

But Nameless was still staring into my soul as he spoke. "It is too much power for one person or being... and usually burns up anyone trying to control it..."

Alyksandre slowly lifted his head, frowning thoughtfully at Nameless. Noticing his boss' attention was on me, he frowned harder. Then he flinched, taking a step back, turning from me to Nameless in rapid succession.

"Nope. I'm not Solomon," I said, shaking my head. "I don't even have a casual acquaintance with wisdom."

"No one ever said you did," Claire offered helpfully.

"I'm not *related* to Solomon," I clarified, my breath quickening. But even as I said it, I realized the flawed logic. I didn't have a single idea who or what I was. All I knew was that my mother had been a wizard named Constance, and I had a Nephilim father.

Nameless shrugged. "Are you so sure? Because I see a Nephilim with powers she shouldn't be able to control – powers not granted to any Nephilim I have ever met..." he let his words echo in the small room. Claire's mouth hung open as she stared at me. I could hardly blink, let alone speak. "It would explain why everyone has been so interested in you."

"I... no," I said, shaking my head, feeling dizzy. "No way. Something like that would be recorded..." I said weakly.

"Your lineage may be in question. I have no proof to this theory, but..." he tapped the symbol on the paper, "I *am* confident your unique powers give you protection from the Seal's dangers."

"And..." I said after a few moments, connecting the dots. "You need my help to do what you intend..." I whispered. "To interrogate the imprisoned demons."

He nodded. Not victoriously. Not angrily. But...

Sadly. Empathetically. "I believe so, although maybe not. Angels do not have the power to control the ring, to abuse it – lest we would be able to control each other, but perhaps we could speak *through* it. To have you as a translator, of sorts." He held up his hands in the universal *I don't know* gesture. "I would like you there, just in case. Maybe you should spend some time brushing up on your... gifts."

I stood, walking away from the desk, pacing anxiously, trying to control my breathing. I couldn't be related to Solomon. That was impossible. But... I did have the Whispers. The Silvers. Were they the same thing? Or was one of them related to this power, this immunity, that Nameless might need? Or maybe it was the two in tandem that gave me the unique chance.

Except my mind kept drifting to the Whispers – the Angelic and Demonic influences that frequently spoke to me. How I had to keep them at bay, control them.

Probably like I would have to do if wearing this Seal. Listen, but keep them at a safe distance.

"Why? This doesn't make any sense. Why would I have anything to do with this?"

He just shrugged.

But what if his crazy plan to water-board demons... wasn't so crazy? I could help put a stop to this impending demon incursion before it ever happened... That would keep my city safe. My friends in St. Louis safe. I could stop a war.

I stared at Nameless, facing him directly. I relaxed my control on my Whispers, hoping for some guidance or input. They were oddly still, as if listening. Or they weren't paying attention.

Damn it.

I let out a sigh. "I need to think on this. We don't even have the Seal yet, anyway. But... yeah. I'll need to think on something like this."

Nameless nodded. "Take your time. I had hoped to earn more of your trust before mentioning this. I only recently connected the pieces – that your unique abilities and the enemies you have attracted might be part of the same element. The solution to my problem in the first place."

I nodded, feeling numb.

Luckily, Claire had driven us over here, because I was pretty sure I couldn't have made a Gateway at that moment. I could barely put one foot in front of the other as I left with Claire, feeling Alyksandre's eyes on the back of my neck.

CHAPTER 22

I had taken a glorious nap, because Claire had threatened to sit on me otherwise. It was early afternoon when I awoke, although it felt like I had slept for a week. Both in the fact that I now felt more relaxed and rested, and…

That I had woken from a coma and that the world might have caught fire in the interim.

The panic hit me like a fist to the gut about ten seconds after I woke up, shattering my smile.

Luckily, Claire had been curled up on the couch in my fluffy pink robe, ready to calm me down. She'd had hot chocolate already poured for me and had *Fist of Legend* – the Jet Li version – paused on the TV at the opening fight scene.

Upon seeing me, she smiled, clicked *play*, and patted the seat next to her.

I lost myself in the fight sequences of the movie, marveling at the choreography until it distracted me enough to think more rationally and to relax.

I muted the screen and turned to Claire, shifting my jacket to the side since something sharp was poking my neck. A buckle or something.

"You better?" Claire asked, smiling encouragingly.

I let out a breath. "I guess," I murmured, staring at the apartment upside down as my head hung over the top of the couch. The place was a mess –

discarded clothes on chairs, empty cups and a dirty bundle of fabric on the table... I blinked, turning to peer over the couch at the bundle.

Then I stood, scooping it up. I hefted it in my palm with a sudden smile.

"I may just be a crazy cat lady queen, but I can do this," I told Claire. "This is normal."

She frowned at the fabric and the broken glass inside from last night in the alley. "It's really not that normal," she said, frowning.

I scowled at her and brought it back to the table, unfolding it to reveal the pieces of blue-stained glass we had picked up from the alley.

I moved them around with my fingers absently, thinking. "I'll need to do some tests, but Roland taught me enough to possibly track where it came from." I moved a few more pieces of glass. "I think."

Claire reached out, inspecting a few of the pieces, her nose bunched up at the noxious smell she had told me about. I still smelled only the earthy scent, so I stood from the couch, scanning my apartment. Did I have what I needed for the spell here? If not, I could always hop over to the training area beneath Abundant Angel Catholic Church – even though I didn't work there anymore, I had helped gather the ingredients in the storage closet—

Claire grunted, sounding surprised. "Maybe we should just go to this address."

I spun, turning to face her. "What?"

She held out one of the larger pieces of glass. "It's got an address stamped on it. Must be from the bottom of the bottle, or whatever this used to be."

I frowned at her. "Who the hell brands their glass?"

Claire shrugged. "An old company?" She inspected it closer, pinching her nose. "All I can make out is the address. No company name. But it's here in Kansas City."

I shook my head. "Too easy. Maybe it's a trap. Or the woman bought it at an antique store and used it to make... magic blue Kool-Aid."

Callie squinted up at me, setting the offensive glass back on the table. "You just want to do your ritual thingy."

I folded my arms stubbornly. "That's not fair." To be honest, rituals and spells like this weren't really my forte. I could do them, but I wasn't great at them. Roland had always insisted upon prioritizing self-defense, stating that there were other easier ways to find information when necessary. Or perhaps that we would be guided where we needed to go if necessary.

Well, I hadn't ever received any texts from God, so I probably should have paid more attention in his introductory lessons.

Fact was, I wasn't sure going to the address would do any good. The glass could have just as easily been left behind by the *pursuers*, not the *woman*. But... Claire hadn't sensed anything magical about them, so what was the harm in chasing down the lead? Maybe we would catch the guys, at least. Give them a talking to.

"Fine. We'll do it your way."

She grinned. "You will grant me estates and titles when you resume your throne, Solomina."

I winced. "I'm fresh out of both estates and titles to grant. And that is a horrid name. Where is this obvious trap set?" I asked her, shrugging on my coat and pocketing a few weapons lying about the apartment – two wooden stakes resting in the candle holder in place of candles, a set of silver knuckle dusters, and the pistols I had picked up at an antique store years ago. Matching Glock something or others.

They went *pew pew* when I pulled the trigger, which was all I really cared about.

Because sometimes guns were better. Shots were loud and could be heard from far away, and the familiar sound usually brought the police down upon the source of the noise. It also alerted any nearby innocents with a familiar sound of danger. Rather than seeing fireballs and bolts of lightning raining down out of a clear sky, inciting a panic, they could mentally process a gunshot and know they should probably run or call 911.

I shoved the pistols in the shoulder holster Claire had tried on yesterday, readjusting it to fit me again. Then I glanced at Claire who was still in my fluffy pink robe, legs curled up beneath her on my couch. I arched a brow at her. "Aren't you going to change?"

She shrugged. "I'm just going to shred what I wear, and I don't want to ruin another set of clothes. I think I'm all out of spares here."

"So, you're going to wear my pink robe to a potential monster brawl."

"The element of surprise..." she said, standing from the couch and stretching lazily.

I sighed. She kind of had a point. And it would be hilarious if we found nothing dangerous and she was forced to assist me in questioning people while wearing my fluffy robe.

I decided I didn't want to talk her out of it. But I did want to talk to

Gunnar Randulf – the Alpha werewolf of St. Louis, and Nate Temple's best friend – to see how he handled the shredded clothes situation. Except, most men were shit when it came to clothing, so I would ask his wife Ashley instead.

Claire read off the address, tightening the robe's sash like it was armor. I knew the general location,but needed to find a less populated area nearby. It wouldn't do to open up a Gateway in the middle of a crowd, in plain sight of everyone.

I remembered once driving by a vacant building about a block away from the address, so pulled up the internet on my phone, searching nearby commercial properties for sale. The one I had driven by was still listed for sale, so I began swiping through the pictures, getting a feel for the general layout so I could open a Gateway there.

Claire was watching me, yawning. "Did you forget what we're doing? The meeting with the real estate agent is tomorrow," she said, referring to our appointment with Paradise and Lost.

I scowled over at her. "No. I'm picking out a drop spot for my Gateway. I need to get a feel for the place. Better results." I swiped through a few more images of the empty unit. "I think."

She watched me doubtfully.

Better off than I had started, I pocketed my phone, took a deep breath, and focused, imagining the empty retail unit. I hoped today wasn't the day that the real estate agent had a hot prospect interested in buying the place. I had to be sure I got it right. Usually, I could Shadow Walk to a place I wasn't as familiar with, but there had been... issues with Shadow Walking lately.

Namely, some giant, robed, Candy Skulled dickwads waiting to slice you to ribbons with glass claws. I would wait until I received the go-ahead from Nate – who said he was *looking into it* – before trying that anytime soon.

Long story short, Gateways were trickier – if you were concerned about being discreet, anyway.

I glanced at Claire, eyeing her robe as if to check that she hadn't changed her mind since we would now have to walk a block through the city streets. Maybe she hadn't noticed that part.

"We should probably hurry. You have a date tonight," she said sternly.

I scowled at her. "It's just a double-date with my dad to meet his girlfriend. Not a big deal."

"It *is* a big deal. And I won't let you be late," she said in warning.

"Fine," I mumbled, not very eager about the whole thing.

"Good. Let's go fuck some shit up," she said, fingering her new pale bracelet in anticipation.

"Or save a victim," I said, opening up a Gateway. A ring of white fire erupted before us, revealing an empty room inside the commercial unit for lease. "Yes! It worked!"

Claire arched a brow at me. "Let's be practical. This is most likely a trap or I wouldn't be willing to wear the robe," she muttered, then jumped through the Gateway ahead of me.

I heard a muffled curse.

"A big fucking man-cow!" Claire shouted in disbelief, out of sight. "I *told* you it was a trap!"

I frowned for a millisecond before jumping through after her. What the fuck was a man-cow?

CHAPTER 23

I landed on a rickety wooden floor, silver knuckle dusters on one fist and a wooden stake in the other, eyes darting about the room for something to hit.

Claire was motionless, staring up at…

Well, a big fucking man-cow.

I lowered my weapons, recognizing him, but my brain short-circuiting at the unexpected appearance.

The legendary Minotaur – a half bull, half man named Asterion – was a reformed Buddhist, according to Nate. And the large set of prayer beads hanging on his bulging chest kind of confirmed it.

"I'm not a man-cow," he snorted to Claire, holding up his massive hands in a peaceful gesture. He was well over seven-feet-tall, covered in long, shaggy, brown fur, and wore a kilt and a pair of huge, custom-made boots. His thick, ivory horns threatened to brush the ceiling if he rose from his slouch, and a fat golden nose ring quivered in his wet nostrils. "I am Asterion, and this is King Midas," he added, pointing to an older gentleman standing beside him.

King Midas – the fabled king cursed with the golden touch – perhaps in his mid to late fifties, judging by the hard lines on his forehead – was watching the exchange with amusement, not the least bit startled. He seemed to have a vibrancy of life to him, something that just made me want to smile as if a ray of sunshine had touched my face on a rainy day. He had crow's feet at the edges of his glittering eyes, and his blonde hair was pulled back into a tight tail. He wore a crisp white suit and polished brown loafers – sans socks. He also wore a pair of tight leather gloves, in case he wanted to shake anyone's hand or touch something. He grinned at Claire. "Nice robe, child. I've got one just like it, in gold," he added, winking.

He might as well have shouted *stupefy* at Claire, for all the reaction she gave him.

Asterion's eyes flickered over to me and he flashed me a relieved smile. "Callie! When I saw that Gateway appear, I figured it had to be you. The white fire," he explained, pointing a sausage-sized finger at the Gateway.

I let it wink out, shaking my head. I knew these two from my trips to visit Nate in St. Louis, but what were they doing *here*?

Midas dipped his chin politely at me. "Miss Penrose. A pleasure." Then he turned to Asterion. "It seems we will *have* to buy the place, now..." he said, sounding only mildly inconvenienced.

"What are you doing here, Asterion?" I asked in disbelief.

"I was escorting Midas through his weekly real estate interests," Asterion said, fingering his prayer beads subconsciously.

"And... one of those interests just happened to be a property in Kansas City where I opened a Gateway," I said doubtfully, placing a reassuring palm on Claire's back. She jumped, so focused on the giant Minotaur that she hadn't paid attention to my approach. She flashed me a demanding look. "This is Claire Stone. A bipolar shifter bear."

"*Polar* bear shifter," she corrected, face flushing slightly as she glared back at me.

I nodded. "Claire, meet Asterion, Nate's pal from St. Louis. And Midas Kingston, also from St. Louis," I said carefully, wondering exactly how I was supposed to formally introduce him.

Claire assessed him, sniffing the air curiously. He smiled back at her, shrugging. "Not a monster. I just like gold, Claire."

I grunted. "This is too much of a coincidence..."

Midas coughed, shooting a look at Asterion. "I'll just go check on the real estate agent. She's probably too busy on her phone to have noticed any of the shouting."

"Didn't she notice the giant freaking Minotaur?" Claire muttered under her breath.

Asterion frowned at her. "She knows us. But your sudden arrival could have been… unnecessarily complicated. She's a wizard, you see…"

"Let's get back to the part where you explain why you're interested in Kansas City real estate. Not that you aren't welcome, but this could have ended very badly. I would appreciate some warning next time."

Asterion nodded sheepishly. "We… have been keeping eyes on certain groups throughout Missouri. One isn't far from here, and Midas liked the idea of having a nearby base of operations just in case we needed to do some digging."

I felt some stars suddenly aligning to ruin my day. "Does this certain group spend time at a building about a block away?"

Claire piped in with the actual address.

Asterion's jaw dropped open, his nose ring quivering at the sudden motion. "You know of the Hellfire Club?" he asked incredulously.

CHAPTER 24

I kept my face studiously blank. "Sure do," I lied. "What do you know about them?"

Asterion was shaking his head in disbelief. "Have they done something to upset you?" he asked, twisting the hair at the base of his chin like a human would twirl his mustache.

"Yet to be determined," I said carefully.

Claire was frowning at the massive set of prayer beads dangling from Asterion's hairy chest, as if only just now noticing the odd necklace. I hadn't told her much about the St. Louis crew, but Asterion was as solid as... well, gold. He worked for Midas Kingston – or King Midas, as he was historically known – and ran the St. Louis Fight Club – a place where Freaks could go to let off some steam.

One could literally pull out all the stops and fight to the death there and wake up the next morning in the comfort of their own beds. Pretty neat, actually. I was eager to test it out, but had also felt the need to keep my abilities under wraps. Having secrets was beneficial. Maybe I could get Midas and Asterion to privately open up the Fight Club for my next birthday party.

Nothing celebrated the gift of life like a birthday cake and friends fighting to the death.

This Hellfire Club sounded oddly familiar, like I had heard about it somewhere.

"I don't see how they could have done anything to upset you. We've been keeping an eye on their members in St. Louis, as well, although they have laid low enough that we almost didn't learn they even had a location there."

"If you don't think they are dangerous, why are you buying this place?"

Asterion smiled faintly. "Nate Temple has taken a sudden interest in his… subjects."

Claire frowned at that, turning back to me. I hadn't brought her up to speed on events in St. Louis, wanting to clean up my own house before worrying about our sister city.

"Who are they?" I asked, realizing too late that I'd just proven I had no idea who they were.

Asterion shot me a puzzled look. "Witches. Fans of the occult. Other supernatural loners."

Claire folded her arms smugly, proud that her assumption that we were going to find trouble at the address had proven accurate. "You don't say?" she said, smiling over at me.

"Witches?" I asked incredulously. "We have honest to god witches in town? How is that not a concern?" I asked, alarmed. Witches were nasty. Well, if they wanted to be, and most did, according to what Roland had taught me. Then again, what I had been told had been fed to me through the objective and altruistic lens of the Vatican.

And we all knew how much they loved their witches.

Maybe it was a knitting circle of retired, middle-aged women who had practiced medicine.

But if this Hellfire Club was really witches, they were capable of brewing a broad array of potions – curses, spells, and healings – with their obscure ingredients. Where wizards typically focused on directly impacting the elements to their will, witches focused on directly combining substances of the earth into something greater.

A difference of semantics, now that I thought about it.

But give a witch a little forewarning, and she could be downright lethal. Curses and potions attached to her belts like Batman's utility belt, ready to shatter vials of unpleasantness upon her foes like nuclear rain. Fighting a witch was tough, because there was no direct element to defend against. You were at the mercy of battling whatever vial or brew she had created, hoping you had chosen the right defensive maneuver when the glass grenade cracked.

With a wizard, you knew – typically – what you were getting into... a street brawl.

With a witch, you were playing a game of cards where they always played ten hands ahead.

Now, given the chance, a wizard could quickly execute a witch with sheer force. But give her even a fraction of warning, and she could curse your entire bloodline for generations. Or turn you into a goat. Or... any number of things, really.

I shook my head, waiting on Asterion to answer, to explain their interest.

Midas came back into the room, whistling softly. "It is done."

I blinked at him. That could be taken all sorts of ways. "What is done?" I asked him warily.

"I bought the place."

Claire grunted. "Just like that. You... bought the place." She shifted her weight from one foot to the other, as if demonstrating the creakiness of the floorboards. Then she pointed at a large hole in a nearby wall. "Hope you got a good deal..."

Midas chuckled. "I *always* get a good deal," he said, chuckling as he walked over to a low-hanging chandelier. He took off a glove and touched it with a finger, closing his eyes. In a flash, the chandelier transformed into gold. Claire gasped in astonishment. Midas was grinning at her again as he slipped his glove back on. "And I know how to get a good return on investment."

Claire shot me a stunned look. "You saw that, right?"

I had figured some of the stories might be true, that whatever King Midas touched turned to gold, but had also considered the fact that it was an exaggerated story. A figure of speech. Like he knew how to always come out ahead in a deal, or something. But to see it *happen* in person.

"In the future, I would appreciate forewarning if you're playing in Kansas City," I told Midas, since he hadn't been in the room when I had said it to Asterion.

The man watched me thoughtfully. Not agreeing, but not denying. Then he put his hands in his pockets and Claire winced, holding her breath.

"It seems I've already crossed the line, so to speak," he said conversationally, indicating the building around us. "You will let me know how I can make that up to you..."

I nodded in appreciation, surprised it had been that easy. Was he being literal? He hadn't put any limitations on his offer, but I was pretty sure I could come up with a few ideas for a man that had no concern for money.

"Thank you. Now, we have some business to attend to at the... Hellfire Club."

"Perhaps we could tag along," Midas offered.

I hesitated. "Um. I don't really know what we're walking into. I'd hate for you to get tossed into the middle of a fight..."

Asterion grunted. "He runs the bloodiest Fight Club in the country – a Den of Freaks who fight to the death on a weekly basis. You'd be surprised at what he can do."

"Okay," I said, not finding any polite way out of it. "We might as well head over there, I guess."

They followed me to the door, and I glanced back at the Minotaur. He had slipped on a long, black coat and was already holding a massive gold – of course – golf umbrella over his head as he squatted low in an awkward shuffle. Well, that worked. I had thought to see something a bit more magical and classy. A way for the Minotaur to conceal his true form. Something majestically wondrous from the legendary Minotaur.

Not a giant fucking man-cow with a gold umbrella.

We made our way across the street, and I caught them up on recent events as we walked towards our destination. I told them about seeing the men chasing a woman into a dark alley before everyone had disappeared. That I had found a piece of glass with the address on it leading us here. They didn't offer comment, just filed the information away.

"I don't know what we're walking into," I said as the building loomed ahead of us. "I just wanted to see if she got away clean."

"But there's always the chance we might need to fuck some shit up," Claire offered helpfully. She arched a brow at Midas. "Maybe you can make something pretty."

"What a novel idea," Midas said, eyes twinkling thoughtfully.

Asterion snorted under his umbrella, but he just looked like a giant golden mushroom, crouched too low for me to even make out his head. Maybe the approaching darkness and rain would help keep him concealed under his golden umbrella.

I sighed. "There's always that possibility in Kansas City," I said to Claire. "Let's hurry before darkness falls."

CHAPTER 25

The three-story brick building Claire pointed out as our destination looked to have once been a hotel – about fifty years ago. I approached the front door, surprised to find it unlocked. I held it open for Claire, Asterion, and Midas, inwardly shaking my head at my gang. What were we about to find, and was it smart for me to involve Asterion and Midas in Kansas City politics?

I entered to find them huddled in a small lobby. Asterion shrugged off his coat and closed his umbrella as he stretched back up to full height, towering over the rest of us. His ears pricked towards the empty space as if searching for threats. Claire had her hands tucked into the pockets of my robe, and Midas was flexing his fingers thoughtfully. I glanced down at my own attire – a pair of jeans, my Darling and Dear jacket and boots, and a long-sleeved tee with a unicorn dragging his ass across the ground, leaving a rainbow trail behind him.

So professional.

I glanced around me, not seeing any furniture, desks, or people. Just a big empty lobby with dust motes drifting in the air. This was the present-day Hellfire Club? Asterion and Midas had caught us up on the historical origins of the group, sparking my memory. To sum it up, they had been a group of occult aficionados who performed rituals, sex rites, and all sorts of ridiculous parties. But it seemed that had just been a front of sorts – that the real Hellfire Club was actually run by real witches. And nowadays, they were kind of like a United Nations committee for their sisters across the globe. A central hub to open lines of communication across great distances.

And the fact that they had laid low for so long – both in Kansas City and St. Louis – was very impressive. They didn't get involved in politics. I hadn't even known of a single witch in Kansas City, let alone a *group* of them. They had restructured their business model and kept their noses clean. Establishing a network for *safety*, not to attack other Freaks.

The woman I had seen running away from those men was likely a member, judging by the glass we had tracked here, and I didn't want to drop the case until I found out her fate – whether she had escaped or not. If she was missing, I wanted to tell this Hellfire Club about seeing her running from those men. Maybe they would know the full story.

Or they were unaware anyone was hunting them.

After recent events, my money was on Templars, but there were plenty of other predators in town who liked chasing down lone women. Even some of the human variety. I was just a little biased.

Either way, the Hellfire Club needed to know they were in danger.

Another thought sent a shiver down my spine. Maybe… the men had been the members, using their blue potion to abduct the woman. I shivered. That would mean we were walking into a very dangerous situation.

Friend or foe?

"Their offices are on the second floor," Midas offered in a low murmur, pointing at a set of stairs to our right. He had taken off his gloves, revealing strong, calloused hands, not the soft, manicured digits I had expected. He looked oddly comfortable, as if he had dusted off an old but familiar skillset from his youth. Maybe he wouldn't be the liability I had feared.

I knew Asterion could handle himself in a fight, but I had been concerned about Midas. Liking to watch fights was different than being good at fighting. Take the UFC, for instance. Everyone who put on an *Affliction* shirt suddenly felt they were invincible, as if the brand was the modern-day equivalent of Hercules' Nemean Lion Cloak – which I knew for a fact was hoarded in Nate's private stash.

Being a fanboy was different than being a fighter.

But Midas' knuckles looked scarred, matching up with his sudden comfort. Then again, he could always just turn his enemies into gold statues with a touch, so he would probably be fine.

"What did Beckett say?" I asked Claire, creeping up the creaking stairs. She had texted him as we walked over here.

"He didn't answer. I gave him the address and said we might have a lead on a missing woman."

I nodded. Hopefully, the *missing woman* phrase would catch his attention. If not, it had only been a courtesy call anyway, since the three men had been human. Might need official handling.

Reaching the top of the stairs, I spotted a tall set of double doors across the landing. I could hear faint music and conversation behind it. I glanced over my shoulder at Asterion. "Do you mind hanging back until I can verify there aren't any Regulars inside?"

Asterion snorted unhappily, folding his arms. I gave Midas a nod, and Claire a wicked grin.

"You're my wild card. If things go badly, drop the robe," I told her.

She blinked at me. "You want me to flash a bunch of witches."

"The element of surprise."

"I think it's the element of indecent exposure, and you had me call the cops ahead of time, so now it's premeditated."

Midas nodded his agreement.

"We have our game plan," I said, as if she hadn't spoken. Then I approached the doors, ignoring her hissed curses behind me.

I took a deep breath, and then called out my black-feathered fan immediately before me – so that it could both protect me if the occupants decided to shoot, but appear to be a normal fan in my hand if they were Regulars.

I gripped the door handles and heaved both open at the same time, hoping to clear my line of vision into the room. A wall of fragrant blue smoke and the haunting sounds of Enya's greatest hits rolled over me as if I had just found Cheech and Chong's love palace.

I blinked as my eyes adjusted, realizing it was actually a small ballroom of sorts, maybe enough for a hundred people to move around freely without feeling liked packed sardines.

A long table sat in the center of the room, but...

Dozens of sheer silk curtains hanging from the ceiling in various pastel hues created the illusion of walls, breaking the area around the table into a handful of smaller areas that were furnished by mismatched lounging couches, daybeds, padded benches, or even piles of thick pillows strewn across the floor. Since the hanging silk walls were basically transparent, there really wasn't any privacy. And there really should have been some privacy police on standby.

About a dozen people had been strutting around the room, murmuring softly to each other as they gazed upon the carnal activities of an equal number of people who were using the furniture like bedroom-parkour props. Many of the pairings were quite unique and imaginative.

I saw a man with long, blonde hair handing out hand towels to two women as they… finished with a dark-haired man who was lying back on a couch, hands folded behind his head as he caught his breath. The two women toweled off, and then tossed the cloths into a nearby bin. One of them pointed at another group, giggling as she tugged her bedmate after her to join in on the second round of fun, obviously not quite fulfilled yet.

I shook my head at the blonde man handing out towels, but he was facing the other direction, so he didn't see my sympathy. Talk about the worst job ever.

One group in particular seemed to be going for the record of how many people they could fit into their orgy, like building a house of cards until it all fell down. They didn't notice my arrival.

But the rest of the room slowly began to notice…

All conversation and recreational activities slowly died out. Except for the record-breakers, who were still bringing their 'A' game to their cause.

I didn't move, just as surprised as the inhabitants. One woman – skin the color of obsidian and not a stitch to conceal it – stared at me from only ten paces away, her white teeth stark against her dark skin. She glistened as if she had just been freshly oiled.

I felt someone step up from behind me, sigh, and then I saw my fluffy pink robe fall to the ground. "Ta-da!" Claire said in a confident cheer. It seemed to have the desired effect, because everyone seemed to relax, resuming their entertainment. Two naked women even giggled as they slipped into one of the areas to join those already having fun.

I groaned, shaking my head. Perhaps now we did fit in better, but I wasn't about to get down to my skin in front of strangers, no matter how much better it made them feel.

A sound made me glance over to spot a man sitting on an elaborate Persian rug.

Except his carpet was hovering about a dozen feet in the air. His bald head was covered in a single large tattoo, and he wore only a kilt. He had a tiger the size of a Yorkie on his lap – and when I say tiger, I don't mean a cub. This was an adult-proportioned tiger, just… miniature. It snarled in my direction, an angry, spitting sound that I almost couldn't hear over the sound of the Reddi Wip can suddenly ejecting its mother-load into the man's mouth.

Sensing the tiger's annoyance, he turned to look as he swallowed the whipped cream. I recognized him from a party at Dorian Gray's mansion. Mike Arthur. I waved at him uncertainly, giving him a crooked smile. "I've seen you bef—" I began.

He chucked the can of whipped cream at me, cutting me short as he slapped his palm down on the rug behind him like he was slapping a horse's rump. I ducked the can, hearing it hit the wall behind me. Mike Arthur's rug bucked once before it zipped across the room in a blur. He hit the large glass window on the opposite side of the room that faced the street, and then exploded through it, sailing off into the night on his magic carpet, shrieking, "FREEDOM!"

Everyone began to scream, swiping up the nearest articles of clothing in a panic.

The human house of cards even collapsed into a sweaty pile.

"Damn you, Mike Arthur," I muttered, watching as all my plans went to hell.

CHAPTER 26

*T*hunderous boots stomping behind me announced Asterion ducking his horned head into the room, blocking off any possibility of escape. Not concerned with hiding magic anymore, I ran through the crowd and over to the window, tearing through the silk walls. I had to hurdle a few bodies still untangling themselves from their romp, but I ignored their shouts. I finally reached the broken window, fearing that I was about to find a dozen pedestrians on their way home from work shouting variants of *What the fuck? Was that a flying carpet?*

What I saw was much worse.

Six figures moved through the gathering darkness, approaching the building from various points across the street, but in coordination. Probably alerted by the fucking magic carpet. They wore dark, practical clothes, and white scarves with splashes of red on the front. I growled furiously.

"Fucking Templars," a familiar voice murmured beside me, also staring out the window. I spun to see Dorian Gray angrily shaking his head at the approaching men. "Are they here for you?"

I continued to stare at him, momentarily forgetting the Templars. "You said you had a *Board Meeting*!" I finally snapped.

"I'm on the Board for the Hellfire Club," he admitted with an easy shrug, as if we had just run into each other at the grocery store. He held his hand out to indicate the crowd of sweaty people frantically tugging on clothes.

"Meeting," he explained absently, "and the best one in town, I might add." He had black lipstick kisses on his face, his hair was messed up, and he wore only a pair of tight – I glanced down – *very* tight leather pants. "I thought you said you had a date tonight," he said in a judgmental tone.

I muttered darkly, turning to check how much time we had. The Templars had seen me in the window and had given up all pretense of stealth, now huddling together, planning their attack since they had lost the element of surprise. We had a few minutes, because they would enter cautiously, alert for threats on their way up.

"I don't know why they're here," I finally said, watching the Templars discussing their options. "Maybe they're following me, or maybe they're hunting one of your members. That's why I'm here in the first place. Checking up on a woman in your group." I briefly took my eyes from the street to see his reaction.

Dorian pursed his lips in concern – as if debating sharing information like that with me. Not that he didn't trust me, but that he didn't want to hand over one of his apparent group members.

The crowd had huddled into one mass near the head of the table, no longer shrieking as they saw Dorian talking to me amicably. They still looked terrified, but not of the incoming threat. Of me and my friends.

I blinked, recognizing a handsome blonde-haired guy. His eyes met mine and he dropped the stack of white hand towels he was holding, face blanching in panic. Faebio. I *thought* he had looked familiar.

Dorian sensed my attention and gripped my shoulder. "Easy, Callie. He's here to earn money to pay off a certain debt. He said he only had forty-eight hours," Dorian said.

I turned to Dorian, blinking. "Are you serious?"

Dorian nodded. "He said you were quite… insistent."

I shook my head disgustedly. "Yeah, but sanitary towels? Good god, I thought *I* was cruel."

Dorian shrugged impassively. "He doesn't mind, and the pay is good. Better than seeking gang protection for when the Templars come calling."

I stared at him. "Wait, he's scared of the Templars? I thought it was a rival *gang*."

Dorian frowned at me as if I were daft. "*Everyone* is scared of them. They've been scooping up people left and right for *weeks*."

So that was the cause of the sudden rise in gang activity. It was lone freaks forming packs. For protection. And I had been hunting them. Just like the Templars. I shivered guiltily.

But… they had been criminals, too. They could have formed gangs without breaking into cars. Still, a small part of me felt responsible.

I glanced back out the window. The Templars were still huddled, but looked to be close to reaching a decision, several of them nodding. "You need to get these people to safety. I doubt they'll listen to me."

Claire was trying to speak to a few of the guests, looking completely comfortable in the nude, of course. They gave her a bit of credit for wearing the right outfit to the board meeting, but I could tell they didn't completely trust her. "How?" Dorian asked. "What if the Templars have more men waiting out back?"

Midas had approached, holding out his hand. "Not the best answer, but I have two dusty old balls, here."

Dorian coughed in an attempt to cover up an outburst of laughter.

Midas must have realized how it had sounded. "Two Tiny Balls," he corrected.

Dorian actually burst out laughing this time.

"It's what he named them!" Midas growled defensively. "Tiny Balls."

I placed a hand on his shoulder in thanks, recognizing the glass marbles in his palm. Instant Gateways. Nate Temple's company, Grimm Tech, had designed them. "Perfect. Only the heavies will be of use against the Templars," I thought out loud. "You can use one for a ruse – if necessary – and the other for your true escape."

Midas nodded, snatching Dorian by the hand and tugging him back to the crowd of frightened naked monsters. I winced, glad that Midas seemed able to control his turning things to gold ability, or Dorian would have become a solid golden statue. Or maybe his painting would have suddenly turned to solid gold, or something.

I snapped out of my thoughts when I noticed that Dorian's pants actually had cutouts to reveal his bare ass cheeks.

I stared, dumbfounded, unable to avert my eyes for a second or two. Three. Four…

I heard glass break as Midas tossed his Tiny Balls on the ground, opening up Gateways to… well, I hadn't checked with Midas on that part, but I was betting St. Louis. Within moments, everyone was jumping through them, not remotely concerned with where they took them.

A distant part of me realized that Midas would appear to be saving the Hellfire Club, possibly granting him their trust. All in all, his real estate purchase had been quite fruitful. I saw Dorian and his bare ass hop through the Gateway holding hands with… I cursed.

A young, brown-haired woman in a long coat that I hadn't noticed participating in the night's frivolities. I couldn't be sure, but it could have been the same one I had been searching for.

Damn Mike Arthur. He'd ruined everything.

I focused back to the task at hand as the Gateway winked shut. I turned to find Claire and Asterion panting, watching me. I nodded at Claire, snapping my fingers.

"It's time to fuck some shit up," I told her.

"Hard and fast," she agreed. "Let's pound them, man-cow," she grinned at Asterion. He grunted his agreement, kissing his prayer beads before extending his fist for her to bump.

She grinned at the gesture, meeting his knuckles with an actual punch. Asterion smiled.

Then Claire exploded into a giant polar bear. I pulled out my pistols as the sound of pounding feet reached the top of the stairs outside the open doorway.

CHAPTER 27

I had fought Templars before, but I couldn't say the same for my allies. I realized that the Templars had no way of knowing who was in the room. Or how many. They had obviously been scoping the place out, so must have been aware there was some kind of... *board meeting* taking place. They'd only moved to action after the enigmatic Mike Arthur and his tiny tiger blew through the window on his magic carpet, quoting Mel Gibson in *Braveheart*.

"It's just me, boys. Come on in!" I shouted out at them.

Asterion and Claire slipped back against the wall, surprisingly fast and silent, hidden from immediate view behind some of the couches and shifting silken streamers hanging from the ceiling, blown about by the wind through the now-broken window.

"Hand over the woman!" a man shouted, voice muffled from his scarf.

"I just told you. I'm alone."

The Whispers chose that moment to chuckle deep within me. I shivered, unsure what to make of it. They had experience with me killing Templars, and were likely recalling the experience, remembering every spurt of blood. *Sinners*, they repeated hungrily, just like last time in Rome.

"I'm entering alone," the same voice called out as I suppressed the Whispers. No matter how true they were in judging the Templars, I didn't want to relish in that judgment.

A few moments later, a man stepped into the open doorway, but he didn't step into the room. I lowered my pistols to my sides and jerked my chin at him.

His eyes flickered about the room, checking for any surprises, but they weren't far enough in to notice the two massive, hairy monsters tucked against the wall.

He met my eyes. "You..."

"Me," I agreed. "Whatcha doing here?"

"This is none of your concern."

"All of Kansas City is my concern, Templar. Just like your men are your concern."

"We know all about you, Temptress," he spat. Literally spat on the floor. Well, it probably wasn't the most unsanitary substance on the ground right now.

"Temptress? That's new. Are you talking about Rome? How's Ol—"

"Do *not* say his name!"

I shrugged. "Okay. How is your new werewolf mascot doing?" I asked instead.

He practically seethed. "This situation isn't your concern," he said, gesturing at the room. "These are the unwashed, the unclean. They are stained. If you get in our way, we will remove you. Permanently."

I rolled my eyes, not pointing out the contradiction of his boss. "Did you really bring six Templars to capture one woman?" I asked. Because I was pretty sure I now knew who had been chasing the brunette. Templars. Just as they had chased Faebio. "And how did you find us?"

"I brought more than six, Temptress," he said, stepping back into the gloomy hallway like a cheap movie villain. "You have five seconds to get out of the room," his voice called out.

I grumbled unhappily, discreetly motioning for my friends to hunker down low.

"One..." he called out.

"Five!" I blurted, rushing his planned schedule.

And I unloaded both clips in a torrent of bullets at the wall above Claire and Asterion. I knew Claire was bulletproof, and I was sure the man-cow knew how to take a stray bullet like a woman, not some whimpering man.

The Templars, on the other hand, began to shout and curse, several shrieking in pain as some of my barrage struck direct hits as they tore through the drywall. My gun ran empty and I held out my hand discreetly to tell my friends to stay low – to wait for return fire.

I openly yawned as I saw a face peer through a larger hole in the wall. Then I very quickly called upon my black feathered fan, placing it before me as I crouched. Their return salvo was almost instantaneous, hammering into my feather fan with sharp *pings* like metal on metal.

They clicked empty and silence reigned. I lowered my fan, peering through the dust from the broken drywall. I spotted the white of an eye before I dropped my chin.

Asterion head-butted the wall, one of his horns taking Mr. Peeper through the eye, producing a bloodcurdling shriek. Then Claire threw herself entirely *through* the wall and screams of surprise and more gunfire erupted. I stared through the dusty air, horrified by the screams, gunfire, and roars, but almost as soon as it had begun, the hallway was silent.

I waited, heart racing.

Then I saw Claire enter the hallway, clutching a boot. She saw me, panted openly, and then continued into the room, revealing that the boot was still attached to a groaning figure. One of them was still alive. I jogged over to her, staring down at the Templar. He was bleeding in a few places, but would probably be fine after a visit to the hospital and a week of bedrest.

I yanked his scarf off, but it wasn't the same Templar I'd spoken with. I called upon a single silver butter-fly to land on the barrel of my pistol. I then carefully scooped up a pair of forgotten panties with the barrel of my other pistol, and dropped it on the butter-fly. Upon contact with the chrome cutie, the fabric sliced in half, fluttering to the man's chest.

I very slowly straddled the Templar, being sure to grind my hips slightly as I held the pistol with the butter-fly before him, smiling. Then I blew a kiss, and the butter-fly drifted down to his nose, resting on the tip like a silver snowflake, wings flapping in slow, measured strokes.

His blue eyes widened in terror.

"Why are you here, little Templar?" I asked in a low, gentle, monotone. I wanted him to confirm my suspicion. That they had been chasing the woman I had seen.

Hypocrite… the Whispers purred in my ears. I let them, agreeing whole-heartedly.

"Chasing down a criminal," he grunted very carefully, clearly pissed off, but knowing he had no other choice.

"You intended to storm a building for one person?"

"Whatever it takes," he muttered.

"And what about Commander Olin Fuentes? His new… changes."

The man looked hesitant. "The Lord works in mysterious ways," he finally said.

I rolled my eyes. "What the hell is wrong with you people? Can't you just leave us alone?"

"When the Lord's work is finished, we will not be needed," he recited.

"Your boss is a fucking werewolf, moron. Can you really not see the double-standard?"

"He was turned into an abomination doing the Lord's work—"

"I know. I was *there*," I said, smiling to twist the barb.

His eyes flashed with anger but he didn't move. "He takes daily penance for his sins, to atone for his filthy blood, but the Lord sees the heart of a man."

I arched a brow, nodding. "Exactly my point. The heart of a Freak isn't inherently bad. You just admitted it. So… stop hunting innocent people in my town."

He sniffed, obviously letting my words bounce off him, but his jaw worked as if he was gritting his teeth.

I glanced up to see Asterion staring down at us with folded arms. "Two of them got away. I picked these off the dead ones," he said, holding out their scarves.

I growled, standing to my feet with a curse. "Take them with you and give them to Nate. They block magic. Do not—" I turned at a sudden sound from Claire, only to see her diving for me. I gasped right before she tackled me to the ground and I heard Asterion bellow a challenge.

Claire picked me up, sniffing me frantically with her big wet nose.

"Claire, I'm fine," I assured her. "What happened?" I asked, confused.

Claire abruptly crushed me to her chest in a bear hug. "Someone took a shot at you," Asterion growled, "but you stood up just in time, so the dart hit your coat."

I shoved Claire back, turning to Asterion who was holding out a tiny dart with a black substance at the tip. The dart had a small crucifix carved into the side. My eyes shot to the Templar on the ground, but he hadn't moved. I saw another dart sticking out of his chest and groaned.

There went any chance of getting answers, and now the Templars knew I wasn't going to back down. "They'll be back," I muttered, shaking my head.

"I hear police sirens," Asterion murmured, cocking his head.

I turned to Claire. "Time to go home. We don't want to be here when they arrive."

Claire nodded. "You have a date tonight," she grumbled, and instantly began panting.

Asterion grunted. "A date?" he asked too-casually, but I knew a spy when I saw one. Nate would know the moment he got back from Fae.

Too tired to explain, I just nodded. "Yeah."

Asterion held out a massive hand to conceal his strained reaction. "I should probably take your guns. You can pick them back up in St. Louis." He studied the room thoughtfully. "But it might be best to just get rid of them. We can help you get replacements without serial numbers."

I nodded, handing them over.

I opened a Gateway back to my apartment, motioning Claire to shuffle through. Then I glanced at Asterion, blushing. "I'm sorry. Do you want a Gateway home?"

He smiled at me, plucking two marbles from a pouch at his side. "I have Tiny Balls, too."

Despite everything, I laughed. "Okay. Thanks, Asterion. We'll meet again soon. Let me know if you need any help with the Hellfire Club."

He shrugged his shoulders. "I think Midas' found a way to turn this bad situation into a golden opportunity. Now, he has them in his clutches. Their savior. And that was Dorian Gray, right?" he asked, as if curious whether he had heard correctly. Not wanting to lie to the person who had just helped me, I nodded. "Him and Temple together..." Asterion said with a shudder.

"I'd send him back sooner rather than later. The others, too. I appreciate you two saving them, but they aren't captives. Tell Midas I said that."

Asterion shrugged, grinning in amusement. "I'll... quote you."

I nodded back, waving farewell as he threw his Tiny Balls on the ground, opening a Gateway. Then I picked up my fluffy pink robe, deciding to dry clean it just in case, before stepping back into my apartment. I collapsed onto the couch mentally exhausted, dropping the robe as questions whirred through my mind like a butterfly exhibit.

Claire had shifted back, but was simply lying on the floor, staring up at the ceiling.

I heard a rattling vibration and frowned down at the robe, realizing it was Claire's phone. I'd forgotten she had tucked it into the pocket. Claire let out an annoyed sigh and crawled over to it, answering it on speaker.

"Claire?" Beckett asked eagerly. "I got your text, but I was in a meeting. I sent over a patrol car. Is everything okay?" he asked.

I shook my head adamantly. If Beckett stuck his nose into this, he was going to get killed.

"We're fine," Claire said, frowning at me uncertainly. "It was just a… false lead," she replied, sounding tired. I nodded at her in relief.

He was quiet for a moment, as if sensing something was off about her tone. "Good. Well, not the false lead thing, but that you're alright."

"Yeah. Just tired," she said. "I'll talk to you later, okay?"

"Sure," he said. "Keep me posted if you're causing me any more problems in town," he said drily. He sounded exhausted. From what Claire said, he'd been working hard lately. Trying to deal with the uptick in gang activity was wearying. He was a homicide detective, but more gang activity led to increased crime, and they'd all had to help pick up the slack.

Claire hung up, staring at me. "Why did I just lie to our only cop friend?" she asked.

I sighed. "I'll tell you while I shower," I said, climbing to my feet. "I have a date to get ready for, remember?" I muttered.

She clapped her hands excitedly, following me into the bathroom to sit on the counter while I cleaned up behind the shower curtain, telling her my thoughts.

Unfortunately, she seemed to agree with my assumptions. Not that it helped us much.

CHAPTER 28

I hissed as Claire tugged the brush through my hair, the merciless blow dryer drowning out my agonized squawks. "Easy! I'm not your childhood Rastafarian Barbie doll!"

She cocked her head at me in the mirror. "I can't hear you!" she shouted, not bothering to turn off the blow dryer. Or to stop yanking the tangles out of my hair. I glared suspiciously, sensing a twinkle of amusement in her bright green eyes.

I suffered the rest of the torture in silence. It was easier to let her do my hair than it would have been to suffer her questions about my date for an extra hour while I tried to get ready by myself, leaving Claire with nothing to do but cross-examine me.

She finally finished, fidgeting a few loose strands with a satisfied smirk. "I'd do you."

I rolled my eyes, snatching the blow dryer from her hands and pretending it was a gun as I mimed blowing my brains out. "No one is getting *done* tonight. I'm only taking a date because I'd rather not feel like the third wheel when I meet my dad's girlfriend."

She smiled knowingly. "I know. But you're so fun to tease."

"I like to look at my date as cannon fodder. A distraction to keep my dad busy while I get a good read on his girlfriend. To maintain even footing with her," I admitted.

She studied me. "How very... Machiavellian of you," she finally said. I shrugged. She glanced down at the folded paper in my hands, dry-washing her hands anxiously. "Any idea what it means?" she asked.

I shrugged, glancing down at it. Claire had gone to check my mailbox after our talk – letting me dry off in privacy, thank god – and had come back with the mysterious letter. It didn't have a stamp or return address. "I have no idea," I admitted. "The graffiti on the wall last night said *Chancery*, remember?" I reminded her, even though I recalled seeing it myself and didn't need her confirmation. But maybe she had read something else on the wall that explained the word.

She snatched the letter out of my hands, reading it out loud again. I let her, turning back to the mirror and checking my makeup.

She cleared her throat, then began to speak in an overly official voice. "Thank you for your service. We will keep a better eye on our own in the future. Regards, the Chancery." She sniffed it thoughtfully but shook her head. "Some kind of perfume concealing the scent," she said, dropping it back on the table. "But who the fuck is the Chancery? And what are they thanking you for?"

I shrugged. "Who cares? They sound polite, which is better than most Freaks in town."

Claire grunted, sounding more upset that she hadn't also received a letter.

I pulled out my phone, glancing at the time. "I'm going to call Haven and give him an update. I meant to do it earlier, but lost track of time."

"Callie?" I glanced up at her worried tone. "What if Beckett comes up against the Templars? If his awareness of the supernatural puts him in their crosshairs?"

I sighed. "We'll just have to make sure that doesn't happen. This is a pretty tenuous relationship we have with his official duties. It's going to take some time getting used to."

She sighed, nodding. "You're right, but you should probably give him a call, Callie. He always asks about you."

I nodded stiffly. "I will. Soon."

"Chicken-shit," she muttered, smiling as she turned away.

I threw a hairpin at her, hitting her in the back of the head. "Why don't you do something useful like replacing my nice underwear you destroyed?"

Claire stopped, slowly turning. "I meant to ask you about that. How did you come to afford two-hundred-dollar panties when you don't even have a *job* anymore?"

I smiled devilishly. "Vatican hush money. Biblery. It's like *bribery*, but not as sinful." At her stunned look, I shrugged. "Meatball made a pretty significant deposit into my checking account in exchange for me keeping my mouth shut about what *really* happened in Rome." Basically, he'd asked me not to make the Shepherds look bad. Word would eventually get out, but he didn't want me starting the gossip.

"Are you *serious*?" Claire hissed.

I nodded. "He even transferred ownership of my apartment to me. They needed to cut ties with me, but were smart enough to not try evicting me out of my apartment. We both win. I guess."

Claire thought about that, still shaking her head. Then she frowned again. "And with all that money, *why* did you buy a brand-new pair of oh-so-expensive *lingerie*?" She didn't bother hiding her suggestive grin as she folded her arms.

I scowled, pointedly punching Haven's contact icon on my phone and lifting it to my ear. She shook her head, plopping down on the couch as she pulled her own phone out.

Haven picked up on the second ring. "Hello," he said in a formal tone, even though he knew it was me from his caller ID. He wasn't alone, then.

"Hello," I said just as formally. "I had a few things to talk to you about if you've got a minute."

There was a muffled conversation in the background and then I heard him lift the phone back to his ear. "You have my undivided attention, Miss Penrose."

I caught him up to speed, then told him that he could probably expect news of a rogue vampire getting jumped in town. I didn't offer the specific details, leaving it to his imagination. I hoped my delay in telling him wouldn't cause future problems between us. Or between Haven and Roland, since he would be returning from Italy soon.

There was a long silence as if he was waiting to be sure I was finished. Or he was gearing up to threaten my life.

Then I heard a slow, dry chuckle, and instantly felt my body relax. I hadn't wanted to add a pissed off Master Vampire to my plate. Maybe it was a sign that things were turning around. "I heard about that already. He will no longer wander the streets without a chaperone. He had the sudden inclination that he needs a family for protection. So, he's undergoing our… new-hire program."

I tried not to betray my relief. "He was that scared about our little confrontation?" I asked, smiling a little smugly.

Haven was silent for a breath too long. "*Your* confrontation?"

I frowned. Maybe he did need details. "Yeah. We had a disagreement. He and a few of his pals across supernatural families. Few shifters. Even a Fae…" I said carefully, not wanting to alarm him of the bigger conspiracy I believed was going on in town.

"That detail must have slipped his mind. He seemed more concerned about a gang of men."

I scratched my chin, mildly ticked off that I hadn't scared him as much as I thought. "Men. It's always the men that get the credit. Claire and I whipped the shit out of them while they were breaking into some cars."

"He just mentioned being jumped, and remembering a few men involved. He wouldn't say who." As I thought about it, it kind of made sense. The vampire had been taken out right at the beginning, and probably didn't recall the details too clearly, and the last thing he had seen was probably the three men jumping over him, before a boot struck him in the head. "Maybe he was just trying to save face? Not wanting to admit that he was really jumped by two women?"

"Yeah. I guess." Claire was pacing back and forth, muttering angrily under her breath, obviously eavesdropping. "Did he say who these guys were that scared him? He did have pretty bad luck. Maybe he ran into someone else that night…" I said, remembering how scared Faebio had been about the Templars. I needed to know if Haven knew anything about that. A test.

"I don't know if it's that important—"

"Haven…" I said in a warning tone.

He let out a breath. "Fine. He said they wear scarves—"

I didn't hear the rest of what he said, anger suddenly making my ears pop. "The scarf had a red cross on it, right?" I growled over him. Claire had stopped pacing and was staring at me.

"Yes," Haven said very slowly. "He was babbling about the Templars, but I'm pretty sure he's just letting his fear of the bogeymen take over. Sees a cross and assumes the worst. They're in Europe anyway."

I was shaking my head. "No, Haven. They're here. I've seen them, too.

Different place. Ever heard of the Hellfire Club?" I asked, thinking back to the men I had seen chasing the woman. *Had* they been Templars? But none of them had worn scarves and they hadn't worn similar clothing to the Templars at the Hellfire Club.

Haven paused hesitantly before speaking. "Perhaps…"

I rolled my eyes. "Relax. I just saved their lives. Half a dozen Templars showed up to harm them – kill or capture, I don't know. But they're safe, now."

"That was *you?*" he hissed in disbelief. "*You* saved the Hellfire Club? Where are they? No one can find them, but I've fielded half a dozen calls in the last hour about it."

"They're safe," I replied carefully. "Don't worry about them."

He grunted in disappointment at me not giving him their location. "Callie Penrose saving the lowest of the low. Isn't that kind of, I don't know, out of character for you, church-mouse?" he said in a lighter tone.

"I'm not prejudiced like some of the zealots in town. If a group of Templars want to attack a bunch of Freaks just trying to get their rocks off in an innocent, consensual gangbang, they're going to find me right in the thick of it."

Claire gasped and Haven roared with laughter. I flushed deep red, my cheeks heating.

"That's *not* what I—" I took a calming breath. "What I *meant*, was that I'm not going to let them have their way." Haven laughed even harder, and Claire just stared at me, shaking her head. "Dorian was there," I said loudly, trying to change the topic. "Apparently, he's on their Board of Directors."

Haven chuckled. "The world's first playboy. Or biggest playboy. The most notorious lecher."

"A *friend*," I said firmly. "The other stuff, too, but he's a friend. And he did us a solid not too long ago. Wasn't about to let some asshole Templars take him out. Without his help tonight, the body count would have been a lot higher."

Haven breathed heavily into the phone. "Callie, the Templars are… like a rumor. A legend. I've heard horrifying tales about them… Maybe you should just let them pass through town. Who knows what kind of casualties a war like that would cause. Haven't we all had enough of that? Maybe they'll get what they want and leave us the hell alone."

I shook my head. "We have history." And by my count, they'd already acquired what they wanted. The Ring of Aandaleeb, also known as the Seal of Solomon. But Haven didn't need to know about that. He sounded scared enough of them already. "And they're actively hunting in our city. That's not okay."

He sighed his reluctant agreement. "Well, keep me posted. I don't like having Roland so far from home, but since you're like his daughter, let me know how I can help."

I blinked. "That's… unusually kind of you, Haven. You sure you don't have a heartbeat?"

He hung up on me.

I set the phone on the table, thinking about the Templars. They had shown up at the Hellfire Club ready to kill a bunch of people in their search for one woman. But were the three men chasing the brown-haired girl from the alley Templars, too? Were they all hunting this brown-haired girl, or were there two women targeted at the Hellfire Club, and two groups of hunters? Maybe those three men were part of this mysterious Chancery – they hadn't worn scarves while chasing a witch, and that seemed like a stupid action on their part. Templars would have worn their scarves if hunting a witch.

And Templars probably would have turned around to fight us when they saw us pursuing.

I grunted. But I also had a reputation. A reputation that could have convinced them – Templar or otherwise – that they shouldn't confront me without solid backup.

I sighed wearily. At least the intended victims were now safe in St. Louis.

Which left me with the Templars hunting the Freaks of Kansas City. I needed to set a trap. Templars stood against magic. Basically, a militia of highly trained – but still human – soldiers. I could bait them, and then have Beckett round them up for carrying illegal weapons or something.

Claire interrupted my thoughts. "You should probably get going or you're going to be late."

I sighed. "I really don't want to do this."

"Fight Templars? We'll take care of them. Just like we did earlier—"

I shook my head. "No. See my dad with another woman," I said in a soft voice.

Claire's face crumpled into a sympathetic frown. Then she wrapped me up in a hug, careful not to mess up my hair.

"I want him to be happy. I really do," I said. "But… it's going to be hard to be nice to her. Hence me bringing a date. Someone to keep me focused."

"Well, I hope you're bringing a good conversationalist. Someone nice and sweet and charming who can get their attention away from you. Someone—"

"I'm bringing Cain," I said, looking up at her.

She stared at me for a few seconds, mouth working, but no words coming out at first. "In the future, you should probably run these things by me first, Callie," she sighed, running her fingers through her hair in a frustrated sweep.

"I'm sure he'll be the perfect gentleman. He knows the situation."

Claire just shook her head. "The world's first murderer wouldn't have even entered my *maybe* list for possible bachelors to take to a family double-date…"

I sighed, nodding. "Better than Dorian, though, right?"

Claire's smile wasn't reassuring.

CHAPTER 29

My dad watched us approach, looking both judgmental of *my* date and anxious he was about to be judged by me for *his* date. It was a unique look on the typically confident man.

I smiled, tugging Cain along behind me by the hand as I approached the table. I smiled politely, not really sure if I was supposed to—

My dad jumped to his feet and wrapped me up in a tight hug, his hands rubbing circles on my back. "I've missed you, Callie," he said, and I could tell he was laughing.

"I've missed you too, dad." I squeezed back before stepping away and holding out my hand to reveal Cain like a Vanna White impersonation.

Cain wore a white dress shirt, stylish jeans, and a pair of polished black boots. I could tell they were less fashionable and more practical, but he'd tried to make them look nice.

"This is Cain," I said. My father studied him critically, not rudely, but in the time-honored tradition of fathers everywhere. *You're on thin ice*, the look warned.

"You've raised a wonderful woman in Callie, Mr. Penrose," the world's first murderer said to my dad. He nodded succinctly, not entirely won over by the compliment, but appreciative.

"And this is Rai," my dad said, holding out a hand to the woman at the table.

She was a raven-haired, buxom woman around my dad's age, but to me she looked ripened by her years. She wasn't overly pretty, didn't wear overly flashy clothes, and wasn't caked in a thousand pounds of make-up. She was just... beautifully normal.

She smiled at me with kind eyes, revealing faint wrinkles on her skin, and she wore a hopeful, but slightly hesitant smile on her face. I reached out on a subconscious level, assessing her for magic, and felt Cain stiffen slightly beside me. But she was utterly normal, a Regular. I let out an inward sigh of relief.

"It's short for Raidia," she admitted, looking embarrassed. "I didn't get a vote on my birth name, but I've always preferred to go by Rai." I knew what it was like to shorten a name, and I figured going through childhood as Raidia might have been rough, so I couldn't blame her. "I've heard so much about you," she said to me, smiling warmly. "You're all Terry talks about."

Terry looked suddenly flustered, motioning for us all to sit down.

"Raidia... like Radiant?" I asked.

She grimaced, giving me a weary look. Then lifted her hands as if to say *what can you do?*

Raidia sighed at something my father had asked Cain. "Seems we're both guilty until proven innocent, tonight." She winked at Cain, smiling at him conspiratorially.

Cain chuckled with an easy shrug. "I'm used to it. Gallows humor is like an old friend."

My smile went slightly stiff, but I quickly relaxed as my dad turned to me with a thoughtful frown. "Cain is a therapist," I blurted without thinking, immediately wishing I had picked something easier for him to lie about – like a nuclear scientist or chemical engineer.

"Oh?" Rai said interestedly, flashing her brilliant white teeth. "How delightful." I subconsciously glanced at her purse, checking for the brand. You could tell a lot about a woman by her accessories. Was she a money-grubber? Not necessarily a gold digger, but familiar to a certain lifestyle, moving on from one man to the next, using each victim to get her just a little bit more, but never taking too much from one. The clever kind of black widow. Wrap them up in the excitement of fresh love, bleed them a little, and then move on.

But her purse was a plain black leather bag, no brand name. Just something that could be found in the clearance section of any department store –

practical and frugal. She even had a pin in the strap that looked suspiciously like that clown that killed kids in the famous horror movie.

Which made sense. She and my dad had gone to a horror movie convention in Chicago for a long weekend as a pseudo-first date.

I wondered if she was a widow or not. Looking to reclaim a household.

Then I realized that instead of simply talking to her, I was trying to find something to pin on her, a reason she might be dirty. Which wasn't a healthy outlook on life. With an effort, I smiled at my dad and turned to listen to her talking to Cain – who was doing surprisingly well for himself. As if he were a normal, plain-Joe Regular, and not the son of Adam and Eve.

Nor the hated Biblical icon who had murdered his brother, Abel.

"Do you have any family?" Rai asked him after taking a sip of her water.

Cain coughed, spluttering his own water – which I hadn't realized had been sitting before us already. My dad must have ordered them ahead.

Cain wiped up the water with his napkin, face slightly flushed. "Sorry, wrong pipe..."

Rai nodded sadly, reading a deeper meaning into his reaction, and I began to hear alarm bells in my mind. "Oh, I'm sorry. I didn't mean to bring up a sensitive subject, and you're probably not used to people asking *you* questions," she said, laughing lightly. "I have a jerk for a brother, myself. I know how annoying they can be." She leaned forward with a playful smile. "Sometimes I could just strangle him!"

Cain nodded woodenly, his lips pale. "Sure. Brothers can be a handful. It's entirely normal to want to kill them sometimes..." He shot me a veiled look. "And I'm a therapist, so..."

I tried not to wince. "Yes. Cain would know." Sweet Baby Jesus. Where was the waiter? I opened my mouth to ask, shooting a sharp look at my dad, but he was obviously enjoying Rai's innocent interrogation of my date, and would be of no use to me.

"What about your mom?" Rai asked instead. "What does she do?" My dad wrapped his arm behind her chair, and I saw the pleased inner smile in her eyes at the gesture of reassurance.

Cain grew visibly uncomfortable, unconsciously twisting his napkin into a ball. "She... likes apples," he managed, as if latching onto the first thing that came to mind.

I wanted to suddenly end this date or find a way to turn the tables back on her. She was also under the threat of judgment. Callie's guillotine.

"She... likes apples?" my dad asked, frowning. "Is she a gardener?" They were both frowning, now.

"You could say that," Cain said in a low tone, failing to make his smile look anything but uncomfortable.

He needed a Knightess in shining armor to save him. I cleared my throat. "Orchards. His mom owns an apple orchard."

Their unease vanished, and they nodded at the simple answer. I almost let out a sigh of relief.

"And your dad—"

A perky, pink and blue haired waitress breasted boobily up to our table. I say it that way because her chest seemed to lead the charge everywhere she went, like a marching band heralding her arrival. I could tell she'd been a waitress for twenty years, and genuinely loved it. And if she used those assets to get better tips, I couldn't blame her.

"Evenin'," she said, flashing us with a dazzling smile, displaying a set of suspenders covered in buttons that only seemed to frame her chest like an art exhibit. At this point, I would have welcomed a streaker. "What can I get ya tonight?" she asked in a southern drawl, as sweet and thick as molasses.

Cain looked remarkably relieved at her arrival, taking a long sip of his drink as my dad and Rai began talking to each other as he held the menu, debating options. Cain shot me a desperate look behind his menu as he pretended to read it.

I grinned, squeezing his thigh with my hand. "You're doing great," I said, leaning closer and pretending to read the menu alongside him.

"Oh, don't be so old-fashioned, Terry. Go ahead and order first," Rai said with a light elbow to his ribs and a lilting laugh.

Terry sighed in defeat, rubbing his ribs to try and get sympathy. "On that note, I think I'll take the ribs. Pretty sure this delicate flower just took one of mine," my dad finally said.

The menu in Cain's hands stiffened as his fingers clenched. My eyes widened in disbelief as I made sure Cain wasn't about to run screaming. Was there no end to the irony of Biblical references? Maybe I *should* have asked Dorian to accompany me instead.

"Mmmm. That sounds delicious!" Rai grinned. "I actually may just steal one of yours for that. Would serve you right," she teased, turning to Cain. "And I'll have the apple and bacon salad, in tribute to your mother's orchard."

Cain gave her a painfully slow nod, attempting gratitude, but looking more like he had felt the first gurgle of an irritable bowel syndrome episode.

"Great choice, honey," the waitress grinned. "And you?" she asked, turning to me.

"The cake. I'll just have a slice of cake. Cain and I can't stay long," I said, picking the last thing I had glanced at. Christ, could this get any worse?

"Would that be the Original Sin Chocolate Delight?" the waitress asked me in an almost bedroom appropriate purr.

"Unbelievable..." Cain breathed into his menu, soft enough for no one else to hear.

I just stared at her for a second. Then I gave her what I hoped passed for a nod.

"And you, sir?" she asked Cain.

"Steak. Rare. And a double whisky. Neat." He glanced over at me. "Two double whiskeys." He closed the menu, handing it over to her as the waitress turned away to the next table. I overheard her stating something cheerful, and laced with sunshine, birdsong, and boobs.

"Let's talk about you two," Cain said, attempting a smile. And I squeezed his thigh in gratitude, turning to Rai and my dad as Cain managed to regain control of the situation.

And the night rolled on pretty comfortably after that.

Rai was... well, she was fun. Lighthearted, quick with the tongue, and obviously playful. I would find myself smiling at nothing in particular several times throughout our meal, and soon forgot the awkward introduction. I did try to get a read on her again, but it was readily apparent that she was just a Regular. She wasn't some demon in disguise – because I had worn my Darling and Dear boots, pointing them at her from under the table. They would give me a slight pinch to the toes if pointed at a demon. But they didn't.

I watched my dad, and found myself smiling happily to see him laughing, not a shadow of sadness crossing his face even once during our meal. Which was enough to make me want to kiss Rai on the lips. For helping my dad relieve himself of the burden of carrying around my mother's memory on his shoulders every day, she had my vote.

But it was also strange to see my dad like this. It had been a very long time since he'd opened his heart back up. Thanks to a request from Nate

Temple, Death had allowed my father to see my mother once more – to clear the air and say a final goodbye.

She'd encouraged him to *live*, to move on, to meet every day with a smile rather than regret.

And it looked like he was giving it his best effort. He caught me watching him and smiled at me, Cain and Rai laughing at some joke they had just shared, seeming lost in the moment.

My dad took a deep breath, and then let it out, signifying the relief he felt. I nodded happily.

I felt Rai watching us and turned to look at her. She was grinning triumphantly, and I found myself grinning right back at her.

"Looks like we passed their tests, apple-picker," she said, lifting her glass of water to Cain.

Cain dipped his head politely at my dad. "Every single day, I consider myself lucky that Callie hasn't tried to kill me. I'm glad I don't have to worry about *two* of Clan Penrose wanting to kill me."

The waitress brought out my cake, drizzled with chocolate syrup, and...

An apple slice with a cutout *bite* mark. The severed *bite* section of the apple was also on the plate, proving that no one had *actually* taken a bite of it.

Or I would have rained down destruction on this establishment.

I winked at Cain, taking a slow, delicious bite of the apple. He shot me a scowl in return. The rest of the night was full of whiskey, laughter, friendship, and a hint of love to come.

But Cain and I just focused on the whiskey and friendship, leaving the love for Rai and my dad to explore.

My dad finally stood with a tired sigh. "We better be heading out, but maybe we can do this again, soon. Now that it's safe to do so, I'll even host it at my place," he said, smiling at Cain. They traded grips, and then Cain moved onto Rai, leaving me facing my Dad.

He placed an arm around my shoulder, smiling as he watched Rai. "Think your mother would approve?" he asked in a very soft voice.

I leaned into his shoulder. "As long as you're happy, dad. That's what she would care about."

He grunted. "We both know you were Sarah's favorite. I was just another dependent for tax write-offs," he muttered playfully. He grunted as I elbowed him lightly. "You doing okay?" he asked.

I nodded. "Yeah. Just tired."

"We should catch up soon. Just us two."

"Sounds good," I agreed, watching Rai and Cain laugh at something. "Where did you meet?"

He chuckled. "Caught her checking out another man so hard that she dropped her bag of lemons. I picked them up for her, clearing my throat politely. She looked more surprised – and embarrassed – than anything."

I smiled, imagining it. "And how did you overcome her interest in the other guy?"

I felt his chest puffing out proudly. "As I set the bag of lemons in her cart, I told her, 'when life hands you lemons, make lemonade... and you look thirsty.'"

I stared at him, impressed. "No. You didn't say that..."

He grinned, rubbing his knuckles on his shirt. "Your Dad's still got it, Callie." I rolled my eyes, shaking my head with a grin. "She tried to push me off for a month, but I was persistent. Must have finally worn her down," he admitted. "She wasn't looking for anything serious. But she couldn't resist my charm," he said, loud enough for her to overhear as she walked up to us.

"Something like that," Rai said in a dry tone, walking up to him. I grinned at her tone and she finally gave me a guilty sigh. "But he's pretty much right. I put up a lot of fight, not sure I wanted to get into the dating game again. But he made each request sound so innocent, though, and before I knew it, we were regularly doing all sorts of things." But she looked genuinely happy with the outcome as she squeezed his shoulder.

"Let's go start the cars," My dad told Cain, and they conveniently left Rai and I standing beside each other, all alone.

"He's too clever for his own good," Rai murmured. I turned to look at her, but she was staring at him as he walked away, smiling to herself, lost in thought. She sensed me looking and averted her eyes, blushing. "Sorry. I'm not very good at this kind of thing," she admitted.

I found myself smiling. "Me neither," I admitted.

"I think we're supposed to hug it out, next. Or you give me a list of demands... What do you think?"

I felt my smile stretching, especially seeing her shifting from foot to foot uncomfortably, like our roles were reversed. "Yeah," I agreed, holding out my arms.

Her eyes seemed to sparkle with relief as she gave me a tight squeeze. "I never thought I'd say this, but he means the world to me, Callie. I feel like I'm young again," she said, squeezing tighter.

I patted her on the back. "Just take care of him. He's all I have left," I admitted, surprised at my openness. But I was pretty good at reading people, and after spending more than an hour with Rai, I'd lost all doubts about what was going on between her and my dad. They both seemed so happy together, and that was enough for me.

Rai released me from the hug, but one of the buckles on my coat snagged her purse for a second, almost ripping it off her shoulders. Luckily, it didn't, but we both apologized over the other – and then cutoff abruptly, laughing lightly as we shook our heads and left the restaurant.

The men sat in their cars, smiling at the two of us in relief.

Maybe they had expected the building to be on fire rather than the two of us laughing as we said our goodbyes.

I was simply glad to have one less stress off my back. My dad was happy, and Rai was pretty fun. Looking at Cain through the windshield as I approached, I remembered the horrible start to the dinner, and began to laugh.

I couldn't wait to tell Claire about the interrogation Cain had received.

CHAPTER 30

*W*e sat in Cain's SUV outside my apartment, having rocked out to *Journey* the whole way home. Cain chuckled, shaking his head as he turned to look at me.

"If a guy ever deserved to get some after meeting a girlfriend's parents, the time is fucking nigh," he said in mock seriousness.

I punched him in the arm, satisfied by his grunt. "Nice try. But we're not – and never will be – boyfriend and girlfriend."

He rubbed his arm dramatically, leaning his head back into his headrest. "I'll take some pity love if it's on the menu," he chuckled, closing his eyes.

I rolled my eyes, but couldn't help smiling. He *had* taken a beating tonight. Who would have thought so many awkward questions could arise that pertained to his real origin story?

I leaned in and gave him a firm kiss on the cheek, startling the living hell out of him.

I pulled back, smiling satisfactorily at the stunned look on his face. It slowly turned to hope.

I held up my palm. "That's the extent of my pity. You earned it."

He exhaled as his momentary hopes and dreams died. He set his hands on the steering wheel, resigned to a night of loneliness. Then he began to laugh. Great big bellows.

And as if it were contagious, soon we were both giggling uncontrollably.

"That couldn't have gone any worse if you had set it up!" he roared, pounding the steering wheel as tears leaked from his eyes. I couldn't help it. I laughed harder.

"Fucking *ribs!*" I hooted.

"And Garden salads!" he shouted back.

It was a long time before he escorted me back up to my apartment, the both of us still giggling as Claire opened the door with a suspicious scowl.

"I'm not leaving," she said, folding her arms.

"I am," Cain said, giving me a quick goodnight hug.

Claire watched him suspiciously as I took a step through the door. I had time to see her sleepy eyes shoot wide before I felt a hard *slap* on my ass.

When I rounded on Cain to punch him in the mouth, all I saw was him hauling ass down the hallway, roaring with laughter. "I earned that, Callie Penrose!" he cackled.

I felt myself laughing along with him, shaking my head.

Claire studied me from head to toe. "Right, missy. Off to bed with you."

"Yes, mother," I said, rolling my eyes as I shuffled past her. I washed my face, brushed my teeth, and threw on a long tee before crawling under the covers.

And that's where *he* found me…

CHAPTER 31

I stood in a vast space of polished marble floors, while thick matching pillars all around me climbed high to support an unseen ceiling. Veins of obsidian and silver streaked the white marble, like faint flickers of lightning. Silver sconces lined the walls, flickering with soothing flames, turning much of the marble into faint mirrors.

I tried to remember how I had gotten here, but my thoughts were hazy and drifting, as if all that mattered was this singular moment. I shook my head, abandoning the attempt to think, realizing the strain was only making my head ache.

I approached an expansive balcony, stopping before a waist-high wall to study the vast, open sky. Gray clouds hung thick enough for me to almost feel like I could reach out and touch them. *Where am I?* The thought drifted up from my mind like a bubble from the bottom of a pond.

Then it was forgotten and the slow ache returned as I tried to recall… I shook my head again.

I stared over the balcony and sucked in a breath, suddenly gripping the marble wall in panic. The marble crunched under my fingers, rubble spilling at my feet. I didn't look down. Just out.

Far, far below was a strange, strange world.

A forest of glowing pink trees flickered with violet flames. Violet embers and sparks erupted into the air as several of the trees crumbled, crashing to the earth. I heard wails of agony and despair, but not from any specific voice. More like… from the trees themselves. Because I saw no one in the flames, just the trees.

A small cloud of sparkling silver mist zipped up to the violet flames, hovered for a moment, and then drifted around it before disappearing behind a rise in the rolling hills beyond the burning forest.

In the distance was the silhouette of a tall, foreboding castle shrouded in sinister fog – harsh spires, keeps, and towers rose above the fog, stabbing at the sky like a fist of thorns.

I saw armies of… creatures marching in the distance, looking like nothing more than black smears of charcoal through the fog, but I heard the distant sound of drums signaling the marching beat. Then I saw two more when I looked a different direction. Then more. And more.

All making their way towards the shrouded castle.

I spun at a sudden sound behind me but didn't immediately see anything in the pillars – which were dim in comparison to the view at the balcony. I walked deeper into the maze of columns, alert for the sound that had startled me.

Suddenly, I was standing before a wide circular depression in the floor, the infinite world of columns behind me. A curving arc of three steps led down into what resembled a royal suite. A wall of uncut diamond bisected the circle, stretching infinitely up and out, before and behind me.

A massive bed of silver and gold backed up against the glittering wall, which I realized was dripping with water like a spring. The entire wall.

Two fireplaces crackled on opposite sides of the bed, one burning with white fire and the other with black. It all felt… natural.

Then I saw *him*.

A masked figure stood directly opposite me, staring at me, with the suite between us. His skin was the same uncut diamond as the wall behind the bed, making him look like a living statue. The black and white flames from the fireplaces reflected off his skin, glittering. Vast skeletal wings rose over his shoulders – no membrane between the spines.

An image flickered into view, and he was suddenly holding an entirely black spear at his side – even the unique sword-axe hybrid blade at the tip was black – with a blazing red orb set in the center of the blade. The spear flickered again, vanishing, and revealed two sets of clawed hands hanging at his sides. He didn't appear to notice the change.

Something about that spear... My head began to ache again so I stopped.

His eyes met mine, and I shivered. They flickered with silver and white fire. I couldn't make out the details of his face, so I took a cautious step down the stairs, closer to him and the suite. Then another.

Like a mirror image, he advanced a step. Then another.

When I stopped, so did he.

As I took another step, finally standing in the bowl, so did he. I finally got a good look at his face and felt a sharp intake of breath escape my lips, my head aching in warning. His mask was majestic and horrifying – a man's harsh features carved into the uncut diamond.

Something about him... That mask... My thoughts felt hazy, fleeting, as if it was taking all my strength to simply exist and observe the moment. I lifted a hand, even though I wasn't close enough to reach him.

He mirrored my motion, and I somehow knew he was just as confused as myself. Or was this literally a reflection of some sort? Some inner monster inside me? Me seeing a version of myself.

I shivered at that, taking another step closer.

So did he.

I frowned, glancing down at some obstruction tangling around my ankles, and saw I was wearing a long white toga that left one shoulder bare. I also wore stained cloth wrapped around my wrists and forearms, filthy compared to the opulent white toga. I was surprised to see my hand gripping a crackling white spear with two bands of shifting black rings on the haft, breaking it into thirds. I gasped, but my fingers didn't release the weapon, as a thought struggled to slip through, searing my mind, no longer giving me a faint warning ache. I pressed against the pain, fighting... whatever it was, allowing the thought to finally break free as I withstood the growing ache.

The Spear of Longinus – the spear that had pierced Jesus' side as he hung on the Cross. I'd also heard it called the Spear of Destiny, and I'd only consciously held it in another vision where I'd confronted a demon named Amira. I'd unknowingly forged the three broken pieces back together during a fight with another demon but had never held the re-forged weapon in the real world. Just in these visions.

"Who are you?" I asked in a cautious whisper, glancing back up at the man as I pressed against the presence in my mind harder, gritting my teeth.

The hold on my mind shattered at the spoken question, and a flood of thoughts rolled over me, drowning out the presence that had been blocking me. I was in a strange vision of sorts. Or a dream.

The man gasped, reaching up to his face to tear off the mask. He flung it to the bed with a violent gesture, and he abruptly changed. A muscularly-sculpted man in a kilt of braided white and silver leather strips stood before me, his now jaw-length hair brushing his chin as he stared at me in disbelief.

"Callie..." he whispered, but it sounded like a question. "What are *you* doing here?"

Nate Temple.

And he was suddenly sprinting at me as if to save me, the marble floor crunching under his pounding feet like thin ice as he held out his hands, a desperate look of pain on his face.

He froze in mid-step, and even the flames in the fireplace halted. As if I was now staring at a room-sized snapshot of what I had just lived. Like a framed picture, what appeared to be a wall of glass rested over the still image of Nate reaching out a hand to save me, only a few feet away.

And in the glass, I could make out a faint reflection of myself superimposed on the scene.

My face was dirtied, smudged, and sported several cuts.

But the most startling aspect was the thick, white bandage covering my eyes, wrapped entirely around my head. Beneath the bandage, liquid silver trailed down my dirty cheeks, gently dripping off my chin to fall to the marble floor, like I was crying silver tears.

I gasped, reaching up to my face, wondering if it was an illusion, but my fingertips touched the bandage and recoiled. It was real. My eyes were completely covered. But... how was I seeing anything with a bandage over my eyes?

As I thought that, the room around me flashed silver, like a filter had been thrown over my eyes, turning everything into chrome lines like I was seeing it all in sonar. Then it snapped back to normal – or what passed for normal in this... place.

A dream?

A vision?

I reached out to touch Nate's outstretched hand on the other side of the glass, and it shattered, crashing to the floor in a pile of shards. Then the shards were gone, and the room as it had been moments ago stood before me – like I was reliving the moment.

Nate stared at me from across the suite wearing his Horseman Mask again.

No wonder we hadn't recognized each other.

As if in replay, he slowly shook his head. Had he experienced the strange reflection as well? Was this real? Or some twisted dream? I'd had strange experiences like this before, but nothing so specific, and never with a person I knew.

Nate tore off his mask again and was suddenly naked other than his white and silver skirt. He somehow pulled it off quite well, and I found my eyes devouring the curves of his upper body. Taking his cue, I reached up to my blindfold and tore it off, letting it flutter to the ground beside me. Nothing changed in my perception of the room, but the air on my cheeks was noticeable, like cold air on wet skin. I reached up, touching the dampness, and when I pulled my fingers away, I saw they were wet with the silver tears.

I also realized that I wore a similar outfit to Nate, except mine was a flowing white, sheer silk skirt, where his was the white and silver strips of leather.

Lucky for him, my chest was also bare, and he took his time acknowledging this facet of the dream – but not any longer than the amount of time I had spent admiring his own bare chest. He didn't leer, but he devoured me with his eyes, and I relished in it.

Then we were hesitantly walking towards each other, as if both fearing the scene was about to freeze again. I arched my back defiantly, not truly understanding why, and I noticed that his jaw was clenched, his hands fisted at his sides.

Like two warriors approaching from opposite sides of a battle.

I was panting in both anticipation and frustration as we reached each other, fearing the vision was about to shatter like glass again the moment we touched, my despair growing with each step.

And I suddenly realized why we had both approached each other like enemies. Not *against* each other, but against whatever was trying to keep us *apart*.

The vision didn't shatter this time, but we didn't relax either. We stood inches apart, the only point of contact was the burning skin of his chest barely grazing the tips of my breasts, which felt suddenly electrified as we both panted, the friction quite literally tearing at my soul and body with a shared desperate need.

He shuddered, slowly lifting his hands to my cheeks. He looked so tired. Exhausted. Resolved.

I lifted my hands to his chest, confirming that he was, in fact, real, and not an image.

I left silver handprints on his body, marking my territory as I stared into his green eyes, which roared like fire in this room of only black, white, and silver.

He gripped my face and leaned closer, his breath like a gentle breeze of anise, or absinthe.

Blue fireflies erupted behind his head, bathing him in a cold glow, showering our hesitant embrace with magical light. Then I noticed green fireflies from behind me mingling with the blue as the swarm began to whirl around us in a gentle tornado. I could feel his racing pulse both through my fingers on his chest and his fingers on my cheeks. We held each other tightly, desperately, squeezing just a hair past comfort and gentleness.

A whisper of violence between us?

Or was it territorial?

Were we *claiming* each other or *challenging* each other?

The fireflies whirled faster and faster, our hair whipping in the steadily increasing vortex of power caused by their passing.

"What is this?" I whispered, digging my fingers tighter into his chest as my lips trembled.

His fingers were slick with the silvery tears dripping from my eyes, but he continued to cup my cheek bones and neck possessively, holding me in the palms of his hands while I clutched at his heart and soul.

"A tale of two cities…" he whispered back, smiling harshly as he glanced over my shoulder, indicating the world I had seen from the balcony.

Before I could respond, fire suddenly rolled over us, immolating the entire world in green and blue flame.

Silver and gold flame.

White and black flame.

CHAPTER 32

I woke up with a gasp, eyes wide and my body drenched in sweat.
Claire snored softly beside me, curled up on half of the bed,
oblivious to my sudden movement. She slept like the dead before she was a
shifter, but now was even worse.

I rushed to the bathroom, frantically staring into the mirror. My eyes
were fine. No marks on my face from Nate's grip. No silver tears on my
cheeks.

But my body tingled with electric fire, every brush of fabric like sand-
paper on my inflamed skin. Especially my lady bits.

I took a *very* cold shower, sitting on the floor, rocking back and forth as
I tried to steady my breathing, to take stock of everything I could remember
about the odd dream, not wanting to forget a single moment for multiple
reasons.

Was someone messing with me? It *had* been like a vision. But those
had only ever happened to me when I confronted an Angel or Demon,
where I would find myself suddenly transported to a different plane of
existence.

Had it been a warning of some kind? Was Nate in danger? Was he still
off in Fae? I'd call him later, not to tell him about the dream – thank you
very much – but to see if anything important had happened to him lately.

With his level of arrogance, I wasn't about to admit to a dream like that.

It would make me look desperate, weak. Like some floozy. He had a big enough head already.

With absolutely no chance of falling back asleep, I threw on some workout clothes, and while Claire continued snoring in my bed, I made a Gateway to a place I wasn't welcome.

I stepped into the familiar training room where I had spent much of my formative years, learning the art of blades, blood, and magic.

Church.

Where I had trained to become a reluctant Shepherd for the Vatican. It had been the only way Roland would agree to teach me about my magic. Of course, as a child I had thought it the coolest thing ever – learning how to use weapons and self-defense like I was the next Karate Kid. I hadn't known about the Shepherd thing. I had known about monsters, unfortunately, and that I had magic, but I hadn't known how to use it.

Or why I had magic in the first place.

Because I had been adopted. Left on the steps of Abundant Angel Catholic Church. The same church that Roland would coincidentally choose to make his home more than ten years later. Shepherds were typically vagabonds, traveling the world from one crisis to another, hunting down those who hunted down the innocent. They didn't put down roots in places, but my presence had convinced him to stay.

Of course, Roland had been put in an impossible situation recently. In order to save two women he called friends, he had been forced to become a vampire. And since Shepherds hunted vampires, shifters, and other monsters, Roland had also been forced to relinquish his duty as a Shepherd.

He was still coming to terms with that decision, but it had forced us both out of our old home. Here. This training room beneath the church.

Glancing around, I realized I hadn't let myself acknowledge how much I missed the place.

A whisper of fabric behind me…

I dropped into a crouch, snatching up a blade concealed in my boot, and threw.

Someone gasped, dropping to the floor.

I called up a ball of white light – a roiling orb of glowing vapor – and approached the assassin, knowing I hadn't killed him.

Only because I hadn't intended to.

He lay on the ground, staring up at me warily, hands open at his sides to let me know he was no threat. I blinked down at the familiar face, clinically assessing the blade sticking out of his upper right chest. It had been a short blade, not intended to be lethal unless thrown at a specific target on the body.

I frowned at him.

"Morning, Callie," Arthur said through gritted teeth. "Guess I asked for that."

Arthur was a homeless man I had shown kindness to months ago, cleaning him up and giving him a place to work here at the church. But upstairs as a janitor and security guard, not in the super-secret Shepherd's bunker below.

"What are you doing down here, Arthur? And *how* did you get down here?"

He looked cautious, as if not sure how to answer, or if knowing his answer might just make things worse. I had trusted this man. Given him a home, of sorts. And he was… robbing the church?

"Roland gave me a code," he said in a rush. "Back before you left for Italy."

I… blinked at him. "He… gave you a code." Arthur nodded eagerly. "For the secret military training rooms underneath the church. The ones that almost no one knows about…"

He nodded again, meeting my eyes. Roland had never told me about that. Was Arthur lying? But… in a way, it sounded like something Roland might have done. Right before we left for Rome, Roland had known he might not ever come back – that he might not be welcome back.

So… choosing a guardian for the place was smart. And Roland had trusted Arthur to visit us after we returned, while we prepared and packed for our final departure with the church. So, this place wasn't a surprise to him. Maybe Roland had forgotten to tell me the full truth. We'd had more pressing matters to be concerned about at the time.

And even if Arthur was lying, he wouldn't have been able to get down here without a code. I could always check the security logs. Maybe he had stolen one of our codes. But that didn't seem likely. I wasn't even sure if our codes worked anymore. Which was why I had made a Gateway here. The Vatican technically owned the place, and for the most part, Roland and I had pretty much severed ties with them after our trip to Rome.

Which meant it was more than likely that Arthur was telling the truth.

"Who knows about this?" I asked him.

"Fabrizio agreed to it this week. Said I would need some training, though," he admitted, eyes flicking to the knife in his chest.

What the hell? The Shepherds had recruited my homeless man? But... he was *mine*!

CHAPTER 33

*J*blinked at him. "Wait, agreed to what? You... you're going to be a Shepherd?" I asked incredulously, eyeing the knife sticking out of his shoulder to pointedly acknowledge Fabrizio's assessment. Arthur would need training. A *lot* of training. But even then... he wasn't exactly a spry chicken. And he didn't have any magic. Not that magic was required, but when going up against monsters, it was always good to have more tools at your disposal rather than less.

"You might need more training than you think," I said, not unkindly, as I helped him to his feet. "Follow me," I said, releasing him and heading deeper into the compound. "If you're anything like me, you'll soon find this is one of your regular hangout spots," I said, finally stepping into the small medical wing, complete with first-aid kits and minor surgical gear.

I'd spent a lot of time here in my training, wrapping myself back up.

He studied the area with familiarity. "I know how to dress a wound," he said softly.

I shot him a thoughtful look. "How about stitching up your own wounds?" I asked with a sarcastic smile.

He didn't miss a beat. "A handful of times."

I assessed him thoughtfully. "Right. Well, you probably did a crap job of it. It's not like putting on a bandage—"

"Looks like this is my first test, then," he interrupted me. "Well, second test, since I failed the first one," he admitted, briefly touching the handle of the blade sticking out of his chest. Now that I watched him, it was surprising how calm he was. Obviously in pain, but not debilitating. "What kind of thread do you have? And needles?" he asked, studying the cabinets in a quick sweep. "Never mind. I'll just have a look myself."

I had no idea. There were different kinds of needle and thread? I usually just found something sharp, and used the thread Roland had shown me to sew up a wound. Doing your own wounds was hard, but Roland had forced me to learn it.

Arthur began digging through the cabinets, grunting when his motion shifted the blade still stuck in his chest. I watched the slow dripping of blood on the counter as he reached up for a small box. He glanced inside, muttered, and set it to the side, reaching back up into the cabinet for another box.

He also set this one aside.

He glanced over his shoulder, face set in stone. "Would be mighty kind of you to lend a hand. I can't reach the top shelf."

I jumped to help and pulled down the items he indicated, surprised to find myself obeying so easily. But I didn't question it. If this was a test, my job was to observe him, study not only his skill at the task, but his mindset, reactions, and inner psyche as he performed the task.

But I'll admit I was more than a little impressed already.

He read a few boxes before finding one that was apparently suitable. He found some latex gloves, snapped them on without even looking, and sat down on the counter. He watched me, meeting my eyes as he expertly weaved the thread through the eye of the needle, tying off a knot from obvious experience.

He jerked a chin over my shoulder. "Any good whiskey over there?" he asked, biting down on a wooden stick he had found in one of the drawers. He was like an entirely different person than the kind, pleasant, harmless man I had first met.

I was already halfway to the sitting room with the liquor decanters he had indicated before I consciously realized it. Instead of making a fuss about it, I picked one up and walked back over to him. He was sitting on a chair, eyes closed, breathing steadily.

I held it out and his eyes opened, even though I hadn't made a sound. He accepted the decanter with a nod of thanks. "Probably not that sanitary," I said, "and I know we have iodine in that dr—"

I realized he had already taken off his shirt and splashed the iodine around the wound. "This is for me," he replied, and took a big swig of the liquor. "The knife, if you please."

"I'd rather you continue the show, Arthur," I said with a faint smile.

He shook his head. "Your knife, your fault. I'm paying the price of being caught off guard, so you'll pay the price of inflicting harm upon a friend, and putting your knife in the wrong… sheathe. Pull it out on my signal," he said, settling the glass decanter down beside him.

I carefully wrapped my fingers around the hilt in a loose grip, ready to withdraw it on his command. He gave me a nod and I pulled out the knife as quickly as it had broken his skin. Blood instantly pooled, but he shoved a wad of gauze over it, pressing down tightly.

I was quite surprised I hadn't seen a flicker of pain on his face. Not even a hint of it.

He took a few more swigs from the decanter, then leaned back into his chair, breathing steadily for a solid minute. Then he set the decanter down and put a wooden stick in his mouth.

He bit down, testing it, before removing the gauze and beginning the stitching. The location wasn't as awkward as I had thought it might be. Now, I had been ready to swoop in if he looked to be making a mess of it, but… he might have done a better job on his own than I could have. He spat out the wood after he crossed his last stitch, then looped the needle through the thread.

I opened my mouth, realizing the wound wasn't closed very tightly and it appeared that he was about finished. Then I stopped as he placed the needle in his mouth, biting down on it. Instead of cutting the thread, he leaned back with his neck, tugging the threads neatly closed.

"Finger," he said in a muffled tone, still gritting the needle in his teeth.

I leaned closer, holding the sutures tight, and he plucked the needle from his teeth to weave a final knot. I cut the thread for him, rolling my eyes at his stubborn grunt. I offered him one of Roland's shirts, even though it was too big, but he filled it out better than I had thought, and for the first time I realized he was much stronger than I had assumed. Hunger and living on the streets had eliminated any excess fat, and he was slim, but covered in tough, corded muscle that had been too stubborn to be starved away. Like a wolf.

I studied him thoughtfully. He studied me back.

"Fine. You did well," I admitted, folding my arms. "But I'm taping you up."

He snorted as I pulled out fresh gauze and began taping it over his stitches. "It just means I have practice stitching myself up. Not a good habit for a would-be-fighter."

I nodded thoughtfully. He had known Fabrizio's name, which kind of verified his claim, because I was sure Roland wouldn't have told him that. "How exactly was this supposed to work? Are you heading off to Rome?" I asked him.

He shrugged. "Fabrizio was considering whether it was wise to send someone here," he said with an amused smirk my way. The indication that Roland and I might not find that particularly reassuring, and rather than doing it anyway, they were sitting on their hands. Probably waiting for Roland to return so they could discuss it with him, first.

Which… was pretty courteous of them.

I shrugged. "Not sure how the majority would feel about it, but maybe I could help here and there with training. Or Roland."

Arthur nodded appreciatively. "I would like that, but I'm not in the decision-making circle. I could offer the option. Might help bridge the gap between you and them. A little."

The silence grew as I thought about it all. "What were you doing down here in the first place?"

He shrugged, eyes scanning the room. "Getting familiar. Maybe work out a little bit. I lived on the streets for a while, as you well know. I can scrap with what's available, but I'm far from a warrior."

I remembered him telling me his life story after we first met. He had made me promise never to share or ask about it unless he expressly gave me permission. As in, him initiating that I could ask about it. I couldn't even pester him. Until then, it hung between us. But it suddenly gave me a lot of questions, especially with his possible recruitment into the Shepherds.

He had left a lot of blanks in his story, but had spoken vaguely enough that I got the feeling Arthur might just be one of the humblest sons of bitches I had ever met. Always polite, kind, commenting about how he didn't know much of this or that.

Then he performed a suture on himself as if he had done it hundreds of times. In war zones. While under fire.

Totally opposite of the calm, polite, almost cute older man who had been ecstatic to receive a small security job working for a church.

I decided I was going to press Fabrizio for a finder's fee since I had brought Arthur into the game, even though I hadn't intended him to become a Shepherd. He didn't need to know that part.

Because if his resolve and calm resiliency under pressure was any indication of his potential, Arthur might just go down as a legendary Shepherd.

"Roland taught me one lesson pretty early on…" I began, speaking softly.

Arthur grunted, climbing to his feet. "May as well get this over with," he said, turning away from me and heading to the sparring room.

My jaw might have been hanging open. Then I was jogging after him. "How did you know what I intended?" I asked him.

"The single most important lesson for a warrior – other than learning which end of the weapon to stick into your enemies – is to learn that flesh wounds, and any other form of distraction, must be ignored during times of crises." He said it simply, not turning to look at me as he inspected a rack of wooden sparring weapons.

I nodded, scowling. Had it been my tone? I had hoped to come off as a wise badass mentor like Roland. Arthur must have sensed my frustration, because he finally glanced back at me.

"Don't worry. You did well. I'm just good at reading people." He studied me thoughtfully. "You haven't told anyone about me, have you?" I shook my head insistently. He studied me for a few tense moments before letting out a breath. "Bless you, Callie. Soon." His eyes grew distant, staring out at his memories. "Soon enough, I imagine." He shook off his memories and managed a sheepish grin. "I'll admit that I'll need a lot of practice with these. My previous skillset was singularly focused."

I studied him suspiciously. "I don't rightly believe you, old one."

He grinned. "That's because you're smart."

"Let us begin," I said, pulling out a staff and letting it thump onto the floor at my feet.

He rolled his shoulders and pulled his own staff, dipping his head respectfully.

$\mathcal{A}$rthur studied me across the mat, the staff held loosely in his fist. I let out a calming breath, bowing back at him.

"We aren't going to start off sparring," I said, approaching him. "We'll begin with drills to loosen up, so you can get a feel for the weapon." He nodded.

I showed him the motions, and he caught on quickly. It wasn't complicated. A simple attack, attack, block sequence with us alternating, to get used to the feel of staff striking staff, familiarizing our fingers to the sensation of the wood buzzing on contact with each blow while not losing track of the sequence.

I thumped him a few times as he lost track, rapping his knuckles twice, but I kept my face a cool mask, emotionless and without sympathy. That would do him no favors, depending on who the Vatican chose as his future mentor. But he didn't seem troubled or overly embarrassed about it, just resolved and determined.

As we fell back into formation, I kept an eye on his chest. I saw blood through the gauze, but it wasn't soaking the bandage, and it didn't slow or distract him.

"Why is it such a secret?" I asked him.

He didn't lose focus, but I sensed his face tighten momentarily. "I'm not who I was. Let people think so, and it's liable to get them killed. Thinking I'll swoop in to save them like some bloody hero."

I nodded, having expected the answer. Still, it was frustrating. He had told me enough to let me know the truth, but also enough to give me a million questions... and since I had promised not to speak about it – even to him – I was toeing a fine line at the moment. His eyes flashed to mine, reminding me of that promise and how close I was to breaking it. I smiled apologetically and focused back on the steady clacking of wood.

After a few more minutes, I struck his staff harder than necessary, and stepped back just enough that his rehearsed attack slipped past my nose, the combination of a solid hit and suddenly finding no resistance in the next motion throwing him off.

But he kept a solid grip on the staff, even dipping his head in amusement.

"Want to show me what you can do with a sword?" I asked mischievously.

He smirked, but lowered his eyes. "I wouldn't know what to do with it."

I scoffed, but he winked at me.

"Another time," he finally said – gently but firmly.

I sighed. "Fine. But you did well today. Get used to the various weapons. You can use the bag to practice striking, and there are several books back in the small library where I got the whiskey. Read over them if for no other reason than to familiarize yourself with the terms. The seemingly useless information will come in handy when you have an actual mentor, saving you time as you begin your training in earnest."

He nodded, glancing past me towards the room. "I like a good book," he said. Then he held out a hand for my staff. I handed it over, years of training with Roland subconsciously preparing me for a sneak attack, but Arthur simply took the staff from me with a chuckle, reading something about my body position that let him know what I was thinking.

As he racked our weapons, I found myself watching him thoughtfully. It would be fun to teach Arthur, but also frustrating. It was hard not to see him as an authority figure since he was older, and I knew about his past. So, teaching him how to spar almost made me feel like a fraud. Not that I wasn't skilled, but...

Knowing his past was making me think of him as a legend, and that would only get someone hurt if he didn't end up living up to the reputation.

His point was valid. But it still made it hard for me to regard him as a simple student.

Whoever trained him would have their work cut out for them, because although I knew he wouldn't be sharing his past with them, he had the molding of an experienced man, and any tutor worth his salt would sense it as well, thinking they were the brunt of a joke.

Maybe it was best if I was the trainer. I was uniquely qualified – I knew his past, and I was good at fighting. Any other trainer would just be good at fighting and might grow suspicious of Arthur's unassuming nature.

I'd think on it.

Arthur walked back up to me, hands behind his back. "You have somewhere to be."

I nodded. "Yes."

"This is good. It will keep you out of my hair."

I arched a brow at him and he smiled. "Be careful down here, Arthur. Stick to the main areas until you hear back from Rome. Deal?"

He nodded. "It was nice seeing you, Callie."

I smiled. "Thanks for... being you, I guess."

He frowned. "I told you, I'm not who I was."

I shook my head in amusement. "I meant *you*, Arthur. You're a good man. I'm glad we met."

He studied me thoughtfully for a few moments, reading my face. "Likewise," he finally said with a smile. "Now be off with you. I've got books to read."

"This might sound strange, but... be careful how much you devote yourself to books. Don't let them change you," I said cryptically.

He laughed. "I won't become a zealot, Callie. In that regard, the Shepherds might be disappointed in recruiting me."

Then he was walking away, whistling as he made his way over to the books.

He scooped up the whiskey on the way.

Picking Arthur might have just been the biggest accidental good choice I'd ever heard of the Vatican making. Or maybe Roland had seen something in Arthur...

For now, I had no choice but to keep his secret, and to teach him how to protect himself from monsters – the ones he would hunt down, *and* the ones he would work for.

CHAPTER 35

I settled on my bed, muscles pleasantly sore from the brief training. A reminder that I had been slacking lately. Too little physical training and too much combat-magic training. I needed to get back to my roots. I closed my eyes, breathing evenly, appreciating the silence of my apartment. I wasn't sure where Claire had run off to, but I was glad for it. I had too many errant thoughts. I needed to clear my head, find my cente—

"How does this one look on me?" Claire asked from only a few feet away.

I gasped, which turned into a coughing fit.

"Claire!" I wheezed, realizing she was standing in my closet.

"Callie," she said in a dry tone. "Does this dress look good on me?" she repeated.

I threw a pillow at her. She frowned as it struck her stomach, not even grunting. "Little crazier than usual. Something on your mind?" she asked, turning to assess herself in the mirror.

"No. Nothing. Just… you caught me off guard. I didn't hear you lurking in my closet like a serial killer."

"Does the serial killer look good in this dress?" she asked, not turning to look at me.

I sighed. I was off my game for sure if I hadn't even noticed her rummaging around my closet. I frowned at her. "Why do you care how my dress looks on you?"

She blushed instantly. "No reason. Just curious."

"Hmmm… Nothing to do with Kenai?" I asked sweetly. He was the shifter bear who had his sights on Claire. She professed disinterest in him, but I always caught her smiling when she complained about him.

"Well, now that you mention it, he did call," she said offhandedly. "Wanted to know when I was coming back to Alaska. They decided to stay up there a few more weeks before returning." The shifter bears were a pretty reclusive group, and those in Kansas City had decided to head out of town for a while after Claire first turned, thinking she would need some time to adjust.

But Claire had caught on quickly – and had grown bored even *more* quickly, not appreciating the concept of living in the woods with a bunch of shifters.

I nodded, hiding my grin. "Well, a dress wouldn't really go with your subzero gear."

She nodded, eyes distant. "Starlight wants to work with me some more."

"Oh?" Starlight was a kind of Shaman leader of sorts for the shifter bears. Like their medicine man. Not an Alpha, but a spiritual guide. He'd also been a wizard at one point before turning. He was kind of an enigma, and he believed Claire showed unique gifts that fit with his area of expertise. Claire hadn't stuck around long enough to learn whether he was right or not.

"Anyway, I was just having some fun since I woke up and you were gone."

I winced guiltily. "I swung by the Church to talk to Arthur," I said. She looked over sharply, as if checking to see if I was wearing my dirty liar face. I held up my hand. "Promise."

She relaxed. "Right. Well, don't do that again. Or at least let me know if you're leaving. Lot of enemies lately. And I promised you I would keep an eye on you. For your own good."

I smiled, waiting until she had turned around again. "Speaking of, I need to head out again, but I need you to stay here. In case anyone shows up to deliver a message."

She slowly turned, placing her hands on her hips. "I disagree with the intelligence of that plan."

"I'm not doing anything dangerous. Promise. And not the promise where I'm really lying to you. The other kind. The one I don't use as often."

Her frown deepened. "Swear it on our friendship. That you are doing nothing where you might coincidentally find yourself in a fight."

I thought about it before nodding. "I swear."

She watched me, her gaze branding the promise onto my forehead. "Fine. Begone, harlot."

I jumped off the bed before she could change her mind. "See you soon. Two hours at the most."

"Make it shorter," she called out as I opened a Gateway in the living room, jumping through before Claire could take a peek at the destination on the other side.

I let the Gateway wink closed behind me and inhaled the scent of cured leather. Peace. Comfort. Protection.

Darling and Dear.

I needed somewhere quiet and safe to clear my head, and since Abundant Angel Catholic Church and my own home were currently occupied, I needed an alternative. And something I'd heard from the proprietors earlier had me thinking.

I'd said something about the gangs in town pissing me off. Darling had replied that both Angels and Demons were vermin, misinterpreting my statement. Because I hadn't mentioned Angels or Demons at that point in the conversation. How much did he really know?

"Hello?" I called out in a loud, cautious tone. I didn't want to have them thinking I was an intruder. Thinking back, I probably shouldn't have made a Gateway directly into their shop. My feet slowed as I thought about that. In fact, I was sure that shouldn't have even been possible. Wasn't the place warded? Hadn't they told me that before? But if it *was* warded, my Gateway wouldn't have worked. Maybe they had given me access, but had forgotten to tell me.

Darling was suddenly walking beside me, entwining his arm through mine so that he held my forearm in the crook of his elbow, escorting me down the aisle without breaking my stride. I stifled my gasp of surprise, not having sensed him appear.

"Thought that would have taken you longer to figure out," he commented conversationally. "Now, we can get down to the affair you desire."

My stomach fluttered at that. "Um, Darling, I didn't come here to have an affair—"

"Your loss, child. He *is* quite talented," Dear said from my other side, suddenly holding my other arm in the crook of her own elbow. "But I do not think that was the affair he meant."

"A double entendre offers so much room for miscommunication. I adore them. One will never get what one does not ask for, and my carefully chosen words could have yielded… sweet, sweet nectar, Dear," he scolded his partner, sounding both disappointed and amused.

"My apologies, Darling. I'll give her a few more moments to flounder before saving our Callie from your seductive clutches," she said apologetically.

"Thank you, Dear," he said, dismissing the matter.

I shook my head, focusing on my task, rather than their bizarre volley. "I came to ask if you had a room I could use. A private one." I swallowed, careful to sound respectful as I continued. "One that is private from even you two," I clarified. "No offense."

They shared a look with each other as if I didn't exist between them, even though they were practically dragging me through their shop.

"That could be arranged," Dear said slowly.

"Indefinitely," Darling added.

"If you agree to our price," Dear said.

I winced. "I just need a few minutes of peace and quiet. I'm not buying an eternal timeshare."

"Privacy is expensive. And you are a dangerous customer. If we aren't listening in, how are we to know what naughty things you could get up to? What attention you might attract."

"Nothing is free," Darling summarized. "We must have plausible deniability. You pay, no one can become suspicious. We do you a *favor*, enemies might ask *questions*."

I sighed. They were right. Why hadn't I been paranoid enough to see this coming?

"And how much is a room?" I asked warily.

"What kind of room?" Darling smiled suggestively.

"If you will need whips, chains, and other tools of pleasure and casual domination, it's one price," Dear explained conversationally, finger lazily pointing out a few leather paddles and furry handcuffs. I blushed, shaking my head. I felt her eyes on me. "If you require a soundproof room with tools for extracting information from your… guests, that is a different price."

I shivered. "I just need a couch. Maybe a fireplace. It's to meditate," I added, wondering if they would decipher some twisted fetish involving a fireplace and a couch.

"Oh, that's much more expensive," Darling said in a somber tone.

I laughed, glancing over at him. But his face was deadly serious. My humor faltered. What the hell? Sex dungeons were cheaper than tranquil meditation rooms?

"What is the price?" I asked, wondering if I needed to find a fourth alternative. A hotel room or something.

"You must make a deal with a daemon," they said in unison.

I stumbled a step, but as if they had anticipated it, they were supporting me almost the moment I began to fall. "I don't think so. I don't deal with demons. I kill them."

They frowned at each other, as if I had spoken gibberish. "Not demons," Dear enunciated the *e* sound. "Daemons," she said, making it sound like *day-muns*.

"Spirit guides," Darling elaborated. "Not good or bad. They offer untarnished, honest advice."

I studied the shop as we continued on in silence, thinking. I hadn't ever heard about a daemon. But it didn't sound bad, and these two had never steered me wrong before. They almost acted like my crazy distant aunt and uncle.

I cleared my throat, careful to sound respectful. "You two are daemons?"

They stiffened as one, their eyes locked ahead as we walked a few paces in silence.

"We… are what we are. *Not* daemons," Dear murmured.

"The world will know soon enough," Darling added in a whisper. "But not yet."

"When?" I asked carefully.

I felt them shift their attention to look down at my hand in each of their arms as if searching for something. "Perhaps when the world is ending," Darling sighed.

"Or when you get better accessories," Dear chimed in, smiling wickedly.

I frowned. "You two sell me my accessories," I said drily.

They released me simultaneously, both pointing at a door that suddenly appeared ahead of me. It looked like it led into one of their small cozy changing rooms. Or a secret sex dungeon. Or a daemon's lair.

Surprise was the spice of life.

"Do you require further assistance?" Dear asked me, ignoring my last comment.

I began walking towards the door, doing a little twirl halfway there, pointing down at the shoes they had made for me. "I think I can manage. These boots were made for walking," I said, turning back to the door.

"Those boots were made for more than *that*, Penrose," he snapped, sounding offended. I spun, startled by the anger in his response.

But the two were simply gone. I walked backwards a few paces, scanning the store, but didn't see them. Just racks and racks of leather goods. I sighed uneasily as I turned and placed my hand on the latch of the door. I took a breath, gathered my courage, and entered the room to speak with a daemon.

I briefly hoped that I wasn't about to end up lying to Claire. Who would have thought a planned meditation could introduce me to a daemon?

Good thing my friend was the forgiving type.

"I've been waiting for you, *Callie*," a familiar voice said, sounding amused by my name.

CHAPTER 36

*T*he Sphinx stared at me, sitting before a fire, wings tucked back neatly against her back. Her eyes glowed purple, as if the firelight was illuminating a set of amethyst stones.

"Hello, Sphinx," I said, letting the door close behind me.

"Hello, human," she replied, sounding annoyed. Because I hadn't used her name? I hadn't been sure if Phix had been a pet name granted to Darling and Dear, so hadn't wanted to seem too familiar with the apparent daemon.

"Do you prefer Phix?" I asked. "I was trying to be polite."

"What I *prefer* is irrelevant. What I *am* called is Phix. I used your name, use mine."

I nodded. "Okay."

"I don't play as many games with my leash holders as I do others," she said.

"It seems I am in for many games, then," I said, smiling crookedly.

She cocked her head, looking interested in my response – that I hadn't assumed she meant me as one of her leash holders. She rose to all fours, walking over to me. Her back was easily as tall as my waist, putting her human breasts not too far below my own, and her piercing eyes at my chin level, which was a little alarming. Much closer to my jugular than I had noticed before.

She licked her lips with a wicked grin, nodding. Then she arched her neck gracefully, showing off the thin skin as if granting me equal status – baring her throat. Her dark hair was cut in a straight line at the jaw, not a hair longer than another, like every Egyptian stereotype I had seen, and she wore long golden earrings of an eagle in flight that had to be worth a pile of money.

The more I thought about it, her actions seemed more animal. Sticking her head in my crotch and sniffing, baring her throat to me. Except… she spoke like Confucius.

"You are wise beyond your years, yet you lack years," she purred, circling me curiously. I didn't turn with her, even when she was behind me. Trust. And despite her intelligence, a big part of her was animalistic. Primal. Like a dog sniffing out a new dog in the yard. Darling and Dear wouldn't have sent me in here as an appetizer. Would they?

"Some people are wise, some are otherwise," I replied as she walked out of view behind me.

I heard her cough, suddenly appearing on the other side of me, grinning widely. "Oh, I could just gobble you up," she said in an endearing tone. At least I didn't think it had been literal.

"Is there another form of affection you could show me?"

She sat down before me, pondering my existence, I suppose. Or considering my question.

"I accept you. But you aren't ready for me yet. You're too innocent."

I arched an eyebrow at her. "I highly doubt it. I've done some pretty dark stuff—"

"I didn't say you were too *light*. I said you were too *innocent*. Too optimistic. Too… hope-full when you should be hope-less," she added with a dry chuckle. "Else how would it all work?"

I felt a chill crawl up my spine. How would *what* all work? Her words also made me think of Nate, the potential Fifth Horseman.

The Horseman of *Hope*.

Phix nodded very slowly, as if reading my thoughts.

I clenched my fists angrily. "I will never be hopeless…"

She dipped her chin. "A play on words, Callie. Nothing more. Balance…"

"If not hope, what should I be?" I asked, fearing the answer.

"Despair," Phix said simply. "It is written on your forehead, after all. Although hidden from others for the time being," she said.

My blood coagulated in an instant, remembering a few times when people had stared at my forehead in alarm. I lifted my hand, as if I would be able to feel it, but found only soft skin.

I glared at Phix. "No. I refuse to be a symbol of despair. It's pretty much the opposite of what I intend to do with my life."

Phix cocked her head, studying me curiously. "Again, you are too innocent. You think of only one side of the coin. Hope can be given or taken, yes? As you well know…"

I frowned, thinking about Nate again. He had vowed to steal hope from the wicked, but to *give* hope to the worthy. I looked at her. "You would have me wield despair in a similar fashion as Nate Temple wields hope?"

Phix sighed. "Would you swing a sword in only one direction?"

I shook my head, kind of understanding her point.

"What I would have you *do* is understand the *difference* before given the *duty*. You must walk through darkness, taste it, feel it, before knowing how to properly wield it. Else it would corrupt you like a cancer. You must break through the treasure chest to obtain the treasure."

I nodded slowly. "I don't want you changing me, making me into something different."

"I would never change you, Penrose. I swear it on my power. I would… open a door for you. Any change would be upon your *own* shoulders. Your *own* decision to make. I will await you on the other side, like a loyal pet. Do not leave me abandoned, Callie Penrose," she warned, suddenly staring into my soul, pleading, begging, fearing.

I nodded, breathing faster.

She seemed to relax. "The only way to balance the whips of hope are to know the blades of despair. The world will require that balance, or all will be lost. Hope is nearing his understanding. The world must birth despair."

I shivered at the casual finality of her words. She *had* to be talking about Nate.

But she was the creature known for riddles.

She could mean anything.

I thought about her proposal. She had sworn it on her power that she intended me no harm. That she would only offer me a doorway to see through. And that she would await me on the other side.

I nodded.

She studied me in silence. "Your decision will require a price. You must sacrifice your purity, your innocence. This sacrifice will not be permanent, unless you will it. The choice will always be yours. For a time, the world will not be as beautiful as it once was, but it is your only chance. The world's only chance." Phix was silent for a time, watching me as I consciously slowed my breathing, considering. I nodded again.

"This is a wise decision. The world may continue spinning a bit longer, now. But do not worry, Penrose. I shall wait for you, and guide you on the other side."

"Will it hurt?" I asked, waiting for some kind of spiritual uppercut.

"You tell me," she said, turning back to the fire.

And I suddenly felt as if the skin over my entire body had tightened – not necessarily in pain, but almost like the third day after a full-body sunburn, when your skin felt just a little too tight for your body. Like I was suddenly wearing a spandex bodysuit.

And... that was it.

I panted, my tension fading. I had made it worse in my head than it had ended up being.

Phix studied me from across the room. "The door is now open, but only you can make it to the other side. How may I serve you, Penrose?"

And there was the catch. I hadn't gone through the doorway yet. I resolved myself to doing whatever it took to get to the other side. To hear, touch, and feel the darkness – to use it, but not to let it consume me.

I glanced down at my hands, wanting to find some kind of sign that I had changed. "How does this work?" I asked her.

"You call, I answer."

I nodded thoughtfully. Like Nate's unicorn, Grimm.

Phix snorted indelicately, reading my mind. Then I flinched, thinking about the Whispers. How many voices could I safely harbor in my mind before I cracked?

"I am not a Whisper," Phix said disapprovingly. "You and I are bonded. They cannot hear me, and I cannot hear them, unless you will it so." She hunkered down onto her front paws. "But I take precedence," she said smugly.

I tucked my hands into my coat pocket, suppressing a sudden shiver at her words – that she was preventing the Whispers from communicating with me. Had been doing so this entire time. I froze after a few moments, and slowly looked back up at Phix. She lifted her head, and ever so slowly, gave me a nod. A vague thought began to take form in my mind.

After a few moments, Phix grinned, appearing amused. "Oh, that is delightful. Despair suits you well, Penrose. You might be better at riddles than you give yourself credit for."

"Will you help me do it?"

She grinned, flashing white teeth at me. "Of course. You need only think a request like this, and consider it immediately accomplished. But to succeed, you will need a talisman. As I am your spirit guide, you must take note of my presence if you see it." She studied me, slowly nodding her head as if proud. "Succeed in this, and I believe I will see you on the other side of darkness sooner than I thought possible."

Well, *that* hadn't been my intention. I'd been thinking about my recent troubles, wondering if this newfound darkness – although I didn't necessarily sense anything different about me – would show me things in a different perspective. "I need to clear my head. Meditation helps me lay it all out."

"I'll follow along in silence. You will not be disturbed," Phix said, standing to saunter over to the door, where she curled up on the floor.

For better or worse, it was done. Now, the real work began.

I took off my jacket, set it beside me, and got comfortable, closing my eyes to meditate.

CHAPTER 37

*a*fter a time, I opened my eyes, finally feeling content and at peace. I glanced over at Phix and she opened her eyes in an instant. I nodded at her. She smiled knowingly and then closed her eyes again, resuming her nap. "Done," she said.

With a guarded sigh, I reached out to them. "What are you?" I asked out loud.

Silence answered me, but I felt them drawing closer, as if they had been far away.

Now she wants to listen... one murmured. *After she let another inside her soul...*

I grimaced guiltily. "I... was afraid," I admitted in a soft voice. "I feel lost. Adrift. Explain it all to me. Help me overcome my fears. What does all this mean?" I asked, opening my heart and walling off my mind.

We are Angels. You have the ears to Hear us.

I shivered involuntarily at the direct confirmation, but was suddenly glad to hear that I didn't actually have them living *inside* of me. I could just talk to them.

"Why do you argue if you are all Angels?" And I hoped that my mind wasn't suddenly going to be immolated for my insolence.

But I merely heard a chorus of amused sighs.

Iron sharpens iron.

We are not all the same.

Strength through diversity.

If we were all identical, why would He have made so many of us?

Not every Angel takes the same path to salvation. We all seek His approval in different ways.

I found myself nodding. That made sense. And they wouldn't be getting along so amicably right now if my initial suspicion had been true. That I had both Angels and Demons in my head.

"I want to try something with you, to attempt to better understand this part of me."

It suddenly felt as if a small group of bodies were huddled around me, focusing on me or protecting me from an enemy. Or simply eager to interact with me rather than each other.

Try... they encouraged in perfect harmony, like, well, a chorus of Angels. A song, of sorts.

With every fiber of my being, I focused on my plan, knowing that small aspects would change, but that it was pretty well fleshed out. I felt a faint throbbing at the strain, the precursor to a headache, but I kept at it until I came to the end of my plan.

Silence met me as I breathed woozily, waiting for their response.

I focused so intently that my head actually began to throb, giving me an instant headache.

Yes, this might just work...

But it is dangerous, another muttered. *Perhaps too dangerous...*

For some reason, I had the sudden suspicion that one of them had remained silent, choosing to observe rather than offer an opinion. But something about the talkative Whispers convinced me that he was no intruder. Just the strong, silent type. The brief pauses of hesitation from the others seemed to be them waiting for him to offer an argument, and when he didn't, they proceeded to speak to me. It was annoying. I was the land-lord here, not him. Then I realized I was basically growing upset that one imaginary friend wasn't talking to me like the others, and muttered under my breath.

I felt a sudden wave of amusement from the silent presence. He didn't talk, but I felt more passion from that sensation than I had from any of the other Whispers' comments.

"Can you help me?" I asked.

No.

Yessssss.

More oppressive silence from the silent emo Angel.

I waited patiently, listening to them debate and discuss my plan. The conversation finally died down, and I felt them shift their attention back to me.

The Whispers felt suddenly closer again, making me cringe. How close would they get, eventually?

We will help you in this... they finally agreed in a serious, but somber tone. All but the silent one. But it seemed the others only cared if he *spoke*, not if he remained *silent*.

Better than nothing.

"Thank you," I said out loud, opening my eyes.

I glanced over at Phix, nodding. She climbed to her feet and stepped out of my way as I scooped up my jacket and tossed it on.

I walked past her, determined. I had some phone calls to make.

CHAPTER 38

$\mathcal{W}$e stood outside an old gothic church building that was borderline blighted. The lot was overgrown with weeds and the concrete slabs were spider-webbed with cracks and loose chunks of rock that had broken off long enough ago to be weathered by later storms.

Paradise and Lost – the stand-in Alpha werewolves of Kansas City – stared up at the church skeptically, trying to see past the shell to find something marginally positive about it. The brick façade was aged, but in good standing, no bulging walls or anything, although it was covered in gangland graffiti. It had only a few parking spaces out back since it had been built in a time when cars were not as common as today.

Spires and stone statues of both Angels and Demons lined the top of the three-story church. The statues were covered with lichen or missing limbs where they had broken off long ago, never having been repaired. The two werewolves let out dual sighs, obviously not seeing the pearl beneath the shell as they made their way back over to me.

"No wonder the real estate agent hates us," Paradise said, kicking a loose stone on the ground, "we drag her out to the nicest properties."

I smiled. "She treats you with disrespect because she probably doesn't believe you have the money to be serious, and that your church is doomed. Because this alleged Father Roland is not present to meet her personally, and his two assistants are named Paradise and Lost, but look suspiciously like smoking hot party animals."

And they were. Both of the women were exotic, tan-skinned brunettes. Paradise was taller than Lost, but both exuded the kind of aura that college boys died for. Home-wreckers. Or, church-wreckers, in this instance.

"Maybe that's why she can't seem to get our names right," Paradise said, frowning.

"You have to admit," I said, "Paradise and Lost sound like a mockery of Catholicism."

Claire grunted, arms folded. She wasn't very pleased with me. It had started off with me taking almost exactly two hours before coming back home. And then, within an hour of my return, news had spread in the supernatural community that I had done something borderline suicidal – and I hadn't notified her as we ate popcorn and hung out at my apartment.

In fact, she hadn't found out until we were on our way here.

"Where is the bitch?" she snarled, glaring out at the street, then up at clouds that threatened to unleash more rain on us any moment, searching for anything to take her frustration out on.

"She's late. Again," Lost agreed, sounding annoyed.

"How many times has she been late?" I asked, frowning at them, not pleased to hear that they actually had been treated poorly by this real estate agent.

"This makes six," they said in unison.

"Maybe she did a drive-by, saw the property, and high-tailed it out of here with a sudden case of explosive diarrhea," Claire offered, eyes leveled on me.

I felt Paradise staring at me and sighed, pretty sure I knew what was on her mind. "Yes?"

She shifted uncomfortably. "You just... don't take this the wrong way, but you look tired. Exhausted, even. Then again, you don't."

"She looks older," Claire muttered angrily, having already told me – in not too pleasant terms back at my apartment – that I looked to have aged a few years. Which had been news to me. I assumed it had something to do with Phix bonding me, but didn't have time to worry about it. Water under the bridge. I had looked in the mirror, noted the difference, and pressed on. It wasn't substantial unless you'd spent time around me recently. Just a few years older.

Lost was studying my face thoughtfully. "That's it. You *do* look older. Only by a few years, but more… mature." Sensing the darkening look on my face, she winced. "Still as cute as a button, though," she affirmed.

"Let me do the talking, this time," I said, changing the topic. "I'll take the heat for this one. It was my idea anyway. She probably doesn't like speaking with what she perceives as Father Roland's minions."

They shrugged, not imagining our conversation would take very long, considering the state of the property. "But we *are* his minions in this. It's going to be his new home when he gets back, yet we're doing all the arranging. Minions," she said, as if she had recited the definition.

"Yep," I agreed. "Definitely minions."

Claire frowned at me. "Why do you look so pleased with yourself, Callie? Let's wrap this up and get out of here, because we still need to argue about Dorian's text blast. Everyone is talking about your stupid idea to—"

As if on cue, an expensive *Look at me, I have money* SUV pulled up to the curb, and a middle-aged woman hopped out of the car, face overly professional. She was layered in make-up and jewelry, and propped up by shiny stilettos with heels that were probably bigger than her rich, country club husband's magic stick. I knew her type, and instantly understood what Paradise and Lost had implied.

This type of woman loved her position of assumed power, and enjoyed lording it over those less fortunate, toasting magnanimously to the poor souls who couldn't afford her services.

She shuffled over to us, and I pointedly stepped in front of Paradise and Lost, making it clear I was the new face of this meeting. I shot her an elitist smile, one she could read like its own language, and her posture visibly changed, picking up on the possible presence of a fellow woman of wealth. Still guarded, but more comfortable.

She didn't even glance at the property. "Hello. Unfortunately, this one is now off the market. Someone scooped it up this morning." She didn't sound displeased as she spoke over my shoulder at Paradise and Lost.

In fact, she sounded hopeful – thinking that this news might convince them that buying an old church in town was a lost cause.

As it should be for their type. The city was better off without it. Or them.

Claire, Paradise, and Lost all cursed loudly, making the real estate agent's eyes climb up to her scalp. She pursed her lips, their outburst only solidifying her predetermined disdain. Three women working for a man of the cloth, wearing tight clothes, and obviously foul-mouthed.

I, on the other hand, kept a polite smile on my face. "You will address me for the duration of our scheduled meeting," I said in a clinical tone, glancing down at my phone before putting it away. Her shoulders locked up at my tone. "We had an appointment to see the place. An appointment in which you arrived abhorrently late. Surely, the paperwork hasn't gone through yet. Could you show us the property, while the property is in..." I smiled in amusement, "purgatory? Might help us better clarify what we do and do not want when you spend hours searching down the next dozen potential properties."

She blinked at me. "And who might *you* be? My contract is with these two... women."

"An interested party," I said, waving a hand dismissively. "I'm sure it won't matter to you," I said in a tone that heavily implied that *she* wasn't worthy of hearing about *me*.

I saw her fingers clench, and no amount of make-up could have hidden the sudden flush to her cheeks. Rather than reaching out to grab a fistful of my jaw-length hair, she plastered on a very bureaucratic smile, shaking her head in mock empathy. "I'm afraid that isn't possible. The paperwork has concluded, and it's no longer available to show."

She waited for me to blow up. I didn't. I just sighed, staring up at the church. "That must have been a nice commission," I mused.

"Yes, well. You win some, you lose some," she admitted, not sounding particularly pleased that she had missed out on the sale – even though she didn't like working with us. But her tone implied that she didn't believe she had actually missed out on anything, because Paradise and Lost either hadn't been good for the money, or serious about buying a church.

"Pity," I said, kicking a pebble on the concrete as I continued to stare up at the tall, imposing church. It wasn't big. Tiny, really, but it definitely had the creepy vibe. Like Count Dracula had built a pool-house for his son.

My three friends were frowning at me, likely wondering why we were still standing here. Especially Claire, who looked about to blow up on me in a fit of impatience.

"I have other appointments, I'm afraid," the agent said. "Let me know if you find any others you would like to take a look at," she said, leaning as if to speak over my shoulder at Paradise and Lost.

"Perhaps if you were punctual you wouldn't need to rush off to your next appointment. Father Roland always says *Proper prior planning prevents poor performance.*"

Paradise piped up. "He does say that quite often."

The agent curled her lip at us. "Yes, well, I wouldn't expect you to know the numerous responsibilities I have running one of the most successful real estate agencies in town. And this was the last one on the market that fit your parameters. Unfortunately." She clicked off the lid to her lipstick, applying a faint touch-up to conceal her triumph.

I could practically feel her purring with contentment. No other listings meant no other dealings with us.

A limousine pulled up to the curb, and I let out a sigh of relief. *Finally*, I thought.

A muscular blonde man climbed out of the limo, wearing tight jeans, boat shoes, and a white tee despite the rain to come. He waved as he approached, muscles bulging beneath the thin fabric of his shirt.

The real estate agent had slid between us like an octopus, flashing him a bright smile. "You must be the new owner," she said excitedly. "Congratulations. I wish I could have helped facilitate this transaction, but if you need anything else in town—"

He stepped around her, not even meeting her eyes as he spoke through the side of his mouth in her general direction. "We don't know each other. I prefer to keep it that way after seeing how you almost bungled this entirely."

He stopped in front of me, handing over a folder and a long, iron key, ignoring the strange sounds coming from the real estate agent's mouth.

I nodded gratefully at Achilles, another friend from St. Louis. Well, Nate's friend, first, but I had commandeered him specifically for this. "Thank you. Father Roland will be pleased."

He rolled his eyes out of the agent's view, but dipped his chin for show before returning back to the limousine and leaving.

CHAPTER 39

*T*he agent finally rounded on me, furious. "I didn't bungle anything!" she hissed. "Who was that, and what did he give you?" she asked, pointing at the items in my hand.

"My bartender. You know how us Catholics love our bartenders," I said, handing the folder back to Paradise and Lost, who were dancing on their toes behind me. "And he brought the signed paperwork for the church. And the key. You can remove your lockbox, now."

She blinked at me rapidly, stunned. "They... bought it?" she whispered, eyes taking in Paradise and Lost furiously. "But... what about *me*? I'm their agent! We have a *contract*!"

I frowned at her. "Did my associate hand Paradise and Lost anything?" I asked, frowning in confusion. Then I nodded, as if recalling the exchange. "No. He didn't. Your contract was with these two upstanding women," I said, pointing a thumb over my shoulder at them. Then I leaned closer. "My new tenants. Not me, Susan. Lockbox, if you please. I want the key. Quickly, now."

"It's Shelly!" she snapped, panting furiously, eyes wild for some form of recourse.

"And *their* names are *Paradise* and *Lost*," I said in a cold tone. "Oh, and you should probably hear it from me, but I offered quite a bit over the asking price to cover the headaches of a rapid closing. It was one... *Hell* of a commission..." I said, glancing up at the church proudly. "That will be all, Sarah. Leave the key by the door." I turned my back on her, listening to her fume and sputter as I walked back to my friends, grinning like an idiot.

They shook their heads in disbelief.

"Roland is going to be so pissed," Claire muttered. "You own it. But... how?"

I smiled at her, miming zipping my lips as I watched the agent storm past us to the front door to get the lockbox, shouting furiously into her cell-phone. It didn't take Claire very long to gasp.

"Midas," she breathed, eyes widening. "You used your favor from Midas. Jesus..." she said, shaking her head. "No wonder Achilles was here. They work together." I nodded proudly.

"Is this really a signed lease agreement for Haven to pay you rent?" Paradise asked.

I nodded. "I also got him to let Roland keep the necklace that lets him walk on Holy Ground."

"*How?*" they spluttered in unison, keeping their voices low enough for only us to hear.

"Because it locks Roland down in Kansas City. Roland wanted a place to himself, and Haven wanted to keep him close. The only Shepherd turned Vampire has a certain... sex appeal that will benefit both of them – Haven gets fame, and Roland gets default protection."

I held up a finger to waylay their next questions, and glanced over my shoulder to see the agent staring up at the old church in horror. She sniffed pompously, sensing my attention. I waved a finger, pointing at the key in her fist. She screamed, throwing it at the door before storming back to her vehicle. The uneven stones made walking in heels a bitch, and she stumbled more than once.

"What's another name that starts with S?" I mused.

"Sally?" Lost chuckled.

I nodded. "Thank you, Sally!" I called out, waving politely.

She shrieked again, climbed into her car, and peeled away from the curb.

"Let's go check the place out," Paradise said, sounding proud.

"Later," I said, thinking about the time. "You three free for a few hours?" I asked. They nodded uncertainly. "Then I have a favor to ask..." And I told them what I had in mind.

For the first time since we had arrived at the Church, Claire finally looked relieved.

And anticipatory. I showed them my phone, revealing a text message from Dorian Gray – who had spread the rumor that I was looking for a little action tonight. "He accepts your challenge. You will fight Olin Fuentes, the Templar Commander, at sundown." It showed an address, too.

Claire's eyes brimmed with barely restrained fury, having heard plenty about the Templar Commander from when I had met him in Italy. I was slightly relieved – and not – to hear confirmation that he was actually in town and that it wasn't some other faction of Templars. It had removed my optimistic hope that this was all some terrible coincidence.

Because if Olin Fuentes was here, he wasn't just looking after his flock. He wanted some Old Testament revenge.

Paradise and Lost were snarling openly. "That hypocrite," Paradise spat. "Lost turned him into a werewolf and he has the audacity to come to *our* town and hunt down Freaks?"

And she was right. At the end of my fight with him, Lost had attacked him from behind, infecting him with her werewolf genes – which the Templar from the Hellfire Club had confirmed. But no one else in town knew that fun fact. Yet.

I turned to Claire. "Bring Beckett up to speed and tell him to make sure the place is devoid of police. Things are going to get loud, and I'll have enough on my plate. But he needs to know the real danger so he can come up with an excuse that makes sense to the other cops."

"Why would he agree to fight you?" Paradise asked, scratching her jaw. "He has to know you have allies here."

"That's just it. I challenged him to a *duel*. This way he knows I *can't* bring allies. If he meets me on the street by chance, he has no idea who else could be lurking in the shadows. I think that's why he's kept his name out of the gossip. Just Templars, never Olin Fuentes. Because he knows that his name would draw me like a moth to a flame."

She nodded thoughtfully. "I get that, but what does he have to gain from fighting you? Other than simple revenge. Especially since he's a werewolf, now. He's risking letting everyone see his deep, dark secret, and shattering his moral high ground."

"How clever of you," I said, patting her on the shoulder. "You're catching on quickly."

"My vacation in St. Louis was… enlightening," she said with a shiver.

I nodded, squeezing her shoulder compassionately. I had been there, too. When Nate decided to wade into a civil war with the dragons not too long ago.

"Winner also gets a fancy ring that was stolen from his base last night."

Claire finally snapped. "But *that's* what I don't understand. You don't *have* the ring!"

"What's so special about this ring? You're saying it like it's capitalized," Lost asked.

"An ancient relic they think belongs to them. It was stolen from them, though. And word on the street says I bought it off the thief. But only the interested parties know what the ring actually *is*. This way, Olin knows it's the one he seeks, but we don't have to worry about alerting the city at large what exactly we're talking about, so we don't attract any additional interest."

"But you don't have it!" Claire hissed again.

I shrugged, smiling wickedly. "He doesn't know that."

Claire just stared at me, shaking her head as she tried to understand what I was planning.

"And that's all you want us to do?" Paradise asked, referring to my request as she folded her arms. "I know it's a duel, but I don't like it. He and I have a beef. I don't like being a lookout."

"Hashtag me, too," Lost grunted.

I shook my head. "This is about more than revenge. If you can't do as asked, stay out of it. I'll find someone else."

"Well, since I don't trust the bastard, I'll be there. For when he breaks the terms. I'll rip off a leg or two before tossing him over to you two," Claire added, glancing at Paradise and Lost.

"That's fine," they agreed.

I gave them a very serious look, shaking my head. "I need to know you guys can stay on point, not see me stumble and assume he cheated. A lot rides on this. More than I'm telling you, obviously. You will do as I ask or you will be a mile away. Even if I have to tie you up myself. This is about more than just revenge. Even I'm not doing it out of a personal vendetta, and I really, *really* want to rip his face off."

They studied each other for a full minute, not speaking.

Finally, Claire growled. "I'll play by your rules, but like I told you before,

I'll always look out for you, Callie. Whether you like it or not. If he cheats and I truly believe your life is in real danger, I won't hold back." She smiled faintly. "Even if you tie me up. Because I just spent a lot of money on your stupid new underwear, and I refuse to have your first time wearing them be in your casket."

I burst out laughing, especially at the puzzled frowns on Paradise and Lost. "Fine," I relented, shaking my head. "But you know your priority, here. I'm serious. Your part is vital."

"Deal," they finally agreed, extending their hands. "Now, can we look at the Church?"

I smiled, glancing up at the sky to judge how long I had until the fight.

"Sure." Why not? We had a little time. "I need to make sure that bitch didn't scratch the door when she threw the key at my new church."

CHAPTER 40

*T*he rain had come and gone, but the clouds still looked past their due-date for another birthing of a heavy downpour. The alley stank, but not as much as some I had wandered recently, hunting down rogue Freaks. Gangster monsters.

I was early and stood in the alley by myself. Luckily, no homeless people had occupied the area, which was why I had arrived early in the first place, to make sure my meeting with Olin Fuentes would go unnoticed by the unwashed of Kansas City.

Thankfully, I didn't see any drunk pedestrians wandering the streets, suddenly interested in a young girl all alone in a dark alley at sunset.

I breathed evenly, checking my blades, straps, jacket, and my boots. My magic would be useless against Olin because he wore a Templar Scarf, which nullified magic. But, to be a bitch, I wore one, too.

Except mine was dyed hot pink. I'd let Paradise and Lost pick the color since they were being such good sports about their job tonight.

I checked it, verifying it was knotted around my neck, and fanning down my chest in a glaring pink stain like I had vomited nuclear Pepto-Bismol. The fat red Templar Cross on the front didn't go with the pink. I looked like Hollywood Barbie gone Catholic.

Perfect.

I checked my phone, wondering how close we were to showdown. It had to be any minute now, but I sensed no one watching, as had been agreed upon. I'd promised not to alert my allies about the fight, even though everyone had heard about my challenge.

Other than my three sentinels, only Dorian Gray had known the location of the fight since he had arranged it.

But he was a filthy gossip and was liable to say anything with his pillow friends – of which he had dozens. I wondered if Olin had considered that, figured he had, and anticipated at least some backup from his side – if for nothing more than to get him out if I tried to ambush him.

Which was technically fine. As long as they didn't interfere with the fight.

The same as I had done.

And since Commander Olin Fuentes of the Holier than Thou Templars considered all Freaks to be devil spawn, my feelings would be hurt if he didn't show up with an army at his back. I wasn't overly concerned about it, either way.

My magic might not work against him, but I had other forms of metaphorical weapons. I had tapped into my Angelic power – to use Silver blades to cut down his men in Italy. I wasn't sure if those blades were related to the Whispers, the Silvers, or if it was all the same thing. Or two entirely different somethings. Since I didn't truly know enough about the origins of my powers – and no one else seemed to, either – I was still in the discovery phase in that regard.

I found myself no longer caring about little details like that.

The Silver blades I could call upon at a thought seemed like magic, and had cut down Templars like surgical scalpels. So, I had a backup. Enough to slice at Olin and then call up a Gateway to escape if I saw a sudden army bearing down on me.

I kind of wanted to go toe-to-toe with this ass clown. This hypocrite. Human versus human. Warrior versus warrior. And if he went werewolf on me, I was ready.

A man stepped into the alley, alone. He studied me, too far away to be a threat. Or too arrogant to care. I motioned him closer like those old Kung Fu movies, dropping into a highly unusual martial arts stance. "Here, boy," I called out, and then I whistled like calling a dog.

He didn't react, just stood there for a moment. Then he strode closer in a casual, calm gait until I could finally make out his familiar face. Our introduction hadn't been long, but it had been memorable.

He stopped about ten paces away, and I studied him. He was tall, fit, and had short, spiky white hair. He wore a sword strapped over either shoulder, about as big as one would dare use single-handed, and his dingy Templar scarf hung down his chest like mine. The power of the scarf worked whether you let it hang free or lifted it above your nose, but it did add a menacing factor when tied around the mouth, like bandits in an old Western.

At least that's how I saw it. His Templars must have felt the same, because they'd worn it up over their faces when I had systematically assassinated them in Italy.

He either didn't consider me with much respect, or he wanted me to see his face. Or maybe they only concealed their faces to hide their identities, and we were well past that.

He grimaced at my scarf, jaw clenching for a moment. "Don't worry. It still works fine," I told him.

"I don't have magic, so there is no benefit to you wearing it. You only soil the symbol."

I arched an eyebrow at him. "Says the wolf in sheep's clothing."

He took a very deep, slow breath, rather than confirming or denying my subtle accusation. "You look... different," he said, studying my face thoughtfully.

"Pink makes me look older," I said, flicking a finger against the scarf at my throat.

I could sense the judgment in his eyes. Not only that I looked different, but that it probably had something to do with me making a deal with a demon or something. A consequence for being a Freak, like the sign of a leper. Because everything fit into a neat black and white world for Olin, or that was what he had told me when we last confronted each other.

Before he had been turned into a werewolf, introducing him to a world of grays.

I didn't hate him because of what he *believed*. I hated him for what he had *done*. He had killed and hunted Freaks all over the world, for quite a long time. If he had been a quietly hateful man of God, I wouldn't have liked him, but I wouldn't have wasted my time fighting him.

But he had spilled blood. For no other reason than that he presumed all

Freaks were monsters and should be eradicated. And he had done it in my city.

"It's okay if you brought some friends with you. Someone will need to drag your body to the pet cemetery. And I will *personally* take care of your *soul*," I winked.

"You still pretend to be an Angel?" he spat disgustedly.

"I don't pretend anyth—"

"Enough!" he growled. "I didn't come here to banter with you. I came here to kill you and retrieve what was offered."

I studied his face, my smile growing. "You *did* bring backup. How predictable."

His eyes narrowed. "They will not interfere. They came to check that no humans were present. I don't want collateral damage when you light this block up with your hellfire." I rolled my eyes. "They seek only for us to have a fair fight. Coincidentally, they learned a few of your own ilk are lurking in the shadows," he added smugly, turning my argument back on me.

"Same story. Just to guarantee a fair fight," I admitted with a shrug, not letting any shame show on my face. "You're already outclassed. I didn't need backup for this. Just someone with a cup of celebratory hot chocolate. So, let's get this over with before it gets cold."

"Yes." He drew only one of the blades from over his shoulder in a practiced motion, never breaking eye contact, and I realized it really was a two-handed sword. He just carried a backup. He held it before him, waiting for me to reveal my weapon of choice.

I drew the long, curved daggers at my waist, almost like machetes, but designed for combat. They went by different names in different parts of the world, but they were a favorite of mine when going against a skilled swordsman – of which I had no doubt Olin was. The blades were long enough to bleed my opponent from a safe distance, strong enough to block his attacks, and short enough to remain light in my hands.

I met his eyes. He acknowledged my blades with mild respect.

Then I tossed them on the ground like pieces of trash, smiling as his lips thinned suspiciously.

I turned my back on him and slowly walked over to a nearby dumpster. A mop in a broken bucket was propped against the wall. I hefted the staff in my hand as if weighing it. Then I nodded, walking back up to him.

He scowled. "Your theatrics do not impress me, and they will not save you," he said.

I pouted. "But I really hoped to hurt your feelings…" The mop thumped into the ground at my feet. Sensing no further comment from him, I sighed, bending over – quite suggestively, I might add – to detach the head of the mop, leaving me with an old staff.

It, of course, hadn't ever really been a mop, but a very special staff. A piece of wood – no matter how well wielded – wouldn't survive one blow from a sword like his. The wood in my hands was an ancient staff Roland had lying around the training area at Abundant Angel. Not magical, but designed to sustain quite a few hits without splintering.

"A staff seemed appropriate," I said. "Like Moses or something," I said, scratching my jaw.

He grunted angrily, took a measured breath, and attacked.

My muscles screamed.

With excitement.

CHAPTER 41

I lifted my staff upright, leaning to the side to let his lunge slide past me, and cracked him on the jaw with a set of silver knuckle dusters I had concealed up to this point. He bellowed in outrage, lifting his scarf into place as he sidestepped out of range.

He squared off, his face now concealed below the eyes, leaving me nothing to read other than his shoulders, because everyone knew following the eyes was a great way to get impaled. I had hoped to see his skin burn on contact with the silver, but he had concealed his face immediately.

To hide the effect, or simply to eliminate the ability for me to read his facial tells. I'd just have to filet him with more silver to find out.

Because I wanted to watch him burn, but I'd settle for hearing him scream through his scarf.

I reversed my grip, leaving the tip on the ground as I waited for him to approach, letting my body go slack, depending on my muscle memory to react in time to his next flurry of attacks. He didn't make the same mistake twice. He knew that since I wasn't using a blade, he had more room to feel me out, since my blows had less chance of being fatal, and as I watched his feet, I could tell that he was experienced – not one to make a rookie mistake like throwing his all into the first strike, letting his anger cloud his judgment.

Which meant his first had been a feeler. Knowing he would either get hit with a secondary weapon or smacked on the head by my staff.

I found myself smiling, and I lifted up my own scarf over my nose, just to mirror his choice to hide his facial tells – even though Roland had beaten most of those out of me long ago.

I waited, grinding the toes of my boots for purchase since the ground was slippery, covered in puddles, uneven, and littered with pieces of trash. He darted forward, slashing for my throat in a wide swing, anticipating my expected block.

Instead, I dropped and rolled towards the blow, using my reverse grip on the staff to pick up additional momentum as I came up in a crouch beside him, but under his attack – a bold, risky move he hadn't anticipated. The tip of the staff hammered into his ribs, with a satisfying cracking noise, but I didn't stop moving, spinning my body to the side and using my free hand to swing into the same tender spot on his ribs in a spinning backfist.

I made contact, knocking some of his breath away before his boot connected with my own ribs below my attacking hand. I grunted, but managed to curl with it slightly, skidding back a few steps with the blow so it didn't shatter my own ribs or break off a few of the floating ones.

My coat could take a beating, though, which helped.

He was already running at me as I glanced over my shoulder, so I darted forward, running away from him. He was too close for anything else.

I sprinted straight at the dumpster, slamming my staff into the mop bucket, and pole-vaulting on top of the thankfully-closed dumpster. Only focusing on my flight, his sword was already swinging down into the dumpster when the mop bucket hit him in the nuts like a fast pitch baseball – since I had used the fulcrum to fling it at him as I jumped. He gasped, dropping his sword instinctively as his hands latched onto his Holies.

That was the thing about men like him. They were too used to fighting other men, and they had an unspoken, cosmic rule about never striking in the family jewels.

I hadn't stopped moving but had spun around as I landed on the dumpster, lifting my boot so that my heel pounded into the brick wall, slowing my momentum. I used that boot as a spring, launching myself right back at him, and thrusting my knee out as I held the staff with both hands before me, aimed over his head.

My intent was to hit him in the face with my knee, wrapping the staff behind his neck so that I could use it as leverage to keep kneeing him in the face, preventing him from drawing his second sword.

It worked.

Kind of.

My knee busted open his jaw since his hands were still clutching his goods, but the moment my staff wrapped around the back of his neck, he went limp – and I wondered if I had knocked him unconscious with my blow.

Then, as we fell back, me riding him like a motorcycle, I felt his boot settle into my stomach, preparing to launch me over him when his back hit the ground.

I immediately dropped my staff, letting it clatter to the ground ahead of us, and gripped two fistfuls of his short hair right as his back hit the ground and his leg extended to throw me.

Which meant that as he succeeded, I ripped out two large tufts of his hair, producing instant screams as I turned my flight into a roll, dropping his hair.

So far, I was impressed. This was a beautiful dance, and my partner – although not winning – was good. Just not as experienced in dealing with talented opponents. Probably too used to being the top dog that he hadn't had to really try in a long while. Still, he was good. And this excited me.

In surprising places, I realized with a distant blush.

I scooped up the staff, not waiting to check on him as I spun, swinging low. His sword was already swinging at the back of my head, but I had remained low in anticipation. His swing whistled over my head right as my staff slammed into his shins, snapping in half as it fractured bone, by the sound of it.

Oh, and he crashed onto his shoulder as his fractured legs were also swept out from beneath him.

He grunted and growled, scrabbling to get to his feet right as I aimed the jagged tip of my broken spear at him, ready to poke and prod until he shifted into a werewolf.

A gunshot rang out, and I jumped back, my black fan instantly appearing beside me in the direction of the sound. I turned up to see a hooded Templar not ten paces away, striding towards Olin, but aiming his pistol at me. His scarf was up, too, showing me only shadowed eyes.

"Enough!" the Templar referee shouted.

I froze in disbelief, but not only because he had interrupted my obvious victory.

Wolves suddenly howling from each direction made him hesitate, aiming his pistol a little closer my way as he realized his interference had not been appreciated by the werewolves he and his backup squad had apparently missed.

Because Paradise and Lost were good. And they had shown up after the fight began, as I had told them to do. Their howls also told me something else I needed to know, but I was too busy staring at the hooded Templar's eyes to remember what it was.

That voice...

CHAPTER 42

*O*lin had climbed to his feet, eyes glinting as his hands hung at his sides, sporting a fancy set of upgrades – long, black claws. I couldn't even bother feeling triumphant, too busy staring at the newest Templar. His pal motioned at the claws subtly, but Olin was beyond caring as he glared back in barely restrained fury at the newcomer, toward the howls, and finally back to me.

Since he was about to kill me, he really didn't care that I had just seen proof he was *in fact* a werewolf. Olin took a step my way before his pal shouted loudly again.

Olin rounded on him this time, claws out to kill. His Templar minion didn't point the gun at his boss, but lowered it, staring at the claws.

Olin glanced down, panting. The claws slowly retracted, revealing normal hands before he glanced over at me, face a rictus of outrage, lingering pain, and pure murder.

"You're through," I said in a soft, distant voice, setting the butt of the broken spear into the pavement at my feet. I felt very cold all of a sudden, and it had nothing to do with the fight. I felt like a fluff of dandelion floating in the wind.

"Not until I get back what's mine," Olin snapped. "You think your wolves scare me? You saw what you turned me into. I no longer harbor the same… concerns about the wolves."

"Meaning you've become what you used to hunt," I said in a dead tone.

"I will use this curse for God, you despicable creature!" he roared. "Your wolves can't get to you fast enough to save you from me, now!"

I blinked lazily at him, not moving. "Did you just call me a *creature?*" I asked, frowning.

"Give me the ring, NOW!"

He was panting again. I shot the assistant Templar a look, sizing him up, but I was pretty sure I knew about as much as I needed to know about him.

I shrugged. "I don't have it—"

His roar abruptly cut me off. Also, the fact that he was suddenly holding me up in the air by the front of my coat, ignoring the jagged spear I had reflexively buried in his gut.

Then he punched me.

I flew back, skidding through puddles as my face flashed with fire. I spat out blood, shaking off my dizziness as I tried to climb to my feet. He kicked me in the ass, sending me sprawling.

"Where is it?" he roared, kicking me again. This time in the ribs. I heard some of them crunch as I slid another few feet.

My heart froze as I heard a very clear chime echo in the alley, the sound of metal striking pavement. *Ping.* I looked up to see three silver rings rolling away from me, but they winked in and out of my vision as I struggled to clear my head.

I flung out a hand, snatching at one of them, but missed as it rolled out of reach.

"The ring!" Olin shouted, sounding as if he was jumping for it.

"No…" I hissed through broken ribs and a bloody mouth, scrabbling to reach it ahead of him.

Which meant I had a perfect view of the blur that suddenly streaked through the air before my face, scooped up the ring, and zipped back up into the sky, out of sight.

"NOOOOO!" Olin roared, screaming up at the sky – the sound half human, half monster.

Then he spun back to me, not holding back this time as he kicked me. I threw my hands out in front of me and felt some of my fingers crack as they took the blow, but I still went sliding.

This wasn't good. I needed to get out of here, but I didn't dare Shadow

Walk. Something was up with that. Something dangerous, but I couldn't remember what.

And I didn't have time to make a Gateway, because I would still have to find a way to get *through* the Gateway, and right now I couldn't even manage to get back on my feet.

Maybe I *had* needed Claire.

But hadn't I done something else? Some phone call... the memory eluded me as I tried to ignore my pain, to think of one last trick to get out of here.

"What is the meaning of this?" Olin demanded from somewhere behind me.

Talking. Maybe that would delay him enough to give me a chance out of this.

"I wanted everyone to see what you've become," I said in a croak.

Silence answered me as floodlights suddenly erupted from an adjacent building, illuminating the clearing in a blinding glow that made me squint.

"What in blaze... you were supposed to check everywhere!" Olin snarled, face livid as he rounded on his fellow Templar.

"We did, sir. They... must have arrived during the fight," the other Templar said. His voice made me cringe, my suspicion confirmed.

I managed to prop myself up into a sitting position, seeing several red laser sights locked onto both Templars. "You didn't anticipate humans wrecking the party," I rasped, adjusting my posture against the agony in an attempt to relieve pressure on my ribs. I needed a few moments before I dared trying to stand.

Bits and pieces came back to me, slowly. I had called Haven. Recruited his security detail to help me out. Hearing the possibility that the Templar in town was actually a werewolf had been too much for him to refuse aid. In exchange for his help and signing my lease for the church, he had wanted undeniable proof that Olin was really a werewolf. His men were here to witness first, and only act as a last resort. Any fuckup could have prevented Olin from showing his hand.

That he was really a werewolf.

And I had made sure to tell Haven that his men had to wait to go to their positions until they were sure they had tracked the other Templar movements, allowing them to sweep the area before sneaking into their positions.

"I wanted everyone to see your hypocrisy. That you're really a werewolf."

I heard a sound behind me and gasped in alarm. Someone was trying to sneak up on me, out of sight from the snipers! And I couldn't even stand, magic being useless against Templars.

A bloodcurdling *yowl* made my ears pop as something slammed into something else behind me. I struggled uselessly to climb to my feet, splitting my attention between the Templars in front of me and the murders happening only paces behind me.

Olin and his Templar buddy stared in disbelief at the wet ripping and crunching sounds interspersed with throaty purrs from something very big. The screams ended abruptly.

Even a few of the sniper lasers darted back and forth nervously.

Giving up on standing, I glanced back to see Phix padding over to me, her semi-furred – but still human – breasts coated in crimson and gore. She hissed through long feline fangs at the two surviving Templars – the sneaky ones were now merely lumps of torn, steaming flesh and guts near the mop bucket, ironically. She hooked the back of my coat with her claws, wincing at my grunts as she pulled me back behind her, standing down the remaining Templars on her own.

"Mine," she said, hunkering low between us.

"Use your boobies to keep them distracted," I murmured, not really caring where the hell she had come from or how. She glanced back, frowning. "They're scared of them." I blinked my eyes several times, trying to block out my pain and clear my head. I spat out some blood.

Something – probably an Angel – had just swooped down to take the Seal of Solomon that had fallen from my jacket pocket, so I was hesitant to try tapping into my Angelic powers. And in my current state, I was scared to try anything new anyway, which left me with regular magic. A Gateway. But I felt too tired to try.

Olin roared at me, pointedly ignoring Phix. Maybe Templars really were allergic to boobies. "I will *kill* you for this! I will destroy every abomination in this town. The vampires, the Hellfire Club, the shifters, and *you!*" I wasn't sure if he was more pissed with me for revealing his secret, or for Phix's sudden arrival.

Phix let out a haunting, high-pitched yowl, arching her back as her claws cracked through the pavement. I waited for her to skip sideways a few steps like an angry cat, but she didn't. I glanced back up at Olin, keeping him in my sight as I placed a hand on Phix's ass to support my attempt to stand. It worked, barely.

I let out a pained breath, finally looking back up at Olin. "It's hard to take you seriously when you're foaming at the mouth like that, werewolf. Can Templars get rabies?"

"We've lost the advantage," the second Templar warned, "unless you want those wolves joining in the fray. Snipers, this... *thing*," he said, indicating Phix, "And the Ring is gone," he added, sounding more concerned about that than anything.

"Because her demon took it!" Olin snarled. I pointedly ignored the second Templar, my mind clearing, but suffering a different form of beating at his words.

"Please, sir. Leave before this gets even worse. I... would like to talk to her for a minute. Alone. I'll meet up with you after, and tell you everything."

"You're already on thin ice," Olin warned. "Don't fail me again." With that, Olin shot me one last look, promising vengeance, before he left, careful to keep his distance from me and inadvertently piss off the snipers or Phix.

The second Templar holstered his pistol and let his hands hang free at his sides.

I patted Phix on the ass. "I can manage a talk but be ready for a quick exit. I probably need a bandage or two." Phix assessed me for a moment, dipped her head, and then retreated to the two dead Templars.

She began eating them in big, fat gulps, not even bothering to chew. She also never broke eye contact with the surviving Templar as she ate his friends. I turned to him, my eyes cold and my soul a pile of ashes.

"So, Beckett, whatcha wanna' talk about?" I asked him.

If I didn't kill him, Phix would. If Phix didn't kill him, Claire would. The list stretched on and on. Beckett Killian was a dead man. I'd let him have his *talk*, first. Last rites.

It was the Catholic thing to do.

CHAPTER 43

*D*etective Beckett Killian lowered his scarf and studied me. "What's it like being a Tit?" I asked him.

He blinked, frowning in confusion. "What?"

"A Templar In Training. A Tit. A boob. A nipple shrine—"

"I get it," he muttered, cutting me off.

"Do you? Do you *fully* understand the depth of what you've done?" I asked, gritting my teeth from both the pain in my broken heart – of betrayal – and that of my injured body.

"They helped me find my wife's murderer!" he snapped. "You seemed too busy to live up to your promise. Helping everyone else *but* me." He was panting, fists flexing at his sides.

I blinked at him a few times. Then I burst into a harsh laugh. "Poor little Beckett. Couldn't wait a few months while I saved *lives* to get his revenge for someone already in the *grave!*" I shouted. "Do you have any idea how childish that sounds? How pathetic? People are dying, *now*! Your petty vengeance can wait just a little bit longer in light of *that*!" My shout echoed off the walls.

He glared back at me. The red dots from the snipers never left his chest, but he didn't seem concerned about them.

"You promised to help me," he rasped, barely restraining himself. "Then you go off on an extended romantic vacation, and when you do finally return, you begin prowling the streets for car thieves and gangsters. Sending me random text messages through Claire about future locations where I might find the broken bodies of monsters, but that I have to be careful how I handle it, or explain it, to my fellow policemen. You relegate me to your personal janitor. Your fixer to make you feel like you're doing some good. And not once do you even *mention* helping *me* find my wife's killer. Like you *promised*. Avenging everyone else but me. While you ask me to help you do it."

I stared at him, my face hot with outrage. "Instead, you use the information I send you to throw Templar hit squads my way. How very *noble* of you. Well, it looks like you have new friends to watch your back." I pointed at the dead Templars behind me that Phix was still munching on. "Practically Saints, back there. Good judges of character. Hunting down evil monsters while *working* for one!"

Beckett grimaced in disgust at Phix's meal. Another thought hit me like a kick to the gut. Judging by Olin's parting comment, I was pretty sure Beckett had been in charge of the Hellfire Club operation, which hadn't turned out well for him.

I shook my head at him. "You were there, at the Hellfire Club, weren't you?" The sudden look on his face confirmed it. "Hiding in the shadows, calling us after you failed, pretending to be concerned." I spat more blood on the ground. "You're beyond saving. You've been doing this for a while now, using me... Your actions literally kept me busy enough to *not* help you," I said in disbelief, shaking my head.

He blinked, as if the thought had only just hit him. Then he gritted his teeth. "They helped me when no one else would," he said. "Their ways may be extreme, but they've all suffered at the hands of Freaks. Now, they fight against the Freaks. *We* fight against the Freaks."

"You work for one, you idiot!" I shouted. Then I took a breath. "What if your wife had been murdered by a human? Would you then turn around and become a serial killer, murdering anyone who shared some of his traits? Perhaps he had dark hair, so all people with dark hair must now be put to the torch. Is that your rationality? One bad person changes the course of your life?" I snapped.

"We should not be enemies, Callie. We both hunt—"

I interrupted him with a harsh laugh. "We..." I said, shaking my head. "Looks like they've got their claws sunk deep, which means they've been brain-washing you for a while, now. Should have known since you already have a scarf."

He nodded. "Few weeks after you left town with Nate Temple for your… vacation," he said it in a tone that let me know just how much my choice in men had bothered him.

Which meant Beckett had been working with the Templars for *months*. He hadn't waited long at all. Or maybe they hadn't waited long in recruiting him. Perhaps I was blaming the wrong person. Beckett was still at fault for being conned, but perhaps the Templars – Olin – had targeted Beckett specifically, wanting to convert one of my allies to his cause to get to me.

That didn't diminish my anger right now, but it was something to consider. It meant that Beckett might be intended as a distraction, something to keep my focus off what the Templars were really doing here – the Ring.

"No matter how justified you think they are, we are not the same. I don't kill indiscriminately. I hunt *bad* Freaks, not *all* Freaks."

"They helped me avenge her. Tracked down her killer," he said, eyes trailing off.

I studied him. "And did you taste your sweet, sweet revenge?" I asked harshly, already knowing the answer from the look on his face.

He averted his eyes.

I let the silence fall between us. I wasn't horrified to hear he had killed. He had taken out a murderer. Unless… the Templars had led Beckett to the wrong guy. Some innocent Freak…

"I'm sure they gave you all sorts of proof. Things you're familiar with as a detective." He kept his eyes down, and I grimaced in disgust. "Do you feel better now?" I asked, deadpan. Then I pointed at his scarf. "That's a trophy, isn't it? For killing your first Freak."

Instead of answering, he set his shoulders. "I didn't expect the world to turn to rainbows and sunshine, after. Just a job that needed doing. I saw enough to know he was the right man."

"I think they get that tattooed on their lower backs after their first kill. *I got the right man.* Then they just add tally marks for every alleged monster they kill after. So their righteous bros can get a good look at it in the sauna. A Temp stamp instead of a tramp stamp."

Beckett's eyes narrowed. "They only kill Freaks," he said, as if it was an answer.

I arched a brow at him. "Oh?" I leaned forward in a mock whisper as if imparting a secret. "What about Olin?"

He didn't rise to the bait. "Maybe you're the misguided one, Callie. Ever thought about that? You're so busy protecting them that maybe you aren't seeing them clearly. They are monsters. They literally hunt humans! Maybe that's why you haven't helped me. Because you choose to protect a fellow Freak rather than aid a weak human!" He grunted, jerking his chin at me as he curled his lip. "You don't even look the same anymore. You look harsher, angrier, darker," he muttered. "Seems like proof to me."

I scowled at him. "That has nothing to do with this!" He grunted dismissively. I shook my head in disbelief, wincing at the pain that flashed through my ribs. "Unbelievable, Beckett. Your oath was *to protect and serve*, not *to threaten and kill*. Easy to mix up, I guess."

He snarled instinctively at my mockery of his oath as a police officer, but then seemed to distantly consider my words. He didn't let that doubt show for long, but I noticed it.

"You're blind with hatred," I finally said.

"In the land of the blind, the one-eyed man is king."

I scoffed. "Don't do this, Beckett. They're *lying* to you. Or not telling you the whole truth."

"They hunt the bad guys, Callie. What's wrong with that? Someone needs to help this city."

"And what do you think I'm trying to do?"

"You've been hunting the bad guys... as long as they're not your friends. Then they get a pass." He held out his hands, indicating my hidden allies and their rifles.

I took an aggressive step closer. "They're using you to try and get to me. They don't care about good or bad. They want us *all* gone."

Beckett met my eyes. "Maybe that's not so bad."

"I'm working with a fucking Angel. And Nephilim! How can you accuse me of being evil?"

"And you think the Angels have clean hands? Do you have any idea how many have tried to take that ring from us lately?" he snapped. "As soon as we found it, we've been under attack. They all want it, and they want it for themselves. The Angels don't care about us. Never have. They have their own agendas and will crush anyone who stands in their way." He stared at me for a long while, his breathing ragged. Then he just shook his head and left.

I turned to share a look with Phix. She was cleaning her blood-stained paws with her tongue.

"That is a riddle I do not pretend to understand," she said softly. I sighed, agreeing with her. At least now I knew for certain how the Templars had been tracking the Freaks. Because I had led them right to each target. "Let's get you patched up. Those wounds aren't life threatening, but I see a hospital in your future unless you know a healer."

Before I could answer, gunfire rang out, peppering the building to my right. I flinched instinctively, spotting a feathered blur swooping down from an adjacent building.

It struck me like a giant fucking pillow and I heard Phix yowling in protest. Rather than carrying me away, the world simply winked out of view like I had fallen asleep.

CHAPTER 44

I opened my eyes, subconsciously holding my side. But my pain was... gone. I stared down at my fingers in disbelief. They tingled, but I could bend them, even though I had been sure I had fractured or sprained them. I took a deep breath, but my ribs didn't hurt either. I felt tired, but I had been healed, apparently. That was a good sign, right?

With a deep breath, I slowly spun to study my surroundings. I was standing in a white circle drawn on polished concrete, a ring of candles just outside of it to bathe me in soft light. Shadows stretched on into the distance, and there was an emptiness to the air that let me know I was standing in a big empty building.

It was much too big to be located in a residential area, so I was guessing a commercial storage building or warehouse. I tried reaching out to my magic and came up against the wall of thrumming energy. I snarled. The circle was blocking my power.

I noticed a hulking, feathered figure standing in the shadows and instinctively locked down my mind. I was surprised to find that the protective circle around me didn't prevent this. Then again, circles trapped energy within their boundaries, so it kind of made sense.

"Who the fuck are you?" I growled.

Nameless and his Nephilim would have taken me to their brownstone, not this... garage.

"He, *the fuck*, is Eae," a familiar voice said, stepping out from the shadows to my right. I hadn't noticed his presence. He looked beaten down. Tired. He hid it behind an easy smile, but I knew him well enough to pierce that façade.

"Nate?" I asked, feeling as if the ground had been taken from under my feet. What was he doing here?

He nodded with a grin. Then his face froze and he leaned closer, studying me intently. "Jesus, Callie. What happened to you?"

Not what a girl wanted to hear from a man who had jumped into her dreams only to leave her high and dry before the dream concluded. I still felt the dream's sensation of his fingers clutching my jaw, wrapping around my neck as he cupped me like a goblet. "Werewolf Templar," I told him, assuming the look on his face meant I was still splattered with blood.

He blinked at me. "No, I meant *you*. You look... older. Only by a few years, but..."

I narrowed my eyes dangerously. "You might want to work on your delivery, Nate."

He cracked a faint smile, but I could tell he was troubled by what he saw. From my deal with Phix. It hadn't seemed alarmingly noticeable to me when I had looked in the mirror, but Nate was pretty perceptive. And he knew subtle changes could have big meanings.

"We'll talk about it later," I said, glancing pointedly at the circle trapping me and then arching an eyebrow at him.

He nodded, continuing to study me like a piece of art he was considering purchasing. "This might sound like a feeble attempt at a recovery," he admitted, "but I think I like the new look. Less innocent church girl, more devil may care chic." A slow grin began to replace my momentary anger. "Are the glowing white eyes new?" he asked.

My smile cracked. "What?"

"Maybe just when you're angry. Like when you first plopped down here. It's gone now."

I furrowed my brows at him, trying to quell my sudden unease. Was it something to do with Phix? "Girls do not *plop down* in places, Nate." He chuckled and I turned back to the winged figure watching us. I scowled at him. Because I recog—

"Asterion mentioned something about a date," Nate said, too casually.

Surprised at the interruption, then all over again for the statement itself,

I slowly turned to stare back at Nate for a good five seconds. "How about we save the reunion until after I kill this Angel?" I said. Because I had seen enough of him to realize he was the cowboy Angel I had fought in the Templar Vaults. Nate had said his name was Eae.

And together, they had trapped me inside a circle.

Eae growled at my comment. Well, maybe a not-so-friendly warning grumble.

"What is the meaning of this?" I demanded, losing any semblance of patience.

"We needed to check on a few things… Precautions," Nate said, pointing down at the circle.

"You two really shouldn't have healed me," I laughed darkly. "Because now I feel strong enough to break this pretty little circle," I said, gritting my teeth.

Eae scoffed in disbelief, but seeing the confident look on my face, his eyes narrowed.

"It's actually for *our* protection," Nate said, pointing behind me on the floor. I turned to see a juice box. I slowly swiveled back, arching a brow at him. He shrugged. "Thought it might cheer you up. A peace offering."

With nothing else to do in my circle, I stabbed the straw into the juice box and took a big sip. They watched me entirely too attentively. I froze, and then threw the juice box to the ground. "What did you do to it?" I hissed, staring down as it leaked juice onto the concrete floor.

They watched me warily. Then they shared a long look with each other. "Well, that pretty much answers that bit," Nate told Eae matter-of-factly. "I told you we could trust her. You can take her out of the circle now." But he sounded relieved, as if a small part of him had feared a different outcome. And I suddenly realized that my change in looks might have made him more nervous than he had initially let on.

Eae shook his head. "Not yet."

"What did you put in my juice box?!" I yelled.

Nate shrugged. "We mixed Holy Water inside it."

I opened my mouth. Then closed it. "*Why?*" I finally asked. "I'm not a demon."

"Maybe because you attacked an Angel the other day?" Nate said, smirking to take away the sting as he pointed at Eae. "Thought *I* was the only one stupid enough to try *that*."

"You thought I was *possessed?*" I asked incredulously.

He shrugged as he began ticking off fingers. "Shutting down the Vatican. Fighting Templars. Fighting an Angel. *I* might have done those things, but you and I have different… genes." He shrugged, alluding to my Nephilim blood. "Those events taken into combination, though, I thought it was at least plausible that someone might try to get to you this way. It would be a clever way to take you down." He brushed his hands together symbolically, turning to Eae. "Callie is rock solid. I trust her. Now that we know she isn't possessed, I can't think of anything else, so she likely has a *very* good reason for attacking you."

Eae shook his head stubbornly, unconvinced.

Nate narrowed his eyes at the Angel. "Well, this is about to get awkward," he said when it became apparent Eae wouldn't budge. And with a flick of his hand, a small jet of fire torched part of the paint on the ground, breaking the circle. I felt the wall blocking me from my magic evaporate as Eae spluttered angrily at Nate.

Nate just folded his arms, smirking absently as the Angel's tirade rolled over him. I shot him a grateful smile that he smugly pretended not to notice.

Eae finally threw up his hands in defeat. "Greta didn't have a high opinion of her," he said.

Nate snorted dismissively, sounding amused. "She doesn't have a high opinion of anyone." He shot me a look. "Eae sent her to convince you something was up."

I sniffed. "Well, she did a shitty job."

Nate burst out laughing.

Eae, on the other hand, looked personally offended. "Greta has impeccable judgment."

I shook my head in disbelief at how arrogant Eae was. "Your Good Samaritan detector seemed to love Cain and Dorian Gray, but not me," I told him, enjoying his reaction. Greta really *had* been one of the good guys. I hated it when the ones I disliked were good guys.

Nate's eyes shot wide open. "Cain? As in, Cain and Abel?" he hissed.

I nodded smugly. "Cool guy if you forgive him his trespasses."

Nate muttered something under his breath about Cain not being able to take a joke, but that couldn't have been right. I remembered Cain saying something about wanting to stay away from St. Louis. The two must have had a disagreement at one point, but Cain was definitely into jokes. I shrugged, turning back to Eae.

He had stepped fully into the light while chastising Nate and I finally took a moment to get a good look at him. He wore jeans and a tee, no shoes. His skin was tanned, and he was very tall. Large wings hung from his shoulder blades, made of what seemed to be dry ice with bits of stone hovering amongst the feathers. They radiated power, since he wasn't bothering to conceal them.

Eae studied me critically. "You *have* changed. Even since I last saw you underground."

I shrugged but didn't offer an explanation.

As I stared into those eyes, I could tell he had spotted Phix in the alley, was curious about it, but had chosen not to bring it up in front of Nate. Which was... strange, since he hadn't seemed to trust me enough to let me out of the circle. An odd way to interrogate someone.

This angry Angel had secrets.

"*You* tried stealing the Seal of Solomon," I pressed. "Why am *I* the one under suspicion?"

His feathers ruffled agitatedly. "And you *lost* the Seal of Solomon. It doesn't belong in the hands of man. It belongs with the Angels!" he snapped, chest heaving angrily.

Nate was watching the two of us glare at each other, frowning. "I wonder what it's like to make a mistake," he mused absently. "I seem to remember an Angel getting his wings clip—"

Eae rounded on Nate, face livid. "That was entirely different!" he snapped.

Nate shrugged. "Bad judgment call, if I recall."

Listening to them, I began to have doubts about Nate's Angel friend. He had tried to steal the Seal of Solomon, and Alyksandre – the most incorruptible Nephilim I had met so far – had seemed confident he was a Fallen Angel. Rather than approaching me – or Nameless – he remained hidden, only showing up again when the Seal of Solomon appeared. When he didn't get it, he kidnapped me, using Nate's friendship to sway me. And rather than releasing me from the circle himself, Nate had had to intervene – which had pissed Eae off. Then, the next real comment directed my way was an accusation... about losing the Seal he seemed so intent upon acquiring.

And now Nate had brought up a blemish in his record.

I decided that these Angels in my life were high maintenance, and I didn't trust a single feather on their wings. They were playing their own game on us. On me. I could play games, too.

I checked my grip on my mental block, making sure it was impenetrable, and I prepared to start throwing wrenches into plans.

CHAPTER 45

J cleared my throat, interrupting their heated argument. They turned to look at me.

"I've got places to be. An heirloom to get back."

Eae spluttered. "You will *not* go after the Seal. It belongs with me, if it belongs with anyone!" he met my eyes, his wings flaring out. "I. Am. Eae. The Demon Thwarter! Of *course* I should have it!" he hissed pompously.

Nate frowned at his display. "I'm pretty sure she can do whatever she fucking pleases, Your Holiness." Eae rounded on him, redirecting his fury into a fresh argument.

"And I'm a firm believer that heirlooms should stay in the family," I said casually.

My words cut them both off like a glass crashing to the floor at a dinner party. They stilled, and then slowly turned to look at me. "What?" Nate asked, staring into my eyes.

"Nameless seems to think that I'm descended from King Solomon, that I can control the Seal all by myself. Wants me to use it for him, but I've got other plans."

"Cool name," Nate muttered almost subconsciously, as his brain tried to process the rest of what I had said. Then he was slowly nodding to himself, as if finding facts to back up my claim – at least enough to merit a debate.

"*Nameless* is not a *cool name*. It is not even an Angel's name," Eae hissed, sounding on the edge of violence.

"He said he changed his name."

Eae blinked. "That wouldn't change who he *is…*" he said, frowning.

I shrugged. "He thinks that the other Angels are too proud, reminiscing about the glory days with their powerful names," I arched an eyebrow at him pointedly, enjoying his resulting scowl, "and forgetting their duties. He chose to adopt a new moniker."

As Eae processed that, Beckett's words came to mind, supporting my suspicion of Eae. As many mistakes as Beckett had made recently, he'd gotten at least one thing right. *The Angels don't care about us. Never have. They have their own agendas and will crush anyone who stands in their way.*

"You believe him?" Nate asked me. "That you're related to King Solomon?"

I met his eyes and nodded confidently.

I didn't, though. Not really. Sure, it explained a lot of weird things about me, but I didn't have any real proof. Thinking about that, I realized that the only real proof would be to slip on the Seal of Solomon and throw myself against the Fallen Angels trapped inside.

Do or die.

But I didn't let any of this show on my face. I needed Eae in a very specific situation.

"It will destroy you," Eae finally said, forcing calm into his voice, trying a new tactic. "Even if it didn't, no man should wield that power. It is too seductive. Too tempting."

I leaned forward. "Not sure if you noticed, but I'm not a man."

Nate smirked, but still rolled his eyes. That hadn't been what Eae meant, and I knew it.

Eae studied me suspiciously. "How did you get the ring in the first place?"

I doubled down on my mental block, making sure it was rock solid. "I didn't know I had it."

Eae studied me with even greater suspicion, and I could tell he was unsuccessfully trying to probe my mind. And his failure was both pissing him off and making him uncertain.

"If you want it so badly, maybe you could just go ask Nameless for it," I offered. "If he declines, you two can go off to a field in Kansas to duke it out. Blame the aftermath on a Superman sighting."

Eae snorted, and I realized that as much as he thwarted demons, allegedly, he was not as confident in his ability to face-off against his fellow Angel. An unnamed one. Hell, Nameless could end up being the Archangel Michael or something, for all anyone knew.

Nate cleared his throat, interrupting us. I looked over to see him staring down Eae. "Kansas City belongs to Callie, and you are an unwelcome visitor. I didn't ask you here to support your own motives, Eae. You promised to share what you found with her." Eae's face darkened, but he didn't speak. "And I'm holding you to that, Angel," Nate warned him in a very frosty tone.

Like Nate had just plucked his feathers, Eae shivered. "As agreed," he said through gritted teeth. "We can discuss the Seal of Solomon at a later time," he added not sounding the least bit pleased about it, but not daring to break his word.

Or possibly to stand up against Nate.

I stared from one to the other. "What are you talking about?" I asked, frowning uncertainly.

Eae lowered his eyes. "It's about your parents," he said in a surprisingly sympathetic tone. I took a step back instinctively, shaking my head. How... had I forgotten about *that*?

Nate had *told* me – what felt like a lifetime ago – that he would get Eae to look into my parents. Had the Seal of Solomon really kept me from remembering such a burning desire to discover their background?

Had Eae been right about the seduction of the Seal?

Nate cleared his throat delicately and I slowly turned to look at him. "I found them, Callie..." Eae grunted meaningfully. "Well, I helped find them," Nate clarified. "If you need me, I'll be outside." He smiled sadly and turned to leave.

I flung out a hand, latching onto his sleeve, stunned that he was just walking away. Leaving me to face this alone. "I might need a... friend to lean on," I whispered, my heart beginning to beat faster. My parents. I had wanted information about them for so long, but...

Right *now*?

Nate was shaking his head firmly. "You don't need to lean on anyone, Callie. In fact, it might do you some good to... wobble a little."

I stared at him in disbelief. *"Excuse* me? It sounds like you're saying I could stand to be knocked down a peg or two."

Nate blinked, caught off guard. "What? No. I meant..." his eyes grew distant, and whatever he was remembering, hurt him. "Look, I've had to have a talk like... this," he said, waving a hand at Eae. "I thought I wanted friends with me, *needed* friends with me, for support. But I learned that using a crutch only delays the healing. Meaning you won't see your fall coming, and it will hit you when you least expect it, knocking you on your ass at the worst possible moment. Sometimes... we need to stand and take the punches. Be prepared to fall at a time of our *own* choosing. The blows will hurt, but..." he smiled encouragingly, "things like this are *supposed* to hurt, right? It means your heart is still open. Not broken..."

I realized I was sobbing softly, irrationally angry at him for being... right.

"You don't need me to help you take off your Band-Aids." He squared his shoulders, lifting his chin. "And I respect you too much to be your crutch, Callie..." He subconsciously scratched at his chest as he spoke, right where he wore the coin necklace that disguised his Horseman's Mask. The Horseman of Hope. Something about that tickled my memory.

Then he was walking away, disappearing into the darkness.

Leaving me with the Angel.

CHAPTER 46

I sat down in the center of my circle, staring as Eae sat directly before me.

I mentally prepared myself for the emotional beat-down ahead. I knew it wasn't going to be a *happily ever after* story, because – spoiler alert – I already knew a demon killed them in the end. Johnathan had bragged to me about it while trying to torture me to death.

But I'd never read the first chapters of their book. Or the prequel.

"Your mother was a dark wizard," he said, watching me with an expressionless face.

I stared at him in silence, imagining ripping off his wings by hand. Luckily, he couldn't read my thoughts, so I relished in it for a few moments. I don't know why the statement angered me so much. It wasn't like I had ever known her. She could have been a polka-dotted owl for all I knew. For all it mattered. She had *abandoned* me. Left me on the steps of the church. And I'd once had the audacity to actually believe that I had been touched by heaven. Eae's single statement had just ripped through that like a paper target at a RPG testing facility.

"Explain," I managed in a whisper.

Eae's face was merciless as he nodded. "A dark wizard," he repeated in a monotone. "She employed black magic. Sacrifices, rituals, murder. A truly despicable person. The works."

I felt myself growing cold, wanting to scream and snarl and hurt something. "Your bedside manner is truly overwhelming," I said in a dangerously calm tone.

He didn't react. He just continued to watch me. I took a deep breath, forcing the rage down. "Fine. So, you think I'm broken. That's why you don't trust me. But you forget that I'm my own woman, *Angel*. I have free will, remember?"

His lips thinned, but he continued to watch me, staring straight into my eyes. It was more than a little unnerving. As if he was trying to read my gray matter, or considering how best to dissect me. Where to slice first. Or maybe he sensed something within me. The Sphinx. The Whispers.

No. I had that part of me locked down. Maybe that was why he was staring at me so intently, wondering why all he could hear was white noise.

"Stop staring, creep. Talk."

He narrowed his eyes one last time, as if not best pleased. "It is good that you accept your mother's past, because that was well behind her when you came into the picture."

I gritted my teeth, barely forcing the words out. "I've wondered how your wings would look nailed to the wall of my living room... But I don't like to be cruel."

His eyes narrowed dangerously as he picked up on my indirect insult. "Let's not pretend that I'm a nice childhood friend. I'm an Angel. Eae, the Demon Thwarter." The room pulsed and I felt an unseen physical force slightly press against me. He watched my reaction, and... didn't look best pleased when he realized that I wasn't sobbing and crying bloody tears of rapture. "You are an anomaly," he continued, frowning pensively. "It is my duty to make sure that anomalies do not put the Realm of Man at risk. So, yes. I'm testing you. Reading into your responses. Tracking your pulse. Trying to read your mind." I smiled smugly and he realized he had inadvertently admitted to failing at the mind-reading thing, which I was betting wasn't usual for him.

"At least I can still ward us," he continued. "No one can eavesdrop with me nearby. I'm blocking them."

I kept my face blank. Was he talking about Phix? The Whispers? Both? I nodded as if I wasn't concerned, although I hoped Phix wasn't suddenly murdering everyone in town in her quest to find me.

She hadn't sounded pleased when Eae kidnapped me.

"I'm still waiting for you to show me why I shouldn't redecorate my living room."

He snarled. "Be careful what you wish for, Little Nephilim. I will *show* you the fable of Titus and Constance. Your father and mother." And he grabbed my entire face with one hand before I could react to hearing my father's name for the first time.

CHAPTER 47

I found myself in the middle of the deep, dark woods – you know the place – creepy tendrils of fog drifting about like a nest of snakes, creepy ravens cawing in the darkened branches, a wolf howling, perhaps, and imagined eyes everywhere I looked.

Except the place was slightly hazy, as if *made* of smoke. A reflection of a memory. Despite it being night, there was an ambient glow to the woods, with neon flashes in my peripheral vision, like little crackles of electricity and motes of sparkling, multicolored dust forming the construct of the scene around us. The details faded into these hazy sparks around the edges, wherever I wasn't directly looking.

I reached out to touch a bush, and my hand went right through it with a small disruption of neon sparks. So, not real. I began to wonder if Eae had designed this whole thing – this virtual reality – to play me. To manipulate me. Only one way to find out.

I walked towards a flickering light around a bend in the path ahead. I came upon a small clearing, the trees forming a thick canopy above, only allowing a fraction of moonlight through to stab the ground like a prison of lunar beams.

A woman knelt before two dead friends. Constance. My mother. I had never seen her before.

And she was sobbing with grief. My so-called evil mother was crying by herself, and it hurt something surprisingly deep inside me to witness it.

Eae's whispered voice rolled across the wind, tickling my ears, narrating the scene.

Constance was a highly dangerous dark wizard. Titus – a well-respected Nephilim – was sent to kill her. He found her like this, crying over these two fallen witches. One dead, one soon on her way to death.

I glanced up to find a man standing across the small clearing, a white glow limning his silhouette. My father... staring at... my mother.

My parents. Enemies.

I shivered, eyes watering with sudden longing. I was so close. They looked so real...

It wasn't clear if the witches had been allies or enemies, Eae's voice continued, *but Titus found this dangerous, dark wizard crying for them...*

Constance slowly looked up to stare at Titus – her executioner. She didn't react aggressively. In fact, she began to sob harder. Not in defeat, but... with genuine grief.

Titus... frowned, unsure what to make of it all. He was a tall, strong, pale-haired man with bright, penetrating eyes. I studied them, recognizing the coolly rational thoughts racing through his mind. Was Constance attempting to deceive him?

The scene warped as Eae continued speaking in my ears, the world rebuilding right before my eyes into a wide cavern, complete with a cell tucked in one corner.

Against all orders, Titus showed mercy to Constance. He decided to capture rather than kill her. He locked her away and allowed her to recover from both her supposed grief and the wounds she had been hiding from him. Even though he didn't properly ward her cell – a test – she never once tried to escape...

I watched as Constance sat silently in her cell. She looked so similar to me that I couldn't have denied our relation if I wanted to. Because in this memory, she looked to be maybe in her early thirties. Her hair was blonde, a beautiful golden color, and despite her captivity in the cell, she was not covered in filth.

Titus knelt before the cell, watching her as if she were a bug in a box. He didn't speak. Only stared unblinking at this evil, dark wizard he had captured. It was easier to make out his features now, revealing an angular, chiseled face beneath his messy pale hair.

Constance stared right back at him, her chin propped in her palm, seeming just as curious and wary of Titus as he was of her. No hatred or romance shone in either set of eyes. They just watched each other, as if trying to understand the actions of their opponent.

A Nephilim who had disobeyed orders to let a dark wizard live.

A dark wizard who had grieved over two dead witches, not fighting her captor.

"Is this a new interrogation technique, Nephilim?" Constance finally asked him in an amused tone, head still propped in her palm as she used her free hand to tap the iron bar with a fingernail. "We both know this isn't sufficiently warded. Do you attempt to offer me hope? Salvation? Only to take it away at the last moment when I try to break free and you shut me down, filling me with despair?" She chuckled mirthlessly, lowering her finger from the bars. "There is no hope for what I've done, Nephilim. Either finish this or give me to someone who will. I don't have the courage to end it myself, and don't appreciate being studied like an experiment."

Titus' eyes might have widened a fraction at her honesty, or perhaps in surprise at her seeing through his plan, but he otherwise continued to sit motionless. But he looked more tense, now.

Something about the vision changed, and I was suddenly watching it in fast forward. Titus never moved. But Constance was now shifting from spot to spot within her cell, sleeping, sitting, standing at the bars to watch her captor, kneeling on the ground, meditating, and even praying.

She never tried to break out and he never moved.

Maybe my father had been trying to break her. With silence.

Eae spoke softly, his voice drifting to my ears like a lover's sigh. *At first, he didn't believe her. Vigilantly waiting for her to reveal her true nature, to show him that he had made a terrible mistake in allowing her to live rather than killing her in the woods.*

That he should have obeyed his command rather than succumbing to her momentary display of compassion for her fallen sisters. That his duty to God had been ignored for no purpose.

He kept her as his captive for months... but never remained in the same place for long...

I gasped as the scene changed, blurring with activity for a moment, slowing only for a few seconds to reveal a startling new scene before blurring again to reveal another.

Them riding camels through an endless twilight desert, staring at each other pensively. *Blur*. Both hunkered back to back in an icy cavern. *Blur*.

Them hacking and slashing through a forgotten jungle with stained, rusted machetes. *Blur*.

Caves, caves, and caves – all different geographies and topographies – one of them always on lookout as the other slept. *Blur*.

Eae continued as more and more visions of their travels whisked before my eyes. *Constance soon realized that they were on the run from his own brothers – the Nephilim – who hunted him day and night for his betrayal in saving her life. It... baffled her.*

He was nothing like she had feared but was an oath-breaking Nephilim.

And she equally baffled him – a remorseful dark wizard...

They had become accomplices, no longer captor and captive.

They had unknowingly freed each other from their bonds of servitude – chains of dark magic and Heavenly fires. Neither understood exactly when it had changed, or why, or how, but they accepted that they had abandoned all prior oaths in exchange for an oath to watch out for each other. Unwitting partners.

The visions slowed again...

Titus carrying my mother's bleeding, unconscious form through a broken, burning city, screaming at her. "Don't die on me, yet, Constance... Don't. Die. Yet!" As tears ran down his soiled, unshaven cheeks. *Blur*.

Constance frantically fighting to paddle a rickety boat through a raging, storming sea, shouting at the top of her lungs over the peals of thunder and lightning. "Wake up, Titus! Please, please just wake up. We're almost free!" As he lay on the seat, unresponsive to the waves that occasionally hammered into him. *Blur*.

I watched, transfixed, tears pouring down my cheeks at hearing them shift from their captor-captive dynamic to using first names – as partners. Begging the other to survive, but never conscious to see that their partner shared the feeling. I tried to burn the memories into my brain. This was the only time I had ever seen them. I had to remember this. No matter what.

The vision blurred again, revealing a wooden hut. Constance and Titus talking to each other over a rickety wooden table with a tiny, almost burnt out candle in the center. Both still looked hesitant, but something deep in their eyes told me they were smiling.

Titus seemed to come to a sudden decision, and reached up with his long, perfect fingers to tentatively touch my mother's face. She gasped, flushed lips opening against her will, as she leaned into his touch, and…

Titus' face lit up with joy, overcome with relief by her response, confirming to me that he hadn't known if she would recoil in disgust or not. A desperate fear that what he felt for her would be unrequited. They slowly, hesitantly, leaned over the table, both licking their lips as they drew closer for their first kiss, and—

The fucking candle on the table burnt out.

CHAPTER 48

I found myself back in the warehouse, facing Eae, who was now smiling faintly at the outrage on my face. I felt as if the power had cut off during my favorite show's season finale. He looked pleased with himself, shrugging mercilessly.

I let out a steadying sigh, my anger slowly fading. Titus and Constance had earned some privacy. To be honest, I'd never even hoped for a fraction of what I'd seen. Just a picture would have sufficed.

"How were you able to show me that, Eae?"

He lowered his eyes, staring down at the ground as he slowly let out a breath, understanding my lack of trust.

"I happened upon them killing a demon, one day. I'll admit that I didn't quite know what to do when they turned to look at me. They were obviously doing a good thing, killing that demon, but… it had been unsanctioned…" he said, recalling the memory. "So, I read their minds in order to understand. Which is when I saw that," he said, waving his hand to indicate the memory reel he had shown me.

I shook my head as I watched him.

"But I knew all about Titus… Everyone did. He was to be taken to trial for his crimes. Still, seeing them there… I didn't know what else to do." My heart rate increased as I began shaking my head in denial. *No. No. NO!* He couldn't have given them up. I'd kill him. No matter the cost. Right here.

He must have sensed something from me because he looked up, eyes widening as he held out his hands, speaking in a rush. "Something about them... the way they moved around each other was like a dance, or two parts of a whole. Their bond was eternal, magical. And I felt I could almost understand why they had traded their prior allegiances for what they found in each other." He sounded uncomfortable as he said it, as if adding an unspoken caveat that he would deny ever saying it in a Godly lie detector test. "When I asked them *why*, they smiled at me sadly as they grasped hands, and in unison, said *Non Serviam*. And a moment later, they were gone," Eae said, admitting his failure to capture them like he had been told.

Just like my father had failed to capture my mother.

My eyes widened in surprise, but I was smart enough not to laugh. They had Shadow Walked!

Then I thought about the Latin phrase. It was from Milton's *Paradise Lost*. It had been written on Lucifer's banner, meaning *I will never serve*. I remembered it from somewhere else, too, but I couldn't place it at the moment, too overwhelmed from the memories that were now demanding new rooms in the limited headspace of my brain.

"I was punished for my failure, of course..." he said, not looking for pity, but stating a fact. "Even though it was an unintentional failure. Something about seeing them together made me hesitate, and in that hesitation, they escaped." He looked up at me, his gaze introspective. "I don't know if I would have let them go," he admitted. But there wasn't even a hint of anger on his face. Just stark truth.

I nodded woodenly, accepting his honesty, but unable to meet his eyes. Because... he was an Angel. He didn't have Free Will like us. Maybe he *couldn't* have done anything else but obey. But he'd still had the courage to admit it to me out loud.

"Don't take this the wrong way, but I've been searching for them for a long time and have never been able to learn a thing. And suddenly you show up with all this..." I said, wiping my nose. I was silent for a moment. "It seems a little too good to be true."

Because every fiber of my being was screaming that Angels were manipulators. Whether against me or each other, I hadn't yet confirmed.

When he didn't respond, I looked up at him.

"I understand, Callie. Believe me when I say that a lot of parties have been looking into this in recent months. Looking into *you*." I hid my surprise at that and merely watched him. "The records of the Nephilim have been scrutinized front to back without luck."

I waited, frowning. "Then what changed?".

He smiled grimly. "I told Nate that I had been unsuccessful, and in a fit of anger, he happened to toss out your mother's name, trying to think of anything that might help me." At the puzzled look on my face, he leaned closer. "The Nephilim records list everyone *except* those considered *disgraced*. Like Titus. We had literally been searching through every Nephilim *except* the right one. Hearing your mother's name brought it all together for me."

Eae shook his head, as if not believing it himself. As if the whole situation stood against everything he thought he knew. Maybe that was why he distrusted me so much.

Or he could be manipulating me. One sad story wasn't enough to change my mind.

I leaned back, not knowing exactly what to make of it all. Nate had... accidentally helped me find my parents. I felt a tear fall, but I didn't cry. I just sat there, not knowing what to do with myself. Was I happy? Mad? There was still so much missing.

But I had learned something. Seen the happy part of their lives. Well, relatively speaking. Eae was still an asshole, but he did have a hint of compassion inside him. It was just buried very deep. Nothing to brag about, but better than I had expected from our initial talks.

"No one ever mentioned anything about them having a child," he said, breaking the silence. "Nephilim typically only mate with other Nephilim. It's their duty." Which made sense. They were bonded to the Angels, after all. "And they definitely do not mate with Freaks. It has happened before, of course, but the pregnancies never survived, so... no one even considered to look for a child. To look for you."

I shivered. "Johnathan did," I said in a very soft voice.

Eae nodded, grimacing.

"They had to know that you would be powerful," he continued after a few moments. "A Nephilim father and a wizard stained by dark magic. Two beings of such diametrically opposed natures successfully producing a child..." He almost sounded as if he was speaking to himself. "They had to have known you would be dangerous. And that both sides would want you – or target you if they couldn't have you for themselves. Heaven and Hell.

Dark and Light. Because you were tainted by both. Your father's light and your mother's dark."

I shivered, trying to imagine the surprise they must have felt.

"With their substantial list of enemies, and not having any allies, they must have warded you, knowing you would be a target. They would have *had* to hide you. To set something in place to keep you safe." He shook his head, in amazement. "The level of planning it took to keep you secret... It's almost unbelievable," he murmured.

I suddenly realized that I was thankful for Nate leaving the room. Not because I didn't want to share this with him, but because his reasoning had been solid. This was crippling news, but being by myself, I could stumble, fall, and get back to my feet. But if he had been here, I might have been tempted to hide my true feelings, masking it behind a calm façade in order to look tough.

Only to be blindsided later as the information drove home at the worst possible moment. A stray comment that suddenly reminded me of what I had suppressed.

The bastard. But I wasn't about to let him know that he'd been right. Well, he'd have to do a little encouraging to get it out of me...

"Did you tell Nate any of this?" I asked him.

Eae shook his head. "He wouldn't let me." I smiled at that. "I have told no one but you."

I stood to my feet. "Thank you for telling me this."

He studied me. "What are you going to do about the Seal of Solomon?" he asked.

I smirked at him. "This wasn't an exchange, Angel. You'll just have to wait and find out like everyone else."

Eae pinned me with a thoughtful look, as if expecting my resolve to shatter.

But that wasn't going to happen. He finally shook his head, as if unsure what to make of this strange, twisted creature before him. After all, I was an abomination.

The spawn of an oath-breaking Nephilim giving up his duty for some dark-magic poontang.

He opened his mouth to press one last time, but froze, eyes shooting past me in the direction Nate had gone. Then he let out an annoyed growl. "It seems we are needed outside... Go on ahead. It's probably best if I don't appear first. People tend to be... frightened when I walk into a room."

I climbed to my feet, frowning at the direction Nate had walked. I thought I could hear shouting, but it was faint, and sounded more like an argument than an attack.

This couldn't be good.

CHAPTER 49

I found Nate holding a young, brown-haired woman by the throat in what looked like a cheap, but once clean, office space. I met her startled eyes for a moment, but didn't speak, choosing to leave her hanging, so to speak. I studied the room casually. Blackened char and broken glass marked the floor in places, and part of the cheap carpet smoldered in the corner near an upturned desk. I sensed a familiar earthy smell to the air, but couldn't tell if it was from outside through one of the broken windows behind Nate, or…

Gee, maybe it was the remnants of the potions that had been thrown around the room.

I had only caught brief glimpses of the woman up until now, but I'd seen enough to recognize her. The only question was, how had she found me? And where were her trackers? Claire, Paradise and Lost had been told to keep an eye out for her during my duel, because I knew she had to have heard about me offering to give up the Seal of Solomon.

Since she had stolen it in the first place.

Knowing Dorian Gray so well, I had specifically chosen him as my mouthpiece to announce my challenge for a duel against Commander Olin Fuentes – where the winner would receive a unique ring. And I had banked on Dorian blabbing his mouth. Especially to the Hellfire Club. Because

Dorian loved to be the center of attention and would do anything for an upraised thumb – online or otherwise. Heh.

My plan had worked. So far.

But I hadn't expected her to find me *first*. I continued to ignore her, noticing a monster standing in the corner of the room. Grimm, Nate's Unicorn, did not look happy. Fog puffed from his nostrils as he stared at the witch. He was as black as midnight and sported a mane of long, almost peacock-like feathers – also black, but with red orbs at the tips rather than the peacock's usual turquoise color. The feathers trailed down his back and into his tail.

A long, barbed horn coated with thorny protrusions extended from his forehead, and his eyes flickered with fire, sometimes orange, sometimes silver, sometimes white. His silver hooves glinted in the remaining fluorescent lighting of the office, because some of them had been knocked from the ceiling during Nate's apprehension of the witch.

Grimm shot me a look out of the corner of his eyes as if to say *I had nothing to do with this.*

I dipped my head at him respectfully, because it was easier to be polite with a unicorn who liked to murder rainbows in his spare time. Much as one would beat up a punching bag – a stress reliever.

I finally turned my attention back to the witch, studying her thoughtfully. In the alley, she'd worn a hood. In the Hellfire Club, she had run away before I could see more than a youngish face and deep brown hair. She was older than me, but only by a few years. Closer to Nate's age than mine. About my height, dressed casually in jeans and a dark jean jacket, and black flats. Nothing that screamed *evil*. No wart on her nose. Just a plain, vaguely-pretty, young woman.

Nate finally noticed that the woman he held by the throat was staring over his shoulder at me. He glanced over casually. "Do you know this crazy bitch? She broke through the window while I was napping in the chair over there and started tossing vials around like I had pinched her ass."

I sighed. "Crazy *witch*, not bitch. Please put her down. She won't attack you." I gave her a stern look. "Will she?" I warned.

She lowered her head with a guilty sigh. "No," she whispered.

"Something about that pregnant pause makes my detective penis tingle," Nate said suspiciously. "You know her," he said, lowering her to the ground, but keeping an eye on her as he took a few cautious steps back.

I nodded stiffly. "Nate, meet Rai... my dad's current girlfriend."

Although she looked entirely different, now.

Nate grunted, impressed. "Go, Terry," he said, openly eyeing the young woman up and down. Her eyes flickered with surprise at my knowledge, but she didn't bother denying it. "*This* should be good..." Nate said.

"That's to be seen," I said, shrugging my shoulders as I stared at her.

CHAPTER 50

*N*ate stepped back from her, folding his arms.

"How did you know?" she asked, sounding both impressed and concerned.

"Your awkward hug after our double-date. You fumbled the handoff. Although I didn't realize it until the next day," I admitted.

Nate raised a hand. "I think I need to hear more about this date in order to understand the full extent of the danger." We both shot him dark looks until he sighed, muttering to himself as he wandered over to Grimm.

"It was nothing," I said, but Rai chose that same moment to be super helpful by saying, "I never thought I would have the privilege of meeting Cain."

Nate swore. "Fucking *Cain?*"

Grimm chuckled, snorting as he stamped a hoof, somehow emitting sparks on the carpet.

I snapped my fingers, cutting Nate off. "Not important, Nate," I said, clenching my teeth.

He scowled at the world in general before leaning against Grimm, folding his arms. The billionaire pouted against his pet unicorn.

Inwardly, I grinned. So, Nate was jealous, was he?

Rai watched us thoughtfully. "If you knew, why didn't you hunt me down? Why haven't your friends hunted me down?" she asked, frowning.

"I didn't tell anyone."

The silence was deafening.

"I'm keeping my trust on a short leash these days," I said, not wanting to go into details. In fact, I currently had about as tight a grip on my thoughts as I had ever consciously maintained. I was mentally exhausted, but it was necessary.

I studied her, frowning thoughtfully. "You're not a dark witch, are you?"

She glanced at Nate as if seeking the best way to answer. Then she turned back to me, shrugging uncomfortably. "Maybe just a little bit?" she said with a hesitant smile, holding up her thumb and forefinger enough for a few pieces of paper to slide between.

Nate roared with laughter. I shot him a murderous look.

"You're *just a little* dark?" I asked, wondering if we were really having this conversation.

She sagged her shoulders. "I'm trying to be honest. I've done some dark things, yes, but only when I had to. Crossed lines, that sort of thing."

"Haven't we all?" Grimm added with another stomp of his hoof.

Rai practically jumped out of her flats, bumping into the door behind her. That sent Nate into another round of giggles. "He can talk!" she gasped, pointing in case we had missed it.

"You should hear my cat," Nate managed between laughs. Then he patted his unicorn's mane in a familiar gesture, as one would thank their pet dog when it barked at an intruder. He swore absently, pausing to glance down at his palm – that was now covered in fresh blood. Because the red orbs on Grimm's feathers actually oozed blood – a weird facet of the feathers. Nate let out a resigned sigh, and resumed petting Grimm, not bothering to wipe it off.

I turned to see Rai staring at the bloody hand in horror, likely assuming that Grimm's feathers were made of razors or something to cut up his hand so easily. She tensed as Grimm suddenly looked up at her, stared at her territorially for a moment, and then nuzzled his face into Nate's chest, careful not to impale his rider with his horn.

Technically, Grimm was an Alicorn – a unicorn with wings – but he currently had his wings hidden from view. He could do that, since they were literally made of shadows. I decided it wouldn't ease Rai's alarm to share that.

"He has a cat?" Rai asked, sounding as if that had been the most important thing he'd said.

"Who's the witch *now*?" Nate muttered back at her, folding his arms. "I've got a cat, a unicorn, a magic satchel," he said, patting the satchel I had given him, "and a long, black staff."

She blinked at him, and then turned to me with a frown, hoping for a more serious response than the juvenile delinquent stroking his bloody unicorn while trying to out-witch the only real witch in the room. I pointed at his satchel. "Like Mary Poppins," I explained to Rai, pretending not to notice the resulting dark look on his face.

I waited, having nothing else helpful to offer. I'd found it was easier to just let Nate rant when he was in the mood. Like a tornado. Some things you just survived.

On cue, he continued, as if to make up for our lack of awe. "I'm also friends with Baba Yaga, but she doesn't carry around all this cool stuff," he muttered.

Rai's eyes briefly widened at mention of the legendary witch. But that was pretty much the extent of Nate's witchcraft resume. Rai glanced down at her own belt – the vials and pouches hanging from it – as if it suddenly felt inadequate. "I've got some crushed starstone, a pinch of sunrise, two chimera eyes, and some sawdust," she admitted. "A satchel would be nice…"

Nate and Grimm both snorted indelicately. Almost victoriously. Nate was becoming a bad influence on Grimm, like two frat brothers left unattended for too long.

I clapped my hands together to end their pissing contest.

"You're going to explain why you stole the Seal of Solomon in the first place, and then why you gave it to me." I took a slow step forward, "and finally, why you are dating my dad." I lifted my palm, a ball of white fire suddenly crackling into existence. "He isn't a part of our world, and I'm a little overprotective. But first, you're going to tell me how you found me, and show me how your disguise works."

Rai took a breath, nodding.

"I used the blood you left behind at the duel with the Templar. I burned the rest of it, don't worry," she added quickly.

I nodded stiffly, not having even considered that I'd left blood behind.

Rai continued. "Your father was never in danger, because the woman he met doesn't really exist," she said. Then, with a murmured phrase, she was suddenly the Rai I had met at the restaurant – an older, raven-haired woman.

Rai lifted her gaze to mine, making sure I was watching. Then she pointed at a strange symbol tattooed on her wrist. "A Druid owed me a favor and made me this secret identity."

I frowned in surprise. "The younger version is your real look?" I asked, wondering all over again why she had decided to date my dad. If the young look was the real her, she could have chosen to date anyone, so why an older man like my dad?

She nodded. "I age well." She murmured the same phrase, and was suddenly the younger woman again, her real self.

I just nodded, having seen too much weird stuff in my life to be overly impressed to hear she was significantly older than she appeared to be. Par for the course in my world.

But she had still put my dad in danger, whether she saw it that way or not. What if one of the Templars had seen her secret identity and connected the two versions as the same person? Seeing her around my dad would have put crosshairs on him, because they likely already knew who he was. Thinking of *that* for the first time, I suddenly felt a panic attack brewing.

I needed to have him watched, protected. It wouldn't be hard for the Templars to connect Terry Penrose as my dad, and Olin Fuentes was currently very, very pissed at me. I wouldn't put it past him. His only saving grace was the fact that he was a Regular.

"You've just proved to me beyond a shadow of a doubt…" I began, nodding as if impressed at her transformation, "that you are remarkable at deceiving people. And that my dad's *life* may now be in danger," I snapped.

Her briefly hopeful face suddenly blanched at my change in tone. "He's in Las Vegas with his friend, Harry." I looked up at her sharply. "I bought him tickets first thing this morning and told him he had one hour to get ready. A boys' weekend. Just in case," she said, nervously.

"Prove it," I finally said, trying to conceal the sudden wave of relief I felt. If he was out of town, he was safe. Olin couldn't find him. And I knew Harry, the boring English teacher my dad usually took with him to the local riverboat casinos every few months or so.

She slowly reached into one of her pouches and pulled out her cell phone. She thumbed through it before holding it out so I could see. I walked a few steps closer, glancing at the screen. There, not an hour ago, was a picture text from my dad. Him and Harry in front of the Bellagio.

I let out a breath I hadn't realized I'd been holding. "Thank you," I managed, not meeting her eyes. "But that doesn't mean you're off the hook. You're the one who put him in danger in the first place," I hissed, wanting to rip her throat out. "Using him to get closer to me. How dare you? I should kill you where you stand. You don't even deserve to utter his name. Let alone think you can date him in the first place?"

Surprisingly, little Rai was a wee bit possessive, and didn't like my tone.

"He was just a charming man in a grocery store!" she snapped, face reddening in fury. "He flirted with me, and I said yes! I had just gotten into town and hadn't even *begun* looking for Constance yet—"

I raised my hand without intending to. My mind went blank and my vision flashed white.

I heard screaming, crashing, and shouting, I think.

Then I felt much better.

CHAPTER 51

I realized something was locking me in place, hugging me tightly, but it didn't feel like arms. I blinked in confusion to see Nate standing in front of me, holding out his hands with a horrified look on his face as he stared at me, mouth moving wordlessly.

I stared at him, not understanding.

But I realized he was blocking my magic.

My ears popped, and sound abruptly returned. "Callie!" Nate shouted at me desperately. I held up a hand, flinching at the immediate increase in volume.

I slowly shook my head, trying to remember what had led to this situation. "What just—"

A pained groan cut me off, and I glanced past Nate to see a woman-sized dent in the wall, and Rai woozily climbing to her feet. I blinked a few times, memory slowly returning. Rai had said something…

Constance. Rai had been looking for… Constance.

My mother.

She stared at me, looking terrified.

"You attacked her. Out of nowhere. You remember?" Nate asked, shifting so that he blocked Rai from my view.

I nodded numbly. I opened my mouth to apologize, but then clicked it shut. Instead, I closed my eyes, breathing deeply for a ten-count. Then I opened them again, meeting Nate's eyes.

"I'm better. She caught me off guard when she mentioned my mother's name."

He nodded, searching my eyes. "I'm going to let you go, now. Okay?" he asked.

"Yeah. But... maybe be ready to jump in again." I met his eyes, letting him see the torment I felt. That it was probably best for someone to play referee. Because I didn't remember consciously deciding to send Rai through the wall.

"Okay. That sounds smart." He released his magic and stepped back, revealing Rai again.

"I'm sorry, Rai," I told her. And I meant it. I had apparently blacked out in a rage, using my magic to hurt her. It didn't mean I wasn't upset right now. I was livid. And terrified. And confused. But those emotions didn't justify what I had done. "I think we need to start from the beginning. To prevent any more... surprises. I'm a little unstable right now," I admitted.

Rai studied me for a moment, still looking startled, but not seriously hurt. "I should have expected it, to be honest. Saying her name like that. But... I lost my cool when you grilled me about Terry."

"Two over-emotional women," I said, lips curling into a hint of a smile. She returned the smile and gave me a single nod. She brushed some drywall off her shoulder, waiting for me to start.

"How did you know my mother?"

She sighed, staring down at the floor sadly. "My sister and I were attacked by Templars many years ago," she whispered. "Outnumbered as we were, we never stood a chance. They tortured us. I watched my sister die and knew I would only survive her by minutes."

Rai's breath shuddered at the memory, and I watched as a few tears fell down her cheeks.

"Just when I had given up, and was bleeding out beside my sister, a wizard appeared out of nowhere, chasing the bad men away." Rai finally looked up at me with a faint smile. "Constance."

The room seemed to tilt beneath my feet, but I somehow remained upright, ignoring the concerned look on Nate's face. I shook my head. The two witches I had seen in Eae's vision. The survivor had been... Rai?

"I remember the Templars all screaming as they fled, slaughtered by their own weapons coming to life as if wielded by an army of ghosts." My own vision blurred as I nodded stiffly. "Everything was quiet for a time as I hugged my sister's body, waiting for the pain to stop. The next thing I knew, a woman was staring down at me with tears in her eyes. She said her name was Constance, and that everything was going to be alright, now."

Rai shook her head wonderingly at her own story.

"She cried for a complete stranger bleeding out on the grass when most people would have simply looked the other way. The last thing I remember is her holding my hand, humming a lullaby to me, and I knew I was about to die as I closed my eyes for the last time." Rai glanced up at me. "I woke up the next morning beside my dead sister, and Constance was already gone. I feared that the Templars had come back for her, that she had sacrificed herself for me... But then she appeared at my doorstep years later, asking for my help—"

Something crashed to the floor behind me, shattering loudly and making me spin instinctively, my pulse suddenly racing as fight or flight kicked in. Eae stood there, wings of stone and vapor flared out wide to touch almost each wall of the office. He had knocked a lamp off a nearby table. Where his wings touched walls, drywall disintegrated to powder. He stared at Rai as if at a ghost. I heard a muffled gasp behind me and turned to see Rai giving him much the same look, except more frightened than shocked. As if suddenly very afraid of the outcome of the next two minutes.

"You..." Eae breathed.

"Me..." Rai squeaked.

I flung my hands out between them. "If *one* more person interrupts my *goddamn* special moment, I'm pinning them to the wall!" I roared as a swarm of butter-flays suddenly hovered above each of my hands.

Eae flinched and I heard Rai gasp.

"Amen," Grimm growled from the corner of the room.

"Got it?" I shouted, letting the swarms of butter-flays rise a foot higher.

Everyone agreed very quickly after that. I released the butter-flays and turned my back on Eae, focusing on Rai's stunned face. "You were saying?" I asked her in a much gentler tone. "My mother asked for your help..." I encouraged, reminding her of where she had left off.

Rai nodded hurriedly. "Constance appeared on my doorstep years later, requesting a powerful blood potion that could ward someone for a very long time. She had heard I was the best at them," Rai added somewhat proudly.

"*You* made the ward?" I asked her, dumbfounded. The ward that had kept me safe my whole life. My parents' parting gift. It had to be.

Rai nodded. "I asked her why she didn't just use magic, but she insisted that it needed to be a blood potion. And she needed it to last for a good long time. I told her I would do it for free, thinking it was the least I could do to repay her, since I wouldn't have been able to make it for her in the first place if she hadn't saved my life. Except she refused my gift, telling me she would rather pay. She even acted like we had never met, even though it was obvious we had."

Nate cleared his throat gently. "That makes sense. A gift could establish a bond. A way to trace the spell. But services rendered are more common, more exchanges to search through. Probably why she pretended not to know you, too," he mused.

Rai sniffed. "I didn't think of that at the time and insisted I would do it for free. She didn't argue further, just held up three glass vials from her pocket and asked if she could be the one to pour the blood in the cauldron when it came time to add the final ingredient. I didn't see any harm in that, and so agreed." Rai's eyes grew distant, recalling the memory with a sad smile. "Took me all night, but it was the finest blood ward I ever created. She never told me what it was for, so I assumed she was wanting it for herself, fleeing dangerous foes…"

I hardly breathed as I listened. My mother had done all that? Why had she wanted to add the blood herself? Had my parents put their own blood in the vials? Then what was in the third vial?

"After she left, I found a pouch of gold hidden beneath her seat, the old cow," Rai muttered. "I never heard from her again, but I sensed the potion still out there in the world, doing its job, and left it at that." Rai glanced meaningfully at me. "Until a few months ago when I felt it suddenly evaporate. Almost gave me a heart attack. If anything, it should have dissipated over time, not disappeared in a blink. I knew something terrible had happened, so I followed it here to Kansas City. She had saved my life, and if she was in danger, now, I wanted to repay that debt. Or avenge her."

She met my eyes warily, and I gave her a nod, knowing what was coming, and silently promising not to smite her again. "I ran into Terry my first day here. We had a lemonade together at the grocery store," she admitted, blushing slightly. "I agreed to a second date just to get him out of my hair," she said defensively, scowling at Nate in particular for some reason.

I glanced over to see a big grin on his face.

"Anyway, I found myself at Dorian Gray's mansion for a casual meeting with the Hellfire Club. I never told them why I was in town, although I heard all sorts of tales about a young woman battling demons. It didn't take me long to realize that my blood ward had never been intended for Constance, but for you. I hadn't even known she had a daughter until I saw you for the first time, jogging right past me down the sidewalk, as healthy as can be..." she said, shaking her head.

"I never knew about the ward until it dropped," I admitted.

Rai nodded to herself. "I'll admit, I wandered the city feeling a loss of purpose, not sure if I should approach you or leave you be. Especially when I realized the man harassing me for dates was none other than your adopted dad. I even convinced him to go to a horror convention, hoping it would send him running and screaming. No pun intended," she smiled faintly, shaking her head. "I hate horror movies."

Unable to help myself, I burst out laughing. "Really?" I gasped.

She nodded, smirking. "I'll admit I'm kind of glad my plan didn't work," she said cautiously.

I smiled at her, feeling a huge weight lifting from my shoulders.

"Then you went off to Italy, and I found myself rather enjoying this city." Her smile faltered. "But then the Templars arrived, and they caught me all over again, just like they had done so long ago..."

CHAPTER 52

I stared at her, leaning forward. "They found you?"

Rai nodded. "Quite by accident. Wrong place, wrong time. They locked me up in a prison below ground, leaving me to rot." She shuddered at the memory. "I heard them talk a lot about a certain Ring they had found, how it would help them regain their power. They didn't bother hiding this knowledge, choosing to rub my face in it, to tell me that my death would be meaningless."

I realized I was clenching my fists. The Templars were going to pay. Beckett was going to pay. Everyone was going to pay.

"It took me two days before I saw a chance to escape – when the guard rotation was delayed by a few minutes." She lifted her shirt slightly to reveal a finger-length slice across her stomach.

"What is *that?*" I asked. It looked fresh, only just crusting over with a scab.

Rai smiled grimly. "After your mother saved me so long ago, I swore I would never be captured again. I sewed a small baggie of traveling powder into my skin for emergencies. Just enough for two people. In memory of my sister," she added sadly. "I used one pinch to hop out of my cell, retrieve my gear, and grab their stupid ring from a pedestal. Then I hid inside a crack in the wall while they ran around like insects for a few minutes. I used the other pinch to get the hell out, but it wasn't enough traveling powder to take me very far."

Nate let out a long whistle. "That is fucking *hardcore*."

Rai shot him a smug look of appreciation before turning back to me. "They were quick to find me, though, chasing me through the streets within minutes. I don't know how. That's when I ran across you, imagine my surprise," she said, smiling at me. "You distracted them long enough for me to throw down a few of the more powerful potions from my pouches and truly escape. I've been hiding ever since. Went to the Hellfire Club to update Dorian about it all, except the Templars found me there, too." I nodded, remembering. I'd been there.

"Wait, did you say *Hellfire Club*?" Nate hooted. "That sounds like a riot! Where—"

"Nate!" I hissed angrily. He pursed his lips.

It looked like Midas hadn't told Nate about them yet. After what I'd seen from their board meetings, I realized that was probably for the best.

I took in Rai's story, thinking about it all. One thing still eluded me. "Why did you slip me the ring?" I finally asked her.

She looked suddenly uncomfortable. "I… when I was in the dungeons, all they spoke about was that ring, and making you pay for your crimes. I knew they would come for you either way, and I figured if they wanted that ring so badly, it must be powerful or dangerous. I thought maybe it would help you. I just didn't know how to tell you about it… When I gave you a hug at dinner, it just kind of happened. I panicked, I guess," she admitted.

I nodded absently, considering. Because as desperate as I was to pry every detail from her – what my mother's smile looked like, how she sounded when she laughed, if Rai remembered the lullaby my mother had sang over her…

I had something a lot more important to deal with right now.

I checked my mental guards, and was mildly surprised to see I hadn't gotten so lost in the story that I accidentally dropped them. That was a relief.

Rai cleared her throat. "If I may say…" she began. I gave her a nod, curious. "I came here to repay a debt to your mother… But I would like to pass that gift on to you. After all, you've already saved my life more times than she did, technically speaking." She dipped her head at me. "Your mother would be very proud of the woman you have be—"

The door suddenly exploding inwards and hammering into Rai ruined the sentimental moment.

She went flying past my shoulder as if hit by a truck. My defensive black fan had instantly popped into existence, shielding me from flying debris, chunks of drywall, and even the lock from the door. I heard Rai slam into Eae behind me, and fire sizzled from somewhere near Nate as I peered over my fan through the cloud of dust, ready to throw down.

CHAPTER 53

J saw the silhouette of a giant white mountain of fur in the shattered, groaning doorway, struggling to peer through the cloud of dusty air.

"Got you now, stank-witch!" the polar bear roared.

"Bear!" Rai wheezed, sounding as if she was struggling to her feet.

"Stand down!" I shouted at everyone. "It's Claire! A friendly," I added, for those who didn't personally know her.

Claire sniffed the air suddenly. "Callie?" she snorted in a stunned growl.

"Clairebear," I said, sighing in relief that we weren't actually under attack. She abruptly shifted back to her human form, squinting through the dust.

"What are you— Hey!" she hopped back, slapping a hand to her hip. Seeing nothing there, she spun back to us. "Who just slapped my ass?"

Nate began whistling innocently, hiding in his corner out of view. I sighed at his childish use of magic.

"That's Nate, isn't it?" Claire snarled, trying to step through the debris to get a good look.

"How did you know?" he asked, chuckling.

"You have woman hands. It makes sense that your magic hands are also dainty."

His chuckle cut off abruptly, and he muttered something darkly under his breath. I caught him discreetly glancing down at his hands, reassuring himself.

"Nameless is looking for you. He left a note under your door," Claire said, finally stumbling into the room. She stood there, naked, looking like some post-apocalyptic prostitute.

Grimm whinnied, shaking his head. "I love shifters," he said appreciatively.

Claire rolled her eyes with a smile. Then she cleared her throat, reciting the message from Nameless, even attempting the sound of his voice.

"The Templars will not leave you alone, now. I have seen what they have become and am disheartened. As I told you before, some battles must be avoided in order to win a war. Help me win my war tonight at midnight, and I'll aid you in your battle against the Templars later. Andy says hello."

Nate chimed in, sounding suspicious. "Who the fuck is *Andy?*"

I ignored Nate and waved a hand in thanks at Claire, motioning for her to give me a minute to think. She nodded and sauntered over to Nate – as far away from Rai as she could get, although not before shooting the witch a dark look for the chase she'd apparently led Claire on. I turned my back on everyone, disregarding the conversation bubbling up as Nate caught Claire up to speed on Rai.

I felt Eae watching me out of the corner of his eye as he spoke with Rai, checking over her for injuries since she had been slapped around three times in this room already and might have a few concussions.

I ignored his glances as I began to pace back and forth, thinking furiously. Thinking *carefully*.

Andy says hello was Nameless confirming that he had the Ring of Aandaleeb – the Seal of Solomon. It was a subtle reminder of what I had called it in the Templar Vault.

This didn't change anything. In fact,…

It might just work *better*.

I finally sighed, motioning Eae to approach me in private. "I'd like you there to watch my back," I told the Angel, low enough so that no one could hear me. He studied me for a moment, thinking. His eternal eyes swept over the group in calculation before returning to mine.

"Okay." He looked relieved that I had asked him – surprised to find that his recommendation about how to handle the Seal had taken root in me.

Then I told him what else I needed, and he stiffened in disbelief. "I need you to do it this very second, and not ask a single question."

He frowned suspiciously, thinking longer over this than the first request, but finally nodded in grim resolve. "If that's the only way…" I didn't reply. "Okay," he finally said. He disappeared between one second and the next.

Rai watched me nervously as I approached. I told her what I required of her, speaking softly so no one else could hear. By now, the rest of the room had gone silent, Claire, Nate, and Grimm watching us suspiciously. Rai frowned nervously, looking shaken. I didn't let my face react at all, just returned her look. "You said you owed me."

She finally nodded, a stiff, jerking motion. "So I did, and I'll honor it…" she whispered.

"Why don't you just tell us what the others are doing?" Claire demanded impatiently.

I turned to look at her. I shook my head. "No." And that was the extent of my explanation.

I turned to Nate, smiling faintly for the first time. "I think it's time for you to let me wobble."

"I'll only ask this once, so really think about it…" he said. I nodded. "Are you sure?"

I focused on my breathing. "Yes," I finally answered him.

He sighed but dipped his chin respectfully. "Okay. Take care, Callie. You know how to call on a friend if you need a quick exit," he said, eyes flicking to Grimm so discreetly that no one else noticed it.

I smiled tiredly. "I won't need it. But the gesture means more than you know."

With that, Nate made a Gateway back to St. Louis with Grimm, and Rai sprinkled a handful of dust over her head as she murmured a word. Her body disintegrated to blue ashes, but not a speck of it remained on the carpet where she had been standing. I grunted, turning to Claire, ready for a fight.

She had her hands on her hips, and she looked determined. "What is your secret plan? Because I can promise you right now, I'll be there, so you might as well just tell me."

I was done playing by everyone else's rules. It hadn't done me any good in the past. I was calling the shots, now.

"Thanks for tracking down Rai," I said. "Didn't expect her to track *me* down, though. Where are we, anyway?"

Claire was frowning at me. "In a warehouse off the Interstate," she said guardedly. "That witch is wily, I'll give her that. It was a pain in the ass to follow her, especially in bear form, which was the only way I could scent her."

I nodded absently, not really caring. "You won't be joining me, Claire."

"Now, you can stop right ther—" she began.

I rounded on her so fast that she cut off, her face paling as she saw my eyes. "No." I let my anger, my frustration, my hatred of the Templars and Beckett's betrayal, all wash over me. "I'm doing this *my* way, Claire! I'm sick and tired of everyone telling me what to do, helping me when it's convenient for them. I'm the one with holy blood, so stop second-guessing me!" I was panting, shaking with anger as I took a step closer to her. "Do you have any idea what Eae told me tonight? What Rai told me tonight. They knew my parents. The *real* story. How – and why – they abandoned me. How – and why – they had to die. You have *no* idea, Claire. This ends *here. Now. My* way."

Claire studied me, trying to find some crack she could wheedle into, some chink in my armor where her compassion and sympathy would find fertile ground.

But I was a barren wasteland.

"And how many will die in your wake, Callie?" she finally asked in a calm tone.

I snorted impassively. "I no longer care. The only ones in danger are those who get in my way."

"And what about Beckett? I think he's still inside there somewhere, Callie. I think he's confused. Drowning in his own grief," she pleaded.

I shrugged. "Too bad for him, then. I'm finding myself agreeing more and more with the Templars these days." Her face paled in disbelief, but I didn't bother to let her reply. "None of them seem to care about me – the monsters, the monster hunters – so I say let them burn. Serves them right. Maybe they'll get the fuck out of Kansas City after they see what I'm capable of."

I could sense Claire failing to restrain her own anger. "I think you might be letting your special magic get to your head," she growled. "I don't give a shit what you learned today. You don't have to do this alone!"

"Just stay out of my way, Claire. You'll only mess things up. You don't have the right tools to stand against Angels and Demons." I met her eyes and she stepped back instinctively. "*I do.*"

She gave me one last furious look before storming from the room and shifting back to her bear form. Then she loped off into the night.

I stared at where I had last seen her, chest heaving as I focused on the whirlwind of news I had received tonight. The history of lies.

I was an abomination – abandoned by my parents' act of sin – hidden away like a dirty family secret. Only to be taken out when guests could not see me. I had spent my life dropped off from one place to the next – my adopted family, the church, and even my friends.

When the powers that be realized I might be a benefit to their cause, they were suddenly available, willing and able to share secrets about my past with me in order to win me over. When before, I hadn't been able to discover even a lick of rumor. Like vultures, they swept down onto the battlefield to feast and then flee. Except I wasn't an ornament to be used and discarded whenever Angels chose to pick me up. Fallen or otherwise.

I wasn't some bauble.

And it was time I let everyone know that.

In one great big pacifying inferno.

Everything else was moving along on schedule, I just needed to let Nameless know the location for our date. So, we could get rid of the trash in this city once and for all.

CHAPTER 54

$\mathscr{I}$ walked into my recently-purchased church, studying the shadows of my new rental property. I didn't even have insurance on it yet. Well, maybe I did. Midas had handled all the paperwork, and I hadn't had time to look over it. It was probably a requirement these days.

"Go light the candles," I told Rai. "Spread them around so there are less shadows. We're about to christen the Church of Callie, after all."

"Okay," she whispered, hurrying to comply. I watched her natural, younger form, the one that the players in town would recognize, not the mature beauty my father had been dating. I couldn't risk anyone making the connection between the two. The young brunette slipped candles out of a backpack, lighting them with a box of matches as she found empty spots on the floor, a serviceable table or stand, a shelf, or a carved niche in the wall.

"Let there be light," I muttered drily, the irony not lost on me.

All will be well... one of the whispers cooed reassuringly. *Soon, all will know.*

I grunted, nodding my head in agreement.

I walked the cleared open space, getting a more intimate feel for my surroundings. It was about to be crowded. I readjusted a few of Rai's candles, but more for something to do as I waited.

Splintered and broken pews littered the floor in places, though most were in working order. The place was dirty and covered with dust, and hoodlums had broken in at some point to tag their signatures, artwork, or gang signs on a few walls. Unsurprisingly, no one had desecrated the pulpit. That took balls, even for hardened criminals.

Rai managed to find a few unbroken candelabras with usable candles in the wreckage and lit them after propping them up and making sure they could stand on their own. Shortly after, she returned to my side, assessing the room dejectedly, waiting.

"You are my pawn in this," I said, not looking at her.

I sensed her resigned nod out of my peripheral vision but didn't bother wasting time to give her false reassurance. There wasn't any point. She would serve my purposes soon and pay the debt she had been so eager to pay. It wasn't like I knew her or cared about her. Just another person involved in the story of my life who had withheld information from me. If she had come to me months ago, I might have felt differently.

But... she hadn't.

She had come tonight to fulfill her promise to my mother. That was the only part of my plan I had decided to reveal to her. That she would arrive with me, wait, and fulfill her debt at a time of my choosing. If I told her anything else, she might have run screaming from the building.

Couldn't have that.

I heard a sound from the back of the building ahead of us and waited, ignoring Rai's uneasy gasp. It had been faint, but noticeable.

Staring ahead, I saw two sets of eyes reflecting the candlelight. "Are you alone?" I called out.

There was a pregnant pause before a familiar voice responded. "Yes," Olin Fuentes growled.

Rai stiffened in recognition, turning to look at me with horrified eyes. Instead of answering her, I held out my hand for her to grab. "Time to pay your debt," I said in a detached voice.

"You... set me up," she whispered from a dry throat, her voice quivering in fear of the two Templars standing in the shadows across the room. "Sold me out," she added. She must have expected me to ask her to fight at my side against my enemies.

I liked my idea better.

"Yes," I told her.

With a shaky breath, she took my hand. Her palm was hot and sweaty as

I led her over to the two figures, who were only now stepping out of the shadows.

Templar Commander Olin Fuentes, and...

His new acolyte, the dirty cop. Detective Beckett Killian.

They were armed and wore their pretty little scarves that covered up their pretty little sins. I halted a pace away, my face uncaring, unafraid, and unyielding. These two were beneath me.

In contrast, their faces were masks of different flavors of anger. Olin looked a breath away from giving up his prize in Rai, and rekindling our earlier fight. Because I had shown the city that he was really a werewolf. A big part of him wanted revenge for that. But he was also mildly intelligent, leery of such an easy setup. Me alone in a church without a weapon on hand had to be a trap.

He had seen how resourceful I could be.

Beckett stared at me with anger as well – upset that I hadn't allowed him to justify his decision. Then again, my perspective had changed. He had been righter than he knew.

I smirked absently. "A dirty cop and a wolf in sheep's clothing. Oathbreakers. Hypocrites. The great unwashed," I murmured, as if reciting from a Biblical passage.

They shouted in unison, fingers clenching, but not reaching for a weapon.

"How dare *you* blaspheme!" Olin snarled, chest heaving.

"I am *not* a dirty cop!" Beckett shouted.

I gave them each an amused look before gently shoving Rai towards them. "Your chance to repay your debt comes. Do not falter, witch," I said, not looking at her. "Be steadfast."

She nodded in numb resignation. "So be it..." she whispered, walking the rest of the way to the Templars like a skittish horse bought at auction.

Olin snatched her up by her collar, putting her in front of him like a shield or a possession. "This isn't all we came for. Where is our Ring? Hand it over or we will burn this city to ashes."

"You should practice patience enough for two this evening, little Templar, for I left mine at home," I replied, my voice flat and emotionless. Beckett studied me as if he had never seen me before. I turned my back on them, ignoring Olin's sputtered protests and growls.

They cut off abruptly as a winged figure dropped from the rafters high above, landing in a crouch that cracked the wooden floor, wings outstretched. Nephilim were suddenly standing up from their hiding places, having snuck in while I addressed the Templars. I hadn't acknowledged their arrival, though I had noticed it – even if no one else had. Every single molecule of testosterone in the room abruptly magnified as weapons were drawn and aimed at each other.

Like two spirits, only Nameless and I remained unconcerned and unaffected. No one attacked, but each man was ready for a fight at the slightest breath.

"You received my note," I said.

He nodded, briefly scanning the building. "The Church of Callie…" he said, not sounding particularly pleased.

"I needed you to be able to decipher it, and not give the location away to anyone else."

He nodded, glancing back at the Templars. "Leave them," he commanded his Nephilim. "They are not your concern. Unless they make themselves a concern," he added.

The Nephilim nodded stiffly, lowering their weapons. I didn't see Alyksandre or Kevin, but didn't really care enough to ask about it. Olin and Beckett looked visibly relieved that they wouldn't have to fight Nephilim.

Turn them on each other…

Show them their sins with a mirror as your blade…

Only the virtuous can prevail.

Repent!

The Whispers bubbled up inside me, not necessarily eager for the impending bloodshed, but resigned, convicted – in exchange for what I had promised.

All parties present had gotten their hands dirty, and that was no longer tolerated in my city.

The Church of Callie was about to be christened.

CHAPTER 55

Nameless stared at me. He knew. That everyone present had crossed a line. He had been the first to admit it to me. That he had tried to manipulate me rather than respect me.

"What is the meaning of this?" he asked in a very calm tone, indicating the Templars.

"All have sinned and fallen short of the glory of God," I murmured. "I wanted to offer an olive branch to get them off my back, to show them we need not be enemies. When they see our purpose – that of Heaven – they will repent and follow our lead. Or they will abandon their sacred duty, but they will do so without the shelter of denial. The truth will be laid bare tonight. Perhaps they will reconsider their hatred when they hear that the thief was working for me the entire time," I said, pointing a finger at Rai, yet not turning to look at her. "To ensure that this moment, here, now, was possible."

Nameless' eyes widened, incredulous. "*You* had her steal the Seal of Solomon?"

Olin was oddly silent for the first time. I could practically hear the questions racing through his mind, though. Beckett looked like he had been struck between the eyes.

And the Nephilim looked murderous. Because I had gone down to the

Catacombs with them to find the Seal of Solomon, telling them I knew nothing of it.

"It's... true," Rai said into the oppressive silence, finally repaying her debt to my mother. "I took it with the intent of giving it to her." She avoided the stunned stares directed her way, taking slow, deep breaths as she stared at the floor, making peace with her decision.

I gave them a few moments to digest that, staring into Nameless' pensive eyes.

I didn't avert my eyes as I pointed up at a darkened loft that looked in danger of collapsing at any moment. "You'll find one of the Fallen up there," I said. "The one who attacked us in the Templar Vaults."

Eae roared defiantly, sounding stunned that I had given away his hiding spot, stunned at my betrayal of his trust. Because I had *told* him to hide there. Told him to bring the Templars here. Nameless had taken off before the words had even finished leaving my mouth, tackling Eae into a wall, sending the loft crashing to the ground. The Nephilim were on Eae in a blink, subduing him with chains designed to restrain an Angel, ignoring his continued shouts of outrage at my betrayal.

"How could you?" Eae bellowed. Nameless landed beside me, watching me thoughtfully. Olin and Beckett stared at me in open disbelief, their bodies rigid as they clutched Rai, who simply stared down at the ground, sobbing softly. Because I had sent Eae to tell them to meet me here.

And I had just betrayed him. There was a lesson in that somewhere. That I no longer played favorites. Even for an Angel.

I stared back at the Templars, showing them my resolve. As much as the consequences of my decisions hurt me – I didn't relish in the pain to come – this was truly the only way. I would deal with my tattered soul later.

I had tried to save them from this, and they hadn't listened. Their greed had been too great. Their desperation for power too profound. Eae wanting the Seal of Solomon. The Templars wanting Rai *and* the Seal of Solomon in lieu of *me*.

The consequences were now on them. At least I had gotten Claire out.

I turned back to Nameless. "It was the only way to get everyone to listen, to entice their greed. I've tried it my way, I've tried it the Shepherds' way, I've even tried negotiating with the various powers in town. Yet they continue to scheme and manipulate. We no longer have time to coddle them." I let my words ring out into the room, even Eae silent as he listened.

"It's time to do it your way. If you're backing out now, then what are we doing here? Stop wasting my time."

"Don't presume to command me, Callie. Only He commands Angels."

I showed him some of my human side, sneering at him. "Then show some backbone. We're on thin ice. We can't afford to hesitate or the demons will sense it. We must be resolved, not display a lack of conviction." I let my eyes rest on Eae, heavily implying what a lack of conviction looked like in an Angel.

Nameless... *did* hesitate, the coward. "Why do you hide your thoughts?"

I gave him a level look. "I realized I don't appreciate unwarranted scrutiny. With two Angels present, I decided it was best to keep you *both* out. Especially considering what we are about to do. I have found my *own* strength. Free will."

He nodded after a few moments. Then he turned to Eae, a last-ditch effort for his fellow Angel to comprehend the big picture. Eae struggled harder against his chains, even knowing it was futile. "What say you, Brother?"

"If you are so righteous, reveal your name!" Eae snarled.

"I gave up my old name when I realized it only held me back, filled me with pride. The pride of all Angels and their petty squabbling that has brought us to this precipice. Now, I am Nameless. The one who will bring us back from that ledge."

Eae stared at him incredulously, but I could see that it was also an inner realization. That a part of him agreed. That Nameless had a point.

"Lucifer take you!" Eae finally spat, shaking his head in stubborn refusal of his own thoughts. "The *both* of you. Do *NOT* do this!" he begged, staring at me.

Like water off a duck's back, I let his anguish roll over me, and shot Nameless a pointed look, letting him see that I had been right, and that his attempt had been futile.

Because no one had known my intentions tonight. I had warned Nate and Claire away. But Rai, Eae, and the Templars had been necessary tools. This moment was for Kansas City itself. And to save my city, I'd do anything. It was all so clear to me, now.

I had been so blind...

The Whispers cooed approvingly, and I let them encourage me, let them fuel my conviction.

"We are wasting time," I finally said. My tone made it obvious that there was the high probability that with all the different parties involved, it wasn't out of the realm of possibility that reinforcements could show up if we delayed further.

Nameless nodded his agreement, though he addressed Eae one last time, sounding disappointed. "We have tried it your way for centuries, Eae. It never worked as more than a delaying tactic. We must go on the offensive. Two demons in just the last two years… No. These are desperate times. I smell our end in the air, Brother. It is coming. The End of Days. Without bold, decisive action, here, *now*, it will arrive sooner rather than later. I would have you see the truth to my words, but either way, I must stop it." Eae shook his head adamantly.

"*We* must stop it," I said, correcting his statement to include myself. Nameless didn't acknowledge my response, but a sudden flash of silver in his palms revealed the Seal of Solomon. I didn't look at it, meeting his stare with a calm, determined look.

"Our purpose is pure," I continued. "We have to stop the demons. Learn of their plans." Then, I pointedly glanced down at the Seal of Solomon. "*That* has the answers. I can almost hear them from here."

I allowed him to see my tightly bottled grief for a fraction of a moment, to prove the price I was paying for this. "It hurts to watch them suffer the consequences of their choices," I admitted, indicating the others in the room. "But that's on them. I can shelter them no longer."

"What finally convinced you?" Nameless asked me, ignoring Eae's arguments.

I lowered my eyes and let out a breath. Then I allowed both Angels to read my mind for themselves. Eae gasped in astonishment, as if having not believed my words up until this moment. I spoke very clearly. "When I truly saw that everyone was working against each other. Especially those that should have been allies. Taking the Ring in the first place was a hope to get everyone to stand down, yet it only made everything worse. And the demons will win if they get us to continue fighting each other. It's probably their plan. The first two were the farmers sowing their seeds of chaos. They understood that we would do the rest to ourselves."

Nameless finally nodded. "Yes." And I could tell that he had read my mind, assessing me for a lie. The look of relief on his face was momentarily bright and expectant, overwhelmed to find proof to my words. Then it was gone again, resolved to the dirty work ahead. "It's distasteful, but necessary, work I do this night," he agreed.

I closed off my mind again, needing as much defense as possible from unwarranted intrusion. I could still allow communication if I chose, but I wasn't handing out unrestricted access. Toeing that line was taxing on me, especially after my long physically and emotionally draining day.

I shivered slightly as I settled my focus back into place like armor – a requirement when dealing with Angels – both Fallen and not. Because soon, I would immerse myself into the Seal of Solomon, and would need every layer of protection available to me as Fallen Angels attempted to scrub my soul raw.

"If anyone should have been on our side, it should have been him, the Demon Thwarter," I said, glancing back at Eae with disappointment. "He wanted the Seal for himself." Eae railed against his bonds. The Nephilim restraining him shifted uneasily from foot to foot, looking disgusted at the act of holding back an Angel, but resolved to follow Nameless' orders – especially at the news that he had wanted the Seal for himself. And Eae was too hesitant to fight back against the Nephilim, fearing to hurt them unless they overtly did anything against God.

Nameless held out his hand, offering me the Seal of Solomon. "Give me what I seek. Help me save the world, Callie Penrose. Interrogate the Fallen for me."

Eae was frowning in disgust at Nameless, momentarily halting his struggle, on the verge of giving up.

With a deep breath, I slid the Seal of Solomon – the Ring of Aandaleeb – onto my finger. It fit perfectly.

Then my eyes flashed white. Or the church exploded in a heartbeat. I wasn't able to determine which, because I was suddenly in a fight for my very soul.

A cage match with Angels.

My Whispers rode with me into the fight, my own personal gang of monsters.

CHAPTER 56

*T*he first thing I consciously knew was that my soul was screaming.

Tears of liquid fire rolled down my cheeks. Even though I wasn't a physical presence here, I still resembled a human form, like a spirit. My soul was laid bare for the Fallen Angels to come and gobble me up.

I desperately gathered my Whispers around me like a blanket. "Protect me, and you shall earn your promised reward," I stammered, spiritual teeth clacking together at the frigid cold and agony that threatened to splinter my mind. They obeyed, and I immediately felt a slight relief in the onslaught.

Very slight.

Unseen power still slammed into me from all angles, wings of claw, bone, stone, and teeth shredding at my mental armor – my last line of protection from the flapping, swooping, stained Angels. Screams, roars, agony, fury, excitement boomed through the world of chrome-tinted glass I found myself standing in – like a tarnished orb with no corners. I could faintly see the church outside the prison, eerily calm in comparison to the chaos inside the Seal of Solomon.

A perfect, circular prison of madness. And the curved glass surface was etched with millions of warding symbols, all identical – as numerous as the stars in the sky.

"FREEDOM!" a voice snarled in a ragged roar. *"You promised US freedom, too!"*

"Not yet," I thought back at it, gritting my figurative teeth. "We have a show to put on, first. Give me something. Anything. Credible enough to convince them, or all of this is for nothing."

They couldn't comply fast enough, spouting out a torrent of names. Details. Locations. Plans. Schemes. They could almost taste their freedom, and would do anything to serve their savior…

Callie Penrose.

Even though their excited frenzy – their very existence – threatened to rip me to spiritual ribbons. I kept a tight leash on my armor, grunting against the wills of the Fallen Angels, because although they were trying to buy back their freedom, they were quite literally too powerful for me to remain for any determinable length of time in the same presence as them. They had been locked here for centuries, and the sweet smell of their freedom was only moments away.

Seconds to them. But they had grown impatient in their captivity.

Like blood thrown into a shark tank, the predators thrashed.

With a ragged breath, I focused on the church that I could still make out beyond the polished chrome glass. I left the Whispers inside with their long-lost Brothers, not sure if I would have the strength to keep bringing them back and forth with me.

The wind, screams, and gusts of power evaporated, and I was standing in the church again, panting heavily.

Nameless was staring at me incredulously, as if stunned that our plan had truly worked – that I had actually survived Round One. The rest of the room was dead silent. My ears almost popped at the sudden silence in comparison to when my mind had been inside the Seal. Nameless grabbed me by the shoulders, shaking me. "What did you learn?" he begged, eyes dancing with eager anticipation.

I recited the list of names and cities I had been given, not all of them, but enough of them. Kansas City had appeared to be the largest target for the Fallen Angels, but St. Louis and Boston had also been mentioned. Some of the names from Kansas City were vaguely familiar to me, but I didn't know much about the other cities.

Nameless' face turned radiant as he demanded more answers of me, tears streaming down his face as he stared through my eyes, trying to peek inside the Seal. "WHAT IS YOUR PLAN?" He screamed at the Fallen Angels, laughing victoriously.

I fell back into the Seal of Solomon, bringing his question with me. The Whispers surrounded me again, but I still grunted and gasped as the swarm of Fallen Angels battered my soul around like a punching bag. They hissed at Nameless' question, howling at me for their promised release.

But they answered the question.

"To cripple the Riders, to burn Eden, to swallow mankind!" I repeated their anguished answers, shouting them out into the Church, feeling like a two-way radio, torrents of power washing through me – first one direction, and then another. My voice was a distorted howl as I hovered between worlds.

"He shall rise!" I screamed, repeating another answer from one of the Fallen. My heartbeat skipped haphazardly for a few moments as I received a mental image of a humanoid figure on a black throne, roaring with his own triumph that seemed to mirror Nameless' in the church.

I knew that figure. I'd seen him before. When I had killed Johnathan, and then again when I killed Amira. But... who was he?

Nameless laughed a challenge, and I forced myself to slip back out of the Seal before there was nothing left of me. I pulled the Whispers back out with me and they immediately fled from my mind. The ring on my finger seeming to buzz as the Fallen Angels within realized I had taken away their chew toys. I ignored them. "And I will defeat him singlehandedly!" Nameless roared, eyes clouded with anticipation as he imagined the battle. "I shall be the most loved of *all* the Angels!"

The Seal of Solomon was a writhing fire of subarctic ice on my finger, slicing, burning, and grinding against my flesh until I was sure the very bone would freeze solid and my finger would fall off, a blackened, frostbitten digit.

I gritted my teeth, grunting as I withstood the torrents of power warring to break free from the Seal of Solomon.

Demanding I follow through with my promises to them.

I flicked my eyes about the church, locking gazes with each and every person, waiting...

Until each face was twisted with terror and despair.

Then I took a deep, shuddering breath, and managed a shaky smile as I attempted to send a message into the Seal of Solomon, rather than jumping back inside myself.

I was relieved that it worked.

It is almost time, I told the screaming, Fallen Angels. *I must neutralize your foes, first...* They screamed in exultation.

With supreme effort – hoping I was strong enough to survive it - I drew deeply from the Seal of Solomon on my finger, attempting to harness the arctic frost of the physical ring itself.

If I was the blood of King Solomon – as it so seemed – it should obey me.

Not just the beings inside, but the ring *itself*.

Scalding fire bloomed behind my eyes, and I heard gasps of disbelief in the church, and I felt more tears cascading down my cheeks at the sheer agony. I glanced up at some unknown instinct, and saw a silhouette watching me from the rafters of the church. I saw wings tucked neatly against the back of a large, four-legged feline, tail twitching absently. Glowing purple human eyes assessed me and gave me a very approving nod.

Phix. And a door creaked open in my mind, revealing sunshine and fields of flowers on the other side. I gasped as a memory slammed into me, making me blink hurriedly.

Yes. I remembered!

I immediately focused on the two Angels before me.

Nameless cackled, head thrown back, relishing in his victory over darkness.

I glanced at Eae to find his own eyes darkening, glaring at the Seal of Solomon on my finger.

Nameless' wings stretched wider as he lifted his arms up to Heaven, weeping. And like he had shrugged off a constraint, energy suddenly crackled around him, buzzing against me as if I stood before a live electric fence. He spun in slow circles, not seeing me, not seeing anyone as raw power washed over the church. He kept his hands out as he laughed, either unaware or relishing in it.

His eyes were storm clouds of power, lightning flashing in their depths as they grew darker – more violent – less restrained. Like he had turned his Angel volume knob up to eleven.

I noticed Eae's fists beginning to pulse, and the chains holding him began to rattle all on their own, steaming and vibrating against his skin. Still, he stared at my ring, his own eyes growing darker with fury, flashing with inner lightning. The Nephilim held fast, but their boots were sliding against the floor, as if magnetically repelled by Eae's loosening of power.

Between the two Angels and the Seal of Solomon on my finger, I panted, grinding my boots into the floor to maintain my footing as pews, detritus, and other trash began to whip about the church, swept up by the storm of power raging within.

There was quite literally an overabundance of epic shit going on.

The floorboards began to rattle in protest, walls cracked, and pews splintered into puffs of kindling like dandelions – the sound swallowed up by the piercing gong of the two Angels suddenly roaring like eternal horns of war.

The Seal of Solomon grew colder against my flesh, if that was possible, the beings inside furious at my delay in fulfilling my promise – and manic that I may have done something to change the ring itself, although they didn't seem to know what. Even though I wasn't inside the ring, they were affecting me, wearing me down. Just like I was somehow affecting them from outside the ring with whatever that bloom of pain behind my eyes had been.

Or it was a combination of everything.

Still, I waited, persevering through the agony with occasional grunts and hisses.

I blinked through watery eyes, assessing the rest of the church.

Olin and Beckett stared at me in awe as their hair whipped back and forth in the raging storm shredding through my church.

Rai stood before the two Templars, eyes squeezed shut, praying under her breath as she rocked back and forth in the chaos. I sensed movement behind them but disregarded it as I turned to Eae. His eyes were crackling with white lightning.

I turned to Nameless.

Between one moment and the next, his eyes shifted from leaden gray to black.

And my Darling and Dear boots – one pointed at Eae, and the other at Nameless – suddenly began pinching my toes like a son of a bitch.

The one pointing at Nameless.

Now, I told myself.

CHAPTER 57

I spun to the Templars, locking eyes with Olin and then Beckett. They recoiled at whatever look they saw on my face, but I didn't take it personally.

"Even Angels can Fall..." I shouted at the top of my lungs over the rampaging storm. "And even monsters can *rise*," I yelled louder.

Beckett nodded very slowly, possibly not even aware he had done it.

But Olin's face transformed into a snarl of outrage – that I would have the nerve to speak against an Angel about to vanquish evil once and for all. Then he seemed to notice Beckett's lack of support. Olin rounded on Beckett, flinging Rai to the ground as he redirected his rage at the source of the betrayal.

"How *dare* you!" he shouted at his acolyte, sensing Beckett's apparent weakened resolve. "You want to side with the monsters over *this*? After what they did to your *wife*? Let me show you what it's like to be a monster!" he shouted. And he raised a werewolf claw over his head.

Which was the exact moment a nightmare flew out from behind a pile of pews – a wall of white fur and inches-long black claws, with teeth as long as my fingers. I couldn't hear her roar, but to abruptly see a greater than ten-foot-tall polar bear with built-in human slicers on her paws suddenly appear out of nowhere, Olin and Beckett both froze for a fraction of a second.

Beckett drew his gun and unloaded it on Claire when it became clear he was her target.

Then Clairebear slammed into Beckett, ignoring the bullets as she sliced into his stomach in a spray of crimson blood before the force of her mass tore him clear of Olin – right before the werewolf's claws slashed through now-empty air. The two smashed through another pile of debris and didn't get up, Claire draped over Beckett, blood staining her fur.

Claire had disobeyed me, too, showing up in time to kill Beckett.

My cheeks felt cold from all the wind as Olin howled in defeat, partially shifted, now. Then he fled, forgetting all about Rai who was sobbing on the floor, curled up in a tight ball.

Stop swatting insects and release us! One of the Fallen Angels bellowed, somehow speaking to me from within the Seal of Solomon, the pulse of raw power making me see stars.

I nodded stiffly. *I'm trying! You're not strong enough to stand against him as you are, now. I must weaken him!*

They railed against the prison in protest, and I felt a part of me being tugged back in. As if whatever I had done to the ring had made our connection a two-way street, not me subjugating it completely.

We are Legion! One Brother is nothing!

But we didn't have just one Angel to worry about. We had two.

Only seconds had passed since Nameless' eyes had blackened and my boots had pinched.

The time to truly open up the Seal of Solomon was now. I couldn't maintain my tentative hold much longer or else I would be consumed.

I gasped as one of the imprisoned Fallen Angels suddenly growled in a voice I hadn't ever heard from the others.

Your games take too long.

I don't know how I knew, but I was certain it was the Silent Emo Angel. Even though he wasn't a physical entity, he suddenly raked at my soul with fiery bone claws, breaking his talons and snapping his finger bones as he threw every fiber of his being into the attack on the Seal of Solomon, and by default, on *me*.

He had seen through my ploy.

I called upon my Silvers with the greatest *need* I could imagine, relinquishing some of my control on the Seal of Solomon, knowing I couldn't do this alone, yet until only moments ago, having been unsure I had *any* allies. Who the enemy truly was.

Or if I instead had multiple *enemies*.

Eae now shone before me like a golden beacon, illuminated in his own sunbeam – pointedly *not* Fallen.

The Emo Angel continued to tear at my mind in the prison, roaring.

Nameless still did his Unholy twirl thing.

My Silver blade of power struck the chains strapped over Eae, shattering them like glass. Fragments of molten metal designed to restrain an Angel struck the Nephilim, burning their faces or cracking bones. They screamed as Eae slammed into them, bowling them out of the way like dolls, sending them flying into the depths of the church as he roared like a lion of God.

I reached out and grabbed Nameless' wings since he had his back turned to me. He spun instinctively, lashing out with his hands to knock me clear. Except they were no longer hands.

His claws slashed across the back of my hands, flashing with fire and a metallic scraping sound where he had made contact, spilling my blood onto the floor.

He stared down at his long black claws in confusion. They were spattered with silver droplets.

Not caring about my sliced hands, I stared down in horror at the Seal of Solomon. A charred line bisected the symbol emblazoned atop the signet ring, breaking the protective ward.

Mr. Emo Angel had used the fragment of time before I could react to break free of his prison.

A black fog zipped up into the air, out of my reach as I frantically rubbed my bloody thumb over the scored line on the protective symbol, hoping that Nameless' claw hadn't damaged the actual metal too greatly. I glanced down at it and let out a stunted breath of relief. Nameless' claw had only scratched and charred it, not destroyed it entirely. It was still intact but had been momentarily broken enough to let out the once-silent Emo Angel. Nameless hadn't been strong enough to permanently damage the seal, only to score a charred line across it.

Essentially, a Fallen Angel had helped another Fallen Angel bust out of Fort Solomon.

And the exhausted Warden Callie Penrose only had time to nail the door back into place – by rubbing off the sooty line – before the rest could escape. The Fallen Angels still trapped within screamed as they rushed toward the weakness in their prison.

I panted in relief when they slammed instead into the prison wall, not breaking free.

But I knew my original plan had officially gone to shit. I had discovered which of the Angels was trustworthy but had accidentally given the bad one an ally.

And I was too exhausted – too unfamiliar with this strange ability of mine – to do anything about the escaped Angel, the black fog.

I knew that as much power as the Seal of Solomon wielded, I was also the weakest link. To use it, I had to wear it. But if I didn't wear it, it was just an impenetrable prison again. As long as that symbol was intact.

I made my decision and yanked it off my finger, panting. The sensation of Fallen Angels railing against my mind abruptly ceased, and the silence in the church felt suddenly oppressive in comparison. I let out a sigh of relief, but it was short-lived as I glanced up to see the black cloud hovering above me.

It regarded Nameless standing frozen beside me. Eae was halfway to us, as if running, but stuck in mid-stride. I quickly realized that *no one* around me moved. Only the fog and me.

The fog chuckled, seeming to inspect his new Brother, Nameless. "You allowed an Angel to Fall, daughter of Solomon. But do you dare try to put the cursed ring back on after he almost broke it?" He drifted back and forth for a moment, as if pacing, or stretching.

An unbidden thought, as clear as a struck bell, bubbled out of my mouth, making me shiver.

"Samael…" I whispered, not knowing how I knew, or where it had come from. But I did know he was powerful. A Fallen Archangel.

He froze for a moment before he began to roil in a slow, circling cloud. "I am He…"

"What… will you do, now?" I whispered, my mind racing. I had done this. Holy Hell.

I'd been so close to trapping Nameless into the ring, locking away his selfish pride into the Seal of Solomon. But I had been too weak to hold him, and as he had recoiled, I'd let him damage the ring – the prison.

I had known it was the only way to take an Angel out. I couldn't *kill* an Angel without risking Armageddon. The only option left to me had been to deceive everyone, to try and find out if Nameless or Eae was corrupt – which of the two was beyond salvation – and then trap that Angel where he could no longer hurt anyone.

Inside the Seal of Solomon, that they had both coveted.

Instead I had driven us into a cozy, quaint little town by the name of FUBAR – or *Fucked Up Beyond All Recognition*, as the locals lovingly called it.

"You impressed me," Samael murmured. "To meet one with such adept skills at deceit, and then witness them using that gift against the *Princes* of deceit…" he truly did sound amazed. "Perhaps we will cross paths again one day, in the dried husk that will be the Garden of Eden… I thought I was the deceiver, but it seems you've bitten from the Apple itself. Eve would be proud…" Then he drifted away, off into the night through a crack in the window high above.

My eyes were blurry with tears, horrified at my failure. I wiped them away, shaking my head, wondering if I had just doomed us all.

CHAPTER 58

*E*verything whipped back to normal speed, and Nameless was still roaring in outrage that his hands were now claws. Eae was suddenly beside me, staring up at the window in horror.

He had noticed Samael, too.

Nameless finally spun to see us, face contorted with a wild darkness of despair. Without thinking, I reached out and grabbed him by the face. His flesh instantly sizzled beneath my touch, and I was startled to realize that my hands were coated in liquid silver, dripping off to splash onto the ground and run down my hands and forearms.

I gritted my teeth as Nameless screamed in defiance, his black eyes dancing with agony, shame, fury – a truly diverse cascade of emotions, refusing to accept what he had become.

A Fallen Angel.

And he currently couldn't move – as if my touch had frozen him.

"LOCK HIM AWAY IN THE RING! HE'S FALLEN!!" Eae screamed beside me, his wings tucked around his body like armor. "I'll hold him while you put it back on!" he shouted in alarm as soon as he realized the Seal of Solomon lay at my feet where I had dropped it at one point.

Eae tried to grab onto Nameless in a bear hug and was promptly thrown across the length of the church by an unseen force, striking the opposite wall about a dozen feet off the ground.

I stepped down on the ring, keeping it under my boot as I gripped Nameless, staring into his black eyes as my own blazed with white fire to battle those depths. Bolts of black lightning slammed into my hands, trying to knock them free. But even as exhausted as I was, I barely felt them. I was on the verge of passing out, yet the strikes of black lightning struck no harder than someone tapping me on the shoulder with a forceful finger.

I didn't dare try to put the ring back on as I would have had to release my grip on Nameless to do so. I knew without a doubt that I couldn't hold back the imprisoned Fallen Angels in my current state. I was too weakened from my ordeal. They would overwhelm me and possibly *all* break free, not even counting that the ring was potentially damaged and might not be able to withstand their combined offensive.

But something about me had changed. I was able to withstand Nameless' mental thrashing, despite what it had done to Eae after only a half a second of contact.

Nameless screamed as liquid silver began to encase his body like a dipped statue, the liquid pouring out of my fingers somehow. If that was my blood, I was going to be bone dry in about ten seconds, but rather than draining me...

I began to feel stronger. As if *I* was draining *Nameless*.

My face still dripped with tears as I stared through blurry eyes, my face a cold, wet mask, like mud. I closed my eyes, rather than trying to blink through the tears, or risking releasing a hand to wipe them away.

I focused on what I had seen before Nameless' eyes had turned black and my boots had alerted me that he'd Fallen. He had gone on and on about him *singlehandedly* vanquishing the demons, using a lot of *I*, and *me* statements. Hubris. Had that been the cause of his Fall? Because my boots hadn't told me he was Fallen until after all of that, when his eyes had finally turned black.

It had been a slow descent from Grace. A calculated walk down a path of good intentions.

Part of me wanted to shed a tear at that, but I was kind of already unintentionally doing that.

I recalled what Nameless had hinted at about my powers, how I was the only one strong enough to use the Seal of Solomon, that it was tied to my powers and my potential relation to King Solomon. But I didn't dare try the ring again, so what did that leave me?

267

The Silver liquid currently pouring out of my hands looked to be part of the Silvers.

But I hadn't known if I could trust them either, which was why I hadn't spoken with that odd version of myself. I'd only used them to break Eae's chains.

I hadn't even known if I could truly trust the Whispers – accepting the possibility that some of those Angelic voices might actually be Fallen Angels. But when I'd first noticed the ring in my pocket while bonding with Phix, everything had changed, and I'd decided to beat the Angels – Fallen or otherwise – at their own game. Because I had sensed the sudden change in their tone – that I was possibly hearing Whispers from *inside* the ring I had just found in my pocket. Or that merely having the ring on my person had possibly attracted the wrong sorts of Angels, suddenly.

I had misled them, promising them *release* for helping me fight tonight.

And the only way to keep that secret from them had been to ask Phix to trick my own mind. To tell her my plan, and for her to then hide it from me. To let me believe and justify my actions as I skipped down a dark path, pretending to fall into Nameless' plan.

Until I had wrought *despair* upon those who knew me. And then without warning noticed Phix hanging out in the rafters of the church.

Phix had done a good job, because until I saw the despair on everyone's faces tonight, I hadn't been able to truly remember the details of my plan, which had been *part and parcel* of my design. She'd said I would need a talisman to snap back out of her block.

My mind finally my own again, I had intended to trap whichever Angel was bad – Eae or Nameless – into the Seal of Solomon. But that path was now closed to me.

I had only the Silvers to rely upon, and they seemed to be doing a fairly good job of restraining Nameless as I felt him thrash beneath my fingers like a struggling snake.

But my grip was firm enough.

With no other idea at hand, I thought back on the Seal of Solomon, how Nameless had scored it enough for Samael to break free. But... wiping my bloody thumb across it had strengthened it sufficiently to keep the others from breaking free.

My bloody thumb.

The blood currently trapping Nameless...

Silver blood.

I suddenly surged against Nameless, forcing more of the liquid silver out of me. Judging by his scream, it worked. I opened my eyes, blinking furiously through the blur to see the silver liquid practically racing over his entire body.

"You have Fallen from grace..." My voice rang out like a soft chime and I felt Nameless stiffen involuntarily. He redoubled his efforts to break free as the silver reached his bare feet.

Nameless roared – a pained, anguished, humiliated sound this time.

"You never once mentioned God," I told him. "It was always *I*, or *me*. You lost your way at some point, too focused on your goal that you lost perspective. You forgot *why*. Your quest for personal fame... to be the most loved of all the Angels brought you to the land of Despair, and now you are mine," I called out in another soft breath that struck like a wind chime.

A burst of wind erupted from Nameless and latched onto my thumb like a coiled snake. The silver statue I held in my hands was suddenly devoid of life.

I gasped at the sudden icy sensation searing into my thumb, and collapsed to my knees.

I glanced down to see a whirling shadow circling my finger like a cyclone.

A ring of smoke.

A Fallen Angel.

What have you done to me? a voice wailed in the back of my mind.

My finger throbbed faintly, but nothing else. Nameless. I was hearing Nameless.

I didn't mean to Fall! I was trying to get intelligence! To break them all! What have I become? His voice trailed off as if he was fleeing deeper inside me.

"You did this to yourself," I told him sadly. He drifted away, the frigid cold from the shadow ring growing more bearable as he retreated from my accusation.

She lied to us! Tricked us! How? The Whispers suddenly wailed, oddly silent until now, waiting until I was finished swatting down the other Angels and possibly – hopefully – weakened.

I released the statue and held up my dripping silver hands, silencing them.

"I promised to *release* you... Unless you prefer to be bound," I said, holding out my thumb with the swirling ring of shadows, "I suggest you take the offer. I have nine other fingers and I didn't bring my patience with me tonight," I hissed at them.

They fled, and Pastor Pillow and Sister Sheets hit me with the Sleep Sermon, knocking me unconscious as I collapsed like a sack of potatoes.

CHAPTER 59

I opened my eyes as I felt a warm presence purring beside me. Gentle hands carefully lifted me slightly – pausing to acknowledge the sudden change in pitch of the purr before settling me back down into a more comfortable position. I blinked back crusted eyelids, my heart racing.

I felt like a wet rag.

I wiped at my eyes with my sleeves to see Eae cradling my head in his lap, brushing my hair with his thumb as he smiled down at me wonderingly. Phix was nestled up beside me, purring.

The Nephilim all knelt before us in a ring, heads down, praying softly in a soothing hum.

Rai stared at me from a few paces away, standing alone, weeping from bloodshot eyes. She gasped, lifting a hand to her mouth as I smiled at her. "I'm sorry, Rai... I never intended to give you up. Not really," I breathed, but she seemed to have heard me.

Claire – sans clothes, of course – and Beckett stood side by side, shaking their heads absently. Beckett's stomach was covered in blood, but he looked entirely fine. Well, his eyes were troubled, and he averted them when I looked into them. "I'm... sorry, Callie," he breathed, shoulders shaking slightly.

I nodded but didn't offer comment.

Claire glanced at Beckett with a tired smile. "I saw what that bastard was about to do, turning Beckett into a werewolf against his will," she growled. "I figured I would turn him, first. Knew his gun wouldn't bother me thanks to this," she said, shaking out the bracelet she had gotten from Darling and Dear. "Hurt like hell, though," she complained.

I realized she was absently fidgeting with something between her fingers. She noticed my attention and held it up for me to see a silver strip. Then she bent it to form a circle, shaking her head in disbelief.

"What is it?" I asked, eyes shifting to the giant silver statue of Angel standing before us like an uninvited party guest. I hid my shiver as Claire spoke. "Um… I think it's your tears. Or blood. Or your holy lady juice." Then she blushed. "Well, not *that*, but something from inside you," she said urgently, pointing at the floor.

I glanced down and gasped. The floor all around me was coated in silver. Like someone had spilled molten metal on the ground to let it harden. It wasn't especially thick, but it didn't scrape off either as I scuffed at it with my heel.

Seeing all that silver, I gasped, hands suddenly reaching out for the Seal of Solomon. I realized it was already in my hand and lifted it, inspecting it in relief.

I blinked, scrubbing my sleeves at my eyes again.

The two interwoven triangles were now entirely whole. In fact, the ring looked as if it had only been made minutes before – stronger than it had ever been. There wasn't even a hint of the scored line that had freed Samael.

I hissed instinctively as I noticed the shifting shadow circling my thumb in an eternal rotation.

"Easy, Callie. It's okay. He can't hurt you." Eae said, looking down at me. He didn't sound particularly appeased by this statement, but more nervous than ever. That I had managed to trap an Angel on my thumb – Fallen or not – was not good table conversation.

I nodded shakily, then relaxed my shoulders, breathing deeply for a few moments as I stared at the Nephilim still kneeling before us. Then I frowned. Were they praying for forgiveness? To Eae? Or… to me?

The woman who had bound an Angel – their old boss – on her finger.

I looked up at Eae. "What have I done?" I whispered.

"I think… you just trapped an Angel on your finger…" he whispered. He studied me for a time, cocking his head pensively. That was when I realized

I still had my mind locked down for protection. Maybe it had been instinctual upon waking up and seeing him nearby. I had done it repeatedly for days, now. With great effort, I uncurled my figurative fingers from the ledge and I opened up my mind, which was hard after clamping it down for so long.

He gasped, eyes wide. "It... that whole thing... was a *setup?*" he breathed. "That's not *possible!*"

I smiled weakly, forcing myself to sit up. "They say the greatest trick the devil ever pulled was convincing the world he didn't exist. I always was a competitive little shit. Wanted to see if I could do one better than old Lucifer. Trick the devil. Or... *a* devil." I turned to glance at him over my shoulder. "In the spirit of honesty, I wasn't sure if it would end up being you or Nameless locked away... But I didn't know it would be on my finger," I said, hefting the Seal of Solomon in my palm. "I thought I would trap one of you in here."

He stared at me as if I had just admitted to plucking Angel wings in my spare time. Maybe I had. "But... the Whispers," he said, shaking his head. "They would have seen through it."

Phix lifted her head, acknowledging Eae with her intense purple eyes. Her purr was like a not so humble brag, now.

I smiled at her. "That was why I had to even lie to myself. I had a... friend help me deceive myself. Phix," I explained.

Phix grinned widely. "The Whispers are now Callie's bitches," she said. Then she reached out with one of her paws to bat around a loose piece of silver on the ground.

I was so amused by this that I didn't realize Claire had walked up to me and was now staring down at me, her face warring between anger, fear, and relief. "Not cool, bitch. How did you know I wouldn't listen to you?"

I smiled proudly, a sob escaping my lips as I remembered seeing her hiding in the shadows, that surprising sense of unconditional love. "You told me," I whispered, reaching up to grasp her hand and squeeze. "You're my conscience. You were the one person I knew I could always trust, even though I couldn't trust myself to remember it."

She squeezed back, shaking her head with a faint smile. "You're very scary, Callie."

"I love you too, honey," I managed, before she wrapped me up in a hug, lifting me to my feet.

"I'll always be there for you, Callie. Especially when you use a legendary monster to wipe your mind to pretend to turn evil for a little while. I'm your Guardian Ang—" she cut off abruptly, glancing at the silver statue, "well, your spirit animal. Your personal guard bear."

I smiled, squeezing her close as I inhaled deeply. It felt so nice to not hold up my shield any longer. The Whispers were gone, for now. I knew I hadn't permanently blocked them, but I had scared them off enough to rethink their plan – whoever they had been.

I turned to Eae. "The Whispers... is there any way to find out who they really are? Will they change as I go to different places? Like radio stations picking up different channels?"

Eae thought about it. "We'll have to test it out. Maybe you and I could practice. We can stand a small distance apart and try to converse. If it works, you should hear me as a Whisper."

Claire shivered at the idea, shaking her head. She squeezed me one last time before walking back to Beckett and speaking to him in low tones. Beckett Killian, brief Templar, now shifter bear. I wondered if I could ever trust him again. He had seen what good intentions led to, if on a much grander scale, and I hoped the lesson had been driven home.

Because Olin was still out there and would need to be put down at some point.

I turned as Rai cleared her throat behind me. "I would have done it," she said, eyes downcast. "I believed you and would have done it. Although... I like this a lot better," she whispered.

I smiled. "I want you to do something much harder. This was just the tryout." Her face paled and she looked up sharply in disbelief. "I want you to *live*. To make my dad happy for as long as you can." She immediately began to cry in relief, hands jerking up to cover her mouth and wipe at her eyes. I let her go for a second, enjoying her sudden relief. "But to do that, you need to first come clean with him..." I warned. "Tell him everything. Hold nothing back. His ignorance puts him in danger." I smiled. "I think he'll appreciate the real you a lot better," I said, pointedly sweeping my eyes over her younger body.

Her exuberant grin was contagious, and I didn't have time to prepare for her sudden hug. Then she held me at arms' length, wiping my cheek with a thumb as she smiled at me, crying. "Thank you, Callie. Your mother would be proud…" Then she kissed me on the forehead and ran through the door ahead of us, laughing jubilantly.

I felt a heavy presence shove against my hip lightly and looked down to see Phix supporting me. I shook my head in wonder, placing my hand on her back and allowing her and Eae to guide me out of the church.

Eae must have already given commands to the Nephilim, because they didn't follow, and he didn't seem concerned about them. Judging by the look he gave them before we opened the door leading outside, I was pretty sure their new Daddy had put them in their place.

And put them on notice.

I took a deep breath of the damp night air, staring out at the crescent moon hanging in the distance through the low-hanging clouds.

A reflection made me glance up at a building across the street, and I froze, breath catching. Two armored… knights with spear and sword stood facing me from the rooftop. When I say armored, I mean full-on jousting armor with helmets, shoulder pauldrons, and everything.

One was gold.

One was silver.

They dipped their heads respectfully at me. Not knowing what else to do, I dipped my head right back.

Eae sniffed at the air suddenly, body tensing. I looked up at him to see if he had noticed our guests. But he wasn't looking at that. He was questing about with his nose, tracking something.

"What is it?" I asked warily.

He smiled absently. "I do not know. Something… beautiful…" he said, sounding annoyed that he couldn't define it. "But it's gone now." He glanced at me suspiciously.

I shrugged, waiting until he looked away before discreetly glancing at the opposite rooftop again. But my beautiful knights were gone.

"I could use a little beautiful after tonight…" I told Eae, leading my two handlers down the steps. A black taxi pulled up to the curb as we reached the bottom, and Roland climbed out. He tossed a bag out of the car, freeing his hands as he saw us.

"Callie…" he said, not looking at me. As if checking to see if I was in immediate danger.

"Vampire," Eae said flatly.

"You're trespassing. This is my church," Roland replied, ignoring Phix entirely – which judging by her suddenly lashing tail, she didn't find acceptable.

"Relax, Roland. We're all friends. And *technically*, it's *my* church."

He continued to stare at Eae for a moment longer before turning to me, not appreciating my technicality. He gasped as he noticed my face. "What *happened* to you?" he practically shouted.

"It's my lady juice," I said, shrugging, hoping to get a rise out of him.

He grimaced at that, but shook his head. "No, you look older—"

I lifted my head to the sky and screamed as loud as possible, ignoring Phix's sudden coughing fit as she battled an Egyptian hairball.

CHAPTER 60

*N*ot knowing where else to go, Eae had agreed to meet us back at Abundant Angel Catholic Church – to the training floor beneath – in a few hours. We needed somewhere safe, secluded, and private to catch Roland up, and I knew Arthur could sneak us in. Even though Roland was a vampire, now, he had an amulet that let him step foot on hallowed ground.

Eae had wanted to give his new Nephilim some commands before he left them unattended.

I had asked after the Nephilim – especially Alyksandre and Kevin – but Eae had only smiled, not sharing my concern about their absence during the fight. Apparently, he'd sought them out after our talk at the warehouse and found them in prayer – troubled over Nameless' plan, but not knowing what they could do since they couldn't directly stand up against their boss. Eae had answered their prayers by… adopting them and sending them to terrorize the rest of the Templars during my knock-out brawl at the church. Leaving him free to bear witness to my confrontation with Nameless.

Before he met back up with us, he wanted to speak with Alyksandre and Kevin, and give them very strict orders for the Nephilim from the church. Sorting the factual wheat from the chaff.

Olin and the Templars had left town, unsurprisingly.

Eae now sat before us beneath Abundant Angel, sipping green tea as we caught Roland up on the night's events. My old mentor studied Eae off and on, looking amazed to meet a real Angel. The feeling had left me quite a while ago, but I didn't rain on his parade. Once finished, he began speaking about his trip to Italy.

But I was too tired to pay attention for long, and actually dozed off at one point.

I dreamed of my silver tears, recalling another dream I'd had with Nate. Because I'd worn a bandage over my eyes and had also had silver tears. Had it been a premonition of some kind? A warning? What did it mean?

And Samael being free...

I had expected that to be practically world-ending, but Eae – although definitely concerned about it – let me know that it would be quite some time before the Fallen Archangel was capable enough to do anything more than terrorize the neighborhood dogs, let alone find a body strong enough to contain him.

And he had been free before. Many demons were free, apparently, and since Eae was the Demon Thwarter, I kind of took his word for it. He seemed to be very familiar with it all and promised me that we had time.

Perhaps I could bond Samael to my finger like I had with Nameless. Thinking of that ring of smoke around my finger, though, was horrifying. The tip of my thumb was constantly cold to the touch, even when the rest of my fingers were warm, which was unnerving. Maybe it was his halo.

But he wasn't answering my calls, even though I was his landlord, now.

Eae had reassured me that the shadow ring held absolutely no power over me, but that he wanted to do a longer study of the statue we had left behind in the center of Roland's church. It would probably need to be moved at one point, and Eae was adamant that I be there when they tried.

Just in case.

I woke to Roland shaking me with a smile on his face. "We have company," he said with a grin. I sat up, wiping my face. I had been drooling and my hair was matted with both silver and probably spittle. I wiped my chin, staring down at my hand nervously, but let out a relieved breath. No silver drool. That would have been creepy.

A heavy thump made me snap my head up to see a large beefy man standing a safe distance away from me, grinning like an idiot.

"Meatball!" I shouted, grinning from ear-to-ear. Then my smile faltered. "Wait, am I in trouble for being down here?" I asked warily.

He rolled his eyes. "Get over here, Girlie Penflower," he muttered, holding out his arms. I ran over to him, throwing my arms around him – well, trying to. He was a big, hairy Italian Shepherd, and he was the one in charge of running the other Shepherds in Rome.

"I love the smell of marinara after a nap," I said, squeezing him tightly.

He grumbled unhappily, but I could tell he was still smiling.

He finally held me back and I realized Arthur was standing a few paces away, smiling. Then it hit me. "You're here to train Arthur?" He nodded. "Kick ass!" I hooted.

He growled at my language, but the sound cut off into a gasp as his eyes widened.

"Good lord, woman! Why do you look so old?"

I stepped back and punched him in the diaphragm, nodding satisfactorily as I knocked his breath away, leaving him wheezing in surprise at the sudden attack. Roland roared with laughter and Phix jumped to her feet arching her back with a hiss at the sudden commotion.

Arthur's eyes widened, apparently not having noticed the Sphinx until that moment.

I calmly turned and walked back into the sleeping area, deciding I was going to take a very long nap. And let the bravest of them dare to try waking me before I was good and ready.

But I heard the familiar padding of feet behind me and knew that they would have to get through Phix first.

CHAPTER 61

*I*t had been a week since the christening of Roland's Church. I had begrudgingly let him choose the new name.

I sat on a bench in a seedy part of town, enjoying the light rain. Almost like déjà vu.

"What are we doing here again?" Nate asked in a curious voice. "Strange place for a date."

I frowned. "This isn't a date, Nate. I'm… broken inside. Not really dating material."

He snorted. "We're *all* broken inside, Callie," he said, dismissing my concern. "I've found the secret is to find the person with the glue."

I smiled at his strange solution, turning to look at him. "Excuse me?"

He nodded, soaked hair swinging at the motion. Neither of us had brought an umbrella, and it had turned into almost a contest of wills – who would break first and suggest heading inside. And it sure as hell wasn't going to be me who broke first.

"You see," he explained, "we're all broken wretches inside, trying to glue our own pieces back together, to become what we always thought we were supposed to be. But we have the wrong glue," he said, turning to wink at me. He turned back to the night, smiling to himself. "The reason so many people fail is because they don't understand that somewhere out there in the world is another broken wretch with the *right* glue. She just doesn't know it because *her* glue didn't work for *her*, just like *his* glue didn't work for *him*." He let that sink in for a moment, grinning at nothing in particular as he continued to stare ahead. "The glue you have inside you is to help put someone *else* back together, not yourself. Chances are, that person probably has the glue *you* need." He laughed suddenly – a bold, challenging sound thrown at the world in general like a glove marking a duel. "Everyone is holding the wrong glue." Then he began laughing, wiping water out of his eyes.

I blinked at him. "That's... ridiculous. We all have glue, but it's not the right glue? You mean people can't fix themselves? I refuse to believe that," I said, folding my arms.

Nate held up a hand. "We can put the pieces in the right places on our own, but without the right glue, it might break again someday. Maybe even worse than before. But with the *right* glue, it will never break again." He shot me a serious look. "Never ever break. It's the balance. Those who choose to only use their own glue don't ever understand that they could be so much more if they found the right partner... the right glue." He sighed. "Like someone claiming they are the best roof maker in the world because the thatch roof they made hasn't leaked. Yet." He shrugged easily, tucking his hands behind his head and leaning back, closing his eyes. "To everyone with a tile roof, his boasts sound ridiculous." Silence stretched between us before he said, "It's just a theory. But I'm usually right."

I rolled my eyes but couldn't hold back my grin. I studied him for a few moments, remembering my dream as I watched accumulated rain drip off his stubbled chin to splash against his throat before rolling down under his collar. I remembered Phix's conversation about Hope and Despair, and my strange dream with Nate in that other place...

I had ordered a book online yesterday but wasn't sure if I would ever give it to him.

A Tale of Two Cities. Like Nate's comment from the strange dream.

But if my dream had just been a normal dream, I would look like an idiot when I tried to explain why I had bought it for him. But if he *had* really shared my dream...

Well, I didn't know what to do about that, either.

Because I was still putting my pieces together, trying to figure out what my picture was going to look like. Apparently, I lacked the right glue.

I quickly turned away to study the night. "An idiotic... romantic theory," I admitted, smiling.

"Speaking of idiotic," he said, opening his eyes. "Why am I holding your stuffed unicorn again?" he asked, patting the drenched unicorn in his lap.

When I didn't immediately answer, he turned to look at me and my breath caught at the sudden intensity in his eyes. It was just how he looked at people sometimes, but it felt like an accusation after fantasizing about the water on his skin. I pointed at the small huddle of thugs loitering against a brick wall across the street. "Hold it up so they can't miss it, and then stand up," I told him, smiling in anticipation.

He frowned at me curiously, but finally complied. He waved the stuffed animal at them, then stood up from the bench. I joined him, straightening my jacket as I watched the thugs.

As if it had been a gunshot, they took off at a dead run, screaming and shouting in a panicked stampede.

Nate turned to me, bewildered. Then I was running after the thugs. "Now, you hopeless romantic, let's go hunt down some Freaks!" I shouted back at him.

And we ran off into the night, chasing down shrieking monsters, laughing, and thinking about the right glue. And maybe even some dreams.

I made my decision to mail the damned book. Let the pieces fall where they may.

~

~

*allie Penrose returns in **SINNER**... Turn the page for a sample! Or **get the book ONLINE!***

SAMPLE: SINNER (FEATHERS AND FIRE # 5)

*R*oland glared at me, actually grinding his teeth as he shook his head in the morning darkness. "No, Callie."

"What? I thought you might need it," I said in a sweet tone, casually sweeping the streets with my eyes, not paying particular attention to the lights in the bakery shop before us. Two young men sat at a table inside, but after a brief look at us through the window, they resumed their conversation. *Only two*, I thought to myself angrily, using my peripheral vision to keep tabs on them as I readjusted my light jacket absently.

We had just climbed out of my truck, prepared to take out the trio of werewolves I had tracked to this bakery. With the local wolves having fled town a few weeks ago, these three had decided they could make a name for themselves and start a new pack. But these frat-boy werewolves were rogues, feral, or just plain stupid, because I suspected them of abducting and murdering young women on their way home from the local bars.

And that didn't sit well with the local Shepherd – the supernatural sheriff for the Vatican.

Or me, the assistant extraordinaire to the Holy Hitman.

"Just because I was injured a few weeks ago doesn't mean I need a walk-er," he seethed, pointing at the contraption I had pulled out of the back of my pickup truck.

I shrugged, feigning surprised hurt. "I was just trying to be considerate. We *are* going after wolves again." I pointed at the walker. "It even has spurs. Maybe you can use them as a weapon or something." He grimaced at the bad duct tape job I had made of attaching the cowboy spurs. I had found the spurs in the same antique shop as the walker yesterday and had known they were meant to go together, for this exact purpose.

"There are dog toys in the basket," he growled even lower. "You're mocking both my injury and the task ahead."

I placed my hand against my chest. "I would *never*."

"We'll talk about this later," he muttered. His eyes flickered over the bakery, and then down the street, making sure we were alone. It was just before sunrise in the Westport district of Kansas City, and it was Saturday, so we didn't have to worry about commuters seeing us on their way to work. The only risk was the occasional walk-of-shame victim stumbling down the street in heels, clubbing clothes, and smudged makeup. But those majestic beasts were elusive, fickle creatures, and apparently hadn't finished sleeping off their bad decisions.

Leaving us all alone. Perfect.

Roland deftly sliced open his palm with a blade, letting his blood fall to the pavement. He pocketed the blade, grasped the walker in front of him, and then stumbled into direct view of the bakery, holding up his bleeding hand. I darted after him, a look of horror on my face. The two wolves inside glanced up, and then froze as they saw his crimson-stained hand.

The blood had the desired effect on the frat-wolves.

The two of them burst out the front door of the shop, eyes excited as they quickly realized the injured man and young woman before them were the only people in sight. They were true bros in every sense of the word, wearing polo shirts with popped collars, skinny jeans, and trendy boat shoes. The one in front was tall and scrawny with dark brown hair and a long, gaunt face. He looked starved, or as if he hadn't hit puberty yet, waiting for that pubescent shot of testosterone that made men, men – or as so many seemed to think.

But the other was short and pudgy, with short, light blonde hair. He looked like a wrestler – a scrapper. I bit back a grin as an idle thought crossed my mind. His choice of pants made his legs look like sausage links. I wondered where the supposed third wolf was – the handsome Hispanic kid, as he had been described. I had visited each bar where the victims had last been seen, and every bartender had remembered three men leaving shortly after each victim left the bar. One bartender had been the victim of Mr. Pudgy's unwelcome flirtations, and had remembered him mentioning they could pick up fresh croissants in the morning at a bakery right next to his place… but he knew just the way to make her burn off those extra calories ahead of time.

She had instantly thrown cold water at his face, and several of the patrons had rushed him out of the bar, lucky for her. He was a dead ringer for her description. As was the scarecrow. But not the third man. Did one of them own the bakery?

"Come inside, Sir," the tall one said, taking a step closer. "We'll get you taken care of in a jiffy." His eyes latched onto the walker, and he somehow managed not to lick his lips at his luck.

"You're always hurting yourself, Grandpa. Let them help you, and then we can go get your coffee."

The pudgy one smiled – to my eyes, a very wicked, hungry smile. "We have coffee inside."

Roland shot them a thankful smile, latched onto his walker, and began hobbling closer to the frat-wolves. "Such kind words, my boy. Thank you. At least *some* of today's youth gives a damn about their elders," he said, shooting an accusing look my way. "My granddaughter could learn a lot from you fine, young men." I averted my eyes sheepishly for the wolves, but it was really so that I didn't kick Roland in the ankle. Bastard. He continued shuffling closer to them with pained steps, playing his part perfectly.

Their faces smiled at me, but their eyes raped me.

There's a difference between a look of honest appreciation and one of dark fantasies, and most girls can sense the difference in an instant, no matter how discreet the boy thinks they are being. It's all in the eyes. These two self-proclaimed badasses looked hungry, and I could tell they considered themselves untouchable.

Whoopsies. Because little did they know, death had arrived this morning, and she fancied a fresh croissant.

I flashed them a shy smile, shifting from foot to foot uncertainly, as if appreciating their personal interest as well as their obvious concern for my grandfather.

The chubby one held the door open, and the taller one stepped through, encouraging Roland to follow. He did so at a glacial pace. The chubby one motioned me closer with a greasy smile that he no doubt thought made him appear handsome. I smiled back at him, forcing a blush to my cheeks as I let my fingers fidget nervously at my hips, unconsciously straightening my shirt at his attention. He sucked in his gut as I neared, puffing out his chest self-importantly.

I took one step inside the door to find Roland approaching the glass display case of pastries, which was illuminated from within by a fluorescent bulb. The room smelled like a new pot of coffee and freshly baked goods. I craned my neck while inhaling deeply for show, using the motion to scan the room. I spotted the light switch on the wall to my left, and managed not to smile. The display case provided more than enough light for this. As if reading my mind, Roland stumbled over his walker and the skinnier wolf darted forward to help him. I hit the light switch beside me, instantly dimming the room so that anyone outside would have a hard time seeing exactly what I was about to do.

Castrating two feral dogs.

I felt a brief pulse of magic, and the walker broke apart, revealing Roland clutching a spur-tipped aluminum baton in each hand. He spun them in his wrists, bringing them up high, and then down onto the taller man's collarbone with a loud *crack*. The boy shrieked and dropped to the ground. I spun, ready to take out the pudgy puppy, but was suddenly yanked out of the way by a thin tendril of magic from behind. I skidded on my ass into the display case of pastries. I quickly climbed to my feet, staring at Roland in surprise as his first victim gasped and cried out on the floor. It wasn't that Roland wasn't a badass, but that he was usually much more reserved.

The metal batons were a blur in Roland's hands as he clocked the pudgy man in the forearms – which were outstretched from the wolf attempting to grab me from behind. The spurred tips scored across his forearms, and the boy howled in pain as he began to shift into wolf form. His clothes exploded into confetti, and Roland dropped the bent batons as he dove at him.

The Shepherd tackled him into the wooden door, causing the wolf to yelp before they crashed together to the ground. Roland grasped for the wolf's throat as they rolled into tables and chairs, each fighting for control of the other. Roland got the upper hand, seeming to wrap something around the snarling wolf's throat, and then he yanked back with all his strength, forearms corded with muscle, causing his veins to pop out under his skin. He was choking him out with...

The rope toy I had put in the basket on the walker.

The wolf whined, snapped his jaws, and scrabbled with his claws on the floor, but Roland scissor-locked his legs around the wolf's belly, pinning him as he hugged him tight. I spun at a sound behind me to find the scrawny guy coming to his feet, snarling as he continued his agonized grunts of pain at the broken collarbone. "We're taking over this city, bitch. No matter what you two think. God is dead, and many of us feel that the days of the wizards are over."

His words reeked of zealotry, as if repeating a mantra.

"Don't take this too personal or anything, but... fuck your feelings." He bared his teeth at me in outrage, and then burst into werewolf form. I grabbed something on the counter behind me as strips of clothing rained down around a tan-colored werewolf. His teeth were still bared as he shook his ruff, but he lifted his front paws gingerly, the broken collarbone still hurting him in his wolf form.

"Puppy want a treat?" I asked in a mocking voice. "Sit."

He didn't.

"Bad dog," I admonished, and I threw the glass pot of coffee at his face. He yelped outrageously loud as the steaming liquid burned his eyes, crashing to the ground as his paws clawed for purchase. I prepared to smash him with a bar of air just as I heard an unsettling *snap* behind me, followed

288

by silence. Before I could turn to look, Roland was shoving me out of the way, and proceeded to stab the wolf through the heart with one spur, and then he swung the other across the screaming wolf's face, breaking his jaw or neck, I wasn't sure.

To put it simply, it was the most violent, heartless, and efficient execution I had ever seen Roland perform. No sympathy. No forgiveness. Just death.

He stared down at the wolf, panting lightly.

I began humming in a low tone. *"Dunna-dunna-dunna-dunna-dunna-dunna-dunna-dunna—"*

"Callie, don't you *dare* finish that stupid jingl—"

"VAT-MAAAAAAN!" I belted out, loud enough to be heard over his protests.

He rolled his eyes and let out a long, patient breath, ignoring my maniacal grin.

Then I heard a door slam in the back of the shop, and was running before I consciously chose to. The third wolf.

∾

Get your copy of SINNER online today!

∾

Turn the page to read a sample of **OBSIDIAN SON** - Nate Temple Book 1 - or **BUY ONLINE**. Nate Temple is a billionaire wizard from St. Louis. He rides a bloodthirsty unicorn and drinks with the Four Horsemen. He even cow-tipped the Minotaur. Once...

(Note: Nate's books 1-6 happen prior to UNCHAINED, but crossover from then on, the two series taking place in the same universe but also able to standalone if you prefer)

Full chronology of all books in the Temple Universe shown on the 'BOOKS IN THE TEMPLE VERSE' page.

TRY: OBSIDIAN SON (NATE TEMPLE #1)

There was no room for emotion in a hate crime. I had to be cold. Heartless. This was just another victim. Nothing more. No face, no name.

Frosted blades of grass crunched under my feet, sounding to my ears alone like the symbolic glass that one shattered under a napkin at a Jewish wedding. The noise would have threatened to give away my stealthy advance as I stalked through the moonlit field, but I was no novice and had planned accordingly. Being a wizard, I was able to muffle all sensory evidence with a fine cloud of magic—no sounds, and no smells. Nifty. But if I made the spell much stronger, the anomaly would be too obvious to my prey.

I knew the consequences for my dark deed tonight. If caught, jail time or possibly even a gruesome, painful death. But if I succeeded, the look of fear and surprise in my victim's eyes before his world collapsed around him, was well worth the risk. I simply couldn't help myself; I had to take him down.

I knew the cops had been keeping tabs on my car, but I was confident that they hadn't followed me. I hadn't seen a tail on my way here, but seeing as how they frowned on this kind of thing I had taken a circuitous route just in case. I was safe. I hoped.

Then my phone chirped at me as I received a text.

My body's fight-or-flight syndrome instantly kicked in, my heart threatening to explode in one final act of pulmonary paroxysm. "Motherf—" I hissed instinctively, practically jumping out of my skin. I had forgotten to silence it. *Stupid, stupid, stupid!* My body remained tense as I swept my gaze over the field, sure that I had been made. My breathing finally began to slow, my pulse returning to normal, as I noticed no changes in my surroundings. Hopefully, my magic had silenced the sound and my resulting outburst. I glanced down at the phone to scan the text and then typed back a quick and angry response before I switched the cursed phone to vibrate.

Now, where were we...

I continued on, the lining of my coat constricting my breathing. Or maybe it was because I was leaning forward in anticipation. *Breathe*, I chided myself. *He doesn't know you're here.* All this risk for a book. It had better be worth it.

I'm taller than most, and not abnormally handsome, but I knew how to play the genetic cards I had been dealt. I had shaggy, dirty blonde hair, and my frame was thick with well-earned muscle, yet still lean. I had once been told that my eyes were like twin emeralds pitted against the golden-brown tufts of my hair—a face like a jewelry box. Of course, that was two bottles of wine into a date, so I could have been a little foggy on her quote. Still, I liked to imagine that was how everyone saw me.

But tonight, all that was masked by magic.

I grinned broadly as the outline of the hairy hulk finally came into view. He was blessedly alone—no nearby sentries to give me away. That was always a risk when performing this ancient right-of-passage. I tried to keep the grin on my face from dissolving into a maniacal cackle.

My skin danced with energy, both natural and unnatural, as I manipulated the threads of magic floating all around me. My victim stood just ahead, oblivious of the world of hurt that I was about to unleash. Even with his millennia of experience, he didn't stand a chance. I had done this so many times that the routine of it was my only enemy. I lost count of how many times I had been told not to do it again; those who knew declared it *cruel, evil, and sadistic.* But what fun wasn't? Regardless, that wasn't enough to stop me from doing it again. And again. Call it an addiction if you will, but it was too much of a rush to ignore.

The pungent smell of manure filled the air, latching onto my nostril hairs. I took another step, trying to calm my racing pulse. A glint of gold reflected in the silver moonlight, but the victim remained motionless, hopefully unaware or all was lost. I wouldn't make it out alive if he knew I was here. Timing was everything.

I carefully took the last two steps, a lifetime between each, watching the legendary monster's ears, anxious and terrified that I would catch even so much as a twitch in my direction. Seeing nothing, a fierce grin split my unshaven cheeks. My spell had worked! I raised my palms an inch away from their target, firmly planted my feet, and squared my shoulders. I took one silent, calming breath, and then heaved forward with every ounce of physical strength I could muster. As well as a teensy-weensy boost of magic. Enough to goose him good.

"MOOO!!!" The sound tore through the cool October night like an unstoppable freight train. *Thud-splat!* The beast collapsed sideways into the frosty grass; straight into a steaming patty of cow shit, cow dung, or, if you really want to church it up, a Meadow Muffin. But to me, shit is, and always will be, shit.

Cow tipping. It doesn't get any better than that in Missouri.

Especially when you're tipping the *Minotaur.* Capital M.

Razor-blade hooves tore at the frozen earth as the beast struggled to stand, grunts of rage vibrating the air. I raised my arms triumphantly. "Boo-yah! Temple 1, Minotaur 0!" I crowed. Then I very bravely prepared to protect myself. Some people just couldn't take a joke. *Cruel, evil,* and *sadistic* cow tipping may be, but by hell, it was a *rush.* The legendary beast turned his gaze on me after gaining his feet, eyes ablaze as he unfolded to his full height on two tree-trunk-thick legs, hooves magically transforming into heavily-booted feet. The thick, gold ring dangling from his snotty snout quivered as the Minotaur panted, and his dense, corded muscle contracted over his human-like chest. As I stared up into those brown eyes, I actually felt sorry...for, well, myself.

"I have killed greater men than you for less offense," he growled.

I swear to God his voice sounded like an angry James Earl Jones. Like Mufasa talking to Scar.

"You have shit on your shoulder, Asterion." I ignited a roiling ball of fire in my palm in order to see his eyes more clearly. By no means was it a defensive gesture on my part. It was just dark. But under the weight of his glare, even I couldn't buy my reassuring lie. I hoped using a form of his ancient name would give me brownie points. Or maybe just not-worthy-of-killing points.

The beast grunted, eyes tightening, and I sensed the barest hesitation. "Nate Temple...your name would look splendid on my already long list of slain idiots." Asterion took a threatening step forward, and I thrust out my palm in warning, my roiling flame blue now.

"You lost fair and square, Asterion. Yield or perish." The beast's shoulders sagged slightly. Then he finally nodded to himself in resignation, appraising me with the scrutiny of a worthy adversary. "Your time comes, Temple, but I will grant you this. You've got a pair of stones on you to rival Hercules."

I pointedly risked a glance down towards the myth's own crown jewels. "Well, I sure won't need a wheelbarrow any time soon, but I'm sure I'll manage."

The Minotaur blinked once, and then bellowed out a deep, contagious, snorting laughter. Realizing I wasn't about to become a murder statistic, I couldn't help but join in. It felt good. It had been a while since I had allowed myself to experience genuine laughter.

In the harsh moonlight, his bulk was even more intimidating as he towered head and shoulders above me. This was the beast that had fed upon human sacrifices for countless years while imprisoned in Daedalus' Labyrinth in Greece. And all of that protein had not gone to waste, forming a heavily woven musculature over the beast's body that made even Mr. Olympia look puny.

From the neck up he was entirely bull, but the rest of his body more resembled a thickly-furred man. But, as shown moments ago, he could adapt his form to his environment, never appearing fully human, but able to make his entire form appear as a bull when necessary. For instance, how he had looked just before I tipped him. Maybe he had been scouting the field for heifers before I had so efficiently killed the mood.

His bull face was also covered in thick, coarse hair—even sporting a long, wavy beard of sorts, and his eyes were the deepest brown I had ever seen. Cow shit brown. His snout jutted out, emphasizing the gold ring dangling from his glistening nostrils, catching a glint in the luminous glow of the moon. The metal was at least an inch thick, and etched with runes of a language long forgotten. Thick, aged ivory horns sprouted from each temple, long enough to skewer a wizard with little effort. He was nude except for a beaded necklace and a pair of distressed leather boots that were big enough to stomp a size twenty-five imprint in my face if he felt so inclined.

I hoped our blossoming friendship wouldn't end that way. I really did.

~

Get your copy of OBSIDIAN SON online today!

~

Turn the page to read a sample of **WHISKEY GINGER** *- Phantom Queen Diaries Book 1, or* **BUY ONLINE**. *Quinn MacKenna is a black magic arms dealer in Boston. She likes to fight monsters almost as much as she likes to drink.*

Full chronology of all books in the Temple Verse shown on the 'BOOKS IN THE TEMPLE VERSE' page.)

TRY: WHISKEY GINGER (PHANTOM QUEEN DIARIES BOOK 1)

*T*he pasty guitarist hunched forward, thrust a rolled-up wad of paper deep into one nostril, and snorted a line of blood crystals—frozen hemoglobin that I'd smuggled over in a refrigerated canister—with the uncanny grace of a drug addict. He sat back, fangs gleaming, and pawed at his nose. "That's some bodacious shit. Hey, bros," he said, glancing at his fellow band members, "come hit this shit before it melts."

He fetched one of the backstage passes hanging nearby, pried the plastic badge from its lanyard, and used it to split up the crystals, murmuring something in an accent that reminded me of California. Not *the* California, but you know, Cali-foh-nia—the land of beaches, babes, and bros. I retrieved a toothpick from my pocket and punched it through its thin wrapper. "So," I asked no one in particular, "now that ye have the product, who's payin'?"

Another band member stepped out of the shadows to my left, and I don't mean that figuratively, either—the fucker literally stepped out of the shadows. I scowled at him, but hid my surprise, nonchalantly rolling the toothpick from one side of my mouth to the other.

The rest of the band gathered around the dressing room table, following the guitarist's lead by preparing their own snorting utensils—tattered magazine covers, mostly. Typically, you'd do this sort of thing with a dollar-bill, maybe even a Benjamin if you were flush. But fangers like this lot couldn't touch cash directly—in God We Trust and all that. Of course, I didn't really understand why sucking blood the old-fashioned way had suddenly gone out of style. More of a rush, maybe?

"It lasts longer," the vampire next to me explained, catching my mildly curious expression. "It's especially good for shows and stuff. Makes us look, like, less—"

"Creepy?" I offered, my Irish brogue lilting just enough to make it a question.

"Pale," he finished, frowning.

I shrugged. "Listen, I've got places to be," I said, holding out my hand.

"I'm sure you do," he replied, smiling. "Tell you what, why don't you, like, hang around for a bit? Once that wears off," he dipped his head toward the bloody powder smeared across the table's surface, "we may need a pick-me-up." He rested his hand on my arm and our gazes locked.

I blinked, realized what he was trying to pull, and rolled my eyes. His widened in surprise, then shock as I yanked out my toothpick and shoved it through his hand.

"Motherfuck—"

"I want what we agreed on," I declared. "Now. No tricks."

The rest of the band saw what happened and rose faster than I could blink. They circled me, their grins feral...they might have even seemed intimidating if it weren't for the fact that they each had a case of the sniffles

—I had to work extra hard not to think about what it felt like to have someone else's blood dripping down my nasal cavity.

I held up a hand.

"Can I ask ye gentlemen a question before we get started?" I asked. "Do ye even *have* what I asked for?"

Two of the band members exchanged looks and shrugged. The guitarist, however, glanced back towards the dressing room, where a brown paper bag sat next to a case full of makeup. He caught me looking and bared his teeth, his fangs stretching until it looked like it would be uncomfortable for him to close his mouth without piercing his own lip.

"Follow-up question," I said, eyeing the vampire I'd stabbed as he gingerly withdrew the toothpick from his hand and flung it across the room with a snarl. "Do ye do each other's make-up? Since, ye know, ye can't use mirrors?"

I was genuinely curious.

The guitarist grunted. "Mike, we have to go on soon."

"Wait a minute. Mike?" I turned to the snarling vampire with a frown. "What happened to *The Vampire Prospero*?" I glanced at the numerous fliers in the dressing room, most of which depicted the band members wading through blood, with Mike in the lead, each one titled *The Vampire Prospero* in *Rocky Horror Picture Show* font. Come to think of it…Mike did look a little like Tim Curry in all that leather and lace.

I was about to comment on the resemblance when Mike spoke up, "Alright, change of plans, bros. We're gonna drain this bitch before the show. We'll look totally—"

"Creepy?" I offered, again.

"Kill her."

～

Get the full book ONLINE!

MAKE A DIFFERENCE

Reviews are the most powerful tools in my arsenal when it comes to getting attention for my books. Much as I'd like to, I don't have the financial muscle of a New York publisher.

But I do have something much more powerful and effective than that, and it's something that those publishers would kill to get their hands on.

A committed and loyal bunch of readers.

Honest reviews of my books help bring them to the attention of other readers.

If you've enjoyed this book, I would be very grateful if you could spend just five minutes leaving a review (it can be as short as you like) on my book's Amazon page.

Thank you very much in advance.

ACKNOWLEDGMENTS

First, I would like to thank my beta-readers, TEAM TEMPLE, those individuals who spent hours of their time to read, and re-re-read the Temple-Verse stories. Your dark, twisted, cunning sense of humor makes me feel right at home...

I would also like to thank you, the reader. I hope you enjoyed reading *ANGEL'S ROAR* as much as I enjoyed writing it. Stay tuned...Callie Penrose returns in GODLESS with her book 7, Nate Temple returns in KNIGHT-MARE with his book 12, and Quinn MacKenna returns in HURRICANE with her book 8—all in 2019!

And last, but definitely not least, I thank my wife, Lexy. Without your support, none of this would have been possible.

BOOKS IN THE TEMPLE VERSE

CHRONOLOGY: All stories in the Temple Verse are shown in chronological order on the following page

FEATHERS AND FIRE SERIES

(Set in the Temple Verse)

UNCHAINED

RAGE

WHISPERS

ANGEL'S ROAR

MOTHERLUCKER (Novella #4.5 in the 'LAST CALL' anthology)

SINNER

BLACK SHEEP

GODLESS (FEATHERS #7) — COMING SOON...

NATE TEMPLE SERIES

(Origin of the Temple Verse)

FAIRY TALE - FREE prequel novella #0 for my subscribers

OBSIDIAN SON

BLOOD DEBTS

GRIMM

SILVER TONGUE

BEAST MASTER

BEERLYMPIAN (Novella #5.5 in the 'LAST CALL' anthology)

TINY GODS

DADDY DUTY (Novella #6.5)

WILD SIDE

WAR HAMMER

NINE SOULS

HORSEMAN

LEGEND

KNIGHTMARE (TEMPLE #12) — COMING SOON…

PHANTOM QUEEN DIARIES

(Also set in the Temple Verse)

COLLINS (Prequel novella #0 in the 'LAST CALL' anthology)

WHISKEY GINGER

COSMOPOLITAN

OLD FASHIONED

MOTHERLUCKER (Novella #3.5 in the 'LAST CALL' anthology)

DARK AND STORMY

MOSCOW MULE

WITCHES BREW

SALTY DOG

CHRONOLOGICAL ORDER: TEMPLE UNIVERSE

FAIRY TALE (TEMPLE PREQUEL)

OBSIDIAN SON (TEMPLE 1)

BLOOD DEBTS (TEMPLE 2)

GRIMM (TEMPLE 3)

SILVER TONGUE (TEMPLE 4)

BEAST MASTER (TEMPLE 5)

BEERLYMPIAN (TEMPLE 5.5)

TINY GODS (TEMPLE 6)

DADDY DUTY (TEMPLE NOVELLA 6.5)

UNCHAINED (FEATHERS… 1)

RAGE (FEATHERS… 2)

WILD SIDE (TEMPLE 7)

WAR HAMMER (TEMPLE 8)

WHISPERS (FEATHERS… 3)

COLLINS (PHANTOM 0)

WHISKEY GINGER (PHANTOM… 1)

NINE SOULS (TEMPLE 9)

COSMOPOLITAN (PHANTOM… 2)

ANGEL'S ROAR (FEATHERS… 4)

MOTHERLUCKER (FEATHERS 4.5, PHANTOM 3.5)

OLD FASHIONED (PHANTOM…3)

HORSEMAN (TEMPLE 10)

DARK AND STORMY (PHANTOM… 4)

MOSCOW MULE (PHANTOM…5)

SINNER (FEATHERS…5)

WITCHES BREW (PHANTOM…6)

LEGEND (TEMPLE…11)

SALTY DOG (PHANTOM…7)

BLACK SHEEP (FEATHERS…6)

GODLESS (FEATHERS…7)

KNIGHTMARE (TEMPLE 12)

ABOUT THE AUTHOR

Shayne is a man of mystery and power, whose power is exceeded only by his mystery...

He currently writes the Amazon Bestselling **Feathers and Fire Series** about a rookie spell-slinger named Callie Penrose who works for the Vatican in Kansas City. Her problem? Hell seems to know more about her past than she does.

He also writes the Amazon Bestselling **Nate Temple Series**, which features a foul-mouthed wizard from St. Louis. He rides a bloodthirsty unicorn, drinks with Achilles, and is pals with the Four Horsemen.

He also co-authors the Amazon Bestselling **Phantom Queen Diaries** with Cameron O'Connell, about Quinn MacKenna, a mouthy black magic arms dealer trading favors in Boston. All she wants? A round-trip ticket to the Fae realm...and maybe a drink on the house.

Shayne holds two high-ranking black belts, and can be found writing in a coffee shop, cackling madly into his computer screen while pounding shots of espresso. He's hard at work on more Temple Verse novels as well as a few entirely new stories outside of the Temple Verse. **Follow him online for all sorts of groovy goodies, giveaways, and new release updates:**

Get Down with Shayne Online
www.shaynesilvers.com
info@shaynesilvers.com